Why YOU love Nancy Revell

'The girls just go from strength to strength. Absolutely brilliant, so many twists and turns. Can't wait for the next book'

'I can't wait to read the next instalment of these incredible women's lives. They're such wonderful characters; I can't wait to see what happens next to them all. September can't come soon enough . . . Thank you, Nancy Revell'

'A cracking saga set in the North East of England during World War 2. I LOVED it and became totally immersed and involved in the story. Can't wait to read the next book in the series'

'It's absolutely brilliant. I read all one to four, I just could not put it down, I got so caught up in the lives of the characters. It's a must read!'

'What a brilliant read – the story is so good it keeps you wanting more . . . I fell in love with the girls; their stories, laughter, tears and so much more'

'How wonderful to read about everyday women, young, middle aged, married or single all coming to work in a man's world. The pride and courage they all showed in taking over from the men who had gone to war. A debt of gratitude is very much owed'

'I absolutely loved this book. I come from Sunderland and knew every street, cafe, road and dock. Have already ordered the sequel'

'This is a book that lets the reader know the way our ancestors behaved during the two world wars. With strength, honour and downright bravery . . . I for one salute them all and give thanks to the author Nancy Revell, for letting us as readers know mostly as it was' *****

'Marvellous read, couldn't put down. Exciting, heart rendering, hope it will not be long before another one. Nancy Revell is an excellent author'

'Everyone's in love with the shipyard girls!'

What the reviewers are saying...

'Well-drawn, believable characters combined with a storyline to keep
you turning the page'
Woman magazine

'The author is one to watch'
Sun

'A riveting read is just what this is in more ways than one'
Northern Echo

'Researched within an inch of its life; the novel is enjoyably entertain-
ing. A perfect way to spend hours, wrapped up in the characters'
lives'
Frost magazine

'A brilliant read!'
Take a Break magazine

'This is a series that has gone from strength to strength ... The clev-
erly weaved secrets and expert plotting had me hooked! 5* Genius'
Anne Bonny Book Reviews Blog

'There is a bit of everything within its pages – drama, heartache, happiness, sadness and the odd dash of humour ... I absolutely loved
this heart wrenching and extremely realistic saga series. A brilliant
5 out of 5*'
Ginger Book Geek Blog

'Nancy creates strong characters that come alive as you read'
Chellsandbooks Blog

'All the essentials of a good saga'
Lyn Andrews, author of *Liverpool Sisters*

'Heartfelt, pacy and gutsy, I adore it already and will no doubt be
devouring the rest of the series with just as much enthusiasm'
Fiona Ford, author of *The Spark Girl*

Victory for the Shipyard Girls

Nancy Revell

arrow books

1 3 5 7 9 10 8 6 4 2

Arrow Books
20 Vauxhall Bridge Road
London SW1V 2SA

Arrow Books is part of the Penguin Random House group
of companies whose addresses can be found at
global.penguinrandomhouse.com.

Penguin
Random House
UK

First published in Great Britain by Arrow Books in 2018

www.penguin.co.uk

A CIP catalogue record for this book is available
from the British Library.

ISBN 9781787460225

Typeset in 10.75/13.5 pt Palatino
by Integra Software Services Pvt. Ltd, Pondicherry

Printed and bound in Great Britain by Clays Ltd, Elcograf S.p.A.

MIX
Paper from
responsible sources
FSC
www.fsc.org   FSC® C018179

Penguin Random House is committed to a
sustainable future for our business, our readers
and our planet. This book is made from Forest
Stewardship Council® certified paper.

To postmaster John Wilson and Liz Skelton at Fulwell Post Office. Thank you so much for all your continued support, enthusiasm and encouragement.

Our greatest glory is not in never falling, but in rising every time we fall
Confucius (551–479 BC)

Prologue

Saturday 10 January 1942

'Will you, Rosie Eloise Thornton, take this man, Peter Archibald Miller, as your lawfully wedded husband, to have and to hold from this day forward, for better, for worse, for richer, for poorer, in sickness and in health, to love and to cherish, till death do you part?'

Rosie looked at her lover, the only man she had ever fallen in love with. The man who might well make her a widow longer than he would a wife, and she smiled. It was a smile full of both happiness and sadness.

'Yes, I do,' she said, looking into Peter's serious, deep blue eyes.

The elderly registrar pushed his gold-rimmed glasses back up the bridge of his nose before turning his attention to the groom, who, he guessed, must be twice the age of his bride. A bride who was very attractive, despite the flecks of tiny scars he could make out underneath her make-up, and who was wearing the most vibrant red dress he'd ever seen. Nothing, however, surprised him these days.

'And do you, Peter Archibald Miller, take this woman, Rosie Eloise Thompson, to be your lawfully wedded wife, to have and to hold from this day forward, for better, for worse, for richer, for poorer, in sickness and in health, to love and to cherish, till death do you part?' the registrar asked.

'I do,' Peter said, not taking his eyes off his bride – the woman who had turned his life upside down, and who had brought him a love that he had never thought existed. A woman he'd thought he had lost for ever, but who had travelled almost three hundred miles to be with him for what might turn out to be their last days together.

The registrar looked down at Peter's hand, which was holding a simple, 18-carat-gold band, one he had bought just that morning from a jewellers a few doors down from their hotel. Peter took his cue.

'With this ring I thee wed.' Peter took hold of Rosie's left hand as gently as he could and slid the gold band on to her wedding-ring finger. Her hand felt cold and he had to stop himself from rubbing it warm.

The registrar looked at Peter and Rosie, cleared his throat and declared, 'I now pronounce you man and wife.' Peter was already bending his head to kiss his new bride as the registrar added rather belatedly, 'You may now kiss the bride.'

Kissing her new husband back, Rosie couldn't stop herself blushing at the public display of affection, even though it was an anticipated part of the short ceremony.

The registrar forced a cough. 'If you can both just sign here … and here.' He didn't want to hurry them, but he was aware that he was running out of time. This particular couple had been squeezed in at the last minute. He looked behind the newly-weds and gave the nod to the two witnesses standing quietly to the side. They were both registry-office clerical workers and this was not the first time they had been called upon to be witnesses of late; in fact, they had been called upon dozens of times in the last year as so many special licences had been granted since the declaration of war.

2

Rosie put her small bouquet of white pansies down on the wooden table. Peter had insisted his wife at least have a wedding bouquet, even if it was just a modest one. After all, she had not even had the chance to go and buy herself a proper wedding dress.

Stepping forward to add their own signatures to the pastel green marriage certificate, both witnesses noted with surprise the descriptions of 'police officer' and 'welder' under the column headed 'Rank or profession'.

Giving the ink a moment to dry, the registrar handed one of the certificates to the groom. Peter folded it up and put it in the inside pocket of the black woollen suit he always wore for work and which had been pressed for this very special occasion.

After Peter and Rosie thanked and shook hands with the man who had just made them husband and wife, Rosie picked up the wedding bouquet and walked out of the small room and into the noisy corridor. Passing a couple dressed in khaki uniforms, his standard army and hers that of the Auxiliary Territorial Service, Peter and Rosie smiled at them.

'Congratulations!' The young man and woman spoke at the same time and laughed, their faces full of excitement and anticipation. Rosie noticed the bride was empty-handed and gave her the small bouquet of pansies.

'Are you sure?' The woman's face lit up.

Rosie nodded.

'Oh, thank you! Thank you! They're gorgeous!'

Rosie stepped forward and spoke to the woman quietly, so that no one else could hear. As she spoke, the young woman clutched Rosie's hand. There were tears in both their eyes.

Just then the registrar stuck his head around the panelled door to the registry office and beckoned the couple in.

'That's one of the many reasons why I love you so much!' Peter said, grabbing both their coats from the wooden stand by the main entrance and helping his new wife into her grey mac.

As soon as they stepped out into the bitingly cold but fresh afternoon, the two witnesses who had slipped away unnoticed suddenly appeared by their side.

'Congratulations!' they shouted, showering the newly-weds with confetti. Rosie jumped with unexpected delight and was taken aback when the young woman gave her a hug and whispered, 'May it be long and happy!'

Hurrying down the steps and onto the wide stretch of gravelled driveway, Peter stopped and pulled Rosie close to him. As there was no one else about, they stood and kissed.

'I love you, Mrs Miller.' Peter pulled back a fraction to look at the woman he had fallen in love with the moment he had first clapped eyes on her.

Rosie stepped closer and told him, 'I love you too, Mr Miller.' She didn't think she had ever felt so happy, so special and yet also so heavy-hearted in her entire life.

Holding hands, Rosie and Peter turned right into a side street, then right again onto a narrow pavement that led to the centre of town. Seeing they were covered in confetti, passing pedestrians smiled and made way for them.

As they neared the main entrance of their hotel, they passed a newspaper stand with the words LIVERPOOL BLITZ written in large capital letters. Peter put his arm around Rosie's shoulders and squeezed her gently to him.

'So, can I have the pleasure of taking my new wife out for a celebratory meal?' he asked, hoping to draw her attention away from the headlines. He was determined that today would be a happy, carefree day. It was just going to be about the two of them. There was to be no war talk.

'Your new wife would love to be taken out for a "celebratory meal", *dear husband*.' Rosie smiled, enjoying their role play, although she too had seen the news and said a silent prayer that her home town would not be next.

Peter and Rosie lay in their sumptuous double bed, wrapped tightly in each other's arms, having made love for the first time as a married couple. Their chatter was interspersed with the occasional silence as they both thought about the romantic whirlwind in which they had been caught these past few days.

'I still can't quite believe you're here – let alone that you are now my wife!' Peter spoke his thoughts aloud. 'And a very kind wife, I have to add.'

Rosie knew Peter was talking about the flowers. The beautiful little bouquet of white pansies had been the only wedding frippery they had been able to indulge in as everything had had to be organised so speedily. They had got them from a little florist just a few hundred yards or so away from their hotel. It had been slim pickings, but they were pleased simply to have found a flower shop still open for business in the present climate.

'They'd served their purpose,' Rosie said, interlinking her fingers with his, enjoying the feel and warmth of his body next to hers. 'I walked down the aisle – or rather the middle of the registry office – with the man I loved, in a dress I loved, holding a beautiful bouquet of flowers. The man – and the lovely red dress – I'll keep, but the flowers, well, they would only be here now, wilting and dying. At least they gave joy to two brides instead of just the one.'

Peter pulled Rosie close and kissed her.

'But had you kept them you could have pressed them and held on to them as the only real memento of your wedding day,' he argued.

'Why would I need dried flowers to remind me of today?' Rosie pressed herself gently against her husband. 'I'll never forget today. Ever.'

'What did you whisper to the young army bride when you gave her the flowers?' Peter asked curiously.

'I told her what the florist told me – that every flower has a meaning and a pansy means *thinking of you*.'

Rosie fell silent for a moment. Turning to Peter, her face was deadly serious.

'I want you to know that I'll always be thinking of you. When I'm working. When I'm not working. Even when I'm sleeping, I'll always be thinking of you.'

Peter kissed her again but worried about the fervour with which she had spoken those words. In different circumstances he couldn't have wished to hear anything more enchanting spoken with such passion and sincerity. But with such an uncertain future, a part of him wished she didn't feel so strongly, for if he didn't come back it would make life so much harder for her. And God only knew, this wonderful, strong, unique woman now lying in his arms had already experienced enough hardship to last her a lifetime.

It was the early hours of the morning and although they had both drifted in and out of sleep it was as though neither of them would allow their bodies to rest, to leave each other for any amount of time – until they had to.

Indulging in a stream-of-consciousness, sleep-deprived chatter, they could not have been happier. They enjoyed the simplicity of revelling in the moment, relishing the time they had before they were forced to part.

'I can't believe you missed me by just a few seconds,' Peter mumbled, sleepily.

Rosie didn't need to ask where her new husband's mind had wandered to. That awful day last week when Kate had turned up at the yard with his letter would be forever etched into her memory. Rosie had run the entire way from Thompson's, across the Wearmouth Bridge and into the town centre, only to arrive at the railway station just as Peter's train was pulling away.

It might have been too late for farewells, but Peter had caught a glimpse of Rosie as she had clattered down the steps to the platform. It had been enough to show him that she still loved him and had made him determined to see her one last time.

'I'm still puzzled as to why Kate didn't give me your letter the night before.' Rosie pulled up the blanket to keep out the cold and snuggled against the warmth of Peter's chest.

'Well, thank goodness she did,' Peter murmured into Rosie's mess of blonde curls, 'otherwise I wouldn't have sent you that telegram, you wouldn't have travelled here to see me, and you wouldn't have agreed to be my wife ... And more than anything, we wouldn't have had these last few days together.'

Rosie stiffened. 'Don't say "last". This is just the start. There's just going to be a bit of a gap for a little while, that's all. Until this war's at an end.'

Peter wished more than anything that he could believe this to be the truth. He knew there was a good chance that when he waved Rosie off at the train station tomorrow, it might be the last time she saw him. He was just so glad he had got the chance to make things right between the two of them; if he didn't make it back alive, he would die knowing that he had done right by Rosie in every way possible.

'I'm so sorry,' Rosie said.

Peter saw Rosie's eyes were wet. 'What on earth are you sorry for? You're probably the most blameless person I know.' He moved a strand of straw-blonde hair out of her eyes.

'For being so awful ... so angry ... for not understanding.' Rosie's voice sounded woebegone, echoing the ache in her heart as she recalled the terrible hurt that had consumed her when Peter told her that, despite being in a reserved occupation, he had signed up.

Peter squeezed her gently. 'You've got nothing to be sorry for. If anyone has to be apologising, it's me. I shouldn't have left it so long to tell you. I should have dealt with the situation better. I was being selfish. I just wanted to keep everything the way it was until the very last moment.'

Deep down, Peter knew that really neither of them was to blame. They were just human – he for wanting to keep the magic of their love unspoilt for as long as possible, she for riling against the injustice of having the only real love she had ever experienced wrenched from her. Rosie had reacted the only way she knew how – with outrage and anger. Peter knew, however, that there was only one real culprit that had caused their hurt and heartbreak – and it was this damnable war.

'But all's well that ends well,' Peter said.

'That's Dorothy's favourite expression,' Rosie said. 'Or should I say Angie's. She's always reminding us that it's a quote from some play by Shakespeare.'

Peter smiled. Thank goodness Rosie had her women welders. She might be their boss, but they were all friends, and good ones at that. If Rosie needed help, he knew they would be there for her.

'Whatever happens,' Peter's voice was serious, 'you have nothing to feel bad or guilty about. You know that, don't you? No regrets – promise?' He could feel Rosie nod.

'We've had the most amazing six weeks together, and all the time before that when we were getting to know each other. And,' he took Rosie's left hand and kissed the gold band on her wedding-ring finger, 'you've made me the happiest and proudest man in the whole universe!'

Rosie propped herself up on her elbow so that she could see Peter's face clearly. It was true – the time they had been together had been magical. After having a variety of obstacles strewn in the way of their love, they'd overcome them all and been so blissfully happy.

So why, she couldn't help asking herself, did it have to be cut short so cruelly? Rosie stopped herself. *No more morbid thoughts!* This was their first night together as a married couple and their last night together for God knew how long. It had to be a happy one.

'I have to say, Mr Miller,' she said in a mock-serious voice, 'your proposal must have been the most business-like one in the history of romance.'

Peter's eyes widened and he let out a loud guffaw.

'Well, there's no arguing there!'

'So,' Rosie said, a smile playing on her lips, 'when my squad ask me how you proposed and are waiting with bated breath to hear how you got down on one knee and wooed me like in the films, I'm going to have to shatter their romantic illusions and tell them the truth.' She kissed him before continuing. 'I can just imagine their faces when I tell them that after meeting me off the train and taking me in your arms, you bought me a brandy in the hotel bar and *told* me – no, actually, you practically *ordered* me – to marry you!'

Peter and Rosie both started chuckling.

'No "Darling, will you marry me?"' Rosie continued through their growing laughter. 'Rather, "Now listen here, Rosie, I'm going to marry you, and before you say another word, you're going to sit there and listen to the reasons why it's imperative you agree to it all."'

By now they were both lying on their backs laughing uncontrollably as they recalled Peter's rather unconventional proposal two nights previously. Rosie was holding her stomach, which was beginning to ache, and tears were rolling down their faces.

'You couldn't have made it up!'

And that was how they would both remember their honeymoon.

Lying in a hotel bed, stomachs aching, crying with laughter.

Enjoying every last minute they had left together.

Chapter One

Borough Road, Sunderland

Monday 12 January 1942

After an epic journey from Guildford to Waterloo Station, a schlep across the capital to King's Cross, then an eight-hour journey back up north, Rosie finally returned home and practically crawled into bed. Yet, as she lay there wide awake, it was clear that sleep was not going to give her body, or her mind, the respite she craved. Instead, she spent the night tossing and turning, her mind spinning with all that had happened, her nerves tingling, her body on some strange kind of high, pumped full of adrenaline, love and excitement. The past five days had been the most magical, the most wondrous, the most loving, and the most surreal of her life.

At half-past five, she finally gave up and got out of bed, pulled on her thick dressing gown and padded into her little kitchenette, where she started to fill the kettle. As she did so the glint of the gold band caught her eye and she found herself standing stock-still, staring at her polished rose-gold wedding ring.

'You bloody well better come back to me, Peter Miller.' Rosie spoke the words aloud, before getting on with the task of making a brew. By the time she had drunk two cups, forced down a slice of toast and put on as many extra layers as possible under her denim overalls to fend off the dropping temperatures, it had gone half six and she was closing the front door behind her.

As she walked the short distance from her flat to the ferry landing down by the south docks, Rosie sensed the fear that had been there these past few days. While she had been with Peter, Rosie had refused to let it contaminate her joy, but as she jostled onto the ferry with the other shipwrights and dock workers, the fear pushed itself to the fore.

Glancing at the large barrage balloons above her, Rosie took a deep breath and forced herself to face the fear – the terrifying spectre of what the future might hold, of what might become of Peter. She stared it down, challenged it, and then pushed it back with all her might.

As Rosie took her place at the side of the boat, she knew she had to stick to the resolution she had made last night as she had lain awake. She would keep herself as busy as humanly possible so that she didn't have time to think. It was how she would cope. She had done it when her parents died, and again when her uncle Raymond had reappeared in her life. And she would do it again.

Rosie waved across to Stan the ferryman, whom she had known since she first started working at Thompson's shipyard. She thought that he looked older; another harsh winter was taking its toll. As the ferry bumped against the north ferry landing, Rosie hurried off and up the embankment to the gates of J.L. Thompson & Sons.

'Mornin', 'n welcome back, Miss Thornton!' Alfie, the young timekeeper, handed Rosie her white time board.

Rosie smiled her thanks and wondered how she was going to tell not just her squad and everyone at the bordello, but also her employers that she was no longer 'Miss'. As she walked through the shipyard's main entrance, with its two huge metal gates, she breathed in the fresh sea air. This early in the morning it was still relatively quiet. She knew she had a good half an hour before the blare of the klaxon sounded out the start of the day's shift and the place was filled with the overwhelming and all-consuming noise of men and machinery.

Knowing that the yard manager, Helen Crawford, was always at work by seven, Rosie decided to go and see her, find out what had been happening while she had been away. As she walked past the long brick building that made up the drawing office, she noticed a light on inside. Looking through one of the windows, criss-crossed with the now customary brown anti-blast tape, she spotted a mop of black hair bobbing over one of the long workbenches. Entering the warmth of the large, high-ceilinged office, Rosie was hit by the distinctive smell of polished wood and the sight of row after row of workbenches covered with rolls of tracing paper, pencil sharpenings and pots of Indian ink.

'Hannah! What are you doing in this early?' Rosie's voice sliced through the quietness.

'You're back!' Hannah hurried over to see her former boss and gave her a hug. Rosie knew that Hannah would always feel grateful to her for getting her a job in the drawing office as a trainee draughtsman once it became clear she was not at all cut out to be a welder.

'How did it all go?' Hannah's dark, almond-shaped eyes were glistening. As she spoke, her boss appeared from the back room. He had both hands in his tweed waistcoat pockets and was looking over his half-moon spectacles to see who it was.

'I'll tell you all about it later,' Rosie whispered to Hannah, before turning her attention to Basil.

'I hope you're not overworking our little bird here?' Rosie's voice was light and jocular, but Basil knew the concern was genuine. Hannah might no longer work with Rosie's squad of women welders, but he was well aware that Rosie and the rest of her gang all kept a close eye on her – and woe betide anyone who didn't treat their former workmate well.

'No, no, Rosie, you know me better than that,' Basil said a little defensively as he walked over and ruffled Hannah's hair. 'Can't keep the wee one away.' Despite living in the north-east most of his life, Basil still retained a slight hint of his Scottish ancestry. 'She keeps badgering me for overtime. I think she'd work round the clock if I let her. She's even got *me* coming in early so she can get cracking at seven o'clock sharp.'

Rosie glanced at Hannah and caught something in her look that she couldn't quite make out.

'Her indoors ...' Basil said with a chuckle, referring to his wife, who he liked to make out was a battle-axe even though she was anything but, ' ... is giving me a right earbashing lately, saying she hardly ever sees me these days.'

'Well, as long as Hannah's getting her overtime pay?'

'Of course!' Basil nodded furiously, as though the mere suggestion that he would have Hannah here working for nothing was an affront.

Seeing Rosie turn to leave, Basil took hold of her left hand and patted it. 'Anyway, it's good to see you, my dear. Yer should pop yer head in 'n say hello more often.'

'You cut yourself?' Hannah perked up, looking at the thick plaster wrapped around one of Rosie's fingers.

Rosie stared at her hand, not quite sure what to say. This morning, as she had got ready for work, she had resolved never to take off her wedding ring. Ever. And so she'd gone to her first-aid box and taped up her finger to protect the band of gold that was so precious to her.

'Eee, eyes like a hawk, this one,' Rosie said.

'Aye,' Basil laughed. 'She has that. Incredible attention to detail. Wish all my apprentices were like this wee bairn.'

Hannah didn't seem to mind being referred to as a child. As Rosie made her way across the drawing office, Hannah shouted out that she and Olly, her 'friend boy', would join her and the rest of the women for lunch.

As Rosie continued on her way to the main administration building, she noticed the familiar sight of Helen standing at a window on the first floor. Her raven hair was surrounded by a swirl of smoke, although Rosie could still make out her perfectly made-up face and bright red lipstick.

Hurrying up the stairs, Rosie found Helen still standing by the window, smoking; she looked lost in her own world. Her hair was pulled back into victory rolls and she was wearing a deep olive tailored dress that perfectly complemented her shapely figure. Rosie had heard people liken her to Vivien Leigh, and after Dorothy had taken them all to see *Gone with the Wind*, Rosie could see why.

'Helen?' Rosie's voice seemed to echo in the expanse of the large open-plan office that was full of desks but devoid of people.

'Ah, Rosie, you're back!' Helen's emerald-green eyes narrowed, scrutinising the woman she had always envied. Her father thought the world of Rosie, and over the years Helen had been forced to feign interest whenever he mentioned how well Rosie was doing, how hard she worked, and how she was the only woman welder he knew. Of course, Rosie had been knocked off her pedestal of late thanks to the war. Now there weren't just women welders being employed to work in the shipyards, but women crane drivers, platers, drillers – even riveters.

'You caused quite a stir, leaving the yard in the middle of your shift last week.' Helen opened the window a fraction and tossed her half-smoked cigarette out into the yard before walking, or rather, sashaying, the short distance to her office.

'Come in,' she beckoned as she manoeuvred herself behind the large steel desk, which, Rosie noticed, no longer had any photographs of her mother and father. In their place was a heavy steel ashtray.

'I was just after a quick word,' Rosie said, panicking that Helen was going to try and grill her about the telegram and why she had been needed in Guildford. 'I just wanted to have a catch-up and see where my squad are at?' Rosie stopped in the doorway to Helen's office.

Helen remained standing as she reached for her packet of Pall Malls, pulled one out and lit it. She desperately wanted to probe Rosie about her four-day hiatus from the yard. She had managed to squeeze a little information out of Harold, the yard's head honcho, and had found out that the telegram had been from a detective sergeant. It had all been very mysterious; even the town gossip, Muriel, who worked in the canteen, had had nothing to offer on the subject. If Rosie had been another worker, Helen would have used her position to bully the information out of her, but she had always been a little wary of Rosie. Perhaps, loath that she would be to admit it, even a little intimidated by her.

Helen blew out a thin trail of smoke. 'Oh, *your* lot have got along just fine without you,' she said with more than a hint of venom.

'Did Gloria manage all right?' Rosie fought to keep the irritation out of her voice. Last Wednesday she'd had to leave straight after Harold had given her the telegram as her train was due to depart at three. She'd put Gloria in charge, but hadn't had the chance to get it sanctioned by her superiors.

'Oh, yes. Gloria managed *just fine.*' Helen's voice had taken on a rather theatrical lilt.

Rosie looked at Helen, waiting for her to expand. She felt uneasy. Something didn't feel quite right.

'Well, are they still working on *Brutus*?' Rosie asked. SS *Brutus*, a 400-foot-long cargo vessel, was one of the Empire ships commissioned by the Ministry of War Transport to replace the growing number of merchant ships that were being sunk by German U-boats.

'Yes,' Helen's voice rose, 'they're all still slaving away on the brute's back.' She paused to take another drag. 'However, I was told at the end of last week that we may be getting in a tanker that's had a hole blown in her bulkhead – apparently you can drive a double-decker bus through it, so your squad may well be needed to do the usual emergency surgery.' Helen expelled more smoke.

Rosie knew that tankers were notoriously hard to sink, aided by the fact that they were really just a collection of self-contained boxes. Providing the engine room or boilers weren't hit, chances were the air in the other compartments would keep it afloat – long enough for it to get its injured hulk back to shore. Since the start of the war Rosie had been amazed by many a ship's resilience and had seen dozens with appalling damage being repaired in the dry dock before being sent back out to sea, almost as good as new.

'But don't worry. I won't split up your squad if your lot *are* needed elsewhere.'

Rosie let out a weary sigh. She wasn't in the mood for any verbal sparring with Helen this morning. If she had been, though, she would have reminded Helen that she'd already tried to split up the squad once and had failed miserably.

17

Just as she was turning to leave, Helen suddenly spoke again. 'Oh, and just so you know – as I'm sure you'll find out soon enough – Mr Crawford's been transferred.'

Rosie looked at Helen. There was something about her manner that was a little off.

'Really? Is he coming back here?' It was a natural presumption. Jack had spent most of his life at Thompson's and had only been sent next door to Crown's on the understanding that he was needed to help with the expected amalgamation of the two yards.

Helen stared at Rosie for a few moments without speaking.

'No, my father has been transferred to one of the yards on the Clyde.'

'Really?' Rosie was shocked. 'Why? I thought they needed him at Crown's for the buyout?' she asked. *Something definitely wasn't right.*

'Well, the Scots obviously need him more than we do.' Helen's voice sounded cold and bitter. The discomfort Rosie felt in her gut was getting worse by the second.

Something had happened.

'Oh?' Rosie stood, wanting to know more, but not knowing what else to ask.

'Anyway, can't stand here chatting all morning.' Helen looked up at the clock on the wall.

'Yes, yes, of course.' Rosie said her goodbyes and turned to leave.

Something was most definitely amiss.

Chapter Two

Rosie walked across the yard to the dry basin where her squad of women welders, as well as dozens of platers and riveters, would soon be gathering in anticipation of the day's work, ready to flesh out the hull of SS *Brutus*.

Something had happened while she had been away.

But what?

Standing still, Rosie looked out at the skyline of cranes, then down towards the wide entrance gates, and saw that there was now a swell of flat-capped workers piling into the yard. As she continued staring down at the miniature tableau showing the shipyard coming to life, she saw what she was looking for – a smattering of colourful turbans. The women's headscarves had been expertly coiled and knotted so that not a strand of hair was able to wiggle free.

A few minutes later her mismatched group of women welders – Gloria, Polly, Dorothy, Angie and Martha – came trundling across the swaying metal walkway.

'Yeh! She's back!' Rosie heard Dorothy shout out as they spotted Rosie standing by a five-gallon barrel fire she had just got started. Rosie mentally braced herself for what she knew would be an avalanche of questions – and those were just the ones coming from Dorothy.

'Eee, am I glad to see you back!' Gloria was the first to reach her. She nodded her head back towards the rest of the squad behind her and rolled her eyes dramatically.

'We've been as good as gold, miss! Just like we promised.' It was Angie, who Rosie thought looked a little pale – and was that another red mark on her face?

Rosie turned to Gloria with a mock-serious look. 'Have they all behaved themselves, then?'

Gloria looked at the four expectant faces, all wanting approval, all excited by their boss's return, and all, she knew, gagging to find out how the trip to see her lover had gone.

'Actually, they've been pretty good. I'll give them that,' Gloria acquiesced. 'But I'll tell you one thing, I wouldn't want your job for the world! Always someone wanting yer attention, or some foreman moaning about something or other. I'm more than happy to hand the reins back.'

Rosie looked at Gloria and tried to read her face. She seemed all right. She didn't seem overly distressed or down. But then again, it had always been hard to tell with Gloria. They had all struggled to know what was really going on with her at the best of times. It had taken months for her to confide in them about her violent other half. And even longer to tell them that she and their yard manager, Jack Crawford, had not only been childhood sweethearts, but had fallen back in love with each other.

'So, come on, Rosie, tell us how it went?' It was Polly, who, Rosie knew, would have given anything to have spent just one day, never mind four days and four nights, with her fiancé, Tommy, a dock diver she'd met here at the yard before he had signed up and joined a special unit of deep-sea divers based in Gibraltar.

'Well, I had a wonderful time.' Rosie looked at all the women and saw a big smile appear on Martha's face.

'Really, really lovely.' Rosie paused. She didn't know what else to say.

'Well? Was he waiting for you at the station?' Dorothy asked.

For the briefest moment Rosie's mind was filled with an image of Peter striding along the platform, his eyes scanning every carriage until he spotted her. The train had barely squealed to a stop before he'd wrenched open the door, lifted her down and wrapped her in his arms, telling her over and over again how much he loved her.

'Well, it was quite romantic, I guess,' Rosie said, hesitating.

As if on cue, the klaxon sounded out for the start of the shift, saving Rosie from further interrogation. The women groaned in unison.

'I'll tell you everything over lunch,' Rosie told them. Her words were met with a chorus of approval, Dorothy clapping her hands in excited anticipation.

As they all headed over to the various sections of the upper deck, Rosie caught up with Gloria.

'Is everything all right with you and Jack?'

Gloria looked at Rosie in surprise.

'Have you heard?'

Rosie nodded. The noise was just starting to gain momentum and she knew that within minutes they wouldn't be able to hear themselves think, never mind talk.

'I'll tell you later.' Gloria cast a quick look around to make sure no one was near. 'But don't mention it in front of everyone.'

Rosie nodded her agreement just as the drillers started up and obliterated anything else she might have wanted to say.

Over the next few hours Dorothy and Angie worked flat out welding braces on to the heavy four-by-six-foot steel doors of the main deck house. Polly and Gloria were doing flat welds on the hatch covers, each sitting with one knee at a right angle, the rubber lead wrapped around their arms to lessen the weight, surrounded by a constantly flashing arc of giant sparks. Martha, like some female warrior from Greek mythology, was standing on the bridge doing overhead welds, her bulky arms not dropping once.

When the hooter sounded out that the workforce should down tools for their lunch break, the women welders did just that.

Martha waved her arm over to Rosie and shouted out, 'Cabin!'

Rosie looked and saw that all the women were beckoning her over to a small steel cabin that had been erected while she was away.

'Bring your flask!' Polly shouted, as she freed her mass of chestnut curls from the confines of her turban. As she hauled her holdall over her shoulder, Rosie saw what looked like a folded-up map peeking out the top.

Arriving in the cabin Rosie was taken aback. 'Gosh, you've made it into a little den!'

'Yeh, miss, and it's *our* den, *no one else* is allowed in here,' Angie said.

'We've claimed it as our own,' Martha added.

'Here they are!' Polly was looking out of the little window at the side of the cabin facing onto the yard.

'Hi, everyone!' Hannah hurried in, closely followed by Olly, who waved his hand self-consciously at the women and blushed.

'Hi, everyone!' he repeated.

'Come on, you two lovebirds! Take a pew!' Dorothy ordered as they all settled around a battered old brazier that had once been used to heat rivets and which had been rescued from the scrapheap by Martha, who was now stoking it up. There was a jangle of metal as they all hung their cans over their make-do stove to heat up their tea, followed by a rustling of greaseproof paper as sandwiches were unwrapped.

'So, come on, we want to hear every minute detail!' Dorothy said, dramatically.

'Yes, come on, Rosie, we want to hear all about it,' Hannah chipped in as Olly handed her half of his sandwich and nodded his own encouragement.

'I don't think I've got much of a choice, have I?' Rosie's question was met by a chorus of 'No!' from the women.

Polly handed Rosie a can of tea from her flask, which was still relatively warm. She could see that Rosie had turned up to work empty-handed, probably anticipating that they would all be going to the canteen.

'Thanks, Polly.' Rosie took the tin cup and took a quick sip. 'Well, I don't know where to start, but I guess the most exciting bit of news is …' She paused, still finding what had happened a little unreal.

'I got married!'

The women all gawped at Rosie in total disbelief. Even Dorothy was momentarily speechless.

'Married? To Peter?' Martha was the first to speak.

Rosie chuckled. 'Yes, to Peter.'

'Oh. My. Goodness!' Dorothy had finally found her tongue. 'You've got married! To your "scrummy detective"?'

Rosie nodded again.

'Eee, congratulations, miss!' Angie stood up and did something she had never done before: she put her arms around her boss and gave her a hug. Her actions started a chorus of 'Congratulations!' and a clamour to follow suit and give Rosie a hug to show her just how happy they were for her.

Martha almost squashed the breath from her, Dorothy's hug was nearly as crushing, and Hannah's skinny arms squeezed her with all their might, accompanied by a few words in her native tongue, something they had all got used to hearing whenever Hannah was excited or worried.

When Polly hugged her, Rosie whispered, 'You'll be next. He'll be back soon. You'll see.' Rosie had thought a lot about Polly since she'd got married. Out of all the squad she knew, news of her nuptials to Peter would affect Polly the most. Tommy had now been away for more than a year and she could tell it was taking its toll. Polly hid it well, but they all knew she was worried sick about her fiancé. She had told Rosie during an unguarded moment that she often wished she and Tommy had got married before he had left.

Gloria was the last to give her friend a bear hug. 'I'm dead chuffed for yer, I really am!' There were tears in her eyes. Rosie thought her second in command seemed more emotional than normal, and again she thought of Jack and his sudden move to Glasgow.

'All right, you lot!' Rosie's voice was thick with emotion. 'Stop now or else I'll be a blubbering wreck!'

'Ha!' Hannah suddenly perked up, pointing to Rosie's left hand. 'I thought it was odd you were wearing a bandage! Show us the ring!'

Everyone looked at Rosie as she picked off the sticking plaster to reveal her gold wedding band.

'Oh, it's lovely, miss.' Angie was staring at the ring as if it was a huge solitaire.

Rosie caught Polly touching the top pocket of her overalls, where she kept the ruby and diamond engagement ring Tommy had given her, and again she felt sorry for her. Polly had recently been the matron of honour at the wedding of her brother Joe and sister-in-law Bel. It must seem to her that everyone was getting married but her.

'So, tell us about the proposal?' Polly asked. If she felt even a touch of jealousy, it didn't show.

'Oh, Polly, I'm afraid it wasn't anywhere near as romantic as yours and Tommy's,' Rosie admitted with a little laugh. She was greeted by a semicircle of disappointed faces. 'Sorry to be so blunt and honest, but it really wasn't.'

'It must have been a little bit mushy?' Dorothy demanded.

Rosie laughed. 'I'm afraid not – not a bit.'

Dorothy opened her mouth to push for more information when the horn sounded out the end of the lunch break.

'Come on, you lot,' Gloria said, naturally taking command, as she had become used to doing this past week.

She looked across at Rosie.

'Next instalment in the Admiral after the end of shift?'

Rosie nodded.

'Definitely.'

Rosie's decision, though, wasn't so much to do with a need to continue being cross-examined about her love life, as for the chance to catch Gloria on her own. She wanted to chat to her about Jack and find out the real reason he was hundreds of miles away building ships on the Clyde.

Chapter Three

The Admiral, North Sands, Sunderland

The women had managed to squeeze just about every last drop of information out of Rosie concerning her nuptials to Peter. They had sat, enrapt, as Rosie told them all about the actual wedding day, how they'd had to get a special licence, that they'd only just had time to get the ring and a bouquet of white pansies, and that she'd worn the red dress Kate had made her for Christmas.

Dorothy and Angie were a little disappointed that Rosie had not been terribly forthcoming about the actual proposal but hadn't wanted to push it. They were conscious that their boss was being more open with them than she ever had been in all the time they had known her. Gloria had also briefed them not to ask anything about Peter's war work, as it was all very 'hush hush', and even Rosie didn't really know where he was going, or what he was doing.

'So,' Rosie said, breathing a sigh of relief that she had done what she knew she had to do, 'enough about me and my love life. I'm bored of talking about myself. So, come on, what's been happening while I've been away?'

Rosie looked at her squad and at Hannah and Olly, who thought no one could see that he was holding his 'friend girl's' hand under the round wooden table. All their faces, apart from Hannah's and Olly's, were flushed from having spent the entire day out in the cold before being propelled into the heat of a packed pub. Rosie looked at Angie and saw that the red mark she had noticed on her face this morning had now merged in with the ruddy blush of her hot cheeks.

'You all right, Angie?' she asked.

'Aye, miss, couldn't be better. Why'd ya ask?'

'Miss *asks*, Ange,' said Dorothy, her expression revealing the depth of her outrage, 'because she's not blind and she saw the mark your dad's backhander left on your face.'

Angie's hand went automatically to the top right side of her face, before dropping quickly to pick up her drink.

'It's like I told Dor, miss, just ma dad in a one ... It was just bad luck I was in the way.' She took a sip of her port.

Rosie glanced across at Gloria, whose face had darkened.

'And what was *the big man* "in a one" about?' Gloria asked. Angie's dad was indeed a 'big man' – pretty huge, in fact – but that wasn't the meaning Gloria conveyed in the tone of her voice. Gloria might have put up with being her ex-husband's punchbag for most of her married life, but since she had got shot of him, hearing about men who used their fists on women made her boiling mad.

'Apparently,' Dorothy answered the question for her friend, something she was wont to do and which Angie didn't seem to mind, 'he was in a mardy because he'd just come in from work and Angie's mum was just going out. *She'd committed the ultimate sin.*' Dorothy's eyes widened to show her incredulity. 'She'd not made his tea, having been called in to do overtime at the ropery.' They all knew Angie's dad worked at the Wearmouth colliery and that her mum was a 'Craven's angel' – the nickname given to the hardy, no-nonsense women who worked at Craven's Ropery.

'So, big gob here,' Dorothy continued, 'decided to make a joke of it and tell her dad that it wouldn't kill him to make his own tea. And as you are all now witness to, it was a joke that was not met with a barrel of laughs.'

'Eee, honestly, Dor, yer don't half exaggerate,' Angie said. 'I keep telling ya, yer should write one of them books yer always trying to get me to read, then ya can be rich 'n famous 'n we can live the high life—'

'Welcome back, Rosie!'

Dorothy and Angie's banter was broken by Jimmy, the head riveter, who was balancing four overflowing pints in his large, outstretched hands. The women all looked up at him.

'And I do believe congratulations are in order!' He had a big smile on his face. 'Yer kept that one quiet, didn't ya!'

The women all looked at Rosie, who was blushing – and it was not caused by the fire that was now roaring in the corner of the pub.

'I'll bring ya a drink over in a minute,' he said, turning away to give his four mates their pints.

'No need, Jim—' Rosie tried to object but found herself addressing the back of his scruffy overalls.

'Blimey!' Polly laughed. 'Talk about quicker than the speed of light!'

They all chuckled and said in unison, 'Muriel!'

'And we didn't even gan to the canteen today!' Angie added.

'Oh dear,' Hannah said, looking unusually guilty, 'I think it might have been me. Olly and I nipped there for Mr B—' Hannah couldn't bring herself to call her boss 'Basil', so had come to a compromise.

'He wanted a cold pie,' Olly interrupted. 'Said his wife wasn't too well and hadn't been able to put up his usual packed lunch.'

'I bet you *she* didn't get a backhander,' Dorothy muttered under her breath.

'We might have been chatting about it in the queue,' Hannah confessed.

'It was my fault,' Olly butted in again. 'I should have kept my voice down. Sorry, Rosie.'

Hannah looked at Olly and shook her head. 'No, it's *my* fault. I should have waited until we were on our own. I was just so excited ...' Hannah gave Rosie a look of remorse.

'Don't worry, you two, it's nobody's fault. Everyone's going to have to find out eventually, might as well get it all over and done with in one go ... Anyway, on a different topic, Hannah, why are you dragging Basil in early and doing so much overtime? It's not very often you draughtsmen are needed to do extra hours.'

Hannah looked at Olly and then back at Rosie. 'I just want to do as much as I can,' she said. 'You know – how do you say it Angie? "To beat the bastards".'

Rosie nodded her understanding. They all knew Hannah wanted to do anything to help win the war. She'd even welded for months on end before she'd nearly collapsed through exhaustion. At least if she was trying to work all the hours God sent, she was doing so with a pencil and paper and in the relative warmth of the drawing office as opposed to outside, in all weathers, working with a welding rod and thick sheets of metal.

'Best of luck, pet!' Jimmy's voice boomed over their heads as he leant over and put a bulbous glass of brandy down in front of Rosie. 'My lot says to tell ya "Congratulations!"'

'Ah, thanks, Jimmy.' Rosie raised her glass in the direction of Jimmy's squad, who were all squashed around a table by the window, and mouthed, 'Thank you.'

Jimmy looked at Martha, who was just taking a big glug of her beer shandy. 'And if Martha there—' He didn't need to finish what he was saying.

'The answer's still no, Jimmy!' Martha said, wiping her mouth with the back of her hand.

'Blimey, you lot never give up, do you?' Polly laughed. Ever since Helen had put Martha to work with the riveters, Jimmy had made no bones about the fact that he wanted her on his team permanently. There was, of course, no way Martha wanted to work with anyone apart from the women welders, even if she was more suited to riveting. The group's gentle giant was as shy and sensitive as she was large. When she'd first started at the yard it had taken months for her to come out of her shell. She had barely even spoken. Now Martha was more verbal than she had been in her entire life and no one wanted to jeopardise that. They all knew that if 'Big Martha', as she was affectionately known by their fellow workers, was put with any squad other than their own, there was a good chance she would shrink straight back into her shell.

'So, Polly,' Rosie asked. 'Did I see a map sticking out of your bag earlier on?'

The question was met with a bluster of 'Tell us about it!' from Dorothy and Angie.

'Polly,' Martha explained, 'has got herself a map of the world.'

'Yeh, so we're all having to learn geography now,' Angie huffed. 'It's bad enough Dor here trying to get me to speak proper and read books, and now Pol's started with all this war talk and where all these countries are that we've never heard of before.'

'Speak for yourself, Ange!' Dor sounded indignant. 'I've heard of most of them, but ...' she smiled over at Polly, who was rummaging around in her bag for the object under discussion, ' ... it *is* actually quite interesting seeing where some of the less well-known countries are.'

'Here we are!' Polly pulled the slightly crumpled atlas from her bag.

'Yes, *Polly here*,' Gloria informed Rosie, 'has been educating us all since Arthur gave her this old map he had stashed away.' Arthur Watts was Tommy's grandfather. He had more or less brought up his grandson single-handedly after his daughter killed herself following the death of Tommy's dad in the First War.

'Like Angie here,' Gloria said, 'I was never really one for school or lessons, let alone geography, but Polly's showed me where the Atlantic Ocean is and which countries it touches on, so I feel I've at least got some idea where my two boys are.'

Gloria's two sons, Bobby and Gordon, had joined the navy before war had been declared. She was used to them being away from home, but not to the fear of what might happen to them.

'Yes, and on Saturday, when all the newspapers were on about the Philips— What do you call them again?' Angie asked.

'The Philippines,' Polly corrected.

'Yes, well, Pol here showed us exactly where they are. And did you know, miss,' Angie informed, 'it's not really a place, just loads of little islands?'

Rosie nodded. She had chatted to Peter about the Japanese attacking the Philippines when the news broke over the weekend.

'Eee, 'n have you heard about Jack, miss?' Angie asked.

'Him being sent to Scotland?' Rosie cast a sidelong glance at Gloria.

'Yeh, just after you left on Wednesday,' Angie continued, 'we ended up being left on our tod when Gloria rushed off to say goodbye to Jack. The bosses said he had to pack his bags pronto and get himself up to Clydeside for some kind of emergency ... Not that he's gonna be gone for long, is he, Glor?'

'Nah, he'll be back soon,' Gloria said, taking a sup of her half-pint of lemon and lime cordial.

'And how's Helen been while I've been away?' Rosie was quick to change the subject, seeing the fleeting look of panic on Gloria's face.

'She's been a nightmare,' Polly said, stuffing her map back into her holdall.

'What? With you lot?' Rosie asked, surprised. Before she left, she had thought that Helen seemed to be mellowing a little. She certainly hadn't been giving any of them a hard time. Quite the reverse. Rosie had thought, perhaps a little over-optimistically, that Helen might well be calling a truce with the women, having bravely saved Gloria from being beaten half to death by Vinnie after he'd found out the baby his wife had just had wasn't his. Luckily, Helen had knocked him flying with the back of a shovel and saved the day.

'Back to being a right old bossyboots,' Martha chipped in.

'And not just with us,' Dorothy added. 'I heard her giving one of the office workers a right old tongue-lashing the other day. Just because the poor girl had made a spelling mistake.'

Angie laughed. 'Good job I don't work there – she'd be hoarse.'

'I think you would have lamped her one if she'd gone at you like she did that Sylvia girl. You know, the one who's just started?' Dorothy looked at Rosie, who nodded.

Surprised that Helen seemed to have reverted back to her old, less amicable self, Rosie was glad that Gloria had agreed to come back to hers after picking up her baby daughter, Hope.

She might finally find out what was really going on.

Chapter Four

'Thanks, Beryl!' Gloria shouted over her shoulder as she manoeuvred the pram onto Tatham Street.

'Nee bother, hinny! Any time!' Beryl shouted back. She had been helping to look after Hope for the day in place of Polly's sister-in-law, Bel, as her three-year-old daughter Lucille had been stricken down with some kind of sickness bug that no one wanted to catch, least of all a five-month-old baby.

'And lovely to see you too, Rosie!' Beryl piped up. 'Pop in any time – you don't need an excuse!'

'Thanks, Beryl! And say hi to the girls. Tell them I'm always on the lookout for more women welders if they don't like it at the post office.'

Beryl's face went stony. 'Over my dead body!' she called back.

Rosie laughed and waved at Beryl, who kept her face grim but gave Rosie a wink before shutting the front door. Whenever the two women saw each other, Rosie would teasingly try to recruit Beryl's two daughters, Iris and Audrey, knowing full well that both Beryl and her lifelong friend Agnes were vehemently against anyone they cared for working at Thompson's, including Agnes's daughter, Polly. They knew only too well that shipyard work was dangerous at the best of times, never mind when the country was at war.

'So, go on ...' Rosie said, getting out her little electric torch to help them see where they were going as the blackout regulations meant there wasn't even a peek of light showing from any of the houses or pubs along the route back to her flat, ' … what's all this about Jack working on the Clyde?'

Gloria stopped to let an old woman shuffle past them.

'Oh, Rosie, I'm not half glad yer back,' she said as they started walking again. Her words were uttered along with a weary sigh. 'I've felt like I've been going to pop, I've had to keep everything so bottled up.' As Gloria spoke she leant forward to check quickly on Hope and was relieved to see she was sleeping soundly, despite the uneven pavement.

'Well,' Rosie said, 'time to uncork that bottle and let it all out.'

Reaching the end of Tatham Street, they both stopped as a tram trundled past, before making their way across the Borough Road.

'I'm just here on the right,' Rosie said as they reached a detached Victorian house that had been converted into four flats. She flashed her torch down a little flight of stone steps.

'I'll take this end.' Rosie grabbed the front of the pram and they both carefully manoeuvred the Silver Cross down the steps. Rosie opened the front door and they managed to get Hope and her grey and silver carriage into the flat without too much bother.

As soon as they were in, Rosie shut the door and switched on the lights.

'Oh,' Gloria said, 'this is lovely!' She looked about the small but cosy basement flat.

'And is that a bathroom I can see down the hallway?'

Rosie nodded and smiled. 'Luxury, eh?' she said, before quickly nipping into the kitchen and putting the kettle on the hob.

'So,' Rosie came back and sat down on one of the dining chairs, 'spill the beans. I'm all ears.' She looked at her friend and saw a mixture of emotions. Relief at being able to talk, but also a deep sadness.

'Well, you know Jack and I were going to come clean with Miriam about everything – and about Hope.' Gloria cast another look over to the pram.

'Mm,' Rosie nodded.

'Well, it didn't quite go to plan,' Gloria said. 'Far from it, in fact.'

'She didn't already know about you two, did she?' Rosie asked.

By the look on Gloria's face, Rosie could see that her guess had been spot on.

'*Oh, yes!*' Gloria let out another sigh. 'I should have guessed she would somehow find out. Although God knows how. Perhaps someone clocked us at St Peter's.' The little Anglo-Saxon church just up from the shipyard had been Jack and Gloria's secret meeting place, both before Jack had gone to America and after his return. Meeting him there had been Gloria's way of helping him get his memory back after his ship was bombed and he'd nearly drowned. 'Or maybe someone who knew Miriam saw Jack visiting me at the hospital that day.' Gloria paused. 'Or perhaps someone from Thompson's came to see me and saw Jack.'

Gloria was quiet for a moment.

Suddenly a terrible thought occurred to her.

Helen!

Helen might well have gone to the hospital outside of visiting hours – just as Jack had done – and seen them together.

'Oh, please let it not have been Helen!' Gloria felt aghast at the thought. 'She would be the last person on earth I'd want to have seen us. Anyone but Helen.'

Rosie looked at her friend and saw her pain and her guilt. Helen adored her father and would be mortified when she found out about his infidelity. But Rosie also knew that Gloria's guilt was exacerbated by the fact that it was Helen who had bravely stepped in and saved her from Vinnie's fists. Helen had risked life and limb for a woman who would undoubtedly be seen as the cause of her parents' break-up.

'Anyway,' Gloria slumped back into the sofa, 'somehow Miriam found out about us. And she didn't *just* know about Jack and me, but about Hope as well. But she didn't act on it straight away. Rather than have the screaming heebie-jeebies like most people would have done if they'd found out their husband was having an affair, Miriam kept it all to herself, stewed on it, and worked out a way that would not only stop it becoming public knowledge, but which would also keep Jack and me apart.'

Rosie's frown furrowed into a question just as the kettle started to scream. 'I don't understand how she can stop it coming out ... Two seconds – let me just get our tea.' Rosie got up and quickly poured a pot of tea and brought it into the living room on a tray with cups and saucers and a plate of biscuits. 'Go on, what happened?'

Gloria leant forward to stir the pot. 'Oh, Rosie, it was awful. About an hour or two after you'd got Peter's telegram and left to catch your train, Billy – I think that's his name?'

'The plater's foreman?' Rosie said.

'Yes, that's the one ... Well, anyway, he came over and said that one of the managers wanted to have a chat with me, but when I got to the admin office, I saw Harold standing by the main gates waving me over. He made some comment about us women welders being in demand and that there was a car waiting for me. He'd walked off before I had the chance to ask him why.'

Rosie listened intently.

'I didn't know what to make of it all. And, idiot that I was, I just went over and got in the car. Of course, it didn't take me long to work out where I was being taken.'

'Roker!' Rosie said.

'Yes. When I arrived at the house, there she was, waiting for me at the doorway, drink in hand.'

'Oh God. What a nightmare!'

'Exactly,' Gloria said, pouring out their two cups of tea and handing one to Rosie. 'When I walked into the living room, Jack was there, standing by the window, looking white as a sheet.'

'Oh my goodness,' Rosie said. 'What did he say?'

'Jack was mortified Miriam had got me to the house, told her it was a conversation he should be having with her on his own. But Miriam wasn't having any of it ... I tried to apologise, said I was sorry – and I *did* mean it. You know me, Rosie. I've felt so terrible about it all, even if I do loathe the woman.'

Rosie knew Gloria had every right to hate Miriam. The woman had just about ruined her life. She'd snatched Jack from under her nose when they were young, pretending she was pregnant in order to get Jack to marry her. If Rosie had been in Gloria's shoes, she knew she wouldn't have felt even a sliver of guilt or remorse. Miriam might look all sweetness and light, with her girlish figure, regal looks, and short, wavy blonde hair, but her heart was as black as coal, she was as ruthless as she was selfish, and when it came to getting what she wanted, God help anyone who stood in her way.

'I didn't know what else to say, to be honest,' continued Gloria. 'The plan had been for Jack to tell Miriam *on his own*. I thought she'd give me a piece of her mind and tell me I was out of a job. Ban us both from Thompson's and probably just about every other shipyard or factory that her father had influence over.

'I didn't mention Hope because I didn't know if she knew, but, of course, she did – made it clear she did.' Gloria shivered as she recalled how Miriam had called her beautiful baby girl a 'bastard'.

'Oh, Rosie, it was just so awful, I wanted to run away. And all the time Miriam just stood there, cool as a cucumber, looking pristine and perfect, sipping her bloody gin and tonic. She said in that uppity way of hers that it didn't take a genius to work out that Jack was going to leave her and set up home with me and Hope. I didn't know what to say, but the weird thing is, I felt a little relieved that everything was finally out in the open.'

Rosie nodded, knowing how much Gloria had hated being deceitful about her affair with Jack, how she had wanted so much to tell the truth.

'Jack told her that he would pack his bags and leave immediately and that it went without saying that she could divorce him on grounds of adultery.' Rosie nodded, thinking that this sounded like Jack. 'But that's where it all went hideously wrong.' Gloria could feel her heart pounding as she relived that awful time just five days ago. 'All of a sudden, all that nicey-niceness, butter-wouldn't-melt act vanished and I swear to God she turned into the Wicked Witch of the West – her mouth was all screwed up and she practically spat as she told Jack and me that we were mad if we thought she'd just stand by and let us "skip off into the sunset", pushing our "bastard child in a second-hand Silver Cross pram".'

'Oh!' Rosie sat up straight, shocked. 'That's vile!' They both automatically looked over to Hope. How anyone could be so vitriolic about such a beautiful and innocent baby was clearly beyond them both.

'Yes, you're right, she was "vile". Absolutely vile. But then when Jack said that she didn't really have any choice in the matter, she let out the most horrible, shrill laugh. I'll never forget it. It sent a shiver down my back, it did. And that's when she dropped the bombshell. Or should I say, bombshells.'

Rosie looked at Gloria. She did not like the sound of this one little bit.

'Go on.'

'Well ...' Gloria took a deep breath. 'She started asking about Thompson's and whether I liked working there ... and about *how close* she'd heard I was to the rest of the women welders, and what a strange bunch of women they were. I was completely thrown. Then she started talking about Hannah and how she had struggled when she first started working at the yard, but had come on leaps and bounds since she'd been moved across to the drawing office.'

Rosie sensed Hope was stirring and went to check on her. Realising she was starting to wake up, she gently took her out of the pram and started swaying her in her arms as she walked around the room.

'I couldn't understand why she was talking about Hannah, until she started saying how Hannah's aunty Rina had got herself into money bothers. You know she works as a credit draper selling clothes and whatnots on tick, don't you?'

Rosie nodded.

'Well, it would seem her customers haven't been paying her what she's owed. Sounds like she's been fobbed off with every sob story going. It's got so bad Hannah's been trying to pick up every minute of overtime just to keep a roof over their heads. And she's only on an apprentice wage, which is nothing.'

Rosie let out air. 'That's why she was in at seven this morning. I thought it was unusual. I thought she looked a bit uncomfortable when I said Basil had better be paying her overtime. Honestly! Why hasn't she said anything to us?'

'I know,' Gloria agreed, 'and I think she's been doing a lot more overtime than we realise.'

'But what's that got to do with Miriam?' Rosie asked, confused.

'Oh Rosie, that woman is pure evil, I swear it. God knows how Jack's stayed married to her for all these years.' Gloria shook her head. 'Anyway, Miriam started going on about how awful it would be for Hannah if she were to lose her job, that her and her aunty would be out on the street or in the workhouse ... That "the little Jewess" wouldn't get work anywhere else, that refugees like Hannah were the last in line for any kind of work, and that she'd heard that Hannah and her aunty Rina were the kind of people who wouldn't accept any kind of charity, even if it was forced on them.'

'Which is true,' Rosie said.

'Oh, I could have slapped Miriam there and then. She put on this mock-sad look. I tell you the woman is definitely a slice short. I'll never forget her words. "From a palace in Prague to the slums of Sunderland. That's quite a fall for your little bird."' Gloria took a breath. 'But Hannah was just the start ... Next up was Martha.'

Gloria shuffled uncomfortably on the sofa, sitting forward with her hands clasped.

'She asked if we'd met Martha's parents.'

Rosie had to stop herself pacing around the room as Hope was starting to get restless in her arms. They'd all met Martha's parents and it was pretty obvious that their only daughter was not their biological child.

'Jack and I just stared at her as she picked up a newspaper from the sideboard. As soon as I saw it I could tell it was old because it was all yellow and crinkled. When I saw the photograph on the front page, though – *and the headline* – I felt sick. There was a black and white mugshot of a woman who looked the spitting image of Martha. If it hadn't been such an old newspaper, I would have bet money it actually was Martha.'

'Her real mother, then?' Rosie asked.

Gloria nodded. 'But it was the headline, Rosie, that knocked me for six.'

'What did it say?'

'Two words,' Gloria said. *'Child Killer.'*

Rosie sucked in air.

'No!'

'The strange thing is, I can remember the court case,' said Gloria. 'You would have been too young. But the irony is I only read about it because I'd become obsessed with reading the marriages and births sections, trying to find out when Miriam and Jack had got married and if they'd had a baby. I know, *pitiful*, but I was only a young girl. I was in bits … Anyway, I remember reading about the court case of this woman from one of the mining villages who was hanged after it was discovered she had killed at least five children – most of them her own. She'd poisoned all these poor mites over months and had made a great show of trying to nurse them back to health.'

'Oh God, and you definitely think it was Martha's real mum?' Rosie asked.

'Yes.' Gloria was definite. 'Miriam told me with great glee how she had a friend who worked in the registry office and she'd confirmed that the woman was Martha's mam.'

Rosie stood still, staring, not knowing what to say. Sensing the disquiet, Hope started to whimper.

'I know, I couldn't quite take it in.' Gloria sighed sadly.

'Poor Martha,' Rosie said, 'fancy finding out that a monster like that is your own flesh and blood.'

'I know, that was exactly the point Miriam made,' Gloria said as she went over to the pram and fished out a bottle of milk.

'Let me guess,' Rosie said, handing Hope over to Gloria. 'She threatened to let every man and his dog know about Martha's mum?'

'That was about the sum of it.' Gloria sat back down and started feeding Hope.

Rosie and Gloria didn't need to say anything; they both knew that Martha would not cope at all well with being the talk of the town and it would send her straight back into the non-verbal world she had previously inhabited. She would be ostracised, stared at in the street, and whispered about behind her back. It would destroy her, as it would her mother and father.

Rosie shook her head. There were no words. She sat back down and topped up her tea, which was going cold.

'So, I'm guessing it wasn't just Hannah and Martha that Miriam dug up dirt on? Mind you, I'd be amazed if she found anything at all untoward about Polly.'

'You're right there about Polly, but what Miriam did threaten to do was get word to Tommy that Polly had found another chap.'

'That's not on!' Rosie exploded. Out of all her squad Polly had always been the most industrious and determined. She was also a lovely girl, who was incredibly kind and caring to just about everyone she met. They had all watched her fall in love with Tommy and seen Tommy fall right back in love with her. Their courtship, though, had been rather tumultuous thanks to Helen's attempts to split them up because she wanted Tommy for herself.

'I think, more than anything, it was Miriam's way of trying to hurt Jack,' Gloria said. 'She knows how close Jack's always been with Arthur, and that Jack thinks the world of Tommy too … And she also knows Tommy's history. You know about Tommy's mam topping herself, don't you?'

Rosie nodded. Most people who worked in the yard knew Tommy and why his granddad had brought him up. Not that anyone ever talked about it openly, least of all in front of Tommy.

'How did Miriam put it …' Gloria thought for a moment. 'That's it … That Tommy might take after his father in looks, but in his mind he was just like his mam – "fragile".'

'God, she really has no soul, does she?' Rosie was aghast.

'Nope, not even a shadow of one,' Gloria agreed. 'The thing is, if Tommy got wind that Polly was off with some other bloke, he'd believe it. Most blokes would believe it. Especially if their sweetheart worked with a load of strapping young men day in and day out.'

Rosie nodded her agreement. It was true. And they'd all seen it with their own eyes, women straying while their fiancés or husbands were away. The war had made people do things they wouldn't normally do.

'What was Jack's reaction?' Rosie asked.

'He was livid.' Gloria looked at Hope, who was falling back off to sleep having drunk most of her bottle. 'He started yelling at Miriam that this was one step too far. I think Miriam knew she was skating on thin ice and tried to smoothe it over, saying she was sure such rumours wouldn't make it all the way over to Gibraltar, but it was obvious the threat was there all the same.'

'So, go on, tell me what she found out about Angie and Dorothy. I'm guessing there was lots to pick from there,'

44

Rosie said, thinking of her two workers – so full of fun and life, but also about as far from saintly as you could get.

'Well, it wasn't them but their *mams* that Miriam – or, I'm guessing, the person she employed – found out about.'

'Really?' Rosie asked.

'Well, it would seem that Angie's mam is having it off with some bloke. God forbid Angie's dad finds out. If he gives his daughter a clobber every now and again for cheeking him back or not getting the shopping in, heavens knows what he'd do if he found his wife was doing the dirty on him.'

Rosie took a drink of her tea and thought about the red mark she'd seen on Angie today.

'But it was what she found out about Dorothy's mam,' Gloria continued, 'that was a real turn-up for the books.' They all knew Dorothy's mother had been married and that the marriage had broken up.

'Well, it seems that Dorothy's mam didn't actually divorce her first husband before marrying the bloke she's with now. The one she's had four more daughters with. And as Miriam was keen to point out, it's illegal to be married to two people at the same time.'

'Bigamy,' Rosie said.

'Exactly,' Gloria said, although she had not known that this was the proper word for it until Miriam had enlightened her. 'Which means if she gets found out, she'll be looking at a spell in prison, or a huge fine. But even if Dorothy's mam got off with a slap on the wrist, it'd be the shame of it all.'

'Blimey.' Rosie whistled out air.

The two women were quiet.

After a few moments Rosie's head suddenly jerked towards Gloria. 'She didn't find anything out about me, did she?'

Gloria shook her head vehemently. 'No, thank goodness. The only thing she'd found about you was that you were "living in sin" with some bloke twice your age.'

Rosie slumped. Relief flooded through her. She didn't think she could handle another threat to the bordello. Not after the last time.

'Thank God for small mercies,' she muttered, pouring out the last dregs of tea into their cups.

Gloria got up and put Hope back in her pram.

'God, Gloria, this really is shocking. What did you do after she'd said all of this?'

Gloria sat back down and took a drink of her tea. 'I just asked her straight. I said she obviously had us over a barrel and what did she want?'

Rosie couldn't help but admire Gloria. Nothing ever seemed to faze her, or at least she never let on that it did.

'I'd pretty much guessed by this stage what she wanted in exchange for *her* keeping shtum – and that was that *I* also keep my mouth shut ... I am never to tell another living soul about Jack and me, nor am I to breathe a word about our "bastard's true paternity".'

Again, Rosie flinched. She hated that word. Not because it was a swear word, but because it was so judgemental.

'She said that if I did that, every one of my "workmates' sleazy secrets" would remain just that – secrets.' Gloria slumped at the word 'secrets'.

'Oh, Gloria ... You were so looking forward to being honest and open, and now here you are not just having to keep your secret – but everyone else's.' Rosie paused. 'I'm guessing that the cherry on Miriam's perfectly iced cake was banishing Jack to Scotland?'

Gloria nodded. Her mind flicked back to how she'd been ordered to leave the house without saying goodbye to Jack, and how she had walked along the coast road feeling punch-drunk. Jack had found her and made her promise to stay strong before they'd said a rushed goodbye. Now Rosie was back, though, she felt she could unload some of that heavy weight she'd been hauling about with her these past five days.

'Yes,' Gloria said. 'Miriam got her father – you know, old Mr Havelock?' Rosie nodded. Everyone knew Mr Havelock. He owned, or at least had substantial shares in, a good majority of the town's businesses and shipyards. 'Well, she got him to sanction Jack's move to the Clyde. The yarn she is going to spin, should anyone ask, is that Jack is the all-singing, all-dancing expert on everything to do with the new Liberty ships, and that, as a result, he's in demand with just about every ship-yard in the country.' Everyone in the shipbuilding indus-try knew the Liberty ships were of massive importance to the war effort. The prototype had been designed by Mr Thompson himself, but the Americans could build them cheaply and quickly, and without the threat of being bombed.

'So, that's why Jack's up in Scotland?'

'Yep, and as far as Miriam's concerned, that's where he's going to stay.' Gloria was unable to keep the despondency out of her voice.

'So, what did you tell the women when you got back? They must have been wondering where you'd got to, and why Jack had suddenly left for the Clyde?'

'You know that lot – always the Spanish Inquisition.' Gloria let out a short laugh. 'Well, I kept it to as near the truth as I could. That Jack had been sent to Scotland at a moment's notice, but that we'd managed to see each other to say goodbye. I just left out everything else.' Gloria sup-pressed a yawn. Now that she had unburdened herself she was starting to feel tired.

47

'Come on,' Rosie said. 'I'll walk you to the bus stop. I'm not surprised you're knackered. We'll work out a solution. Might take us a little while, but we'll think of something. Miriam's a nasty piece of work, but she's not going to win. *Mark my words.*'

'I wasn't a total pushover, though, you know? With Miriam,' Gloria said, puffing as she and Rosie carefully got the pram up the steps and onto the pavement.

'I can well imagine,' Rosie said. Gloria was about as far removed from a pushover as you could get, although it still surprised her that her workmate had put up with her husband's violence for so long.

'I didn't exactly have the last word, but I did manage to give her the length of my tongue before I was booted out the front door,' Gloria said. The cold night air had woken her up.

Rosie looked across at Gloria as she pushed the pram along Borough Road and past the towering stone pillars of the town's municipal museum, still open despite it now being early evening.

'She tried telling me I'd shot myself in the foot by telling Vinnie about Hope and that I'd be called all sorts now as everyone would know that I had an illegitimate baby and there was no father around. She said I'd be known as the yard's "bike"!'

Rosie tutted as she wrapped her old work coat around her denim overalls.

'Oh, I thought it was quite funny actually,' Gloria said, peering in the pram as she walked, checking on Hope. 'Told her I didn't give two hoots about what anyone thought of me.'

Which was true, Rosie thought. Gloria had only ever been worried about people finding out she was being beaten by her husband. For some inexplicable reason that was still a source of shame to her.

'She didn't like the fact that I laughed in her face and told me I should be careful as she might well inform the authorities that I'm an unfit mother and get Hope put into some kind of care home.'

Rosie could feel her own anger rise, so she knew how this must have made Gloria want to explode.

'Well, red rag to a bull or what?' Gloria said as they continued up Holmeside in the direction of the bus depot at Park Lane.

'So, I told her straight – that if she even *threatened* to do that ever again, I would make sure that every man, woman and child in this entire town and beyond knew that her husband had had a child with another woman ... That I would make damn sure that *she* was never able to lift *her* head high ever again in this town without a trail of salacious whispers following behind her. And, to top it all, I would make sure that everyone who is anyone got to hear how she tricked Jack into marriage, how she pretended she was pregnant, how she conned him and dragged him down the aisle faster than the speed of light – and then how she faked a miscarriage! I told her she'd be the laughing stock of polite society. That she would be known as *Desperate Miriam Havelock*. The woman who had to pretend she was up the duff to get her man!'

'Good on you, Glor! What did she say?'

'Oh you know, tried to make a joke of it and say she was quaking in her boots, but I knew I had got to her. At least when she slammed the door in my face I felt like I'd won a very minor victory.'

Rosie squeezed her friend's arm. Miriam might well have the upper hand, but this was by no means the end of the matter. The hostilities, Rosie was sure, would continue for a long time to come.

After Rosie had helped Gloria put the pram onto the double-decker bus that had been waiting, she waved her goodbyes and hurried home. She'd never really thought about how far Gloria had to trudge to work and back each day, but helping her bang that boat of a pram about, well, it had got her thinking. As she walked back down Holmeside she resolved to have a word with her landlord, old Mr Brown who lived in the flat above her, as well as a chat with George. Once, that was, she had told everyone at the bordello about her new marital status, something she felt a little nervous about and was happy to leave until tomorrow.

She was certainly in no rush to tell Lily that she was now a married woman. George, of course, would be the perfect gentleman and get out the best brandy and demand an impromptu celebration, but she was sure Lily would find some reason to throw a bucket of cold water over the celebration. Rosie loved Lily to pieces and knew Lily loved her too, but Peter had been, and still was, their one bone of contention.

Passing the museum, Rosie saw that there was some kind of event on as there were people hurrying up the wide stone steps and disappearing through the main entrance. The people who were attending looked well-to-do, which again brought Miriam to mind.

As she and Gloria had trooped to the bus depot they had agreed that at the moment, they had to do what that horrible woman wanted. There was nothing else they could do. Interfering in any of the women's lives would probably just make matters worse. They couldn't exactly tell Dorothy, Angie, Hannah and Martha what they knew.

And as for Polly, if she thought there was even the remotest possibility that Tommy might be fed lies about her and some other bloke at the yard, she'd worry herself into an early grave. The girl was as anxious as hell about her fiancé. And who wouldn't be? Handling unexploded bombs did not bode well for a long life.

Such morbid musings about Tommy had Rosie's thoughts slipping back unguarded to Peter. He mightn't be handling live mines, but she was pretty sure that what he was about to embark on was just as dangerous.

Chapter Five

Tatham Street, Hendon, Sunderland

'*Nooo!*'

Lucille pushed the thermometer that Bel had been trying to ease gently into her mouth out of her mum's hand before flinging the blankets in her cot to the side with great gusto.

Bel looked at Maisie, rolled her eyes towards the ceiling, and sighed heavily.

Maisie considered taking the thermometer and trying to give it a go herself, but then decided against it as she didn't want to catch whatever horrible bug it was Lucille had. The poor mite had been throwing up, sweating, and tossing and turning since the early hours.

Maisie had arrived at the Elliots' with the intention of taking her little niece into town for their regular sojourn to the Holme Café for some hot chocolate and one of Mrs Milburn's famous patisseries, only to find Lucille languishing in her cot in the downstairs bedroom that was now Polly's.

'I think it's safe to say you've had a wasted journey,' Bel said to her half-sister, putting the blankets back over her daughter. 'Why don't you come back at the weekend when madam here should be back on her feet?'

'*Noooo!*' This time Lucille's wail was even longer and was followed by another eruption of snotty tears. ''Aisiee stay!' she pleaded, eyes watering with tears, her little button mouth pursed defiantly at the aunty who was abandoning her in her hour of need.

'Nothing wrong with her hearing, then,' Bel said, wearily. She had been up half the night and was starting to feel more than a little under the weather herself.

Chuckling, Maisie took off her coat, grabbed the chair that was by the dresser, positioned it next to the cot and took hold of her niece's hot little hand through the wooden bars. Children had never interested Maisie; she had certainly never yearned for a daughter or son of her own, like most women she knew, but she did love Lucille. Her niece was full of life and fire, and sometimes, Maisie swore, she saw herself in the little girl.

'I don't know, LuLu,' Maisie said softly, 'what *are* we going to do with you?'

Lucille now looked at her aunt with wide, adoring eyes and grabbed for the toy bunny that Maisie had brought back for her from a trip to London. She started sucking her thumb at the same time as squashing the cloth bunny to her tear-stained face.

'You're going to have to get better soon,' Maisie said, keeping her voice low and cajoling, 'because I can't go to Mrs Milburn's tea shop on my own, can I?'

Lucille shook her head, hypnotised by Maisie's softly spoken, southern accent.

'You don't *have* to stay, you know?' Bel said, tucking the blankets around Lucille, who was now calming down.

Maisie laughed quietly. 'I think the whole street will get a right earful if I go now.'

'Well,' Bel whispered, 'as soon as she starts to drop off, you can make your escape.'

Bel was secretly pleased Maisie was staying, a feeling that was relatively new to her as their relationship had not got off on the right foot. It was at Bel's and Joe's wedding that Maisie had decided to declare that she was Bel's sibling, and Pearl her long-lost mother. The very public reunion had taken an even more dramatic turn after a shunned and very distraught Pearl had gone on a bender, only to be found in the nick of time as she was taking a midnight dip on Hendon beach.

On that day in November last year, Bel and Maisie had exchanged more than a few harsh words, but they'd reached a truce of sorts. They had spent an entire day and night searching for Pearl and had got to know each other, warts and all. Now they both accepted that they were to be a part of each other's lives, whether they liked it or not. And lately, it felt as though they were liking it more often than not.

'Joe out with the Home Guard?' Maisie asked.

Bel nodded as she glanced down at her daughter, who looked as though she might finally be drifting off to sleep. 'He said he'd be popping back to check on Lucille, and to grab something to eat, but then he'd be straight back out. They're doing the night watch over at Bartram's.'

Maisie knew Bartram's was one of the shipyards famous for launching straight into the North Sea, but she didn't realise that this evening's duty bore particular significance for Joe, as Bartram's was where he and Teddy had done their apprenticeship together, working as riveters from the age of fourteen.

'His leg bearing up?' Maisie's question was genuine. She had known quite a few young men who had come back from war with shrapnel injuries, and was aware that they could cause a lot of pain even after the wound had healed.

'It seems all right,' Bel said. 'It gives him a bit of gyp if he's been on his feet for a long time, but you know Joe, he never complains.'

Maisie nodded, although she didn't really know Joe. Whenever she saw him it was usually just a quick hello or goodbye, but he seemed a decent enough bloke. Bel and Joe had got together after Joe had been medically discharged from the army. He and his twin, Teddy, had both been Desert Rats, but only Joe had made it home. Teddy had caught a landmine, leaving Bel a widow with a young daughter.

'Talk of the devil,' Bel said. 'This sounds like him now.'

They both listened to the front door close, and the sound of Joe's walking stick on the tiled hallway before he quietly opened the bedroom door.

'Ahh,' he said, seeing both Maisie and Bel by Lucille's cot. 'Two Florence Nightingales to tend to one poorly little patient.'

Bel always felt herself flush when she saw Joe. He looked so handsome in his khaki uniform. Dorothy and Angie were right: her husband did look the spitting image of Errol Flynn.

Hearing Joe's voice, Lucille's eyes flickered open and she immediately stretched out her arms. 'Doey! Daddy!'

Joe hobbled across the room that used to be Bel's. He could never come into this room without recalling the time he and Bel had shared their first kiss. It had been the start of their love affair, although one that initially Bel had fought against ferociously.

Bending down to give Bel a quick kiss, Joe then leant his stick against the cot and scooped Lucille out of her bed. As soon as he lifted her up, she wrapped her legs and arms around him like a little koala bear.

'Go on, you two,' Joe commanded. 'Get yourselves a cuppa while I read this one a story.'

Bel handed Joe the shabby hardback picture book of 'The Lambton Worm' – Lucille's favourite bedtime story.

Lucille let out a jubilant cry followed by a rattling cough. Bel sighed inwardly. She had tried to get her daughter to enjoy something that wasn't about fighting and killing, but to no avail. Perhaps it wasn't so surprising, since all Lucille had known for her three years on this earth were air raids, bombed buildings and a world at war.

Maisie touched her niece's hot cheek. 'Get better, LuLu. Aunty Maisie loves you loads,' she told her.

''Aisiee ...' Lucille gave her aunty a forlorn look, but her attention was soon focused on the one person she adored more than anyone – Joe.

'God, she really is a proper daddy's girl, isn't she?' Maisie said as she and Bel stepped out into the hallway and headed into the kitchen.

Bel nodded.

'You all right with her calling Joe "Daddy"?' Maisie asked. She had noticed that when she and Lucille were on their own the little girl would always call Joe 'Daddy', but when she was with Bel, sensing her mummy's disapproval she would oscillate between calling her stepfather 'Doey' and 'Daddy'.

'I'm not sure, to be honest.' Bel leant over the kitchen table and felt the brown ceramic teapot with both her hands to see how warm it was. 'I don't want her to forget who her real dad is, but in her eyes, Joe *is* her dad. He's real, and he's here and he loves her. And she adores him. Always has. And how do you explain to a toddler that her real daddy's dead and that the man she sees as her da is actually her uncle? Of course, it doesn't help that he looks identical to Teddy.' Bel gave a sad laugh. She had fought her feelings for Joe and part of her had hated him when he first came back because he was a constant reminder of the husband she'd had taken from her.

'Cuppa?' Bel retrieved two cups and saucers from the side cabinet.

'Please,' Maisie said, sitting herself down at the kitchen table, glad that there was just her and Bel, and the two dogs, of course, who were both flat out in front of the hot range. It always amazed her how so many people could live under the one roof and that they would all invariably congregate in this small kitchen-cum-living room. When everyone was at home – Agnes, Arthur, Joe, Bel, Lucille, Polly and Pearl – there was barely room to breathe.

'Talking about fathers,' Bel said, trying to sound casual as she poured them each a cup of tea, 'you found out any more about *your* real da?' They both knew that Maisie's dad had been a stoker whose ship had docked in South Shields, just up the coast, and that young lads like him, often from Africa and India, were used as cheap labour on the ships. Other than that, though, they did not know much.

Maisie looked at Bel. They might still be getting to know each other, but there were times, like now, when Maisie could read her sister like a book, and she knew exactly where this conversation was headed.

'Well, I hate to admit it, but I've hit a bit of a dead end. Ma seems convinced that when he went back to the West Indies, he had no intention of returning. I think if I really want to meet him, I'm going to have to travel across to the other side of the world, which, at the moment, is clearly an impossibility. But even if this war does end sometime soon, and I do spend weeks on a ship travelling there, it's going to be like looking for a needle in a haystack ... And then there's no guarantee he's even still alive.' Maisie took a sip of her tea and relished it; her sister did know how to make a good brew. 'No, I think travelling all the way up north to find the woman who gave birth to me will have to do me. At least I found one of my parents ... I often wonder, though, if Ma had known she was pregnant before her sailor boy went back home, whether or not they would have stayed together?'

Bel looked at her stunning half-sister, and at her caramel-coloured skin. She had met a man from Africa once, but never anyone from the West Indies. She hadn't really known where that was until Polly had shown her on the map Arthur had given her.

'Would have been hard in those days, I reckon,' Bel said. 'Bad enough now a coloured man being with a white woman, but back then ...'

'I know, especially up here. It probably wouldn't have been so bad in London, but I don't think I've even seen another coloured person since I've been here.' Maisie suddenly started to chuckle.

'What's tickled your fancy?' Bel asked, getting up to put the kettle back on the hob.

'Ah, that mad mother of ours. Did she tell you that when she first met my dad, she had no idea he was coloured?'

Bel turned back from the stove and shook her head.

'Apparently he'd just come off the ship and hadn't had a chance to wash and was covered from head to toe in coal dust. All the stokers came off looking like they had been scrubbed with black shoe polish. But she said she took one look into his hazel eyes and that was it, she wouldn't have cared whether he was all the colours of the rainbow, she fell for him hook, line and sinker.'

Bel felt a shot of envy that Maisie had been treated to such a wonderful story about her da, and yet her ma had never uttered a word about *her* father.

'You know, I still want to find out about *my* da.' Bel came right out and said it.

Maisie looked at her sister. 'Honestly, Bel, you've got it all here. A lovely husband, an adorable daughter.' She would have liked to add that Bel also had enviable looks, with her perfect pale skin and naturally blonde hair – not a dark complexion that needed the aid of expensive cosmetics to look lighter, or tightly coiled hair that required hours to oil and straighten. 'And the best mother-in-law anyone could want. One who more than makes up for you having a "ma" whose mothering skills are lacking, to say the least.'

Maisie had learnt that the idyllic life she had imagined Pearl and Bel enjoying had been just that – a fantasy. She should have known that such perfect families simply didn't exist, but her bitterness at being given up as a baby had clouded her thinking. It hadn't taken her long, however, after meeting her mother and sister to realise that her imaginings could not have been further from the truth, and that if it hadn't been for Agnes, Bel would most likely have ended up in the workhouse.

'You've got this lovely life here,' Maisie argued. 'So why are you bothered about who your father is? Besides, Ma says he's dead. Died when you were a baby.'

Bel let out a hollow laugh, causing both Tramp and Pup to raise their heads slightly.

'God, pull the other one, it's got bells on.'

'You really don't believe her then?' Maisie's question was genuine.

Bel shook her head. 'I never believed Ma when I was a little girl and I certainly don't now. For someone who's told a load of lies her whole life long, Ma's never really mastered the art of being good at it. I've always been able to tell when she's trying to pull a fast one or telling porkies. And I always knew she was telling a great big whopper whenever I asked her why I didn't have a da like all the other children ... Dead my backside!'

'Who's dead?' It was Pearl's distinctive gravelly voice announcing her arrival in the kitchen.

Both Maisie and Bel turned in surprise to see their mother's scrawny frame blocking the doorway; as usual, she was heavily made-up, and dressed in a short skirt more suited to a twenty-year-old than a forty-two-year-old.

'Honestly, Ma, you can't half be quiet and stealth-like when you want,' Maisie said before taking another sip of her tea, drinking it down quickly as she knew Pearl's arrival meant it was time for her to go.

'Ha!' Pearl let out a boisterous laugh, which suggested she might have had a few whilst working the afternoon shift at the Tatham. 'That's me – what's the saying? *Hidden depths*. Anyway, what poor sod's dead?'

'My da, apparently,' Bel said, watching her mother's face drop, as she knew it would.

'Gosh, is that the time?' Maisie looked up at an imaginary clock and stood. She knew exactly when to get out of the line of fire. This was a conversation for her mother and her sister alone. 'I'd better get going.' Maisie gave Bel a quick hug and a kiss on the cheek. 'I'll check in on LuLu tomorrow, if that's all right? See if I can get her some sweeties to help that bad cough.'

'Oh, she'll love you even more than she does already if you do!' Bel said.

'I'll just grab my coat and say my goodbyes. Don't worry, I'll see myself out,' Maisie added.

'What about yer auld ma!' Pearl said, arms akimbo. 'Doesn't she get a hug 'n a kiss goodbye?'

Maisie looked at her mother. They were about the same height and build, quite small and petite, but where Maisie would be described as slender, Pearl might, at best, be classed as skinny.

'Ma, we are not huggers. *You* are not a hugger,' she said, opening her handbag and pulling out a packet of Winstons. 'Here you are – instead of a hug.'

Pearl's face lit up, happy to swap love for a packet of fags. 'Eee, thanks, pet.' She took the cigarettes off her daughter and immediately opened them, took out two and gave one to Maisie.

'I'll save it for the walk home,' Maisie said, grabbing her coat and hurrying out of the kitchen, just as the kettle started to scream.

'Fancy a cuppa, Ma?' Bel asked, taking the kettle off the hob and topping up the pot of tea on the kitchen table.

Pearl looked nervous. Her daughter had mentioned the dreaded 'D' word. Something she had mentioned more than once these past few weeks. Bel didn't normally offer her tea, and she had clearly been talking to Maisie about her da. Pearl was no clairvoyant, but she knew exactly what Bel was going to say next.

'I'd love a cuppa, pet,' Pearl said, trying to sound convincing, 'but I've gorra get back to the pub. Bill needs us to open up so I cannot be late.'

There was a moment's silence before Bel looked at her mother and said, 'Ma, you're going to have to tell me, you know.'

Pearl was now reaching for her handbag, which she had dumped on the table, and scrabbled around for her lighter.

'Tell you what, pet?' she asked, stalling for time.

'About my da!' Bel replied, exasperated.

Pearl gave up her search for a moment and took a deep breath. She knew she couldn't keep running away from this for ever.

'And don't,' Bel said, 'even try and give me that old baloney about him being dead, because you and me know

61

that's an outright lie. I didn't believe you as a child and I don't believe you now.'

Pearl looked at Bel but was struggling to think of a response.

'You know, Ma,' Bel said, more gently this time, which Pearl found even more disconcerting, 'I *need* to know. It's not fair that you've told Maisie everything about her da and yet, for some reason, it's like you've been sworn to secrecy about mine.'

Mother and daughter looked at each other.

Finally, Pearl broke their stand-off.

'Yer right ... He isn't dead ... or rather, he *wasn't* dead then. I'm not sure about now, though ...' Pearl let her voice trail off.

Bel waited. Her eyes glued to her mother.

Just then the front door went and the sound of Polly's hobnailed boots could be heard hurrying down the corridor.

'You wouldn't guess what happened at work—' She stopped in her tracks as she reached the doorway to the kitchen. She hadn't anticipated Pearl being there. Polly was never keen to be around Bel's mother for any length of time, and she certainly didn't want to tell her about Rosie's newly-wed status.

'Oh, is that a cuppa begging?' Polly asked, not waiting for an answer and quickly pouring herself some tea.

'Well, dinnit keep us waiting, Pol,' Pearl said. 'What happened at work? We're all ears.'

'Ah, it's nothing important. I'll tell you all later when I get myself out of these scruffy overalls and cleaned up.' Just one glance at Bel and Pearl and the serious looks on their faces told Polly to leave them to it. Slopping some milk into her cup, she braced herself for her trip to the washhouse in the backyard, which she knew would be near glacial.

Bel turned to her mother, eager to continue their conversation, only to find Pearl looking at her watch.

'Bugger! Is that the time?' She looked at Bel, who was about to say something.

'Look, pet, yer right. It's not fair I've talked to Maisie about her da and not to you, but this isn't the right time. And I've got to get back to the Tatham. There's only me and Bill on tonight so I need to get there early and help set up. We'll chat about this another time.'

Bel kept her eyes on her mother. 'Promise?'

'Aye, pet, I promise,' Pearl said, picking up her bag and gas mask and hurrying out of the kitchen. Stepping out the front door and crossing the road to the Tatham, she'd never thought she would be so glad to go to work. Telling Maisie about her da had been a walk in the park. Enjoyable, even. Maisie's father had been such a gentle soul. And even though they had been so young, really just children, they had loved each other. It had only been fate and the expanse of the Atlantic Ocean that had parted them.

Isabelle's father, however, was a *very* different ball game. And as much as Pearl wished he were dead, she knew for a fact he was very much alive and kicking – men like him had the knack of living to a ripe old age.

Chapter Six

When Pearl climbed into bed that night it was well past last orders. She had insisted on helping Bill clear up and had persuaded him to have a nightcap, not that he needed much persuading. It was clear to just about everyone, apart from Pearl, that he was sweet on her. Her delaying tactics had paid off, though, and everyone was in bed by the time she crept through the front door and up to her room.

Lying in her bed, inspecting the cracked plaster on the ceiling, Pearl realised it didn't matter how many nightcaps she had, tonight sleep was not going to come easily. She also had an awful feeling that what was keeping her awake would continue to do so for many more nights. Pearl might have avoided answering her daughter's probing queries about her da this evening, but she *had* promised they would chat about it later. Something she had never done before.

When Bel had been a child, for a good while she had pestered Pearl relentlessly about who her father was. Her playground friends had started chattering about mams and dads and who hadn't got any, or was missing one, and the whys and wherefores. Pearl had always batted away Bel's questions with the same trotted-out response: *Isabelle, yer da's dead. There's no more to say.* When the pestering had worn her down, she'd made up a vague story that her da had died of some illness. Pearl was of a mind that she was not going to glorify his fictional death in any way. She certainly wasn't going to pretend that he was some kind of war hero, or that his death had been anything even remotely commendable. Not like some women she knew whose lovers had, in reality, simply buggered off when they'd realised they'd got their bit of stuff in the family way. No, Isabelle's da did not deserve a praiseworthy death. She would never grant him that, and there was a perverse part of her that enjoyed imagining he had died a lingering and painful death.

When Maisie had declared herself Pearl's daughter, Pearl had been forced to relive a part of her life that had been so very painful for her. It had been so painful that she had tried ever since to erase that day twenty-eight years ago when she had handed Maisie over to Evelina, the midwife at the Salvation Army's hostel for unmarried mothers. But being reunited with the daughter she had given up had ended up being the best thing that had ever happened to her. Pearl had revelled in telling Maisie all about her father – how theirs had been a young love, which had ended when he'd left to travel back to his homeland without knowing that she was carrying their child.

Perhaps spurred on by Maisie's chatter about her da and how she had thought about trying to find him, Isabelle's childish determination to know the truth about *her* own father had been rekindled. Isabelle and her sister might be chalk and cheese, but they shared one trait – they were both stubborn as hell, and when they wanted something, they wouldn't stop until they got it.

Maisie had realised that it was highly unlikely she would ever get to meet the man who had sired her – unless she was prepared to travel halfway round the world.

Isabelle's da, however, was another matter entirely.

And worst of all, he was not living on the other side of the world, but much closer to home.

With a sinking heart, Pearl realised that this was not going to be some passing fancy of Isabelle's, and the questions about her da were not going to go away. Pearl was going to have to deal with this, whether she wanted to or not. She just needed more time to think and to work out a plausible lie – one that her daughter would believe.

Either that or she was simply going to have to tell her the awful truth.

When sleep finally came to Pearl it did not bring her any kind of repose. Far from it. Instead she was flung back into the dark depths of a nightmare in which she often found herself entombed and which had haunted her for almost twenty-eight years. The horror it forced upon her had never abated or lessened over the many years it had come back to torment her.

And like tonight, it always began the same way – with an impenetrable darkness, a bottomless, inky blackness that slowly became infused with the faint odour of a sickly-sweet perfume mixed with a foul-smelling sweat that became stronger and more overpowering.

And then came the fear. A fear that, once let out of the starting blocks, raced through her unconscious body, alerting every part of her to the danger that had snuck up on her so quietly, so surreptitiously. Forcing her eyes open, Pearl strained to see what it was – but there was nothing there.

Just the inky blackness.

The smell.

And the fear.

Until she sensed a presence nearby. Another being. She knew there was a face in the darkness, but try as she might, she could not see it. Every nerve in her body told her that the being was not good. It was the opposite of goodness. It was greed. Powerful greed. A greed that was determined to be satisfied. Dark, unnatural and perverted.

A moment's deathly silence followed until suddenly Pearl felt a dead weight on top of her. A fleshy, panting, human mass that seemed to be crushing the life out of her.

And then came the pain. The terrible, unbearable pain – along with the slow, almost gentle squeeze around her neck, increasing in pressure, trapping the breath inside her, depriving her of air.

Desperate for oxygen, her body started to thrash around. But it was all in vain.

The pain and the choking continued.

Her head screamed, enough to wake the dead, but silent to the living.

No one could hear her.

Just as she thought that her body could not take any more, and believing that she would surely die, Pearl woke from her nightmare, as she always did, heaving for air, her hand around her throat – lathered from head to toe in sweat.

Chapter Seven

Park Avenue, Roker, Sunderland

'I *know* what you did, Mother.' Helen lit one of her Pall Malls and wandered over to the drinks cabinet in the lounge. She started making two gin and tonics. One for her mother and one for herself.

'What do you mean, darling? You *know* what I did? Honestly, you sound like you're accusing your poor old mama here of some dreadful crime.'

Miriam wandered over and took her drink from her daughter.

'I heard you, Mum. Heard every word that was said.' Helen blew out smoke and tapped her cigarette in the heavy crystal ashtray she had taken from the top of the sideboard.

'Really, Helen, you're talking in riddles. What are you going on about?' Miriam took a sip of her drink. She had a good idea what Helen had 'heard' and she was cursing inwardly. She'd thought Helen had been at work that day. Clearly not.

'Mum, I know you're getting on a bit,' Helen smiled as she spoke, knowing that her age was her mother's Achilles heel, 'but you must remember what you said. Here. In this very room. Last Wednesday?'

Miriam took another sip of her drink, forcing back the resentment and annoyance she felt towards her beautiful – and young – daughter.

'You know,' Helen continued, walking over to the fire and putting her drink on the black marble mantelpiece. 'When Jack and Gloria were here, and you were all having a rather interesting tête-à-tête?'

'You're going to have to learn how to mix a decent G and T, my dear,' Miriam said, stalling for time and going back over to the cabinet to add more gin to her glass tumbler. Returning to the leather Chesterfield by the fire, Miriam sat down. She was glad she'd told Mrs Westley to put some more coal on the fire. This looked like it was going to be a long conversation.

'Come and sit down, dear.' Miriam patted the cushion next to her.

'I'm fine standing, Mother,' Helen said, her voice sounding strained. 'I'm not staying long anyway. I'm going out this evening.'

Miriam's face brightened. This was what she needed – her daughter out of an evening. Not moping around the house, and more importantly, not putting any kind of spanner in the works.

'Good for you, darling. Some nice young man taking you out?'

'It doesn't matter where I'm going, Mum. Or with whom. I want to talk to you about what you *did*.' Helen was inwardly fuming. She had held back all of her anger and grief these past five days, but it was no good, she had to have it out with her mother.

Miriam looked at her daughter, not sure how to tackle the situation. What she did know, though, was that it was imperative she kept Helen onside – and well away from her father.

'Helen, darling, you're going to have to explain to me just what it is you think I did?' Miriam needed Helen to tell her exactly how much or how little she knew.

'I know you've basically blackmailed Gloria into keeping silent about her affair with Dad.' Helen took a drag of her cigarette. 'And about Hope.' It still pained her to say the baby's name. The name of her father's daughter. *The name of her sister.*

Miriam took another sip of her drink to quell the fury that rose up in her whenever she even thought about her husband's bastard. If it had just been an affair it would have been so much easier to deal with. But when Helen had told her Jack had been stupid enough to get Gloria pregnant, she knew that this problem wasn't just going to disappear.

The bastard baby had changed everything.

'I know,' Helen continued, 'that you got him moved to Scotland. That it was all a ruse for you to get shot of Dad.'

'Ah,' Miriam said, 'well, my dear, what I "did", as you keep putting it so aggressively, was actually solve a rather huge problem, and one that wouldn't just affect me – but you as well.' Miriam was trying to keep her voice gentle. She needed her daughter to believe that she had acted in her best interests – that it was really Helen she had been concerned about.

'Like you say, darling, I am getting on a bit. I've *had* my life.' Miriam sounded sincere but didn't mean a word she had just uttered. She put down her drink and stood up. Straightening her skirt, she carefully stepped across the thick Persian rug in her peep-toe shoes towards her daughter. Helen automatically took a step back. Her mother rarely came this near to her.

'What I did, Helen, I did for you.' Miriam took her daughter's hands in her own and squeezed them gently. 'That terrible day you came back here, crying your eyes out after seeing your father with that woman at the hospital. That day that will be forever etched in my mind, when

70

you told me that your father had had a baby with that woman ...' Miriam paused as if to compose herself. 'That night, after we had chatted down here in this very room, I went up to my room and lay awake all night and cried.'

Miriam, of course, had not shed a tear; nor had she lain awake all night, thanks to her sleeping pills. She had, however, spent much of the evening working out what to do.

'All that crying and heartache,' Miriam tried to force tears into her eyes, 'was not for myself.' She looked her daughter straight in the eyes and could see that she had succeeded in bringing the hurt of that day to the fore. 'It was for you,' Miriam said, both hands clutching those of her daughter. 'For all the degradation you were going to have to endure when it came out that *your father* was having an affair with one of *your* workers – and not even some pretty little office worker, but some haggard, middle-aged woman welder.'

Helen automatically tried to pull her hands away but her mother had a tight grip. She didn't know why but whenever her mother demeaned Gloria something inside of her fought against it. It irked her. She couldn't help it. Perhaps it was because she had seen Gloria beaten like a dog by her mad ex, or because the image of her bloodied face as she'd looked up at her to thank her for helping would never leave her.

'I kept thinking of how you would be the laughing stock of the whole of Thompson's. But most of all,' Miriam let go of her daughter's hand and touched the soft, young skin on her face, 'I cried because your father has committed the worst sin possible. He has had another baby. A daughter with another woman.'

Miriam knew this was what had really hurt Helen more than anything. More than the affair with Gloria, more than the indignity she might suffer if it came out and became

71

fodder for the gossipmongers. The real dagger in her daughter's heart had been plunged deep when she had realised that her father had a new daughter. Helen had always been the centre of her father's world. Miriam knew that if it hadn't been for Helen – the daughter he adored so much – Jack would have probably walked away from their marriage years ago. He thought the world of Helen. Just as Helen did him. Or rather just as she *used* to. Now Miriam just needed to cement her daughter's rejection of her dear papa. Remind her that she had been forsaken, cast aside for this new baby.

She needed Helen to believe that Jack loved his new family more than he did her.

Miriam knew that was the only way she would keep her daughter on her side. The only thing that would stop Helen going to Scotland to see Jack. The only way she could keep this rather precarious stack of cards she had built upright.

'So, you see, my darling ...' Miriam stepped away from her daughter and sat back down on the sofa as though she was defeated, a martyr, exhausted and tired, '... I did what I did for you. For your future.'

Miriam watched her daughter as she walked back to the cabinet to retrieve the drink she had barely touched. She knew the words her daughter uttered next would tell her if she had succeeded in doing what she knew she had to do.

'Oh, Mum ...' Helen's voice had lost its accusatory tone. She was a child again, needing her mother's love and care. 'Why did all this have to happen? Every morning I wake up and I wish I could just put the clock back. Turn back time. Make everything the way it was before. But I can't, can I?' Tears were now falling down Helen's cheeks.

Miriam knew this was the cue for her to do what a normal mother would and go comfort her daughter. She stood up and walked over to Helen.

'Darling, everything's going to be all right. But you're right, we can't turn the clock back. But at least by doing what I've done, I've been able to stop it going forward. No one's ever going to find out. Everything is going to be exactly the same as before this whole abomination came to light. Nothing's really going to change.'

Miriam put her hands on her daughter's shoulders and squeezed them gently. It was as near to a hug as she could manage. What she really wanted to do was to give her daughter a good shake and tell her to stop snivelling and harden up. The girl was like a wet blanket. And that was another thing that was Jack's fault.

'I just keep thinking about the baby.' Helen was trying not to cry, knowing what her mum thought of tears, but she couldn't stop herself. Her mother was being so nice to her.

'I just keep thinking,' she repeated, 'that I've got *a sister*.'

Miriam instantly took her hands off her daughter. She walked over to the sideboard and pulled open one of the drawers, where she found a small pile of freshly laundered and pressed handkerchiefs. She walked back over to Helen and handed her one.

'Now, listen to me.' Miriam tried to keep the infuriation she was feeling out of her voice. 'That baby is *not your sister*. It has nothing to do with you. Nor you with it. So, just wipe that thought right out of your head.'

Miriam gently took Helen's chin in her hand and lifted her face so that they were looking at each other.

'Nothing. You hear me?'

Helen nodded.

'Now, dry those tears and get yourself out on your date.' Miriam walked over to the lounge door and opened it.

'I'm not going on a date, Mum. When do I *ever* go on dates?'

Miriam looked at her daughter and realised this was true. She had courted a few boys in the past, but never for long. Perhaps that was what she needed. A bit of a distraction.

'Well, then perhaps you should start? Where are you going tonight, if not out with some eligible young bachelor?'

'The charity benefit at the museum. You know? The one to raise funds for the Royal?'

Miriam shuddered at the mention of the town's main hospital on the New Durham Road. It was where Jack had been taken after he had fallen into a coma. *God, she wished he'd never woken up.*

'Well,' Miriam said, 'if you see your grandfather there, send my apologies. Tell him I've got one of my heads.'

'He didn't look the picture of health the other week when I went to see him,' Helen said, 'so I'm not sure he'll definitely be there.'

'Oh ...' Miriam let out a rather cynical laugh ' ... the old man will be there, without a doubt. Anything to do with the hospital always gives him his fix of adulation – even if such reverence *is* bought with the money he keeps throwing into their coffers.' Her face clouded over. 'Mind you, if he keeps on chucking money at them the way he does, there'll be nothing left for his own family.'

Helen looked at her mother. Her grandfather was one of the town's most well-known businessmen and charitable donors. Everyone seemed to love him, apart from his own daughter, although her mother was always nice enough to the old man – to his face, anyway. And she always made sure she kept in his good books.

'Well, go on then! Go and have some fun! Find yourself a nice, eligible young man!' Miriam put her hand on her daughter's back and guided her out of the room. 'Put on that lovely dress you've just had made. You'll have all the men falling over you.'

As Helen left the room and started walking up the stairs to freshen up, her mother's voice followed her.

'Forget all this *other stuff*. And just enjoy yourself!'

As Helen put on her new cream-coloured rayon dress, she tried to focus on the evening ahead and, like her mother had said, 'have some fun', but her mind kept pulling her back to that awful afternoon last week when she'd spotted Gloria leaving the yard in a chauffeur-driven car and, sensing something was up, had hurried home. With her ear pressed against the closed door of the living room, she had listened to her mother and to the occasional interjections of her father and Gloria and had been proven right.

What she had heard had been shocking: Dorothy's mother's bigamy, Angie's mam's infidelity, Hannah's aunty's money woes – and Martha *the offspring of a child killer!* Only Rosie and Polly had come out of it unsullied by scandal. Her mother had put Gloria well and truly into a corner, with not even the possibility of escape.

Up until that point Helen had thought her mother a veritable genius, but then she had dropped her second bombshell, and it wasn't just Gloria who was devastated, but Helen too. Her father was to be banished to Glasgow.

Sitting down on the small stool by her dresser, Helen reached for her make-up. Her hand trembled as she applied her ruby-coloured lipstick and her eyes started to sting with the beginning of tears. But it was the feeling of guilt that was unbearable. Guilt had continued to weigh her down this past week, for it was *she* – the daughter her father doted on – who had been the cause of his exile. It was *she* who had told her mother about Gloria and the baby.

If she hadn't, her father would still be here.

When she had originally told her mother about the affair, Miriam had made Helen promise not to utter a word of what she knew to anyone. Especially her father. Helen knew the only way she could do that was to avoid him, which she had done for weeks, terrified that she would break down and confess that she knew about Gloria – and about the baby. So, Helen had worked all the hours possible and then forced herself to go out most nights. And it had worked. She had spent next to no time with her father and adhered to her mother's wishes and not spilled the beans. But it had pained her dreadfully, and she knew that her father had also been confused and hurt by his daughter's unexplained rejection of him.

Helen put down her lipstick and picked up her compact, dabbing a loose layer of powder onto her face. As she did so she felt breathless. Her perfectly fitted dress all of a sudden felt too tight and she fought the urge to undo the zip. She could feel the panic she'd felt when her father had left the house for the last time. When she had fought with herself, not knowing what to do, whether to rush down the stairs and fling her arms around him and beg him not to leave, beg him to forgive her, for this was all her fault, she was sorry – if she had just kept her mouth shut, not told her mother what she had seen at the hospital that day, none of this would be happening, and he would not be leaving her now.

Or would she only have ended up slapping him and screaming that she hated him, and how could he do this to her? How could he have an affair? Worst of all, how could he have another child – another daughter?

She had been pulled by love and hate equally. Guilt and blame.

And so she had remained crouched down, on her haunches, gripping the bannisters as though they were the bars of a prison cell, trapped by her own emotions, not knowing what to do – and then it was all too late. Her father had told her mother that she was 'pure venom', 'tainting' everything she touched. The front door had slammed shut, and he had gone.

As Helen applied her mascara, forcing back the tears, she looked at her reflection. Her mother was right. If Gloria and her father *had* sailed off into the sunset together, she would be the equivalent of front-page news for the town's gossipmongers. Her father might not be here any more, but at least she could hold her head up high. She had been so wrapped up in thoughts of her father's deception that she had not thought about the stigma she would suffer should it all come out. It would be unbearable. She would be a laughing stock.

Her mother was right.

But more than anything, her mother had done what she had done *for her*.

Helen took a deep, shaky breath and dabbed her eyes. She stared back at her reflection and thought of her mother's words – how she had said she was 'young and beautiful'. She didn't often give her compliments, but lately her mum had been really kind, treating her to a lovely dress that had been designed and made especially for her by the young woman everyone was calling 'the town's very own Coco Chanel'. This was the first time she had felt that her mother was really looking out for her. Caring for her. Loving her.

Perhaps, Helen wondered, in losing her father, she had gained a mother.

Hearing the front door close and the jangle of the wrought-iron gate as Helen left for her evening out, Miriam walked over to where she had put her handbag by the side of the sofa. She had kept it well hidden; not that Helen would have opened or looked in it for any reason, but it was better to be safe than sorry. It was imperative that her daughter did not find out about this, especially now it was clear that Helen was more than capable of snooping around and eavesdropping. Perhaps her daughter was more like her than she'd given her credit for.

Thinking about it now, perhaps it was even a good thing that Helen had overheard what had gone on that afternoon. Helen could learn a thing or two about winning.

Miriam sat down on the sofa and picked up her handbag. She took a quick sip of her gin and tonic and put it down on the little coffee table. She should have guessed that Helen knew something when Miriam had told her that her father had had to leave for Scotland and hadn't had the chance to say his goodbyes. Helen hadn't grilled her like she would have normally done, but, instead, had just accepted it.

She was quite surprised, though, that Helen hadn't said anything until now – it had, after all, been almost a week. Mind you, they had both been busy. Helen had been at the yard morning, noon and night, and Miriam had been quietly celebrating the success of her perfectly executed master plan by gallivanting with her friend Amelia – revelling in all the attention she and her friend were getting from the newly billeted Admiralty at the Grand Hotel.

Miriam undid the clasp of her handbag and pulled out a letter that had arrived that morning. She silently counted her lucky stars Helen had got herself off to work before the crack of dawn and had therefore missed the postwoman and, more importantly, the letter that had arrived for her.

Miriam turned the unopened envelope round and looked at the writing on the front. Miriam had been married to Jack long enough to recognise his scrawl at ten paces. He wasn't the most educated person in the world, and although he could read and write, his actual handwriting left much to be desired.

Sliding a well-manicured finger underneath the seal of the envelope, Miriam opened her daughter's post. Straightening out the single sheet of thick paper, she took a deep breath and read the letter her husband had written two days after his arrival in Glasgow.

Lithgows Ltd. Shipyard
Kingston
Port Glasgow
Scotland

Friday 9th January 1942

To my dearest daughter, Helen,
I am so sorry that I had to leave so quickly and was not able to say goodbye to you.
I am so very sorry about so much, but these are things that I need to talk to you about personally. I am not such a good writer as to put it all in a letter, I'm afraid, and would rather talk to you in person, so as best to explain to you what has happened.
This is really just a brief letter to tell you that I love you very much. I hope above all else that what has happened will not change anything between us. You are my daughter and I love you and always will.
I will write again soon and hope that you too will write to me here in Glasgow.
With all my love, Dad x

Miriam looked at the letter for a moment before reaching over to the coffee table and picking up her glass and finishing her drink in one go. Still holding the letter, she stood up and walked over to the fire. Reaching for the poker, she stoked the coals, which responded by giving off a burst of heat and a vibrant orange glow. She then took the letter and held it over the flickering flames for a moment until it caught alight. Dropping it into the fire, she watched to ensure every part of the paper was burnt to a crisp and had turned to ash.

Chapter Eight

Sunderland Museum and Winter Gardens, Burdon Road, Sunderland

'Helen, how lovely to see you here!'

Helen turned and came face to face with Dr Matthew Gilbert, consultant in neurology at the Sunderland Royal Infirmary. She knew his voice before she saw him. He had only a trace of an accent, his boarding-school education having taken away all but a hint that he hailed from the north-east. As always when she saw her father's neurologist, her heart lifted, and she felt a tingle of excitement.

'Oh, Matthew! How *lovely* to see you too.' Helen stretched out her hand. She could feel his warmth as he shook it. 'I wasn't sure whether you would be able to make it – with you doctors being on call just about every minute of the day and night.'

'Ha! They allow us out occasionally!' he chuckled. 'How are you doing, my dear?' His voice was sincere, as it always was. And as usual he asked about her. Not her father. Not her mother. But about *her* well-being. He had once told her that often when people were seriously ill like her father had been, those nearest and dearest to the patient tended to get overlooked or neglected their own health. He had told Helen on a number of occasions that she had to look after herself.

'Oh, I'm very well. Thank you, Matthew.' Helen knew she was blushing and wondered if the very handsome, but unfortunately also very married, doctor had realised that her sudden rosy glow was due to his presence. Helen had nursed a rather large crush on him for most of the time she had known him, ever since her father had been transferred to the Royal in August last year. It was a crush that hadn't diminished with time, and if she was honest, the only real reason she was here this evening.

'And your father? How's he doing? It's been a while since I've seen him, which is always a good sign.'

'Oh, he's ... he's fine.' Helen hesitated, aware of a slight tremble in her voice, and unsure of what to say. So many thoughts were racing through her mind: how miserable and guilty she really felt because it was her fault that her dad had been banished to Scotland; how angry she was because of what he had done; how lonely she had been ever since she had seen him kissing Gloria that fateful day. And to top it all off, she actually had no idea *how* her father was.

Helen looked at Matthew. He was smiling at her. His deep brown eyes seemed to see right into her, making her want to pull him aside and tell him everything that had happened. She envisioned Matthew listening, reassuring her that everything would turn out just fine, before taking her in his arms and kissing her.

Matthew looked at Helen. He had got to know her quite well during her father's convalescence; after all, she had been by his side constantly, and had accompanied him to all of his appointments. Tonight, though, she seemed a little peculiar and not quite herself.

'When I saw him last,' Matthew said, 'he seemed to be making quite major steps towards getting his memory back. He's been quite the success story.'

Helen nodded, thinking how desperate she had been for her father to regain his memory, how elated she had been when she realised it had started to slowly come back, helped by the time he was spending with Arthur – time, she now realised, which had actually been spent with Gloria.

'Yes, yes, I do believe he's not far off making a full recovery,' Helen said as they were offered a glass of wine by one of the young waitresses.

Matthew looked at Helen again, trying to work out what was different about her. She was certainly looking particularly stunning this evening. She clearly took after her mother in the looks department, though her thick black hair was most definitely Jack's. Helen had caused quite a stir amongst the younger doctors while she had kept a constant vigil by her father's bed. He had heard many a complimentary word said about her, despite the fact she'd looked pretty washed out most of the time. Matthew couldn't help thinking that if he were ten years younger and a single man, he would have been quite happy to spend the evening by her side – possibly even the night.

'So,' Matthew forced his mind back to more chaste matters, 'did you have a nice break up in Scotland with your aunt and uncle?'

'Yes.' Helen took a sip of wine, wanting to gather up her courage. 'I did, thank you.' She had seen Matthew since then, but it had only been a fleeting exchange of pleasantries at a social do, not unlike the one they were at today. But on that occasion his wife had been there, which had prevented Helen from spending time with him on her own, as she fully intended to do this evening.

'I'm back at Thompson's. Nose to the grindstone.' She let out a tinkle of laughter, reserved for moments like this when she was putting her woman's wiles into top gear.

'But tell me, Matthew, what's happening in the world of medicine these days?' Helen knew that as much as she could have chatted on for ages about the latest happenings at Thompson's, it was unlikely to interest Matthew much and that men generally liked to talk about themselves. 'I heard that a lot of our wounded soldiers are being taken to the new Emergency Service Hospital in Ryhope?' she asked.

For the next twenty minutes Matthew chatted on about the medical huts that had been erected near the local lunatic asylum in Ryhope to treat soldiers back from Dunkirk and how it had been these temporary outbuildings that had inspired the building of the new state-funded military hospital. As Helen listened and asked more questions, she subtly took another two drinks from the waitress circulating the room and gently took Matthew's empty glass from his hand, replacing it with a full one. As she did so, she made sure her hand casually brushed his.

What had her mother said? *Have some fun! Find a nice, eligible young man.* Well, Matthew might not be that young, or eligible, but he was the only man with whom she wanted to have fun.

Taking a sip of her wine, Helen looked around casually before moving closer to Matthew. When he stopped talking, she said in a low voice so that he had to lean into her to hear, 'I'm guessing you are here on your own this evening?'

Matthew suddenly realised how much he'd drunk, and that he had been chatting away to Helen quite happily – perhaps a little too happily. Now they seemed to be in very close proximity to each other. Enough for him to smell the rather lovely perfume she was wearing.

Seeing Helen here tonight and talking with her so freely had taken him a little off guard. Glancing at her now in her ivory dress that was both classy and rather ravishing, he couldn't help but feel physically drawn to her. She was an incredibly sexy woman and, he now realised, she also knew how to use it to her advantage. What surprised him the most, though, was that he should be the focus of her amorous intentions. He was not only married, but twice her age.

'I *am* alone,' he said, taking a slightly nervous sip of his drink. 'My wife's at home. We weren't able to get a babysitter.' It was a lie. He and his wife had had an argument and she had refused to accompany him, but he hoped by mentioning his wife and children that he would remind Helen – and himself – that he was a married man.

'Well, I may not be married myself,' Helen said, her voice still low as she leant in a little closer, 'but I would guess that husbands – especially doctors – need to go out occasionally on their own to let off steam.'

Matthew knew he had unwittingly wandered into dangerous territory. He had been completely faithful to his wife during their fifteen years of marriage. All the doctors he'd ever known regularly received romantic overtures – some more tempting than others. It was what they called the 'white-coat effect'. None of the overtures Matthew had been privy to, however, had been from someone quite as young and as attractive as Helen.

Knowing that the conversation needed to be halted in its tracks, he looked around the room, desperately trying to spot someone he might know. The place was full of consultants and those high up in management, as well as lots of 'captains of industry', but most were with their wives or girlfriends. Looking back to Helen, he could see that there was only one option. He had to be honest with her.

'I'm so sorry, Helen,' Matthew began. Helen picked up the change in his voice. 'I feel that I have done you a disservice ...' He paused, trying to choose his words as carefully as possible. 'I might have let you think that perhaps I am happy to be here on my own this evening.'

Another pause.

'Without my wife.'

Helen felt herself starting to turn a bright shade of red. She could feel her heart pounding. She knew what was coming next.

'I'm afraid I have to be totally straight up with you, as I really don't want you to feel as though I have strung you along in any way. You are an incredibly beautiful young woman, and I am quite an older man. But I am also a happily married older man.'

Seeing her blush and sensing her mortification at his words, Matthew softened his voice.

'Sometimes patients, or the loved ones of patients, can feel very close to their doctor. It's a known phenomenon and quite understandable, but also one that needs to be viewed as what it is. The patient – or a patient's loved one – simply ...' He stuttered, now totally embarrassed. 'Oh ... how can I put it? ... I suppose you could say they can develop a bit of a soft spot for the doctor who has helped them.'

Helen had gone from feeling like a femme fatale to some silly little schoolgirl. She could feel her cheeks burning and she started fumbling around in her bag for her cigarettes.

Matthew could see her embarrassment and felt awful. Poor girl. She'd been through so much. Had sat by her father's bedside just about every waking moment. She'd been so overjoyed when he had come out of his coma, only to be told that he had no memory of her or of his past life. She really had been through the mill these past five months.

Matthew looked about the room and almost jumped for joy when he spotted two guests entering the room. One was 'young John', as he liked to refer to him, otherwise known professionally as Dr Parker, who worked at the same hospital. He had got to know Helen when Jack was recovering, was about the same age as her as well, and more importantly, he was single.

The second person he saw, looking radiant and, to his eyes, very beautiful, was his wife, whose presence showed she was willing to make up.

'Helen, do you recall Dr Parker from the hospital?' Matthew was talking to her as though nothing had happened.

Helen forced a smile at the young doctor, who she remembered well. All of a sudden she felt surrounded by memories of her father. They were suffocating her. She had that feeling of breathlessness again and felt the need to escape.

'And I do believe you have met my wife, Rebecca, before?' Matthew's tone of voice gave nothing away of what had just passed.

Helen and Rebecca smiled at each other and exchanged a rather limp handshake.

Helen wanted the ground to swallow her up there and then. Part of her wanted to run out of the room. She had come there tonight to have fun. When she had seen Matthew, her heart had leapt. She was a glamorous woman. Her arrival that evening had been met by admiring glances. Matthew must be about the only man in the place not to find her attractive.

God, the humiliation of it all. Could her life get any worse?

'Can I have your attention, please?' The loud, booming voice of the organiser demanded quiet. Everyone acquiesced apart from a baby whose sudden piercing cries cut through the air. Helen's eyes scanned the room. God, what mother in her right mind would bring a baby to an event like this? Helen finally spotted the offending woman and child over on the other side of the room. Suddenly an image of Gloria and Hope – her *sister* – sprang to mind. The image caught Helen off guard, and along with it came that feeling again – that awful sense of yearning. It annoyed her, confused her. As she pushed away all thoughts of her father, Gloria and Hope, her heart started pounding in her chest. She took a large slug of her drink, hoping it would make it stop. As she did so she noticed her hands were shaking.

'Are you all right, Miss Crawford?'

Helen nodded at the fresh-faced Dr Parker, whose first name she had never bothered to find out. She had always thought he looked far too young to be a doctor and had told him that one day when he had been in the middle of giving her an update on her father's condition. He had laughed good-naturedly and said that was what most people told him, but that he was actually fully qualified and nearer thirty than he was twenty.

Dr Parker made a movement towards her, as though he was going to either check her over or engage her in conversation. Helen quickly made a show of raising her chin as though she was desperate to hear what the speaker was about to say. As she did so, though, she caught Matthew's wife giving him a kiss and whispering something into his ear. It took every bit of Helen's reserve not to scream louder than the bawling baby and run out of the building.

Somehow Helen managed to hold it together. The overweight, balding man standing at the front of the room suddenly stopped talking and turned to his left. 'Ladies and gentlemen, please give a round of applause for our main benefactor.' Helen looked at her grandfather as he raised his hand in acknowledgement and slowly walked over to the compère.

Great! That was all she needed. If she didn't go now, he'd spot her and she'd end up spending most of the evening being introduced to all his old cronies.

The bald dignitary started his introduction about what a great philanthropist Mr Havelock was, how he was an accomplished businessman and, of course, a veteran of the First War. And, most importantly, how he had yet again come to the hospital's financial aid during one of the most important times in the nation's history.

'I'm so sorry,' Helen said during a short break when the speaker stopped to take a drink of water. She tried to sound as normal and as sincere as possible. 'But I'm afraid I'm going to have to go. I completely forgot I said I was going to meet an old friend for a drink at the Grand.'

'Can I walk you there?' Dr Parker asked. He didn't look particularly keen to stay at the do himself.

'No, no. But thanks, anyway,' Helen said in her sweetest, most polite voice.

'Lovely to see you again, Matthew.' She turned, forcing herself to do what she knew she had to do for appearance's sake before she made her escape.

'And Rebecca.' She extended her hand to the wife of the man she had just more or less propositioned and wished her an enjoyable evening.

As Helen made her excuses and left, she was unaware that her departure was being watched by one of the surgeons Matthew had been telling her about who had been drafted in to operate on the wounded soldiers at the new military hospital.

Mr Theodore Harvey-Smith, a specialist in burns and reconstructive surgery, had struggled to take his eyes off Helen as soon as he'd spotted her not long after arriving. He had seen how she had not left his colleague's side for the entirety of her time at the museum. He had been too far away to eavesdrop, but their body language as well as their facial expressions were enough to give him a good idea as to what had passed between the two.

If he'd had a chance to chat to Helen beforehand, he would have saved her the embarrassment she had clearly suffered before she'd suddenly decided to leave. He would have told her that Matthew was a damn near perfect husband and father and would never stray. And that he had seen Matthew become the focus of attention for a few very charming women, but he had not allowed himself so much as a quick kiss or cuddle.

Theodore looked at his watch. Helen had left just a few minutes ago. He turned and apologised to the company he was with and weaved his way quickly and quietly through the throng of partygoers.

Dr Parker watched as Theodore went to collect his coat from the little cloakroom next to the display of the town's Garrison pottery and Hartleys glass. Ever the sharp eye, Dr Parker also noticed that as his fellow medic was shrugging on his overcoat, he was also easing his gold band off his wedding-ring finger, sliding it quickly and unobtrusively into his trouser pocket as he left the museum.

Helen was out on the main road, gulping in air as though she had been underwater for too long.

Why was her life turning into such a disaster? Before her father had gone off to America, her life had been almost perfect. Helen wrapped her full-length woollen winter coat around herself and pulled the belt tight, glancing across at the bomb site where Binns, the town's main department store, had once stood.

Damn this war! Helen cursed. She'd loved that shop. *Damn! Damn! This war!*

If it hadn't been for this wretched war her life would be very different. Women would not have ended up working at Thompson's, which would have meant that little Miss Perfect Polly wouldn't have stolen Tommy from her, and Gloria would not have taken her father. More than anything, though, it would have meant she would not now have a baby sister and her father would not have been ousted from the town – and, moreover, from her life.

Her life, just like the whole of her home town, was being deconstructed bit by bit.

As she turned right and marched along Borough Road, she slowed down. She had escaped her humiliation at the museum, and her heart rate was returning to normal.

After crossing the Toward Road, she heard a door open and the sound of laughter drift out along with a shard of light. It was a public house, one she had not been in before, not that she had actually been inside many pubs at all. Her social life had been mainly charity dos, like the one she had just fled, or stuffy dinner parties.

Stopping to look up at a sign that read THE BURTON HOUSE, in a moment of madness Helen considered going in, before swiftly turning away. As she did so, she bumped into a man whom she recognised as one of the guests at the museum.

'Go on!' he laughed, pushing a thick mop of auburn hair away from his face. 'I dare you!'

'Are you following me?' Helen demanded in her most hoity-toity voice.

'I might be,' Theodore responded, raising his eyebrows slightly. 'And if I was, would that be such a terrible thing to do?' he asked, cocking his head to the side slightly, making no effort to hide the fact he was admiring her.

It was on the tip of Helen's tongue to demand who he thought he was, speaking to her so, daring to suggest she enter such a common pub. But something stopped her. The wine and the hit of cold air had made her feel a little giddy, and braver, or perhaps more foolhardy.

Helen looked at the man. He was not what she would call drop dead gorgeous, but he was rather attractive in a slightly roguish way, with dancing eyes that glinted with more than a little mischief.

Helen allowed herself a slight smile and threw him a look that said she was no coward. She walked towards the pub door and stood aside, waiting for him to do the gentlemanly thing and open it for her. He responded to her unspoken demand, stepped forward and pulled open the door.

'After you, milady,' he said, sweeping his arm theatrically before her, and returning Helen's half-smile with one of his own.

Feeling a shot of nerves, Helen took a deep breath and stepped into the packed pub. Once they were in, he leant over and whispered into her ear, 'You find a seat, and I'll get us a drink. What's your poison?'

Chapter Nine

J.L. Thompson & Sons Shipyard, North Sands, Sunderland

Tuesday 13 January

'Eee, I thought the blower was never going to go off!' Angie stretched out both her arms in front of her.

'I think we're all gonna have muscles like dumb-bells if this war doesn't end soon,' Gloria said, causing everyone to instinctively look at Martha.

'We're not gonna stop working here when the war ends, you know,' Polly said, looking around at everyone.

'I don't think we'll have a choice,' Gloria said. 'There was a big enough stink when us "fairer sex" started to work here. The only reason they gave it the thumbs up was on the condition that the jobs would be kept open for the men when they come back. When they do, we'll be sent packing quick as Jack Flash.'

'Well, they'll not get rid of us that easily,' Polly said, outraged. Working at Thompson's had been a dream come true for Polly. She came from a long line of shipbuilders, but because of her gender had never thought she too would be able to become part of the town's revered shipbuilding heritage.

'I'll be staying put!' she added, adamantly.

Gloria let out a hoot of laughter.

'We'll see if that's the case when Tommy's back. He'll be dragging you down that aisle even quicker than Peter did Rosie here, and then before you know it you'll be bigger than one of those five-gallon barrels over there.' Gloria pointed over to a row of metal drums to make her point.

'I don't mind being dragged down the aisle, as you put it,' Polly laughed. 'Although I think we'll be pushed to do it quicker than Rosie and Peter. I reckon they set some kind of a record!'

Everyone laughed.

'But as for starting a family, well, that can wait. I'm in no rush for all of that malarkey. I have no illusions about the joys of motherhood, living under the same roof as Lucille, and my ma having turned the house into a nursery. And much as I love Hope,' Polly looked at Gloria, 'she's certainly got a good set of lungs on her!'

'Yer right there!' Gloria chuckled. 'She used to save it all for me after work, but nowadays she seems to be allowing others to enjoy her vocals!'

'I will be like Rosie here,' Polly declared ostentatiously, 'and, though I hate to even say her name, *Helen as well*. And I shall become a fixture in the yards – married or not!'

'Hear, hear!' Rosie encouraged. 'And I hope you will *all* take a leaf out of Polly's book when the time comes and not leave me here on my own.'

'Never!' Martha said in earnest.

'Yeh, they'll have to haul us out of here kicking and screaming.' Dorothy laughed.

'Talking about the old cow – ' Angie never called Helen by her name ' – she looked rough as a dog this morning. Did yer see her? I reckon she'd had more than a few jars last night. Looked like she was ganna chuck up on the spot.'

'Honestly, Ange,' Dorothy said. 'She may have this awful winter bug that's going around. You always think the worst. Not everyone's living it up and drinking like fishes every night.' They both looked at each other and burst into raucous laughter.

'*Like us two!*'

Gloria rolled her eyes at Rosie and said in a voice loud enough for the squad's two comics to hear, 'I swear them two are getting worse!'

'Well, you know what they say,' Dorothy trilled, nudging Angie.

'*You're only young once!*' they sang out in unison as they swung their haversacks and boxed gas masks onto their backs.

'Thank God!' Gloria shot back.

As the women welders all started to make their way over to the main gates, Rosie hung back to speak to Polly.

'How's Lucille? She any better?'

'Yes, I think she's over the worst now. She's started to play up and demand even more attention than she normally does, so she must be. And no one else seems to have caught whatever it was she's had. Touch wood.'

'Well, just to be on the safe side, keep a handkerchief over your mouth when you're around your niece. I don't need you ill. I don't need any of you off poorly.' Rosie dropped her voice before adding, 'Any more word from Tommy?'

Polly shook her head. 'No, I'm trying not to pester the poor postwoman every morning. I think she dreads coming to our house.'

They both chuckled.

'What're you two in cahoots about?' It was Gloria. She'd been chatting to Martha, who had just headed over to see Hannah in the drawing office.

'Just asking Polly if she's had any word from Tommy.'

'It's not been that long since his last letter, has it?' Gloria said as the three of them stood in line to hand over their time boards to Alfie.

'No. Not really,' Polly admitted. 'I'm terrible. I don't think I'd be happy unless I got one every day.'

'See you all tomorrow!' It was Dorothy and Angie shouting over at them from the other side of the main gates.

Rosie, Gloria and Polly waved back over a sea of flat caps.

'So, I'm guessing you're off to tell Lily and George your good news this evening?' Gloria asked.

Rosie grimaced. 'I am, but I don't know if Lily will see it as a reason to celebrate.'

Polly looked puzzled. 'Why not?'

'Well, let's just say she's never been overly keen on Peter, and she can be incredibly pig-headed. When she's decided something, *she's decided*. And it's nigh impossible to get her to change her mind.'

Gloria didn't say anything. She was the only one of Rosie's squad who knew exactly why Lily was not particularly enamoured with Peter as she was the only one Rosie had confided in when there was a concern – before they'd become an item – that Peter might report the bordello to the authorities.

As they all trooped down to the ferry landing, Gloria cast a look at her boss and couldn't help but feel for her. Rosie had met the love of her life and they'd had a rather stormy courtship, during which she had fallen out with Peter more than the once, before finally kissing and making up.

Then, just as it looked as though she was going to get her happy-ever-after ending, she'd had to wave it all goodbye.

This bloody war. It had a lot to answer for.

Chapter Ten

An hour later Rosie was shutting the front door of her flat and heading along Borough Road. She had just been up to see her landlord, old Mr Brown, who lived on the ground floor, in the flat above her, and she was pleased with how their little chat had gone.

Normally Rosie would have turned left up Toward Road, but she had somewhere to go before she went to Lily's. Jumping on a single-decker bus that was headed for Tunstall, she sat by the window and looked out into the darkness. She could just make out the shops as the bus drove up Holmeside. Scrutinising the front of the Maison Nouvelle, she couldn't tell if Kate was still there. Rosie hoped she wasn't working late this evening as she wanted her to be at the bordello when she made her announcement. Out of everyone, she knew that Kate would be the most overjoyed.

As the bus turned left and started making its way along Tunstall Road, the roads became quieter. The tree-lined residential streets and well-kept Victorian terraces were evidence that they were crossing over into the more affluent part of town. A few minutes later, Rosie rang the bell and the driver pulled up at the bus stop. Stepping onto the pavement, Rosie didn't bother getting out her little torch; she couldn't see much, but she knew the way well enough now to find Peter's even if she were blindfolded. She heard another bus coming in the opposite direction before she saw its dimmed, hooded front lights. She crossed the road as soon as it had passed and walked down the side street to the little wooden gate that heralded the start of a pretty stretch of houses called Brookside Gardens.

It felt strange coming here, knowing that Peter was not going to be there. Her heart felt heavy as she clicked open the gate and walked down the wide gravel pathway. The last time she had come here she had not gone through the gate. Her stubbornness and anger had stopped her coming to see Peter. It was something she had berated herself for, hated herself for, but now she was glad she hadn't, otherwise, like Peter had said, they wouldn't have had the time they'd just spent together in Guildford.

When Rosie reached number four she walked up the short path. She had the key ready in her hand and had just turned the lock when Mrs Jenkins, the next-door neighbour, suddenly appeared. Rosie silently cursed. If she had just been a bit quicker, she might have got in before being spotted. Peter was right. The woman didn't miss a trick.

'Ah, it's Rosie, isn't it? Peter's told me all about you! Lovely to finally meet you!' Mrs Jenkins wiped her hands on her pinny, then stuck one out.

'You too, Mrs Jenkins.' Rosie shook hands. 'Peter's told me all about his neighbours and how lucky he is.'

'Oh, we're the lucky ones, having Peter.' She glanced down at Rosie's hand to see the front-door key in it. 'How's Peter? He never really said where exactly he was going? Is he due back already?'

Rosie wondered how many questions you could ask in one breath.

'He's fine,' Rosie said, removing her gloves and taking a step into the house to show she didn't want to hang about. 'Hopefully, he'll be back soon.' Peter had primed Rosie on what to say to his inquisitive neighbour, which basically amounted to as little as possible.

'Oh!' Mrs Jenkins took a sharp intake of breath, causing Rosie to look round quickly, thinking her neighbour had seen something shocking.

'Goodness gracious me!' Mrs Jenkins's slightly arthritic finger was pointing to Rosie's bare hand.

'Is that a wedding band I see?' Mrs Jenkins's mouth had dropped open in sheer astonishment.

Rosie looked at her own hand as if she herself had just noticed the gold wedding ring, then back up at Mrs Jenkins. 'Yes,' she said. 'It is!'

'Oh! This is wonderful news, my dear! Wonderful! Congratulations!' Stepping over the little row of shrubs that divided the two pathways, she grabbed hold of Rosie and gave her a bear hug. Rosie didn't think she had been hugged so much in her life as she had these past two days.

'I'm so pleased.' Mrs Jenkins held on to Rosie's shoulders with both hands. 'I never thought Peter would get married again. Not after what happened to his poor wife. Ah, I'm so pleased. You must tell him I'm over the moon! I guess you'll be moving in here now? How wonderful. I'll have a new neighbour!'

Rosie looked at Mrs Jenkins's animated face. Her goodwill and joy were infectious and Rosie smiled back.

'Yes, I'm hoping to move in properly in a few weeks' time. It's all been rather a whirlwind,' she confessed.

'Come in for a cuppa,' Mrs Jenkins beckoned, 'or a tipple of something stronger. Kenneth's out with the Home Guard, so we'll have the place to ourselves for a good natter!'

'That's a kind offer, but I'm afraid I've got to go straight back out. I was only popping by to check on everything.' Rosie felt guilty seeing Mrs Jenkins's face drop in disappointment. Peter had said he thought she was lonely. It was a supposition Rosie agreed with.

'I tell you what,' Rosie said, shifting herself further across the front doorstep of the house, which, in normal circumstances, she would have been entering for the first time as a married woman with her husband by her side, 'let's have a cup of tea, and a catch-up, as soon as I move in properly.'

Mrs Jenkins's face lit up. 'That'll be grand, my dear! I shall look forward to it.' She was just opening her mouth to ask another question when Rosie suddenly looked down at her watch.

'Oh, look at the time! Sorry, Mrs Jenkins, I must dash. But a cup of tea – soon!'

And with that Rosie managed to get her whole body into the house. Giving Mrs Jenkins a quick farewell wave, she gently shut the front door behind her.

Turning around and looking down the hallway, Rosie took a deep breath. The house was dark and cold and she was suddenly struck by a huge upsurge of sadness that Peter was not there with her now. Stepping forward and switching on the light, she felt something under her foot. Looking down she saw that some post had arrived and automatically went to pick it up.

When she saw the name *Mrs Rosie Miller* in Peter's neat handwriting on the front of the envelope, her heart leapt. Hurrying into the kitchen, she switched on the light and sat down at the little Formica table, carefully opening the envelope and taking out the letter to read.

To my dear wife,
What an absolute joy to be able to write those words to you!
My dear wife.
There, I just needed to write them again!

I can't tell you just how very proud, and so incredibly happy, I am that you have made me your husband. I just wish I was there now so that I could pick you up and carry you across the threshold like any self-respecting newly married man is expected to do to his new wife.

But knowing you, Rosie, my love, you would have insisted on walking across the threshold anyway. You are the most independent, toughest, most beautiful person I have ever known – in both nature and looks.

I need you to remember just how resilient you are while we are parted.

I will try my damnedest to get back to you, and if there is any way possible that I can get word to you that I am alive and well, I will.

As I have said to you before, though, if I don't make it back into your arms, you must keep your promise that you made in Guildford and you must live this wonderful life we have been given. With or without me.

My thoughts are, as always, with you, and as I think you know well enough by now, I love you truly, more than any words can express.

Yours,

Peter x

Tears rolled down Rosie's face unchecked. Reading his words had transported her back into his arms, to when they had lain together after they had made love, and after she had agreed to be his wife and he had made her promise that she would live her life to the fullest, even if he did not come back to her. She had done so only because she knew he had needed to hear that; because, in all honesty, she didn't know if that *would* be possible if he was not a part of it.

Chapter Eleven

Twenty minutes later Rosie was quietly shutting the front door, terrified she might alert Mrs Jenkins that she was leaving. Hurrying down the gravel pathway, she pulled out the small torch she kept in the pocket of her mackintosh. She switched it on and as the weak beam swung to her right and onto the grassy borders, her heart skipped a beat.

Pansies! There were small bunches of pansies growing amongst the other weeds and wild flowers that bordered the vegetable patch, which had recently been cultivated under the push to grow your own and 'Dig for Victory'.

Rosie forced back more tears.

'Come on!' she muttered to herself. 'No more tears. You've got to be strong. If Peter is being brave and putting his life on the line, you're not going to mope around weeping into your hankie!'

And with that she swung open the wooden gate and practically marched the half-mile up the steep incline of Tunstall Vale, turning right on to West Lawn before arriving at Lily's. She was just looking for her front-door keys when the wide black oak door swung open. As always when Rosie arrived at the bordello, she was hit by the sweet smell of perfume and a mixture of cigarette and cigar smoke, together with, of course, a lovely blanket of warmth. Lily's was always well heated. It was one of the house rules. If it was cold, like this evening, then every fire would be burning, regardless of shortages. Lily, they'd all learnt, had her ways of getting hold of just about anything that was either rationed or in short supply.

'Rosie!' It was Kate who opened the door. 'I've been watching out for you!' She tugged Rosie's arm to pull her in from the front step, then shut the door behind her.

'How did it go? How's Peter?'

Rosie looked at Kate's expectant face, and knew it was important for Kate to know that her time with Peter had gone well. She knew how guilty her old school friend still felt about not getting Peter's letter to her in time.

'The wanderer returns!' It was Lily making her way down the final flight of stairs from her room on the second floor. Rosie could hear the rustle of the taffeta she was wearing. She was clearly in a flamboyant mood tonight as her hooped skirts always made a show when Lily was feeling particularly extravagant. Rosie went to greet her at the bottom of the stairs and Lily gave her the customary two kisses on each cheek.

'I'm hoping your detective treated you well whilst you were away? Of course, I might have worried you'd run off to join the circus – *or worse still* – had our Kate here not informed us that you had hopped on a train down to Guildford!'

Rosie gave a look of exasperation.

'Lily, you know I would have come here myself and told you if I'd had time.' As Rosie spoke she guided Lily towards the kitchen She could hear that some 'guests' had already arrived and were in the reception room, chatting and drinking and singing along to George's piano rendition of the popular, and rather risqué, cabaret song 'I've Got the Deepest Shelter in Town'.

'George! *Mon cher!* Our errant child has returned to the fold!' Lily shouted through to the back reception room in her best faux-French accent. Rosie and Kate exchanged looks and made their way through the swing door and into the kitchen where they all liked to relax and unwind.

'She's been like this since you left,' Kate whispered to Rosie. 'Like she's been abandoned.' She let out a little chuckle. 'I've never known such a drama queen.'

Rosie knew Kate thought the world of Lily, who had not only given her a roof over her head when Rosie had brought her in off the streets, but had also cared for her, giving her elocution lessons and a new wardrobe. Most importantly, though, Lily had given her an old sewing machine and encouraged her to do what she loved more than anything else in the world – designing and making clothes. Recently, Lily had taken over the lease of the Maison Nouvelle, bought whatever stock had been left there by the previous owner, and told Kate to get on with doing what she had 'clearly been put on this earth to do'.

'Ah, she's back!'

Rosie turned to see George hurrying into the kitchen, his ivory walking stick striking the tiled flooring.

'Thank goodness!' He gave her a gentle hug, and whispered in her ear, 'She's been like a bear with a sore head this past week.'

'The *bear* might have a sore head, but it also has very good hearing!' Lily scowled over at George, and then at Kate, just as Maisie and Vivian came bustling through the door.

'Rosie! Welcome back!' Maisie came over and, like her boss, kissed Rosie lightly on both cheeks. As she did so she whispered, 'Don't you *ever* leave us again!'

'Is everyone all right next door?' Lily asked Vivian, who was now the official head of the girls. 'I thought you were with the Brigadier?'

'He's having a kip by the fire,' Vivian said defensively, her Liverpudlian twang sneaking through her usual Mae West persona.

Lily looked at George for confirmation.

'Yes, my dear, like a baby. And the rest of the girls are looking after the other guests. Everything's fine and dandy, so ...' George hobbled over to the armoire ' ... I think a celebration is in order.' He pulled out a bottle of Rémy Martin.

For a moment Rosie thought they all knew.

'Celebration?' she asked, as Maisie squeezed past her with a tray of Lily's best cut-crystal tumblers.

'To celebrate your return,' Maisie said, setting the glasses down in the middle of the large farmhouse kitchen table.

Lily settled herself at the top of the table as she always did, and they all sat down in their usual places as George tipped generous quantities into everyone's glasses, bar Kate, who didn't drink and was pouring herself a cup of tea. She still hadn't told anyone about the night she had fallen well and truly off the wagon and drunk almost half a bottle of cheap cooking brandy. It had been the reason she'd forgotten to hand over Peter's letter, although she was still too ashamed to admit it openly.

'So, here's to the return of our Rosie!' George's words instigated a circle of raised glasses and one china teacup.

'To Rosie's return!' everyone chorused.

'So,' Lily said, taking centre stage. Her bosom seemed to be desperately trying to break free from the tight corset she had pulled herself into this evening. 'I'm sure I'm not alone in wanting to know exactly how your little holiday in Guildford went?'

Everyone murmured their agreement.

Rosie took a deep breath, followed by another sip of her brandy.

'Well, I had a wonderful time,' she said. Vivian gently nudged Maisie, who pretended not to notice. The pair of them were now firm friends and had become quite inseparable. 'But I do have some rather unexpected news ...' She hesitated. 'Actually, some rather exciting news to tell you all.'

Rosie looked at Lily and then at everyone else's expectant faces.

She pulled off the gloves she had purposely kept on when she had arrived and showed everyone her left hand.

'I got married!'

Chapter Twelve

Just like when she had told her women welders, Rosie was met by five shocked faces and a moment of silent disbelief.

'Never!' It was Vivian who spoke first.

'Well, I'll be damned!' It was George, who was smiling from ear to ear. 'Now this really *does* call for a celebration. Sod the Rémy! Let's get the old champers!' He pushed his chair back. 'Well, I'll be damned!' he said again, taking a few ungainly steps towards Rosie.

'Congratulations my dear!' he declared, embracing the young woman, who was like the daughter he'd never had.

'Oh, Rosie!' Kate was waiting her turn behind George. 'This is the best news ever!'

Rosie could feel herself becoming emotional as she looked at her old friend and saw that her eyes were brimming with tears. 'Stop it or you'll start me off!' she scolded.

Maisie and Vivian crowded around and gave Rosie a quick hug in turn.

'Congratulations!' Vivian said in her best Mae West accent.

'Thank heaven for some good news for a change!' Maisie said. She would never admit it, but the thought that they might feel the long arm of the law pulling at their collar was still not quite a distant memory for her. The fact that Rosie was not only back with her detective but had also married him made her feel much more secure.

'If the sirens go off now, I'm not budging an inch!' Vivian declared as she helped Maisie set the champagne glasses on the table.

'Here goes!' George warned as the pop of the champagne cork caused everyone to duck automatically.

As the glasses were filled, Rosie looked at Lily, who had remained seated at the top of the table and was looking decidedly shell-shocked. Rosie would never admit it, but she needed Lily's approval and she couldn't keep this from showing on her face. Lily saw it and stood up, opened her arms wide and beckoned to her with her heavily jewelled hands.

'*Ma chérie*, this is the most wondrous news! Congratulations!' She stepped towards Rosie and gave her a big hug. It was the last thing Lily felt like doing, but she knew it was what Rosie wanted – and needed. She had known Rosie since the age of sixteen, when shortly after the death of her parents she had come to Lily seeking work. Lily had to bite her tongue to prevent herself from saying what she really thought about this latest turn of events.

George coughed and clinked the side of his champagne glass with a silver teaspoon to get everyone's attention.

'A toast!' he declared. 'To the best woman anyone could hope to be married to, *our Rosie!*'

He paused dramatically.

'Mrs Rosie Miller!'

Everyone raised their glasses, including Kate, who had put some tap water in hers teacup.

'To Mr and Mrs Miller!' he said. 'Congratulations!'

'Congratulations!' everyone chorused.

'*Félicitations pour ton mariage!*' Lily said in a convincing French accent, before adding, 'Now, tell us all about it! We want to hear every detail.'

Rosie smiled. There was a part of her that hated being the centre of attention, but another part that wanted to relive her four days with Peter over and over again. Regaling the story of her rather unconventional, last-minute marriage would allow her to do just that.

After Maisie and Vivian had returned to their guests in the back parlour, and Kate had gone up to her room to work on her latest design, Rosie started to clear up the empty glasses.

'Leave that,' Lily told her. 'Milly's due in soon. She'll sort it out.'

Rosie didn't pay Lily any heed and quickly washed up the glasses.

'Gawd, might as well just talk to the wall,' Lily huffed.

Rosie left the glasses to drain and sat back down.

'I'm thinking of buying my flat off Mr Brown,' Rosie said, her eyes flicking from Lily to George to gauge their reactions.

'What a good idea!' they said in unison.

Rosie chuckled at their unintended double act.

'*Ma chère*, I would say that not only is it a very good idea, but it is also a very astute move. Wouldn't you agree, George?' Lily looked at her fiancé with eyes that showed she expected both agreement and enthusiasm.

'I most certainly would. Splendid idea! And, I might add, a financially savvy move.'

George had already told Rosie that he and Lily were looking towards building a more legitimate business infrastructure by using the profits from Lily's and La Lumière Bleue in Soho, putting any extra cash into 'bricks and mortar'. His friends in finance had told him that property was the next big thing.

'I'm sure it's going to be more than possible, my dear,' George continued, 'what with the money you'll be saving when you move to Brookside Gardens and are no longer paying rent. Even more so when you factor into the equation the money you'll be gaining from renting out the flat yourself.'

'My only worry,' Rosie said, 'is buying property at a time like this, which, let's face it, is pretty unpredictable to say the least.'

'Darling,' Lily said, pulling a cigarette out of her packet of Gauloises, 'in business one has to take risks. What's the phrase you're so keen on, George – *you have to speculate to accumulate*?'

Rosie sat back in her chair. 'I suppose my main worry is that the flat's not far from the docks and the town's already been heavily bombed.'

'True. You might buy into bricks and mortar and be left with just that – a load of rubble,' Lily mused, blowing smoke up to the ceiling.

'Well, that's where insurance comes into it,' George said. 'It might be expensive, but it'll be worth it.'

'Mmm, and it'll give peace of mind,' Lily added.

'God, I hate to even say this, but what if we lose the war?' Rosie said, taking a deep breath.

'Well, if that *does* happen,' George pushed himself out of his seat, 'it wouldn't matter either way as we'll all be living under a dictatorship, with absolutely no freedom, no rights, no money, and certainly no property. Everything will be owned by the Third Reich.'

A chill seemed to descend on the room.

'Regardless,' George made his voice upbeat, 'it's worth the gamble, and if we win the war, *which we will*, then you, Rosie, my dear, will have got yourself a very healthy little nest egg ... Do you know how much your landlord – what's his name again?'

'Mr Brown.'

'Yes, of course, Mr Brown ... Do you know how much your Mr Brown wants for your little flat?'

'We had a very brief chat about it before I came out tonight,' Rosie said, 'and it was clearly something he'd been thinking about for a while now. He said he'd asked around and been told that £175 would be a fair price for each flat.'

George nodded slowly. 'Well, I would say that sounds about right. He's not giving it away, but he's also not being greedy.'

They were all quiet for a moment before Lily spoke.

'That may be reasonable, George, but I'm not sure our Rosie's got that much ready cash.' Lily looked at Rosie for an answer.

'I was thinking of getting a small mortgage,' Rosie said.

'That might prove difficult, my dear,' George said. 'I believe you would have to get your husband's consent, which is probably going to be difficult given Peter's present situation.'

Rosie's shoulders slumped a little. She had feared this might be the case.

'So, what *then* happens,' George said, casting a quick look across to Lily, 'is that I will loan you the outstanding amount you need just like a bank would.'

'Oh, I couldn't—' Rosie started to object.

'Rosie, *ma chère*,' Lily stubbed her cigarette out, 'George has more than enough money – and it's just sat doing bugger all in the bank at the moment.'

'Agree wholeheartedly!' George said. 'Lily's right. It's just sat there gathering dust – and very little interest – so you'd make me feel better knowing it's actually being put to good use.'

Rosie looked at them both.

'All right … But I'll only accept your kind offer, George, *if* I pay interest – like I'd be doing if I borrowed it from a bank.'

'Good God, girl, I'll hear nothing of the sort!' George went over to the decanter and sloshed a measure of brandy into his tumbler. 'I'm actually insulted you've even suggested it!'

Rosie knew there would be no changing George's mind. She sighed. 'That's very kind of you, George, and not at all "financially savvy". Thank you.'

George raised his glass in the air.

'So, that's all agreed. Our Rosie is going to take her first step onto the property ladder!'

Lily raised her glass and winked across at Rosie.

'Hear! Hear!' she said.

Rosie looked at them both and felt a sudden rush of excitement that it was possible.

She was going to buy a flat!

She took Kate's empty teacup and raised it in the air.

The smile on her face said it all.

After Rosie had left for the evening, along with most of the guests, Lily and George retired to bed.

'Well, this has been an evening to remember, hasn't it?' George said, making himself comfy in the armchair next to the little open fire. 'Our Rosie, a married woman … and now about to become a landlord. Or should I say, landlady.'

'It certainly has been, my dear.' Lily sat on the cushioned stool in front of her dressing table. 'Buying the flat is a very wise move …' Her voice trailed off as she removed her jewellery.

'So, why do I sense there's a "but" coming?' George asked.

'Well,' Lily huffed, 'I have to say I thought she might have told us first that she'd got married. It would appear every Tom, Dick and Harry got to know about this bleedin' wedding before we did.' Lily had been bursting at the seams to say those exact words since Rosie had mentioned that her squad of women welders had been the first to hear her news.

'Even this Mrs Jenkins, *the new neighbour*,' Lily shook her head with indignation, 'even *she* knew before us! If Rosie had left it much longer, we'd have been reading about it in the births, marriages and deaths section of the bleedin' local paper!'

George laughed. It always made him chuckle that Lily's cockney twang came rushing back to the fore when she got irate or had one too many. And tonight, both had happened.

'Lily, my dear, our Rosie could have come straight from the railway station as soon as she'd arrived back to tell us she'd got hitched, and you'd *still* not have been any happier about the situation.'

Lily puffed out air and reached for her packet of Gauloises. 'I just don't understand why they had to get married!' She pulled a cigarette out and lit it, inhaling deeply. 'I just hope to God he's not swanned off to be a hero and left our Rosie with a little Peter or a little Rosie to bring up on her own.'

George looked at Lily. He had wondered himself if this was the case for the sudden nuptials.

'I don't think so. I saw Rosie's reaction when you ever so subtly asked her if we might soon be converting one of the rooms into a nursery. She dismissed it out of hand straight away.'

George had thought she had done so a little too quickly. And there had been something else he had picked up on when Lily had been prodding Rosie for information. Was it sadness that he saw in her eyes? Or anger? Or both? He wasn't sure. But what he was certain of was that they wouldn't be knee-deep in nappies any time soon.

Lily blew out a plume of smoke. 'Well, if she's not in the family way, I really don't understand why she married the bloke.'

George almost spluttered on his whisky. 'Honestly, I think I'm about to get married to the most unromantic woman on this planet. I thought you were marrying me for love – or are you really just after my money?'

'Both!' Lily said, poker-faced.

'Lily,' George sighed, 'has it never occurred to you that Rosie's married "the bloke" because she loves him? Because he's the only bloke she's ever loved?'

'Pah!' Lily dismissed the idea with a wave of her hand. She looked at George's reflection in the bevelled mirror as she smothered her face with cream.

'Rosie might have been lovelorn enough to marry for love, but that's not the reason *he* asked her to be his wife. *That much I do know!*' Lily tapped the end of her half-smoked Gauloise into the silver ashtray. 'My reckoning is that it's because he wants to make sure no one else gets a look-in while he's away.'

'I think, my dear, you might be right on one count and there *is* another reason for wanting Rosie to become his wife, but I don't think it's because he wants to fend off any other potential beaux. I think you're too hard on Peter. There's much more to that "bloke" than meets the eye.'

Lily turned around to look at George. 'Please, don't go all rose-tinted glasses on me. I can read you like a book, George Reginald Macalister. You think he's married our Rosie so that she will get whatever's his, should he die a hero's death out on some godforsaken battlefield.'

George nodded. This was exactly what he believed. Although he knew that if Peter was killed, he would not be revered as a hero, nor would he breathe his last breath on some stretch of foreign land that was being openly fought over. If Peter did die for the greater good of his country, it would be behind enemy lines, and his death would probably not be a quick one. He was pretty sure that Peter had volunteered to become part of what was being nicknamed by those in the know as 'Churchill's Secret Army'.

George just hoped for Rosie's sake that Peter's French was a damn sight better than Lily's, and that luck and God – if there was one – would be close by his side.

When Rosie climbed into bed it had gone midnight. She was tired and glad of it. If she could just keep herself as busy as possible – throw herself into work, both at Thompson's and at Lily's, and now with this new venture of being a landlady – it might just be possible to outrun the ache in her heart caused by her separation from Peter.

At least now, she thought, as she plumped her pillows and sat up in bed, everyone knew about Peter – her squad of women welders and, thank goodness, Lily. Rosie had expected a frostier reception to her news, but Lily had put on a good show, which made Rosie love her all the more. Just about everyone who needed to know had been told – she'd even taken the bull by the horns and gone to see Harold. He had been taken aback, but had seemed genuinely happy for her – and he seemed even happier that he now knew the mystery surrounding Rosie's telegram.

'Love and war,' he'd declared, standing behind his desk and puffing on his cigar. 'Let there be more love and less war, that's what I say!' He had then taken her hand in both of his, squeezed it, and told her, 'I'll make all the necessary name and status changes, *Mrs Miller*!'

There was only one other person to tell and that was her little sister, Charlotte. There had been a time not so long ago that Rosie could have predicted how her younger sister would have reacted – probably even the exact words she would have used – but not now. Over the past few months Charlotte had changed. She had gone from having an easy-going, happy temperament to being a rather moody and angry young girl, demanding that she leave her posh boarding school in Harrogate and come back to their home town. Lily had said it was simply down to her age, that, having just turned fourteen, she was 'no longer a child, but not quite a woman'. Rosie's intuition told her that it was more than that, but as she was not due to see Charlotte until the Easter break, she resolved not to worry about it until then. At least she knew her little sister was safe and out of harm's way there.

Rosie leant over to her bedside cabinet and reached into the top drawer, where she had put Peter's letter. She smoothed it out and read it slowly, digesting every word.

Her eyes became heavy as she read it for the second time, and she fell into a deep sleep, still clutching her letter of love.

Chapter Thirteen

Wanborough Manor, near Guildford, Surrey

As Peter lay in his bed in the large, high-ceilinged room that was his new sleeping quarters, he knew by the cacophony of snoring around him that he was the only one still awake.

He and thirteen other 'students', as they were referred to, had just completed their second day of an intensive three-week course that the former Coldstream officer, Major Roger de Wesselow, had called an 'instruction in the school of subversive activity'.

Their 'school' was the secluded Wanborough Manor, a country house in a small, secluded parish lying between Guildford and Farnham. Those who lived in the few cottages and houses nearby had been told the former family home had been requisitioned as a commando training base.

Peter had little knowledge about the workings of the Special Operations Executive before he arrived, other than the sketchy details his old university friend Toby had given him when he had 'dropped by' to see him – a visit he now realised had been for the sole purpose of recruiting him. He knew, however, that the manor was being used exclusively to train French operatives.

Peter had anticipated that his fellow recruits would come from all walks of life, but he hadn't expected such diversity – there were two brothers who had been travelling acrobats, a chef, a fashion artist for *Vogue* and *Country*

Life, a hairdresser who had once been a colonial boxing champion, a hotelier, an industrial chemist, a county council surveyor, a ship's chandler and a diplomatic consul. They all had one thing in common, though – French was their second language, and one they were expected to use all the time from now on, even at meals. His mother's refusal to speak English was something for which Peter was now eternally grateful.

Peter had thought he might well be the oldest, being in his early forties, but it seemed that age was no barrier. Philip, who was in the bed next to him, had recently turned fifty. Today he had quietly told Peter that he worried he wouldn't be fit enough for the job, but Peter knew he wouldn't have been approached unless the powers that be had something specific in mind for him. Just like he suspected they had for each of them.

The Major, who must have been in his fifties himself, and who they all knew to be a veteran of the First War, had explained yesterday that their training here would consist of lectures and practical exercises in map-reading, demolitions, weapons training, Morse code and close combat. He had stressed that once they were put into the field, it would be a 'tough and solitary' life. No one was to know what went on at the manor.

Their training officer had briefed them on exactly what was happening in France in both the occupied and unoccupied zones. He had drilled into them that security was paramount. A poster showing a sexy blonde in a red dress under the heading YOU FORGET BUT SHE REMEMBERS had been put up in the dining hall, although for Peter it only served as a painful reminder of Rosie looking ravishing in her own red dress.

They'd been told there was to be no leave, no phone calls, and any post would be checked and censored.

It was why Peter had sent Rosie that one final letter, posting it just hours after they had said their goodbyes on Sunday.

Staring up at the elaborately decorated ribbed plaster ceiling of what had been the master bedroom, Peter hoped there hadn't been any disruptions in the postal service and that Rosie would now have the letter. He had wanted it to be on the doormat when she let herself into her new home. He would have given anything to have been there, to have picked her up in his arms and carried her over the threshold, for Rosie to have spent her first night at Brookside Gardens as a married woman with her husband by her side. But it was not to be, so a letter was the rather poor alternative.

As he lay there knowing sleep was still a long way off, Peter ran over their precious time together. His anxious wait at the train station, unsure whether or not she'd come, then seeing her at the carriage door, looking stunning, tears of joy in her eyes, and how they had talked and made love and talked some more.

He realised now that Rosie would have said yes to his proposal of marriage without his carefully thought out arguments as to why she should become his wife. She had said yes simply because she loved him, because she wanted him to be her husband. A part of him wished he had tried the romantic approach first, and if that had failed *only then* gone on to the practical reasons for doing so. But he had been so convinced that Rosie was not the marrying kind, he had just presumed she would say no. He had decided on the honest, no-nonsense approach and told her straight up: if she married him now, should anything happen to him while he was away, she would inherit everything he owned. He had no children of his own (his wife's cancer had robbed him of that chance), nor did he have any living relatives that he was particularly close to or who were in desperate financial straits.

Of course, he could have left everything in his will to Rosie without her being his wife, but he didn't want there to be any kind of ambiguity. A legally binding union made everything black and white. Now she was his wife, she would inherit everything, as well as his police pension.

Rosie had listened quietly without interrupting as he had explained that by marrying him she could also move into his home. He knew how much Rosie loved the house, and it was a safer area of town to live in, not to mention the money she would save on the rent of her flat. He had added that it would also put his mind at rest if he knew the house would be looked after while he was away, but he knew Rosie wasn't a fool and realised he was only saying that to make her think that she would be doing him a favour.

One advantage of getting hitched that he didn't mention, however, but which brought him some comfort, was that should he be killed, as next of kin she would be the first to be informed. She wouldn't have to hear it second-hand, or worry that he might be dead, but no one would know to tell her.

When he had finally finished what felt like the opening argument in a taut court case, he had been bowled over by her response.

'Peter,' she'd said with a smile and a sparkle in her eyes, 'I have listened to every word you have said and taken on board all of your very well-rehearsed arguments for me agreeing to be your wife.' She paused and her smile widened. 'I will agree to be your wife for one reason and one reason only. And that is because I love you. Because I want to be your wife. Because I want you to be my husband. You could be a pauper for all I care; I'd still want to marry you.'

Her words had shocked him and for a short moment he'd been speechless, then he had leant across the little round table they were sitting at, cupped her radiant face in his hands and kissed her. She had got embarrassed, as she always did when he kissed her in public, and pulled away, blushing, but her joy at agreeing to become Mrs Miller had been almost parallel to his own at her agreeing to have him as her husband.

He had told her that she could and should spend his savings, which he had put in both their names – regardless of whether he lived or died. He hadn't said as much but there was more than enough to enable her to leave the bordello and still be able to keep Charlotte at her school in Harrogate, or at the Sunderland Church High School should Charlotte get her way and persuade Rosie to let her come back. Something told him, however, that Rosie wouldn't leave Lily's and her cuckoo's nest of waifs and strays.

The few days they'd had together had been a dream – the most wonderful, happy and loving dream imaginable. They had barely left their hotel other than to nip into a jewellers to buy the ring, and to the florist for the bouquet of pansies. Even the registry office had just been a short walk away from where they were staying.

It amazed him how happy they had been, how they had been able to simply enjoy each other in the here and now, without the sadness of their parting creeping into their precious time together.

What had been so important for Peter's own peace of mind was that Rosie understood *why* he was doing what he had signed up to do. Not that he had told her anything specific. He had explained there was very little he could tell her about where he was going and what he would be doing, but he sensed she had an idea. She had told him that

George had 'talked some sense' into her and helped her to understand 'certain things'.

He hoped one day to be able to shake George's hand. Peter knew of men like George, those who had survived the so-called war to end all wars, who had returned to their homeland but had never truly been able to go back to the lives they'd lived before. Peter had a lot to thank George for. Not only for 'talking sense' to Rosie, but also for loving Rosie dearly and being there for her should he not make it back.

Despite the risks, though, there was still no doubt in his mind that he had done the right thing in signing up. The situations at home and abroad were far from good. Not only was it clear that Hitler was committed to continuing his Blitz on all the major industrial towns and cities in this country, he was also making inroads into North Africa and Russia, and now the Japanese were attacking the Philippines and were doing so very successfully. The scales of war were swinging heavily in favour of the Axis. Anyone who read a paper or listened to the BBC Home Service could see the future was looking decidedly dark – even with the huge dollops of propaganda being doled out to dilute the seriousness of the situation and safeguard national morale.

Peter knew there were no blurred lines in this world war. It simply came down to a battle between good and evil. And Peter would be damned if evil was going to win. He would sacrifice his love and his life to help his country win this godforsaken war.

As sleep finally started to draw him down, Peter pictured Rosie as they had said their goodbyes. They had stood on the station platform with their arms wrapped tightly around each other. He'd told her that it was unlikely that he would be able to write to her and she'd said she understood. He had kissed her, taking in the smell of her skin and the scent of the hotel soap that she had said was 'pure heaven', but then he'd said something he immediately regretted:

'If there's any way I can get word to you, I will. I promise.'

The words had just slipped out and he had immediately chided himself. He had been determined not to give Rosie false hope. It was unfair. But it was too late, the words had been said.

When the stationmaster's whistle pierced the air, Peter had opened the carriage door and helped his new wife into her compartment, placing her one piece of luggage by her feet and closing the door. Rosie had opened the sash window, leant out and grabbed Peter's hand. She had smiled but Peter knew her too well – knew that she was trying so hard to keep back the tears.

The second blow of the whistle had filled the air, along with the hiss of the engine and a rising billow of steam. They had held hands as the train had edged its way out of the station, only relinquishing each other's touch when they absolutely had to.

'I love you, Mrs Miller!' he had shouted out.

He clung on to the last image he had of Rosie – her face disappearing behind a veil of smoke as she blew him a kiss and mouthed back to him:

'I love you too.'

Chapter Fourteen

'So, just show me again, where is Malta exactly?' Polly looked at Arthur. It was getting late and they were now the only two still up in the Elliot household. Even Tramp and Pup were gently snoring, curled up in their favourite spot by the warmth of the range.

Arthur's long, bony finger circled the small island that was presently being subjected to a blitzkrieg of epic proportions.

'And Malta is a British colony?' Polly asked.

Arthur nodded.

'Which is why it's under attack now?' Another question.

'Well, pet, from my understanding, it's where it *is* – geographically – that's important.' Arthur sat back in his chair and put his hands on his knees. 'Have yer ever played chess, pet?' he asked.

'I tried, but it wasn't one of my favourite games.' Polly had never really liked games that required sitting for long stretches of time, preferring to run around playing tag and hide and seek.

'But yer know the principle o' the game, don't ya? What the pawns dee – and the bishops 'n the queen? And that where they're positioned on the board is important?'

Polly nodded.

'Well, Malta is in an important position. The British air force 'n navy based there can attack enemy ships transporting supplies 'n troops. Obviously, life would be a lot easier fer Hitler if he had control of the island 'n that's why he's presently trying to bomb it into submission.'

'So,' Polly had a frown on her face as her tired mind tried to make sense of the strategies of war, 'Malta is a bit like Gibraltar then?'

'Aye,' Arthur said, '*where* they are is important – especially when it comes to North Africa. The Germans 'n Italians are gonna struggle to win the Desert War if we keep control of Malta 'n Gibraltar. It's like if you had yer bishop 'n yer knight protecting yer queen, the queen's safe, providing yer opponent doesn't take either or both of those other two pieces.'

Polly sighed.

'Oh Arthur, it's all very complicated.'

The old man looked at his grandson's fiancée and felt her pain and frustration. She didn't care about the complexities of warmongering – or chess. She just wanted to know about Tommy. Where he was. What he was doing. And, more importantly, if he was safe.

As Arthur looked at Polly studying the map, he felt his heart break a little at the thought of what might happen to this lovely young woman if Tommy did not return. She was strong and feisty, but she was also fiercely loyal. He'd seen enough of life and knew enough of people to see that Polly would never love another. Tommy would be her one and only love.

As if sensing his stare, Polly looked up.

'He's going to be all right? Isn't he?' Polly knew her words sounded desperate, that Arthur did not have a crystal ball and could not see what the future held, but she needed to just hear him say the words.

'That lad's a born survivor.' Arthur forced his voice to sound strong and certain. 'He'll be back, pet. Yer mark my words.' He looked at Polly and saw her eyes had started to glisten with tears. 'I know that lad 'n I know nowt's going to stop him making it back home to his sweetheart. He made a promise.' Arthur looked down at Polly's left hand and at the ruby engagement ring she wore of an evening. The ring that had once belonged to his own wife, Flo. 'And he's not one to break it. Jerry or no Jerry.' Arthur put his gnarled, veiny hand on top of Polly's and squeezed it.

Polly wiped under her eyes with her free hand; she would not cry, at least not in front of anyone.

'I just don't understand why we're at war at all.' Polly's worry about Tommy had started to morph into anger, as it was wont to do. It was easier to deal with. 'Why couldn't Hitler just be happy with ruling over Germany? Why does he think he's got the right to just stomp into another country and claim it as his own?'

Arthur sat back in his chair again and sighed. 'That's why we're at war, Polly. Because it's not right. And he hasn't got the right to just do that. We're fighting a wrong to keep everything right.' Arthur paused for a moment, not sure whether to say what he wanted to say next.

'And that's why we must both keep telling ourselves that our Tommy is where he should be ...'

'Fighting a wrong to make it right.' Polly repeated the old man's words.

They both sat in quietness for a few moments, until they heard the creak of the wooden floorboards on the stairs.

'You two still up?' Bel's head appeared around the kitchen door, which had been pulled ajar.

Arthur got to his feet as Bel padded into the kitchen, pulling her dressing gown tightly around her.

'Come and sit down here.' Arthur pulled the chair out. 'The seat's warm if nothing else. This old man's talked enough for one night. Time for some shut-eye.'

Polly smiled up at the old man. She had always liked Arthur, since first meeting him when she and Tommy had started courting, but now she loved him like he was family. The granddad – perhaps even the da – that she had never had.

Arthur shut the door behind him and walked down the hallway to his bedroom at the front of the house; a room that had been a front parlour many moons ago, then more recently Joe's, after he'd come back from war.

'You all right?' Bel asked, looking at Polly. It wasn't often she caught her sister-in-law looking so subdued and also a little teary.

'Yes, I'm fine,' Polly said, trying to sound more cheerful than she felt.

Bel looked down at the map and thought that it had become a kind of comfort blanket for Polly; as though being able to look at the part of the world where she knew her fiancé to be somehow brought him closer to her.

'Can't you sleep?' Polly asked, folding up the map, wanting to steer the conversation away from Tommy, knowing that if she didn't her peak of anger might well dissolve back into tears.

'No. Tossing and turning like I'm lying on a bed of coals,' Bel said, looking round and spotting the kettle on the hob. 'Thought I'd give up and at least allow Joe to get some sleep.' Bel got up and felt the kettle's pot belly to gauge how recently it had been used to make a brew. She picked it up and topped up the teapot on the table.

She looked at Polly.

'Are you sure you're all right?'

Polly nodded.

'You know I'm here whenever you need me. Always got time to listen to my best mate.'

Polly could feel the tears starting to ease their way back.

'Don't be nice to me, Bel.' She let out a little laugh that was anything but joyful. 'I don't want to start blubbering. Can't be doing with it.' Polly got up and fetched two cups from the sideboard. 'Now pour us both a cup of watery, lukewarm tea and tell me what's keeping you up. Something's playing on your mind. I know you too well.'

They both took a sip of tea.

'Remember when we were little and we used to top and tail it in bed?' Polly said. The two women chuckled at the remembrance. 'I always knew if something was up with you because you'd be flinging yourself from side to side. I'm surprised I never got a black eye from those stubby toes of yours.'

Bel spluttered on her tea. 'Eee, there's nothing stubby about my toes!'

Polly looked at Bel.

'So, come on. Out with it!'

Bel sighed.

'It's my ma.'

'When isn't it!' Polly joked.

'I just wish she'd be upfront and tell me about my da.' Bel took another sip from her cup. 'Then I argue with myself that it's not important. Whoever he is, he has never been a part of my life, and never will be, so what's the point? But I just can't seem to let it go.'

Polly looked at her best friend, her sister-in-law twice over, and knew she wouldn't be able to let it go. And nor did she want to.

Chapter Fifteen

Two weeks later

Tuesday 27 January

'Eee, thank goodness for that!' Pearl exclaimed as she walked out of the Tatham with Bill, the two barmaids, and her neighbour Ronald. They had been cooped up in the basement of the pub for the past hour or so waiting for the all-clear to sound out. The cellar made a perfect air raid shelter. It's only downfall was that it was small and could only just accommodate half a dozen people – enough for Bill and his staff and a couple of regulars.

Fortunately, the air raid had only been precautionary, and the skies had remained clear of Hitler's harbingers of death. It had been over a week since the Luftwaffe had paid the town a visit, the earliest after-dark raid to date. Four bombs had been dropped, creating a 40-foot-deep crater in one of the main roads leading out of town, bursting a water main, and breaking just about every window in the town's revered art school. But no one had been injured or killed, which during the usual clear-up the next day everyone had agreed was all that mattered.

'See you all tomorrow.' Bill looked down the street as he waved off his staff and Ronald, who might as well be an employee – he was always propping up the bar and would often swap sides and help out if they got really busy. Bill wasn't a fool, though, and knew Ronald would not be such a constant presence in his pub if it wasn't for Pearl.

'See ya tomorrow,' Pearl shouted back, puffing on a cigarette.

'Ma!' A voice sounded out from the darkness. Pearl looked around to see Bel hurrying towards her. Behind her she could see Joe, Agnes, Arthur and Polly, who was carrying a sleepy Lucille in her arms. Pearl noticed her granddaughter was still managing to clutch on to her new toy rabbit. She guessed they'd all been holed up in the shelter around the corner under Tavistock House.

'You all right, pet?' Pearl asked as Bel caught up with her and started walking by her side.

'Mm,' Bel said, 'just tired. At least the house is still standing, eh?'

They'd reached their front door and Pearl nodded her farewells to Ronald.

'Aye, there is that,' Pearl said, eyeing Bel with suspicion. Her daughter wouldn't normally have made an effort to come and talk to her. Not after being stuck for an age in the shelter at this time of night.

'Eee, home sweet home!' It was Polly's voice coming through the front door behind them. 'I'll let this one sleep with me tonight. All right, Bel?' she asked. Lucille's head was buried in the crook of her aunty's neck.

'Yes, that's great, thanks, Pol,' Bel replied before quickly turning her attention to her mother, who was fidgeting about in her bag trying to find her packet of Winstons.

'I can't remember smoking them all,' she muttered to herself.

'Honestly, Ma, I don't know why you don't just hang them round your neck.' Bel was hovering over her mother.

'Night all!' It was Joe, heading straight for the stairs. The sound of his walking stick on the wooden treads could be heard as he made his way up to the top of the house, where his and Bel's new room was now fully furnished.

'Aye, night all!' It was Arthur, who was more than happy to have swapped bedrooms with Joe; his legs had been stiffening up of late and he had struggled to make it up and down the steep staircase.

The final goodnight came from Agnes as she trudged up to her bedroom on the first floor.

'Found them!' Pearl raised her cigarettes half-heartedly in the air and made her way to the back door.

'Ma,' Bel said, 'I'm sure Agnes won't mind if you have a smoke in here tonight.'

Pearl looked at her daughter, unable to keep the shock from showing on her face. Not once since she had arrived at the Elliots' had she been allowed to have a fag indoors, and she knew it was Bel who had laid down the law, not Agnes.

'You know what, pet, I feel like I've been stuck in that smelly cellar for ever. I feel like I need a bit o' fresh air.'

Bel looked at her mother.

'Anyone would think you were avoiding me, Ma,' Bel said, her eyes scrutinising her mother. 'I've hardly seen hide nor hair of you since you got back from London with Maisie.'

And it was true. Since Pearl had returned from the 'mother-daughter bonding trip' to London, when she and Maisie had gone to see Evelina and the place of Maisie's birth, Pearl was rarely at home unless it was to sleep. Her time was spent either working at the Tatham or taking Lucille out, usually to the park or to see Wallace, the museum's famous stuffed lion, which amazed Bel as her ma had not once taken her to any of the town's parks, never mind into a museum, when she had been a little girl.

'Eee, there's no pleasing some,' Pearl said. 'You'd be moaning at me if I was indoors all the time, getting under your 'n Agnes's feet.'

Bel had to admit to herself that this was true. During the day the house was full to the brim with children and laundry. Aggie's nursery was now attracting desperate mothers from beyond the immediate vicinity, all in need of someone to look after their offspring while they went out to work. Bel had commented a few times that even if they charged just a minimal amount, they would be a lot better off each week, but Agnes wouldn't entertain the idea. She was adamant that this was her way of 'doing my bit for the war effort'. As a result, they had continued taking in bags of laundry from some of the local small businesses in order to make ends meet, spending most of their days up to their elbows in soapy suds.

'You're probably right, Ma,' Bel had to concede, 'it just feels like you've been avoiding me?'

'Dinnit talk daft,' Pearl said, heading towards the back door.

But they both knew it was true. And they both knew why. It was the elephant in the room that Bel was desperate to point out, and which Pearl was equally desperate to ignore.

'Shall I put a brew on? Have a cuppa after you've had your fag?' Bel asked.

A look of slight panic crossed Pearl's face.

'Eee, Isabelle,' Pearl said, 'that's sweet of ya, but yer auld ma's knackered. I just wanna have this smoke 'n hit the sack. I'll be out for the count as soon as my head touches the pillow.'

Bel looked at her mother as she sloped off out the back door and into the yard. She knew her ma couldn't keep running away from her for ever. The time was near when there would be no other choice but for them to talk openly – and, hopefully, honestly – about the man who was her father.

This wasn't going to go away.

Chapter Sixteen

The Slums, Sunderland

1915

Pearl listened to the silence and panic shot through her exhausted, sweat-drenched body. The small back room she was in seemed so dark and gloomy. Was it night already? She was sure it had still been light when she had arrived here, knowing her time had come. She strained her head up. It shouldn't be this quiet. Something was wrong.

And then she heard it.

It started off as a whimper and grew rapidly into a fully formed wail, and Pearl's body sank back onto the thin mattress.

Her baby was alive.

It was then that she sensed movement and she turned her head to the side to see the vague outline of an old woman, dressed head to toe in black, moving around in the shadows. The baby's cries died down, and the sound of the old woman's coarse voice could be heard as she shuffled back towards Pearl.

'Well then, pet, yer did well there,' she cackled.

There wasn't a trace of kindness or comfort in the words that had just been spoken, and for a moment Pearl thought of Evelina. *Lovely Evelina.* Who had spoken the same words, but with such gentleness and reassurance. Not like the old witch presently stooped over her.

'Like you've done it all before.' The old woman's voice was croaky and this time it was full of mockery.

She knew. Knew, without Pearl having to say a word, that she had, in fact, done this all before.

Pearl turned her head, which felt like a lead weight, and glared at the old hag's wrinkled face. She would never admit to this craggy, callous cow that she was right – that she *had* done this before. She had not told a soul about the baby she had been forced to give up, and never would. The old woman could think what she wanted.

'My baby?' Pearl's words were little more than a mumble, her eyes scanning the darkness for sight of the child she had just given birth to.

There was a sudden flare of candlelight as the old woman opened a small window, and for a split second Pearl caught a glimpse of two tiny little arms reaching out for comfort but finding only air.

'My baby!' This time it was a demand.

'Yer can't have her!' the witch hissed. *'We're not done yet!'*

Pearl moved slightly and as she did so, she knew something wasn't right. She felt wet. Instinctively, she craned her head forward. The old woman was lighting another candle on the table by the side. As it burned and flickered, it threw light on Pearl's body. She looked down and gasped in horror. The lower half of her body was saturated in blood. Pools of blood.

This hadn't happened before! Not with her Maisie. Not when Evelina had been her midwife!

'What's happening? Why's there all this blood?' she cried out, afraid. She felt like a helpless child.

The little light there had been was suddenly blocked out as the old woman hunched over her, and Pearl's fear was replaced by pain. A terrible, stabbing pain. The old woman was doing something down there. And it hurt.

Pearl screamed but no sound came out. The stabbing pain kept on. And on. And during it all she was aware of a baby, out of reach in the corner of the room.

And the little bairn was whimpering.

Finally, after what felt like too long, the pain ended and the silent screaming in her head ceased.

Pearl watched the back of the grey-haired witch as she washed her hands in a bowl, pouring water over her thick forearms before reaching for a piece of rag and drying her hands.

And all the while the baby was crying quietly in the corner.

'This'll be yer last, bonny lass,' the old woman said. 'There'll be no more babs fer yer.' Now there was a hint of sadness in the old woman's voice as Pearl struggled to comprehend what she was being told. The old woman had moved away, but returned seconds later holding a glass jar of watery white liquid.

'That might not be a bad thing, eh?' the woman told her, putting the jar to Pearl's dry lips. 'Drink it. It'll make yer feel better,' she commanded.

Pearl did as she was told. The cold liquid tasted bitter. And all the while she could hear the baby crying.

After Pearl had forced down the drink, the old woman turned and padded across the small room. The concoction Pearl had just consumed took immediate effect, and she could feel the pain ebbing away. She watched with increasingly heavy eyelids as the old woman came back to her – this time with her baby in her arms. Pearl felt the weight of the newborn as the old woman placed her on her chest, but at the same time it felt as though her own body was being dragged down.

Sleep was coming, but she didn't want to sleep!

I want to see my baby!

Pearl forced her eyes open and tilted her head forward. Her arms were now so heavy she could barely move them, but she knew she was holding her child in them.

Again, she strained her neck and head up from the mattress.

There! She could see her baby!

Her vision was now blurred. Her mind felt tired and confused.

She gasped in shock.

This isn't my baby! She wanted to scream out, but the words stayed within her.

There's been a mistake! This is someone else's baby! The old witch had tricked her.

This baby had ivory skin and big blue eyes!

Where was her other baby? the voice in her head screamed. *My 'special' baby? The one they said I couldn't keep?*

Pearl looked down again at the babe in her arms and then up again, expecting to see the fresh, kindly face of Evelina, but instead she saw the old woman.

'Where've yer taken my baby?!' Pearl cried out. Her own voice sounded loud and the words banged against her throbbing head.

The old woman looked down at them.

'What do you mean, hinny?' the old woman asked. '*Here's* your baby.'

Pearl looked again at the child now at peace in her arms. She had a thin veil of white-blonde hair. Her breath caught when the baby looked up at her, opening her eyes wide as if startled, showing her large, round, sea-blue eyes. She was beautiful. So very beautiful.

But she looked like him.

As Pearl finally gave in to the opium-induced oblivion, she knew that this *was* her baby.

'Yer gonna sleep now,' the old woman said, putting a damp cloth on Pearl's brow. She was surprised she wasn't calling the undertaker. The girl was still burning up, but she'd got through the worst. She was stronger than she looked.

She'd make it.

Chapter Seventeen

The Ford Estate, Sunderland

Sunday 1 February

Gloria took one last look at the lounge, which now seemed bare despite all the furniture still there – everything apart from the battered and worn-out armchair that she had nicknamed 'Vinnie's throne' as no one but her ex was ever allowed to sit in it. Even after she'd chucked him out, she could still not bring herself to use it, although it had brought her immense joy to see others plonk themselves down in it, drink tea and drop biscuit crumbs down the sides.

As Gloria closed the lounge door, she had a great sense of finality. She was leaving what had once been her marital home. These four walls had been witness to too much violence and bullying, too much unhappiness and too much sadness.

She walked down the hallway for the last time and as she opened the front door an image of her waving off her two sons suddenly sprang to mind. They couldn't wait to leave home and join the navy, not because of a deep yearning to go to sea, but to escape an atmosphere that had become increasingly charged as they had grown into young men. Thoughts of Bobby and Gordon brought with them the now familiar sharp stab of worry. Gloria reminded herself of the letter she'd received from them the previous week; it took the edge off, but only a fraction.

Stepping out of the house and looking at the street that she very much doubted she would ever return to, Gloria shielded her eyes against the midday sun that had come out as if in celebration of the end of an old life and the beginning of a new one.

'Come on, Glor!'

Gloria squinted as she saw Dorothy and Angie, both in their work overalls, their hair tied back in ponytails. They were standing in the small, open-backed truck that was now full of old suitcases stuffed to the brim with clothes, tablecloths and bed linen, as well as a number of large wooden tea chests overflowing with household utensils, framed photographs and rolled-up rugs. And, of course, there was Hope's cot.

'Is that everything?' Martha shouted out. She was dressed in a pair of men's dungarees and was standing at the side of the truck, her arms akimbo. She looked sweaty and out of puff.

'Yes, thanks, Martha, that's everything!' Gloria turned back, taking one last look before closing the front door for a final time. She then pushed the key through the letter box. The landlord had an extra copy and had told her that he would be meeting the new tenants there later on in the day.

Dorothy caught her workmate looking unusually emotional and shouted out, 'Now don't be getting all sentimental on us, will you?'

'Yeah,' Angie added, 'yer dinnit want us all thinking you've gone soft on us!'

Gloria laughed, but found she wasn't able to bite back with a quick retort. Her throat seemed to have gone tight and her eyes were smarting with the beginnings of tears.

As she walked down the short pathway and through the little wooden gate, making sure she closed it behind her, she felt an overwhelming sadness that Jack was not with her now. That this was not the start of a new life for the two of them as they had planned and hoped at the beginning of the year.

Stop it! she reprimanded herself. *This is not the time to get all maudlin.*

None of the women, bar Rosie, had any idea that Jack wasn't coming back. She had let them believe that he'd *had* to go to Glasgow but that it was just temporary, and then they would tell the world – or rather, Miriam – about their love. And their love child.

As Gloria reached the van she was greeted by Jimmy, dusting himself down after helping Martha with some heavy lifting.

'You ready for the off?' he asked.

Gloria nodded, still not quite trusting herself to speak. She looked at Dorothy and Angie, who had hold of Martha's hands and were helping to haul her into the back of the truck.

Climbing into the passenger seat, she sat quietly as Jimmy pushed the truck into first gear, released the handbrake and drove steadily down Fordham Road. Gloria looked out the window she had wound down and saw that Martha and Jimmy had done as she had asked and hauled Vinnie's armchair to the small stretch of derelict land where the kids from the estate loved to run riot.

She smiled as she saw they had already discovered the new addition to their makeshift playground. There were screams of excitement as the little ones took turns to jump up and down on it as though it was a trampoline, while the older boys and girls ran around it playing tag.

All of a sudden Gloria started to laugh and then cry. She couldn't stop the tears and through her blurred vision she saw Jimmy's hand reach for her own. He squeezed it hard before putting his big calloused riveter's hands back on the steering wheel. Jimmy didn't say anything, but he had heard about the beating Gloria's husband had given her in the yard that December afternoon, and he knew it was unlikely that it was the first Gloria had had to endure during her marriage. Fortunately for Gloria, though, it looked as though it might well have been the last, as the gossip doing the rounds was that her husband had been conscripted back into the navy and was gone for the foreseeable future. If not for good.

'Here they come!' Polly shouted down the small flight of stone steps that led to Rosie's basement flat, or rather, to what had been Rosie's flat and was now Gloria's.

Rosie came hurrying up the steps and onto the Borough Road. She was glad the sun was out, even though it was still bitterly cold. She was closely followed by Bel, who was carrying Hope. She had been babysitting at home in Tatham Street, but had wanted to be there with Hope to welcome Gloria to her new home.

'Shame Jack couldn't be here,' Bel said quietly to Rosie as she shifted Hope on her hip and brushed the baby's mop of thick black hair away from her eyes.

'I know,' Rosie agreed, but didn't say any more. She wondered how much longer Gloria could get away with telling people that Jack was coming back 'soon'.

'He hasn't seen Hope since just after the New Year, and this little girl is changing by the day. And getting bigger by the minute.' Bel jigged Hope up again and onto her other hip. 'But still,' she added, 'at least she knows who her da is.'

Rosie looked at Bel and wanted to say something, but thought better of it. Polly had told her about her sister-in-law's determination to find out who her real father was, but Rosie knew Bel was quite a private person and she didn't want her thinking that she was prying.

'Eee, honestly, look at them two!' Polly pointed at Dorothy and Angie, who were standing up in the back of the van and waving their hands in the air as though they were on a carnival float.

'Poor Martha, having to put up with them all morning. As if she doesn't get enough of that pair of jokers at work.' Rosie laughed as she took in the comic sight of her three women welders in the back of the truck.

As Jimmy pulled up onto the pavement, Gloria waved at the little welcoming party standing there. Before getting out, she turned to Jimmy. 'Thanks so much for doing all this. I don't know how I would have managed otherwise.'

'No worries,' he laughed. 'I've not done too badly out of it myself.'

'What do yer mean?' Gloria asked, puzzled. In the corner of her eye she saw that Martha was carrying a wooden tea chest down into the flat, followed by Angie with Hope's cot, and Dorothy, who was lugging two suitcases, one in each hand.

'They didn't tell you?' Jimmy let out a hoot of laughter.

Gloria shook her head.

'I did a swap. The truck in exchange for Martha. She's agreed to fill in for Frank next week, but only if I got some kind of transport sorted and helped you move.'

Gloria gave Jimmy a playful shove. 'Cor, and there was me thinking yer were doing this through the kindness of yer heart! I might have guessed!'

'Never one to pass up an opportunity,' Jimmy said. He stuck his head out the window and saw that the women had cleared the back of the van.

'Well, you're not getting her permanently,' Gloria said, climbing out of the passenger seat and shutting the door. 'Martha's not daft.' She stuck her head through the open window. 'She knows the future's welding. Riveting'll soon be a thing of the past!'

'Pah!' Jimmy said. It was their familiar banter. 'You'll never get better than a riveted ship!'

Having successfully got the last word, Jimmy honked his horn and drove off.

When Gloria walked through her new front door, she was greeted by a gang of happy faces all cheering 'Home Sweet Home!' in front of a banner hanging from the ceiling that had those exact words written on it.

The flat was just as Gloria remembered it. When Rosie had suggested she take over the flat as she was going to move into Peter's house in Brookside Gardens, Gloria hadn't hesitated. Looking around the living room now, with its little settee and armchair and oblong coffee table, Gloria thought that it looked exactly the same. The three-bar electric heater was still on the hearth in front of the blocked-off fireplace and was, as usual, kicking out the heat. Even the walls still had the two gold-framed paintings of flowers, and a large hexagonal mirror hung above the mantelpiece.

Gloria looked at Rosie, who had told her that she had been taking 'bits and bobs' over to Peter's the past week, and had now more or less moved in.

'Haven't you taken anything with you?' she asked.

Rosie laughed. 'No, not really.'

Rosie had told Gloria that she was leaving most of the furniture she had bought when she first moved in, but had refused point-blank Gloria's offer of buying it off her. Gloria had also questioned the amount of rent as it seemed very low – she would have thought Mr Brown, the landlord, would have wanted to get as much as he could in these hard times. It was easier to put up the rent a little with a new tenant than it was with an old one, but again Rosie had been adamant that this was the going rate for such a flat in this part of town.

'Are you sure you don't even want to take any pictures or lamps with you?' Gloria asked.

'Honestly,' Rosie reassured her, 'I've got everything I need at Peter's.'

'Well, don't just stand there gawping!' The conversation was interrupted by Dorothy, who was taking control of the move. 'Let's 'ave a butcher's!' Dorothy and Angie had been on a few dates with a couple of merchant sailors from London and were enjoying learning the odd cockney word and rhyming slang. Dorothy tugged Gloria by the arm down the short hallway.

'First of all, the back bedroom, which Angie, Bel and I have converted into a little nursery for my goddaughter!'

All the women welders had helped to bring Hope into the world when Gloria had gone into labour unexpectedly during a midday air raid, but it was Dorothy who had actually delivered baby Hope. Afterwards, Gloria had asked if her less than angelic workmate would be her baby girl's godmother. It was an offer Dorothy had gleefully accepted and a role she both cherished and took very seriously.

Peering into the room, Gloria saw Hope's wooden cot in the middle of a spotlessly clean room. She noticed that the baby gas mask, which was almost as big as Hope, had been placed out of the way in the corner of the room, but near enough to grab if needed. In the other corner Bel was putting some of Lucille's hand-me-down baby clothes into a chest of drawers, on top of which there was a little night light and a small vase of flowers.

'Ah, this is gorgeous.' Gloria looked at Dorothy and Angie and back at Bel. 'Thank you.'

Gloria walked over to look at the little pile of baby outfits Bel was carefully folding and putting away.

'Aren't these lovely?' she said, holding up a particularly cute pink romper suit to show Dorothy and Angie, who nodded but didn't seem overly interested. Looking back at Bel, she said quietly, 'Shouldn't you be keeping them for yourself?'

Bel smiled. It wasn't the first time someone had made a subtle reference to the possibility that she and Joe might soon be giving Lucille a baby brother or sister. It was three months since they had said their wedding vows to each other, and they had both agreed to let nature take its course. Bel had thought Mother Nature would have done so already, especially as she had fallen with Lucille within a month of her marriage to Teddy – Lucille's birthday was almost exactly nine months to the day of their wedding – but it would seem this was not to be the case this time round.

'Hope needs them now. They're not benefiting anyone stuffed away in my wardrobe back home. Anyway, I'm determined to have a boy this time.' Bel tried to make a joke of it. In truth, she didn't care what sex any baby she might have was.

'Well, that's you with another girl for certain,' Gloria laughed. 'If you want a girl, you'll get a boy. If you want a boy, you'll get a girl. It's sod's law!'

'So, you think this is good enough for my goddaughter?' Dorothy butted in, walking to the blackout curtains and making sure they were shut properly.

'Most definitely!' Gloria looked down at Hope, snuggled up in her cot, clutching a bottle of milk and staring about her in wonder. 'Your goddaughter, Dor, is a very lucky little girl.'

They all looked at Hope for a moment, before they were distracted by the sound of the front door going.

'That'll be Hannah,' Dorothy and Angie said in unison.

'She said she was bringing some of her aunty's special Jewish pastries,' Angie shouted back to Bel and Gloria as she and Dorothy hurried down the hallway.

Hannah's arrival had the same effect as the klaxon at work – everyone stopped what they were doing and started organising their tea break. Rosie made a big ceramic pot of tea, which Martha then carried into the lounge-cum-dining room, putting it on a small table. Rosie staggered in with a tray laden with cups and saucers, a jug of milk and a bowl of sugar. Dorothy and Angie upended empty wooden boxes, grabbed all the available chairs and put them around the table. Bel saw to Hope who had started to cry, having been left alone in her cot while there was clearly something exciting happening within earshot. And finally, Hannah put the pastries on plates and made them the centrepiece of their impromptu tea party.

As they chatted through mouthfuls of crescent-shaped rolls of lightly sugared pastry filled with raisins, nuts and jam, a rare treat in these times of rationing, Hannah explained that there had been a bar mitzvah at the synagogue on the Ryhope Road and, as was always the case at such ceremonies, there had been a celebration afterwards. Hannah's aunty Rina, who was well known within the Jewish community as a master baker, had been tasked with baking bread and making sandwiches and pastries, which Hannah told everyone were called 'rugelach'.

'I think these are the best cakes I've ever tasted!' Martha said.

'They're *pastries*, Martha, not *cakes*,' Dorothy corrected. 'And I agree, they are simply scrumptious!'

For a moment they all sat quietly and devoured the delicious delicacy.

'Perhaps *we* could have a – what did you call it, Hannah? A barmits—?'

'A bar mitzvah,' Hannah said before letting out a little chuckle. 'I don't think we could. For starters, you have to be twelve or thirteen years old, and secondly you have to be a boy.'

'And thirdly,' Martha added, 'you have to be Jewish!'

They all laughed.

'I never thought I would utter these words ...' Bel took a quick sip of tea ' ... but I do believe these surpass Mrs Milburn's and that's saying something.'

Rosie suddenly stopped drinking her tea and looked at Hannah before casting a glance over to Gloria, who returned her look in such a way as to show that she knew exactly what Rosie was thinking.

'Here, let me take her.' Gloria got up and took Hope off Bel. 'Give you a chance to enjoy your tea.'

Bel looked at Hope with adoring eyes. 'It's going to be great having you both practically living on the doorstep,' she said. She would never admit it to Gloria, but she often felt that Hope was half hers. She dreaded the day that, for whatever reason, Gloria stopped working.

'It's going to be so much easier,' Gloria said, wiping some cream from the side of her mouth. 'Just a few minutes' walk to drop Hope off with you and then just another few minutes' walk to the ferry. No more hiking to and from the Ford Estate every day. Yes,' Gloria raised her teacup, 'this is a fresh start, and I have to say, it really would not have been possible without you all. So, a really big thank-you!'

'Ahh, you're welcome,' the women chorused.

'And,' Gloria added, 'an even bigger thanks to Martha here, who, I don't know if she told you all, did a swap with

Jimmy – a week with his squad for the use of the truck today.'

They all nodded and looked at Martha, who was eyeing up the last pastry. They had all known about the swap. There had been a slight concern that Martha would be on her own, or rather, without the security blanket of her friends around her, but she had seemed genuine in her reassurances to them all that she would be just fine.

'I think that means Martha deserves the last cake – I mean *pastry*,' Gloria said, looking at Hannah, who nodded enthusiastically. Martha didn't need telling twice. She was just taking her first bite when there was a knock on the front door. They all fell silent and looked at each other.

Rosie jumped up, having guessed who it might be. She opened the door to an old man who was standing there in a frayed brown cardigan with patches on the elbows, leaning heavily on a wooden stick.

'Mr Brown, come in, meet your new neighbour!' Rosie stepped aside as Mr Brown hobbled in and gave the women a toothless smile.

'Hello, Mr Brown, so good to meet you!' Gloria got up and went to shake his hand. 'We can offer you a cup of tea, but I'm afraid the last *pastry* has just been devoured.' She looked across at Martha, who was clearly in seventh heaven and knew she'd just managed to get her reward by the skin of her teeth.

After everyone introduced themselves, the chatter continued, and Gloria took her new neighbour into the kitchen to make another pot of tea.

'So, Mr Brown, are you happy if I pay the rent on a weekly basis? I know some people pay monthly these days, but I prefer weekly if that suits you? Stops me spending it!' Gloria chuckled, although she was actually very astute with her money and had even opened up her own bank account, something George had suggested she do with the money she had saved up for her divorce from Vinnie but hadn't used after George had refused to let her pay.

'Sorry, my dear, I'm not sure what you mean?' Mr Brown looked puzzled. 'Of course, if you want to give me some money, I wouldn't object,' he laughed, pulling out a large hankie and blowing his nose. 'But I'm guessing your daughter needs it more than this old man.'

Now it was Gloria's turn to look confused.

'But I thought you owned this building? This flat?'

'Ah,' Mr Brown said, stuffing his hankie back into the pocket of his cardigan, 'I did … I do … I mean, I own most of it, but dear Rosie – now, of course, Mrs Miller – well, she has bought your flat. So,' his face brightened up at having made some sense, '*she* is your landlord.' He dropped his voice. 'And hopefully she might be buying the whole house as time goes on.'

Gloria nodded and didn't say anything, but her mind was working overtime. It would explain why the rent was so bloomin' cheap!

Wait till she had Rosie on her own.

Chapter Eighteen

'And thank you!' Gloria shouted out as Polly, Martha, Hannah, Dorothy and Angie all waved their goodbyes from the top of the stone steps. It was a little after four o'clock and darkness had just about covered the town.

Martha was off to do her fire-warden duties, for which, she had told them, she was being paid twelve shillings, Hannah was going to help her aunty with some door-to-door credit calls, Bel was headed back to Tatham Street to help Agnes with a stack of laundry she had taken in and needed to be ready for the morning, Polly was going to see Arthur at his friend Albert's allotment to help him carry back whatever vegetables had survived the week's plummeting temperatures, and Dorothy and Angie, of course, were going to get themselves 'togged up' to dance the evening away with their cockney merchant-navy sailors at the town's main dance venue – the Rink.

'A quick cuppa before you head back to *your* new home?' Gloria asked Rosie as she shut her front door and walked back into the warmth.

'Go on, then,' Rosie said. 'Actually, I'm dreading going back.'

'Why?' Gloria was immediately concerned.

Seeing the look of worry on her friend's face, Rosie laughed. 'Oh, I'm just being dramatic – it must be spending too much time around Dorothy.' She went into the kitchen and put the kettle on. 'It's just that I agreed to go around to

151

my new neighbour's house. You know, Mrs Jenkins? The one I told you about?'

'Ah,' Gloria smiled. 'Mrs Nebby-Nose.'

'It's the neighbourly thing to do,' Rosie said. 'And there's a part of me feels a bit sorry for her. She's obviously really lonely.'

'She should get herself a job, or some kind of war work, that'll sort her out,' Gloria said. 'She wouldn't be twitching her curtains all day then, that's for sure.'

Rosie put the fresh pot of tea on the table, sat down and poured out two cups while Gloria quickly tiptoed down the short hallway to check on Hope, now sound asleep after all the activity of the day. 'Talking of neighbours,' she said, coming back into the living room and sitting down, 'I had a chat with *my* new neighbour, Mr Brown, when he came round earlier on.'

'That's good.' Rosie looked up at Gloria, before pouring milk and adding sugar to their tea. 'He's a sweet old man, isn't he? This house used to be his family home, you know? But he lost most of his family in the First War – he had five sons and lost every one, poor man – so he and his wife made it into a B & B, and when Mrs Brown passed away he divided the place up into flats.'

'Yes, he told me a little about his life.' Gloria's heart had gone out to the poor man and his wife. She couldn't imagine what it would be like to suffer the loss of *one* of her boys, never mind all of your children.

'He also told me he wants to sell the whole building.' Gloria looked directly at Rosie. 'Wants to get himself a place out in the country.'

'Oh, I'm so sorry, Gloria ... He told you I've bought the flat?'

Gloria nodded. 'Didn't you want me to know?'

'Of course I want you to know. I should have mentioned something to you before now, but I guess I didn't want to jinx it all. It's been very last-minute and I wasn't sure if it was going to go through. All the legal stuff that needed doing – it only just got sorted on Friday gone.' Rosie paused. 'It doesn't bother you that I'm your landlord – or rather landlady – does it?'

'Course not!' Gloria said straight away. 'I couldn't want for a better landlady. And I think it's great you've bought the flat. Bloody brilliant actually. I don't know of another woman that even owns their own shed!' Gloria stopped for a moment while she looked for the right words. 'I am a little concerned, though, that you've set the rent so low. I don't want you feeling like you have to because I'm a mate, or because you think I can't afford any more. I'm not doing too badly moneywise, you know? Especially since I got shot of Vinnie. I get to keep all my own wages now. I've only got myself and Hope to feed, and all the house-keeping money isn't being spent down the pub. Honestly, I feel rich!'

Rosie thought how much Gloria had changed since she had started working at Thompson's. She had been a closed book then, rather like herself really, but for different reasons. Out of all her women welders it had surprised her that it was Gloria who was being knocked about by her bloke. Rosie knew that working at the yard, and every-thing that came with that – learning a new skill and forg-ing such firm friendships – had given Gloria the strength to stand up for herself and change her situation.

'I know you're as far from a charity case as you can get,' Rosie said. 'And I'm also not the softie you might think I am. Buying this flat is the start of a possible new busi-ness venture and having you as my first tenant, someone I know and can trust, is perfect.'

'Well, then, here's to a perfect tenancy!' Gloria raised her cup to clink china with her new landlady.

'And a happy home for you and Hope!' Rosie hesitated. 'And perhaps for Jack too, some day in the not too distant future.'

'I'll drink to that,' Gloria said.

Rosie put her cup back in its saucer before tentatively asking, 'Do you think he'll be able to come back and perhaps visit you on the sly?'

'I don't think so. His movements are being monitored, by the sound of things. If he didn't turn up for work, Miriam would be one of the first to know.'

Rosie shook her head in disbelief at the power Jack's wife wielded.

'She can't stop us writing to each other, though. So that's some consolation. At least I can tell him all about Hope and what's happening at the yard. And his memory has really improved. He reckons it's just about back to normal. How did he put it ... He said, well, *wrote*, that he feels "truly awake" ... that he feels he's been half asleep these past few months and only now is really conscious, *really alive*. He's determined Miriam's not going to win. Oh, I nearly forgot! He said to tell you how happy he is for you and to tell you "Congratulations!" I hope you didn't mind me telling him?'

'Of course not,' Rosie said. 'That's one secret we don't have to keep, thank God.'

'Talking about secrets,' Gloria said, 'were you thinking what I was thinking earlier on when Hannah was telling us about her aunty's pastry-making skills?'

Rosie was taking a sip of her tea and nodding at the same time. 'Yes! That Hannah's aunty ditches her dire attempts at being a credit draper and does something she's good at – *like baking cakes and making pastries*—'

'—for someone like Mrs Milburn! It could be the perfect solution. But does she need someone?' Gloria pondered.

'That's just the thing,' Rosie said. 'Kate was telling me that Mrs Milburn was having a moan to her the other day that Michele, her baker, who everyone thought was French, is in fact Italian and has been taken off to the Isle of Wight as a prisoner of war.'

'So, it could be a case of Mrs Milburn's loss is Aunty Rina's gain,' Gloria mused. 'But how do we go about it? It would be good if Hannah doesn't know that we know about her aunt's money worries – she's so damned proud. I thought us northerners were bad, but it looks like the Czechs can give us a run for our money.'

'It might be a case of roping in Kate,' Rosie suggested. 'And getting her to have a word with Mrs Milburn. The pair of them are pretty tight. Shop owners up against it in hard times and all of that.'

'Good idea,' Gloria said.

'I'll have a chat with Kate.' Rosie finished off her tea. 'Shame we couldn't get our hands on one of those rugelach or whatever they're called. Give it to Mrs Milburn, proof of the pudding and all that ... Well, I'd better get going. Mrs Jenkins awaits.' She looked down the hall and could just see the corner of Hope's cot through the open doorway. 'I won't disturb the little one in case she wakes up.'

Gloria laughed. 'Oh, don't worry, she'll be clapped out and will only wake up when she senses I'm drifting off into a lovely, deep sleep.'

Rosie picked up her gas mask and her holdall and gave Gloria a hug.

'Say hi to Jack when you write to him next.'

'I'll be writing to him tonight, telling him all about today.' Gloria looked at Rosie and was going to say something about Peter but didn't. What could she say? Rosie couldn't write to him, nor Peter to her. And from what she had gathered from the little Rosie had said, she didn't even know where Peter was.

'You enjoy your first proper night in your new home too,' Gloria said as Rosie walked up the stone steps. 'And Rosie,' she called out from the doorway. 'I can't thank you enough for everything you've done.'

Rosie turned and looked as though she was about to say something, but didn't, before disappearing into the darkness of the blackout.

What Rosie had wanted to say was that what she was doing for Gloria – and anything else she might do for her friends – would never match what they had done for her, for they had all saved her life the night her uncle Raymond had tried to take it.

Had they not gone looking for her that cold and foggy November evening just over a year ago when she hadn't turned up at the pub, she would no longer be here. Rosie's squad of women welders had prevented her suffering the most torturous death over a spitting weld; the scars on her face forever a reminder of that moment.

And not only would she have lost her own life, but the life of her little sister would also have been ripped apart. Charlotte would have been left totally on her own and, with no one to pay her fees, would have had to leave school. But worst of all, she would have become her sick and twisted uncle's latest victim.

The women's rescue, which had resulted in her uncle's accidental death, had freed her from the man who had not only killed her parents in a hit-and-run accident, but had also raped her on the eve of their funeral.

Rosie would be forever thankful not just for the brave actions of her squad, but for their reaction when she had gone back to work after recovering from her injuries. She would never forget the joy on their faces when they'd welcomed her back. But what had meant more than anything to her was that she had not seen even a flicker of judgement on any of those faces – the women knew what she did for money, they knew about her 'other life' at Lily's, yet it was clear they did not think any less of her. It was the first time in her life she had felt that she had real friends. The first time she hadn't felt alone in this world since her parents had died.

As Rosie walked up Burdon Road she recalled the vow she had made to herself at that time. A promise to herself that she would always be there for each and every one of them. They would have her love and her loyalty for as long as she drew breath.

And woe betide anyone who tried to do them harm.

Thinking about that awful day in November made Rosie realise just how much had changed since then. She would never have thought in a million years that she would go from being a working girl to managing and part-owning Lily's and becoming a married woman whose husband was a detective sergeant at that – and all in such a short period of time.

And now she had made her first property investment and bought a flat!

It would always be a worry that the bordello could be exposed. It was a risky business; Rosie knew she'd been lucky that whoever it was that Miriam had employed to dig up dirt on them all had not found out about her involvement at Lily's. Building up what George had referred to as a 'property portfolio' would be a very good safety net if they ever had to close the bordello. And when Charlotte came of age, she could transfer it all into her name.

As Rosie walked along Grange Terrace, her mind jumped from thoughts of her new venture as landlady, to Hannah's aunty and Mrs Milburn, to Thompson's, to Lily's, and, of course, to Peter.

Rosie had accepted that Peter would always be there in her head, but she was thankful that life had been so hectic since her trip to Guildford that she hadn't been able to stew too much on the ins and outs of what was happening in Peter's life.

That might not be so easy, though, in a few weeks' time, when she knew that it was unlikely Peter would still be on British soil.

Chapter Nineteen

When Gloria went back into the flat she saw that Rosie had left her grey woollen scarf on the coat peg on the back of the door. Grabbing it, she opened the door, put it on the latch and hurried up the stairs. Turning immediately right onto the main pavement of Borough Road, she walked slap bang into a couple coming towards her.

'Oh, I'm so sorry! I—' she started to apologise further, but stopped as her eyes adjusted to the darkness and she took in the face of the woman she had almost pushed onto the road and under an oncoming tram.

'Gloria!' Helen said, equally stunned. 'Gosh, I thought I was being mugged for a moment there! What are you doing?' She looked down from where Gloria had suddenly appeared and saw the steps to the basement flat and the front door that was slightly ajar.

'You don't live here, do you?' Helen's mind was racing. She had not talked to Gloria since the day she had seen her having the living daylights beaten out of her by her ex. 'I thought you were living up on the Ford Estate?'

Helen was staring at Gloria, her heart hammering, and not just with the shock of almost being bowled over, but because she had been doing her utmost to avoid Gloria since that fateful day at the hospital.

'Yes, that's right; I *was* living up on Fordham Road.' Gloria looked at Helen, who had even more make-up on than she normally did, and at the man she was with, who, Gloria noticed, had quickly taken his arm from around

Helen's shoulders when he'd realised they knew each other. 'Until about five hours ago when I moved here,' she said, trying to keep her voice friendly and light-hearted.

'Why?' Helen couldn't seem to stop herself asking questions, despite sensing that Theodore was getting restless.

'Oh, you know, nearer to work ...' Gloria was taken aback by the question. Helen had not spoken two words to her since the day Vinnie had attacked her. Not that she had spoken to her much before then, but that day Helen had saved her there had been a connection between them – a closeness. Gloria had asked Helen to come into the back of the ambulance so that she could thank her personally for being so brave, for putting herself at risk. That day Gloria had seen the other side of Helen – a kind and compassionate side. She hadn't seen it since, but knew it was there, well hidden behind her fancy clothes, elegant hairdos and expensive cosmetics.

'And, of course,' Gloria added, 'it's nearer to Hope's childminders.'

As soon as Gloria said Hope's name, she saw the change in Helen's face. It was at that moment she knew for certain: Helen knew about Gloria's love affair with her father and the child she had borne. A child bound to her by blood. Her sister.

They stood and looked at each other. Neither knowing what to say next.

'Well, I don't know about you two, but I'm freezing my socks off here.' Theodore's well-spoken voice broke the awkwardness.

Gloria thought the voice a little harsh, despite the smile playing on his lips. There was something about the bloke that made her bristle.

'Yes, yes, of course.' Helen looked at Theodore and forced a smile. 'We better get off.' And with that Helen turned, quickly checked that there was no traffic on the road, and hurried across to the other side. Theodore followed but made no effort to take hold of Helen's hand, or put his arm back around her shoulders.

Gloria stood staring, still holding Rosie's grey scarf, and watched as Helen and her date disappeared into the Burton – a nice enough pub, but not one she would have thought Helen would have chosen to frequent, nor the snooty bloke she was with.

'So, who was your friend?' Theodore asked after Helen had ordered their drinks. It was quieter this evening, being a Sunday, and he was glad of it. He'd been in theatre all day and didn't feel like he had the energy to raise his voice to conduct a conversation.

'Friend? Gloria?' Helen almost spat the words out. She'd managed to shake herself out of the shock of seeing her father's lover. *The mother of her sister.* 'God, no! Gloria's not a friend. She's one of the women welders at work. Why on earth would you think she was a friend?'

'Heavens knows.' Theodore's reply was curt as he looked around for a seat. He was shattered and didn't need this attitude. Helen was normally the epitome of refined womanliness, never even the slightest hint of a bad mood. He didn't give a jot who this person was. All that mattered was she was a nobody. She didn't mix in Helen's circles, and she certainly didn't mix in his. His secret was safe.

But this accidental meeting of someone Helen knew, even if it was just a lowly employee, had made him think. He had been taking Helen out for nigh on three weeks. Well, 'taking out' were hardly the right words to describe their meetings. He didn't take her out anywhere other than this pub and a few other dives around town where he was guaranteed not to meet anyone he knew. All the other medics he worked with went to either the Grand or the Empress, both known for their sophistication and class. Most of them, thankfully, stayed local and went to the pubs in Ryhope. Helen still had no idea that he was a married man, but she wasn't totally stupid. Naïve and innocent perhaps, but she had a brain on her, and it wouldn't take her long to realise that he really was just after one thing. He just had to make sure he got what he wanted before the penny did eventually drop.

Perhaps tonight was the night to push things along a bit.

'Be a sweetheart and grab us those seats over there,' he asked Helen, nodding in the direction of a free table by the window.

As Helen did as she was told, Theodore caught the barman's attention.

'Make that one a double, my old man,' Theodore said, pushing Helen's gin and tonic back across the bar.

Helen found a seat near the window, which, if not for the blackout shutters, she would have liked to have stared out of, inspecting the large detached Victorian house where Gloria and Hope now lived.

It felt strange sitting here, just a few hundred yards away from her little sister. Standing there, talking to Gloria, she had wanted to ask her so many questions. But, of course, she couldn't – she wasn't even sure if her father or Gloria knew she was aware of their love affair and of their 'bastard', as her mother liked to call Hope.

Well, if Gloria hadn't known before, then Helen was fairly sure she did now. She'd caught the look Gloria had given her, knew Gloria had seen something in her face that had given her away. But what did it matter anyway? Her father wasn't here, and couldn't even be bothered to write to her. What did it matter if Gloria knew or not? It wasn't as though she could utter a word to Helen – or anyone – about her father and Hope. There was no way Gloria was going to rock the boat, not with all those secrets her mother had threatened to expose if Gloria didn't play ball and keep her mouth shut.

Helen got out her Pall Malls and lit one, forcing back the tears that wanted so desperately to come trickling down her face. She had tried to hate Gloria, but how could she after seeing the bloodied mess of her face that day in the yard when her deranged husband's fist had pummelled into her again and again?

'Here you are, gorgeous.' Theodore put Helen's drink down. 'Now why are you looking so downbeat? What can I do to put a smile back on that beautiful face of yours?'

Helen looked at the man sitting opposite her. He was so lovely, so thoughtful and so considerate. She took a sip of her gin and tonic and it caught her breath. The cheap gin they used in these places seemed to taste stronger than the one her mother had at home.

'Do you know what I think we should do this rather dark and, dare I say it, slightly gloomy evening?' he said.

Helen shook her head and took another drag on her cigarette. Being told she was gorgeous and beautiful was improving her mood, and she did *so* want to be happy. To be carefree like other women her age. God, she had reached the age of twenty-two and had barely even kissed a boy. Not that anyone would have believed her. She knew how to act the part, to walk the walk, talk the talk, and behave like a woman of the world. She had watched enough Hollywood films. But the truth of the matter was that not only was she still a virgin, she had only gone as far as kissing. And she hadn't even done an awful lot of that.

Helen took another sip of her drink.

'What do you think we should do on this "dark and gloomy evening"?' Helen asked, pushing back the residues of confusion and sadness still lingering after her meeting with Gloria.

'I think we should go back to my rather cosy little flat, where I have one of those wonderful gas fires that will get us warm instantly, and then I can put the wireless on and we can listen to some music and there'll be just the two of us.' He looked around at the other customers in the bar as if to highlight how unpalatable it was to be surrounded by people. 'And I can make you a nice cup of tea and perhaps put a splash of brandy in there, just to take the edge off whatever it is that's bothering you.'

Helen looked at Theodore. The picture he was painting was rather enticing.

'But,' he lowered his voice and whispered into her ear so that she could feel his breath on her bare skin, 'most of all, I can take you in my arms and simply hold you until you stop feeling so blue.'

When Helen got back that evening her head was swimming. It was late and when she passed her mother's bedroom door she could hear her gentle snoring. Tiptoeing up to her own room, Helen shut the door behind her and sat on the bed, breathless and more than a little tipsy. She didn't think she'd had that much to drink, but she hadn't eaten much during the day, so perhaps it had gone to her head more than normal.

The evening had started off so dreadfully. Bumping into Gloria had caused all those feelings of hurt and anger to come rushing back up to the surface. And then there was that yearning feeling again. That was what she hated the most. It was as though she missed something. A strange kind of homesickness. It just didn't make sense. Whatever it was, though, a sense of sadness – and of being alone – always followed.

Thank goodness she had Theodore. Being with him this evening had brought her out of her depressive mood. If she didn't have him in her life she would feel completely wretched all of the time. And what was so lovely was that he had seen she was troubled and had done his utmost to lift her spirits, to make her feel better.

When they had left the pub, they had caught a tram, something Helen rarely did as she always had the use of the family's chauffeur-driven car. Theodore had pulled her close to him in the semi-darkness of the carriage and she had pointed out local landmarks and areas of the town, even though they couldn't really see them due to the blackout.

In turn he had told her about where he lived in Oxford, on a wide, tree-lined street called Banbury Road, and about all the city's beautiful buildings, parks and university colleges.

'Perhaps I can show you around *my* home town one day soon?' he had said, kissing her.

And it was then that she had felt a sense of hope.

Hope for a happier life.

His words – his suggestion – had switched on a light in her mind, and it had illuminated a picture of another life, different to the one she was living now. A life away from Gloria and Hope. Away from her home where she and her mother were living a lie. A lie of a life that was being held up by a stack of secrets kept in place by her mother's blackmail.

Getting off the tram, Theodore had continued to speak about 'the city of dreaming spires' as he had shown her into his ground-floor flat. It was not unlike the one Gloria had just moved into – something Helen had had to force from her mind and replace with images of her and Theodore punting along the River Cherwell, laughing and carefree.

As he had taken her coat and made her a cup of tea with brandy, she had asked him more questions about his life in Oxford before the war. Before he had been sent up north. It had sounded idyllic. Even the picture Theodore painted of his family – his parents and his brother and sister, Stanley and Tamara – seemed so perfect, so homely.

And as the brandy relaxed her, she allowed herself to sink into his world and enjoy a respite from her own. As they had cuddled on the sofa, she had let him kiss her for a long time, and let him do more than she had ever let any other boy do. Helen knew that Theodore had wanted her. He had not hidden his passion from her and it had felt wonderful to be so desired. So wanted. He had made her feel good. She had been transported into another world, one that had given her hope for a different – and much happier – future.

Chapter Twenty

One week later

Saturday 7 February

The tinkling sound of the little brass bell above the doorway of the Maison Nouvelle had Kate hurrying out from the curtained-off back room where she had gone to make herself a quick cuppa. When she saw it was Bel and Lucille, relief washed over her and the pounding of her heart started to die down. It annoyed her that she was still a bag of nerves whenever anyone entered the shop. She had been like this since Sister Bernadette's surprise visit at the start of the year. She hadn't been able to shake the fear of her return, no matter how much she argued with herself that the nun who had treated her worse than a dog no longer had the power to hurt her.

'Oh, come in! Come in!' Kate hurried through the shop to greet them. Bel had been her first real customer, Rosie having asked Kate to make Bel's wedding dress. The pastel pink silk dress was still on display in the window. She had offered countless times to remove the dress so that Bel could have it at home but she had refused, saying she loved standing and looking in the window with other shoppers as they oohed and aahed over it.

'My favourite small person!' Kate crouched down as Lucille let go of her mum's hand and ran to Kate. Bel thought she showed surprising strength in picking the little girl up, twirling her around and plopping her on the high stool next to the wooden workbench.

'You now lurgy-free?' Kate asked Lucille, who nodded excitedly.

'Yes, she's what you call fighting fit!' Bel joked.

'That's what we like to hear,' Kate said, pushing Lucille's blonde locks out of her eyes. 'Your aunty Maisie was telling me all about it and how poorly you were.'

The bell rang out, causing Kate to jump. Seeing that it was Maisie, she relaxed. 'Talk of the devil,' she said.

'I thought my ears were burning,' Maisie quipped but she didn't step into the shop. 'Can we leave the little monkey with you for twenty minutes? Bel and I were just going to have a quick cuppa and catch-up next door?'

'Of course,' Kate said. 'I'm actually working on a design for a girl's party dress and Lucille would be a perfect model.'

Lucille had become somewhat of a regular at the Maison Nouvelle since her aunty Maisie had become a part of her life. Whenever they were in town, or next door having their hot chocolate treat, Maisie would take Lucille in if the boutique was empty, and each time Kate would give her the 'grand tour'. Lucille loved every moment, looking at the fabric-draped mannequins and touching all the different cloths and ribbons that were within her reach.

'Thanks so much, Kate,' Bel said, 'but if she misbehaves, or you get a client in, just bring her next door.'

As Bel shut the glass door laced with brown anti-blast tape, she saw Kate pull out a basket full of colourful ribbons, causing Lucille's little face to break into a look of wonder.

'Kate's brilliant with Lucille. She's a real natural with children,' Bel said as she followed Maisie into the café.

'I think Lucille adores her almost as much as she does you,' Bel added as they sat down at a little table by the front of the shop.

Maisie brushed the compliment away with her hand as she looked around for the waitress to give her their order. 'I think it may have more to do with the toys and sweets I spoil her with,' Maisie said, before turning to the young waitress. 'Two teas, please – and a piece of cake to take away. Victoria sponge if you have it, if not, whatever you've got. Thank you.'

Bel looked at her sister and thought how gracious she was, and also how well she pretended not to notice people staring at her. Maisie was a stunner, there was no doubt about that, but she knew it wasn't just her good looks that drew people's curious glances.

'Honestly, I think I'm seeing more of you at the moment than I am my own ma who I live with! She's like the female version of the Scarlet Pimpernel lately.'

Maisie chuckled. Her sister had a way with words. And could be quite the comic, in a dry kind of a way.

'I've never known her to put in so many hours,' Bel continued. 'Ma's always been work-shy, to put it mildly. But lately it's like she's been going for some kind of barmaid of the year award. I'm sure Bill thinks he's in with a chance. Poor bloke doesn't realise the only reason she's practically taken up residency behind the bar is because she doesn't want to be at home.'

'And all the free booze she manages to consume when she's there.' Maisie chuckled.

'Yeh,' Bel agreed, 'and if she's not supping away the pub's profits, she's drinking every last drop of liquor Ronald may have stashed away.'

'And smoking all his contraband,' Maisie added quietly, aware that the couple of old biddies at the next table had gone quiet since she and Bel had sat down.

'And since Lucille's been on the mend, she's had her out and about, here, there and everywhere. God, she even took her into the museum the other day – and not just to see Wallace the lion, but to an actual exhibition! She used to refuse outright to take me anywhere near the place when I was little, saying it was just for the posh folk!' Bel was enjoying their joint condemnation of their ma.

Maisie poured a little milk into her cup and added a good heap of sugar. She knew now that Pearl hadn't bothered much with Bel when she was growing up. Even Pearl had admitted to her that she had been a 'waste of space' as a mother, which made it all the more surprising that Pearl enjoyed spending time with her granddaughter. If Bel felt a little jealous, Maisie could understand it, but her sister wasn't like that. Maisie wished she could be more like Bel in that way, but try as she might, the green-eyed monster frequently reared its ugly head.

'Knowing what you know now,' Bel asked, her voice unusually serious, 'do you think you would swap the childhood you had for one growing up with our ma?'

'Well, that's a question and a half,' Maisie said, blowing out air. 'Gosh, I would really have to think about that one.' She took a sip of tea, not liking to think about the childhood she'd had. Although it had not been poverty-stricken and neglectful like Bel's, it had also not been a bed of roses by any stretch of the imagination either. She had suffered badly, albeit in a different way to the suffering Bel had had to endure.

'I think the scales would be quite evenly weighed,' she said finally. She paused for another moment, before looking at Bel and asking, 'What makes you ask that?'

Bel looked at the front door, checking that her daughter was not about to come in. 'I don't know. I guess I've just been thinking about us both. Our lives. And how different they have been. *Are.* I know Ma chats to you more freely than she does to me. Does she ever tell you anything about the time after she came back from London?'

'What? After she handed me over to complete strangers?' Maisie said with a slightly bitter laugh. She still carried some residual resentment about being adopted out, and much as she had tried to shift it, she had accepted it didn't seem to want to budge.

'I know she came back here after she left me at Ivy House,' Maisie said, keeping her voice low. 'I know she didn't go back and live with her mother and father – I don't think they were exactly model parents, reading in between the lines. I'm sure she said something about being some kind of a maid. Not a chambermaid, though, I think it was something more downstairs than upstairs.'

'So, let's work this out,' Bel said. 'Ma was about ... what, fourteen, fifteen, when she had you, and there is about a year-and-a-half age gap between us two.'

'Sixteen months to be precise,' Maisie said.

'Sixteen months.' Bel thought about it. 'So that means I must have been conceived within seven months of her coming back to Sunderland.'

'Sounds about right,' Maisie agreed.

'So, the question is, what was Ma doing during that time, and who was she courting?'

'I suppose she might have been seeing someone from the place she worked?' Maisie volunteered.

'Mm,' Bel mused.

'Why don't you just ask her?' Maisie said. 'Just sit her down and ask her point-blank.'

Maisie looked at Bel and cocked her head to direct her attention to Lucille, whose face was pressed against the glass doorway of the café.

The bell above the tea-room door jingled and Lucille entered, followed by Kate. The little girl was determined to show her mother and aunty her new hair ribbons, which had been tied to the bottom of two perfectly woven pigtails.

'Sorry, you two,' Kate said. Bel hadn't said anything, but it had been obvious she'd wanted to chat to Maisie about something important and not appropriate for little ears to hear. 'But Lucille just had to show you her new hairdo.'

Bel and Maisie looked at the beaming little girl proudly standing up straight, her two plaits placed on her shoulders to show off their new crimson bows. Maisie smiled at her little niece, thinking how lucky Lucille was.

At least there was one little girl who was getting to have a happy childhood.

As Maisie and Bel walked back to Tatham Street with Lucille swinging like a little monkey between the two of them, Bel cast a glance over to her sister.

'Don't suppose you could subtly quiz Ma, do you?'

'What, about where she worked when she came back up north?'

'Yeh, and if there was someone special in her life then?'

Maisie nodded. She could pose the question, but she knew Pearl would suss out straight away what her daughters were up to. Maisie sympathised with her sister; she knew only too well what it felt like to want, more than anything, to know who your real mother and father were. She would have suggested that Bel try and get a look at her birth certificate – it was how Maisie herself had found out her ma's name and had been able to trace her. She'd paid some shady bloke to find her certificate, check that her mother had not died, and find out where she was living. Her present whereabouts had been the hard part, and for this she'd had to shell out more money; her mother had moved about more than your average gypsy.

But this was not the path that would lead Bel to her father. For starters, Maisie would bet her savings that Pearl had not put any name down on Bel's birth certificate. So, even if Bel was able to unearth the certificate, something Pearl had apparently lost, it would not get her any nearer to finding out her father's true identity.

No, the only way Bel was going to find out the name of the man who had fathered her was through Pearl. And for some reason Pearl was not looking all that amenable to disclosing the information. From what Maisie had gathered, there was something about Bel's father that Pearl wanted left well and truly in the past. And Maisie was astute enough to know that meant one of two things. Either Pearl had had her heart broken so badly she could not bring herself to relive the pain of it all, or she hated the man so much that she was determined he would not play any part in her life, or her daughter's.

Experience told her that it was the latter.

'I'll pop by later on in the week,' Maisie said, giving her sister a quick kiss on both cheeks. 'And I'll see what I can find out,' she added quietly.

'And you, cheeky little monkey, behave for your mummy? Promise?'

Lucille looked up at her aunty and nodded vigorously.

After Bel and Lucille had gone inside, Maisie crossed over the road and headed towards the Tatham.

'No time like the present,' she said to herself.

'Ta, Bill.' Pearl took the two drinks from Bill, who had brought them over to their table, telling them they were 'on the house'.

'Yes, thank you, Bill. That's very kind of you,' Maisie added, making a mental note to bring Bill a bottle of some decent brandy she could subtly suggest be used whenever she popped in to see her mother.

'So, Ma,' Maisie said, taking a small sip, 'you know when you came back up north, after *abandoning* me—'

'I never abandoned you!' Pearl was quick to snipe back. 'I gave you a chance at life. Money, warmth, food in your belly, security. Acceptance.'

Maisie could see that she had rankled her mother and knew if the conversation was to go the way she wanted, she had to pacify her.

'Let me rephrase that. After you did what you thought was the best thing for your baby, when you came back here – to your home town – where did you work?'

Pearl gave her daughter a piercing look.

'Why do ya wanna know?' she snapped. No one asked about her life. No one had ever really shown an interest in anything about her. Unless they were after something. Apart from Bill, who had asked her a few questions after Maisie had turned up out of the blue. She'd told him a little about her past, but that was because he was a friend.

'You've never been bothered before. Why now?'

Maisie was taken aback by her mother's sharpness and she knew then she had hit a sore spot.

'Just curious, that's all.' Maisie tried to sound nonchalant. 'Just want to get to know a bit more about *me auld ma*,' she replied.

Pearl gave her a look that said she did not believe her for one moment. Maisie was like her mother and as much as Pearl loved her daughter, she also saw her for the person she was. She was a beautiful, streetwise, determined young woman who took no punches, but she was also only really interested in anything that might affect her. Pearl knew that what her 'auld ma' had done and where she had worked were of no real interest to her.

Whereas they might well be of interest to her other daughter.

'Isabelle's asked yer to ask me,' Pearl said, looking Maisie straight in the eye. 'Hasn't she?'

'Blimey, Ma, what's that expression you're so fond of? "There's no flies on you."' Maisie let out a nervous laugh.

'Don't forget I've been on this planet twice as long as you.' Pearl's eyes squinted as she looked at Maisie. 'So, it *was* Isabelle. Yer little sister got yer doing her dirty work fer her, has she?'

Maisie hadn't quite viewed Bel's request as 'dirty work', or thought that her sister was using her, but now her ma put it like that ...

'Honestly, Ma, you make it sound like Bel's trying to do one over on you – and I'm her dogsbody accomplice!' she defended. 'Bel was just curious, that was all,' she added, in what she hoped was a placatory manner.

'Curious my foot!' Pearl took out her cigarettes, pulled out two and handed one to Maisie, who got out her silver-plated lighter and lit Pearl's and then her own.

'That girl's *obsessed* with finding out who her real da is,' Pearl said, puffing away angrily and looking over to see where Bill was so she could signal to him she wanted – no, *needed* – another drink.

Maisie finished off her own brandy and lemonade, grimacing slightly as she did so. The lemonade hadn't managed to disguise the taste of the cheap brandy.

'She just wanted me to find out where you worked, that was all, and to see if there was anyone, you know, *special* about at that time?'

Pearl pursed her mouth, only opening it a fraction to take another long draw on her cigarette.

'God, why that girl can't just get on with her life and stop mithering on about the past!' She spat the words out with a flurry of smoke. She looked over at Bill, finally catching his eye. He nodded, pulling out two brandy glasses and turning back to the optics lining the back of the bar.

'I don't understand why you don't just tell her. Put her out of her misery,' Maisie said. 'I mean, you've told me about *my* father. Why not Bel hers?'

'Different kettle of fish,' Pearl said bluntly.

'How? What's the big secret about Bel's da?'

'Can't say,' Pearl said, even more tersely. 'Anyway,' she added, 'I couldn't tell you if I've not told Isabelle. Wouldn't be fair.'

'Well,' Maisie said, 'I'm getting to know my little sister and I'll tell you this for nothing, she's going to keep badgering you until you tell her. You think *I'm* stubborn! Bel won't let this go. She's not stupid. She knows you're trying to avoid her. She made a joke of it earlier on, but I could tell it was bothering her.'

Pearl didn't say anything. Since Bel had made her promise that she would tell her about the man who had fathered her, she'd been making sure she didn't have a minute to spare, working every shift going at the pub, and when she wasn't there, going out and about doing chores, seeing Maisie, taking Lucille out. And when she did tip up back at the house she'd sneak straight up to her room, even forsaking her last fag of the day.

When Bill leant over with the drinks, Maisie insisted on paying. 'You must be struggling to make a profit with this one working for you. Drinking the bar dry every night, I'll bet!' she said, walking with Bill back to the till. Maisie was pleased that nowadays no one in the pub batted an eyelid at her. The Tatham was one of the few places that had accepted her, or at least not made her feel like she was walking around with two heads.

Going back to the little table she was sitting at with Pearl, Maisie wished she had kept her mouth shut. She shouldn't have got involved. This was between her sister and her mother. They had a very tenuous relationship at the best of times and she should have known that it would have been wiser to steer well clear.

Chapter Twenty-One

September 1913

Pearl knew she would never be able to give her baby girl any kind of life. She was fifteen with no money, no home, no husband, and no family. Her mam and dad were unaware of her condition and would, without a doubt, thrash her to kingdom come if they found out. And if all that wasn't enough, she had given birth to a coloured baby. Pearl knew that if she really loved her daughter, which she did – with every bone in her body – then she had to let her go. She had to give her a chance. A chance at life that she simply would not have if Pearl kept her.

And so she'd handed her baby over to Evelina, but as she'd done so, the overwhelming love she felt towards her baby was replaced by the most soul-destroying sorrow. Left on her own in her bed, Pearl realised she couldn't bear being at Ivy House a minute longer. She certainly didn't want to stick around to meet the wealthy coloured couple who were to have her baby – no matter how lovely Evelina had reassured her they were.

So, she cleaned herself up the best she could, got dressed, packed what few belongings she had into her small hold-all and cleared off in the middle of the night without as much as a goodbye. She walked for miles and miles from Hackney to King's Cross, crying on and off the whole way. She sat huddled under one of the stone arches in the main entrance of the station, not caring whether she lived or died as the cold crept into every part of her body. She was joined by a down-and-out who offered her a drink from a dirty bottle. The burning liquid brought her some respite from the unbearable grief and sorrow she had been choking on since being parted from her baby.

Pearl caught the early-morning train up north and slept on the hard wooden bench of the third-class compartment for most of the journey. Arriving back at her home town in the afternoon, walking out of the main entrance she was greeted by a bright, autumnal sun, but despite nature's cheerful welcome, Pearl felt a huge dark cloud of depression descend on her.

She knew she couldn't go back to the house in Barrack Street – back to the life she'd had with her ma and da and six brothers and sisters – back to all the dirt, drink and constant screaming and shouting, so instead she headed over to the other side of town and knocked on the doors of the big houses overlooking Backhouse Park where all the rich families lived, and asked in the most polite voice she could muster if there were any live-in positions available. She trooped up each driveway and stood for a few minutes while she plucked up the courage to lift the knocker or pull the bell on the doors of what could only be described as mansions. She must have heard the words 'Sorry, pet,' at least a dozen times in the space of an hour.

She had got halfway down a road called The Cedars, presumably after the thick-trunked trees that lined the pathway, when she spotted another street that veered off to the right, following the perimeter wall of the park. Pearl looked at the cast-iron street sign embossed with the name *Glen Path*. This street also consisted of a long row of beautiful detached homes, all with sweeping drives, although many were cordoned off by huge metal gates. Not daring to knock on these doors for fear she would be chased off the property by the master of the house, or worse still, by one of the snarling hounds she'd heard rich people tended to keep to guard their homes, Pearl opted for those with nothing that suggested prohibited access.

Knocking on the first two houses at the start of the street, Pearl was not even given the courtesy of a 'Sorry, pet,' but simply had the door slammed in her face. Following the road round to the left, she saw that it stretched right up to what looked like a main road.

Looking up at the darkening sky and the huge trees, most of which were now almost bare of leaves, Pearl felt total despair. Her mind kept flitting to her baby. Her Maisie. She wondered if the couple who had adopted her had kept the name. She had almost begged Evelina to persuade her baby's new parents to keep the name, and Evelina had promised Pearl she would do her utmost to fulfil her heartfelt request.

Walking away from another house, and another rebuttal, Pearl suddenly felt exhausted. Her breasts felt sore and heavy with milk, her legs as though they were made of lead. She didn't think she could walk much further. Her body urged her to sit down on the kerbside on top of the blanket of crisp yellow leaves covering the grass verge. She wanted – needed – to rest, but knew if she did, she might not have the energy to get up again.

'Get to the end of the road and then you can give up.'

Pearl spoke her words aloud to the crows above her who were squawking from the very tops of the surrounding trees – trees, Pearl thought, that brought to mind an army of skeletons, their bony arms stretching out to the charcoal-scrubbed skies above.

Pearl decided if she had no joy by the time she reached the end of the road, then she would climb over the mossy wall and bed down in the park. If she didn't make it through the night, she didn't care. The thought of waking up and not having to face another day was almost a comfort.

The housemaids who answered the door to Pearl at the next couple of houses simply shook their heads and waited until Pearl was back on the main pavement before closing and bolting the door.

Walking up the wide, gravelled entrance to the next house, Pearl stared in awe at its magnificence. All the houses she had been to were extremely grandiose, if a little dark and foreboding, but this house – this palace – was striking in its elegance. Pearl had never thought a building beautiful until now. She had to rock her head back to see the very top of the three-storey, red-brick house and couldn't help but count the number of windows. There were twelve. And they were all as tall as they were wide.

When Pearl brought her head back down she felt a little dizzy and had to grab on to the iron railing that led up the half a dozen stone steps to the red front door. Pearl had never seen such a brightly coloured door in her life. She looked to her right, where there was a long brass rod that must have been at least two, if not three feet long. She hesitated before pulling it. The effort of doing so made her feel weak and light-headed. Pearl doubted she would keep her promise of making it to the end of the road before she gave up and sought sanctuary in the park.

Pearl heard the bell chime in the house and counted to ten. She wiped her nose, which had started to run. After the sunny day, dusk was falling and with it the temperature. Pushing some strands of blonde hair behind her ears, she pulled her grey woollen shawl tightly around her body in an attempt to hide the shabby blue dress she was wearing underneath.

Hearing the click of the door latch, Pearl took a deep breath and put what she hoped resembled a smile on her face. Her hands were clasped together, unwittingly giving the impression she was either praying or begging.

When the door swung open, Pearl's eyes widened in surprise. Thinking a house this grand would surely have a butler, she was surprised to see what could only be the mistress standing in the doorway; no servant would be allowed to wear such outrageous clothing.

Pearl couldn't tear her eyes away from the woman now standing in front of her. Her huge skirt and tightly fitted bodice were a mass of crimsons and purples, and made up of what looked like a variety of different fabrics. A knot of rich reddish brown hair was piled chaotically up on the woman's head, thick strands hanging loose around her narrow neck. But it was the woman's heart-shaped face that really captivated Pearl. A face that looked unreal, mask-like, due to the garish make-up she was wearing – a thick layer of powder, generously applied cherry lipstick, a smudge of rouge on each cheek, and a dab of cobalt blue on her eyelids.

She reminded Pearl of one of those Russian dolls she had seen in a shop window in London. She had watched, fascinated, as the owner had taken the colourful wooden ornament from the shelf and opened it up to show a customer that there was another one inside, exactly the same, only smaller. Pearl had stood transfixed, her nose almost touching the windowpane until the shopkeeper had become aware of her gawping and pulled down the roller blind.

'Oh my!' The Russian-doll woman spoke first. She too could not hide her fascination at the curiosity in front of her. 'It's the little match girl!'

The woman stared at Pearl standing rooted to the spot on the top step.

'Den Lille Pige med Svovlstikkerne!'

'Sorry, miss?' Pearl finally managed to speak.

'The little match girl!' the Russian-doll woman repeated, as if that explained everything. Pearl was still none the wiser. She could only think that the lady thought she was selling matches, but what would make her think that, she did not know. Pearl's confusion must have been apparent on her face as the mistress of the house smiled at her and beckoned her to come in. Pearl hesitated.

'Come in! Come in!' the woman cajoled.

Pearl bent down and grabbed the cloth bag that contained what few possessions she had and stepped over the polished brass threshold.

'You must be freezing stood out there! We don't want you suffering the same fate as the poor little match girl, do we?' Seeing the continued blank look on Pearl's face, the woman put her hands on her hips and sighed. 'When dear old Hans wrote his story, he must have had a picture of you in his mind,' she said.

Pearl had no idea what the strange lady was talking about and was just opening her mouth to repeat her set little speech enquiring as to whether or not the mistress's household might need another maid or the like, when she saw a man who she guessed was the butler come charging down the long, polished parquet hallway.

'Ma'am, what have I said about answering the front door!'

Pearl stared at the man, stunned that he was speaking to the mistress of the house in such a reprimanding manner.

'And to strangers of all people!' He looked down at Pearl and could barely hide the shock that she had let such an undesirable through the front door.

'What's your business, girl?' he demanded, his hands held firmly behind his back, his face a scowl.

'Now, now, Heathcliff, don't frighten the poor thing. What do you think she's going to do? Go on a rampage and murder us all? Look at her, there's barely a picking on her. I was just telling her that she must have been Hans Christian Andersen's inspiration when he wrote "*Den Lille Pige med Svovlstikkerne*".'

Pearl looked at the manservant and then back to the mistress. They were talking about her as though she were blind, deaf and dumb. They stood in silence for a moment, before the mistress turned to Pearl and extended her heavily jewelled hand.

'My dear, my name is Henrietta. Well, actually, if I'm to be totally honest Henrietta is my middle name, but I refuse to be called by my first name. It's far too boring. So, *little match girl*, pleased to make your acquaintance.'

Pearl heard Heathcliff sigh heavily.

Pearl extended her own hand and returned the handshake.

'I'm Pearl, miss.'

'Oh, what a wonderful name!' Henrietta exclaimed, clapping her hands together, but not so forcibly as to make any sound. 'So, Pearl, what is the reason for your visit?'

Heathcliff coughed and Henrietta cast him a look of reproof.

'I wanted to ask if yer needed a maid or cleaner. Or owt?' Pearl had been put off track and had forgotten to trot out her practised and more refined spiel.

'Well,' Henrietta said, smoothing down the outer layers of her huge, swaying skirt. 'It just so happens we do. Follow me, *Pearl*.'

The unlikely trio walked in a line down the stairs and into the warmth of the huge kitchen. Introductions were made to the rest of the staff, who were sitting round a long wooden table enjoying a pot of tea.

'So, ma'am, what exactly is the position that you say needs filling?' Heathcliff asked. It was a genuine question, for as far as he was concerned there was no position to be filled. They had just replaced the last girl who had got herself in the family way and they already had more staff than they needed.

Henrietta put a finger to her lips and looked around the kitchen as if trying to locate something she had misplaced, before perking up:

'Scullery maid! Pearl shall be our new scullery maid!'

Chapter Twenty-Two

Wednesday 25 February

When Helen hurried out the front door she quickly looked at her watch. It had gone seven already. She would normally have been at work by now. She had been out with Theodore last night and hadn't got back until late. She felt rough. A mixture of too little sleep and too much brandy, too many cigarettes and too little food.

As she went down the four stone steps that led to the entrance gate, Helen stopped mid-flight and looked to her right, where there was a brand-new postbox. She was surprised she hadn't noticed it last night when she had come back home. Still, it had been dark, and she had to admit to having been a tad blurry-eyed.

Helen shook her head in slight disbelief at her mother's solution to what she saw as a problem with their mail. Their usual postie had been called up and replaced by a woman, much to her mother's chagrin. 'You'd think she was stuffing a chicken the way she rams post through our letter box!' had been her main complaint, but her mother had also been disgruntled by their mail not being delivered at the same time every day, as it used to be. Helen had tried to point out that there was, in fact, a war on, and the GPO was lucky to be running at all.

Helen couldn't give two figs if there was any post or not. It had become quite clear that her father was not going to bother putting pen to paper. She knew he wasn't the most proficient letter writer, but he might at least have sent a postcard? It was clearly the case, as her mother had so succinctly put it, that her father now had 'another family'.

'It's abundantly obvious,' she said one evening when they had both been in, a rarity these days, 'that if he can't have his other woman and their bastard, he isn't going to bother with his own legitimate daughter.'

Helen had at first thought her mother was speaking out of bitterness and hurt, and that her father would never forsake her. But it looked as though her mother was right. The proof being the post – or rather the lack of it.

Every time she thought of her father she was hit by the most awful guilt, and she would go through the same mental argument to convince herself she had nothing to feel guilty for.

He was the one who had chosen another woman over her mother.

He was the one who had had another child.

But then another voice inside her head would argue that it was *her* fault he had been banished from the town.

What would have happened if *she* had confronted her father first? She had been the one to keep quiet and let her mother take control of the situation. God, she had hardly spoken to her father since that day at the hospital, pretending she was either too busy working or out socialising. And he had been so kind to her, telling her not to burn the candle at both ends.

The voices in her head argued.

And the more they argued, the more her chest tightened and the more she felt as though her world was closing in on her and there was no escape.

But there was an escape, wasn't there?

Theodore.

*

187

Lovely Theodore was her safety net. Her sanctuary. When she was with him, she didn't have the tight chest or the feeling that her world was collapsing. She just heard nice words, felt his soft, gentle hands on her body. He made everything all right again.

'Morning, Miss Crawford!' Nicholas tipped his cap and opened the car door for Helen. 'Thompson's, miss?'

Helen nodded and took another look at her watch. She would make it there well before half past. God, why did she fret so? She was allowed to be a little late every now and again. Like Theodore kept telling her, she had to let her hair down more. 'Live a little!' was how he put it. Helen guessed the seriousness of his job had given him a different outlook on life. Operating on the war-wounded, she guessed, would make you that way. She was thankful her job dealt with steel and not skin.

Over the past few weeks they had become increasingly intimate and Helen felt herself finding it harder and harder to say no at the time she knew she *should* be saying no. But Theodore could be very persuasive, and the more he talked about life in Oxford and how she would love it there, the more Helen began to see it as her future home. Her new life.

She had suggested he meet her mother, but he thought it might be better to meet both her parents together. And what could she say? That her father was unlikely to cross the county boundary ever again?

The problem was, if he was going to ask for her hand in marriage, she would have to think of something.

'Here we are, miss.' Nicholas was opening the door and in doing so snapped Helen out of her reverie.

She got out of her car and hurried through the main gates, just before another wave of workers disembarked from the ferry and started striding up the embankment for the start of the shift.

Rosie was standing at the main entrance of the admin building. She had already been up to the offices in the hope of seeing Helen about ordering in some new welding equipment, but when she'd got there she had been surprised to find the place empty. It must have been the first time Helen hadn't been at her desk by seven o'clock sharp. Rosie knew Jack had been Helen's work mentor when she had first started working at Thompson's, just like he had been Rosie's. His words of advice over the years had certainly helped them both navigate the male-dominated world of the shipyard. If you wanted to get on, you had to work harder and longer hours than everyone else – and more so if you were a woman. Rosie wondered if Helen's recent tardiness was because of this new fella Gloria had seen her with.

'Ah, Helen. Morning,' Rosie said, standing up straight.

'Good morning, Rosie.' Helen's tone was far from friendly. 'Or should I call you Mrs Miller now that you are a married woman?' This was the second time Helen had made reference to her relatively new marital status.

'No, no, Rosie's just fine.' It was six weeks since her nuptials to Peter, and the initial flurry of excitement over her unexpected marriage had now settled down, thank goodness. Rosie was particularly pleased not to have to field any more questions about what many thought had been a shotgun wedding. Those rumours had subsided as it became clear Rosie's waistline showed no signs of expanding.

'I'm guessing you're waiting to see me?' Helen asked as she pulled open the front door.

'Yes, it was just about ordering in some more equipment.' Rosie didn't make any movement to show she was keen on following Helen into the building.

'Well, come in then!' Helen demanded, keeping the door from slamming shut in Rosie's face. 'We can't talk about it out here, can we?'

Rosie reluctantly followed Helen through the entrance and trudged up the stairs to her office. Shrugging off her coat, Helen fished out her cigarettes from her Schiaparelli handbag and looked around for her lighter. Watching her, Rosie thought she looked as though she had lost a bit of weight, which had diminished her normally noticeable bosom.

'Right,' Helen said, lighting up her cigarette. 'What was it you needed?'

After Rosie had talked Helen through her rather lengthy order – which amounted to just about everything: new protective glass for their helmets, a selection of rods, a new welding machine and some electric wiring for a couple of the machines that were on their last legs – the two women then talked through some issues with SS *Brutus*, as well as some spot-welding that had to be done on a collier that had just been dragged into the dry dock.

By the time Rosie left, the klaxon had already sounded and all of the office workers were at their desks.

Hurrying down the stairs and back out into the yard, Rosie sucked in the fresh air. Helen had more or less chain-smoked during their meeting and Rosie could hardly breathe. Still, at least that was done. Dealing with Helen was never the most pleasant of tasks. As Rosie approached her squad, she was glad to see that Gloria had taken charge and got them started on the funnel that had just been lifted into position.

Picking up her mask and pulling on her thick leather gloves, Rosie was glad to be back in her own working environment. Since Gloria had told her she suspected that Helen knew about her relationship with Jack and baby Hope, Rosie had felt even more awkward around Helen than normal. It must be awful knowing that the father you have hero-worshipped all of your life has been having an affair with a woman from work. If Helen had been a more likeable person, Rosie might perhaps have felt a little more sympathy for her.

At ten o'clock Rosie tapped them all on their shoulders and made the sign of a T. The day was relatively mild so they sat on a metal girder and drank their tea out of their tin cups. Most of the other workers also took their break at this time so the noise was bearable and they were able to hear each other speak.

'Guess who we saw last night?' Dorothy looked at Gloria and then at Rosie.

Dorothy, Angie, Polly, Martha, Hannah and Olly had all gone to the Cora picture house last night to see the latest film, *Ships with Wings*. For once it hadn't been Dorothy who had been keen to see the film, but Polly, as a number of scenes had been set and shot on the *Ark Royal*, which had been sunk off the coast of Gibraltar.

'Who?' Gloria asked, taking a sip of her steaming tea.

'No, you've got to guess!' Angie piped up.

'Humphrey Bogart!' Gloria joked.

'No!' Dorothy was clearly bursting at the seams to tell them.

'I thought he was in the film?' Gloria was enjoying winding them up.

'No, he wasn't, Glor. That was Leslie Banks! And I didn't mean who was in the movie.'

'She meant a real live person!' Angie chipped in.

Polly and Martha chuckled, knowing Dorothy and Angie had been chomping at the bit to tell them. They had tried to persuade Gloria and Rosie to see the film but both had declined. Rosie had her usual commitments at Lily's and Gloria had Hope to look after.

'Go on then,' Gloria said, 'spit it out. Who did you see?'

'Helen!'

'The duchess!'

Dorothy and Angie spoke in unison.

'Well, isn't the girl allowed to go out of an evening?' Gloria asked.

They had all got used to their workmate defending Helen.

'Agreed, Glor, but that's not the *goss*, is it?'

'Honestly, Dorothy,' Rosie piped up, 'you make a mountain out of a molehill you do.'

'So, go on then,' Gloria was now genuinely intrigued. 'What *is* the real "goss"?'

'Drunk as a kitty cat!' Angie declared before taking a big slurp of tea.

Gloria looked at Polly and Martha for confirmation.

'I don't know if I'd go that far,' Polly answered Gloria's unspoken question.

'But,' Martha added, 'she did look a bit tipsy. Even Hannah thought she was.'

Gloria gave Rosie a look that spoke of her concern.

'Well, I saw her this morning, so she can't have been that bad,' Rosie reassured her friend quietly.

'Angie might be putting it a bit too harshly,' Dorothy said, 'but she was clearly a few sheets to the wind. But what surprised us all,' she looked at Polly, Martha and Angie, who all nodded, knowing what she was going to say, 'was the pub we saw her coming out of.'

'Where?' Now it was Rosie's and Gloria's turn to speak in unison.

'The Wheatsheaf!' Dorothy declared.

'Well,' Rosie conceded, 'I wouldn't have thought that was her scene.'

'Us neither, miss!' Angie agreed.

'Was she with a bloke?' Gloria asked.

'Aye, looked a right toff,' Angie said.

'Yeah, you could tell he was moneyed by what he had on,' Dorothy chipped in.

'And by his manner,' Polly added.

'Dear me, right lot of Sherlock Holmeses we have here!' Gloria said, but she still had a look of concern about her.

Any more conversation was ended by the pneumatic drills from the gang of riveters they were working alongside. Rosie tossed the dregs of her tea onto the ground and stood up, showing them all that it was nose back to the grindstone.

When the horn sounded out the start of the lunch break, Martha asked if they would accompany her to the canteen. They all happily agreed. Dorothy and Angie were particularly keen as they wanted to ask Muriel if she had heard any more about the 'overpaid' and 'oversexed' American GIs, and if they were going to get themselves 'over here'. The first batch had already arrived in Belfast a few weeks back, but there was still no word as to whether they'd be coming across to the north-east and, more specifically, to Sunderland.

As Martha, Polly, Dorothy and Angie hurried on ahead, full of chatter about last night's film, Gloria hung back to speak to Rosie, who had been checking one of the welding machines.

'I think there's something funny about that bloke Helen's seeing,' Gloria said, grabbing her gas mask and haversack. 'I saw him taking Helen into the Burton opposite mine, and now, by the sounds of it, she's been drinking in the Wheatsheaf. That's not normal behaviour for a courting couple. Not of Helen's standing, anyway.'

Rosie had to laugh. 'Honestly, Gloria, if I didn't know you better I'd say you were a class-one snob!'

'Yer know what I mean,' Gloria argued. 'People like Helen just don't go to pubs like that. They go to the Grand or the Palatine ...'

'I know what you mean,' Rosie agreed, 'but the places she's going to are not really "dives", are they, just normal, common or garden pubs.'

'I know, but still, the *Wheatsheaf*? It's hardly the most romantic of places to take a date, is it?'

Rosie had to agree. When she and Peter were courting they had tended to go to tea rooms and the Victoria Arms just off the Villette Road, which was more of a family pub.

'Perhaps Helen and this fella of hers want to see how the other half live?' Rosie said as they both circumvented a huge mound of chains that had been dumped next to one of the yard's cranes.

'She's not replied to any of Jack's letters, you know,' Gloria said.

Now that did surprise Rosie, much more than Helen having a predilection for drinking in slightly down-at-heel pubs.

'She's just hurt.' Rosie tried to help assuage her friend's unspoken guilt. 'She'll come round, you'll see.'

'Mm, I'm not so sure. This goes deep with Helen.'

As they caught sight of their squad chatting away to Hannah and Olly outside the canteen, they both fell silent.

Chapter Twenty-Three

'Polly, do you think Bel would mind looking after Hope for an extra half-hour or so? It's just that I've got some stuff to sort out with Gloria about the flat,' Rosie asked as they made their way off the ferry and up the short embankment from the south docks.

'Of course she won't. Hope's part of the family now.' Polly chuckled. 'And Bel does adore her. I think she needs to have another little 'un herself soon, or one day she might not hand Hope back.'

'Tell her thanks, Pol. We won't be long.' Gloria knew Polly was joking, but she did sometimes worry that Hope might begin to think that Bel *was* her mam; after all she did spend more time with her, certainly more waking hours. And if her daughter didn't see Jack soon, she might even start to see Joe as her dad.

'Have we really got stuff to sort out about the flat?' Gloria asked Rosie as Polly hurried on ahead. Within seconds she had disappeared from sight, having jogged past a particularly loquacious group of shipwrights heading into one of many pubs that made up this part of the east end.

'No,' Rosie said, grabbing her friend's arm and tugging her against the tide of workers as they turned left along High Street East. 'Remember Peter and I used to always go for tea and cake at the little café just up the road here?'

'Vera's? The one run by that grumpy old woman?'

Rosie laughed. Vera was known as much for her un-friendly demeanour as her mouth-watering sandwiches and cakes.

'That's the one,' she said as they both checked for trams before crossing the road. 'Well, that's where we're going. I've got an idea.'

When they reached the café, the blackout blinds were down, but as soon as they opened the glass-panelled door they were hit by warmth and the unbeatable smell of fresh baking.

Hearing the bell sound out above the door, Vera auto-matically looked up from behind the counter where she was pouring steaming-hot water into a ceramic teapot. She immediately flicked up the tap and left a long line of customers waiting in a queue that ran the length of the display counter.

'Rosie!' She bustled over, her large girth squeezing its way round her seated customers. As always the café was packed. In place of a hug, Vera took both of Rosie's fore-arms and gave them a squeeze. She stepped back and inspected Rosie from top to bottom. 'Yer still too skinny for my liking!' Then she turned her attention to Gloria. Like Rosie, she was dressed in scruffy denim overalls and still had her hair tied up in a turban.

'Workmate?' she surmised.

'How did you guess?' Rosie chuckled. 'Vera, this is Gloria. Gloria, Vera.'

The women nodded at each other but neither offered up a smile.

'Go to your table and I'll bring yer tea o'er.' She pointed to the corner of the café where there was a small round table with just two chairs. When they got there they both saw the piece of folded card with *Reserved* written on it.

'Did she know you were coming?' Gloria asked.

Rosie looked across at Vera, who was sorting out their tea tray. 'Well, I try to come every Wednesday.'

'Like you and Peter used to?'

Rosie nodded. 'He made me promise to keep coming.'

When Vera banged the tin tray down on the table and plonked two cups of tea and two huge slices of pound cake, Gloria realised why Peter had made the request. Not only did Vera clearly care for Rosie an awful lot, but she was also making sure she wasn't going to waste away. It wasn't the first time Gloria had thought Peter a rather clever – and very caring – man.

'Vera.' Rosie grabbed her arm gently. 'When you get a spare moment, would you mind coming over for a quick chat, please?'

Vera gave a curt nod and left.

'So …' Gloria took a sip of her tea. 'Spill the beans. What's this all about?'

'Well, you know we had decided I would see if Kate could have a word with Mrs Milburn to take Hannah's aunty on?'

Gloria nodded.

'Well, it took a while for Kate to speak to her as she's been visiting relatives over in Rochdale, so she only managed to see her the other day, and unfortunately it would seem that Mrs Milburn brought back a cousin who is going to replace the Italian baker she thought was French.'

'Bugger! Bloody nepotism!'

'I know, bloody families, eh!' Rosie chuckled. 'Anyway, I got to thinking, and I know it might be a strange mix, but I wondered if Vera could take her on. I know she mightn't be everyone's ideal choice of employer, but underneath her brusque exterior is actually quite a nice woman.'

Gloria looked across at Vera.

'She could certainly do with some help by the looks of it,' she agreed. 'It has to be said, though – Hannah's aunty couldn't be more different to Vera. They look about the same age, but I'd say that's where any similarity stops.'

'I know,' Rosie said, 'that was my initial concern. But I thought it might be worth a try. Vera's been a stubborn old mule and despite some heavy hints, she just dismisses the idea with a wave of her hand.'

'Why do I feel that my ears should be burning?' It was Vera, pulling up one of the few free chairs. She had managed to get through her queue, although this was partly because a good few customers had given up and left.

Vera looked down at Gloria's cake, which hadn't been touched. 'Dinnit yer like it?' As she spoke, Rosie quickly forked her own untouched piece of cake and put it in her mouth.

'Far from it!' Gloria looked longingly at her plate. 'It's just that I owe someone a real favour 'n I thought I'd give it to her, if yer don't mind, that is?'

'Nah, course not. This one here's always doing it.' She looked at Rosie, who had managed to demolish half of her cake and was washing it down with a big glug of tea.

'So, haddaway,' Vera said. 'What did ya want? Can't sit around here all day. Work to do.'

'Well, that's exactly what we wanted to chat to you about,' Rosie said, swallowing hard and wiping her mouth quickly with her napkin. 'We've got someone who we think would be perfect for this place.'

'What? Working here?' Vera asked, folding her arms across her large chest.

Gloria noted Vera's immediate defensive reaction and didn't hold out much hope that Rosie's idea would come to fruition.

Rosie leant forward, abandoning the rest of her cake. 'This woman is not just some waitress who will clear up teacups and serve, although she would be able to do that as well – *she's a brilliant baker*. She can really help out in the kitchen. What she can do within the limitations of rationing is second to none.'

Rosie looked at Vera, who still looked very sceptical.

'You, of course, are still the best cake-maker in the whole of the town,' Rosie said with a cheeky smile.

'*And butty-maker*, dinnit forget!' Vera's arms had dropped to her sides. She looked around and saw another queue had formed. Every day it seemed to be getting busier and she wasn't getting any younger. Every night she went upstairs to her flat above the shop and fell into her bed, exhausted.

Vera pushed back her chair and stood up. 'What's this "master baker's" name then?'

'She's called Rina,' Rosie said. 'She lives up Villette Road.'

'She Jewish?'

Rosie nodded.

'Oldish woman? Sells stuff on tick?'

Rosie nodded again. 'Do you know her?'

'Know *of* her. Why does she want to work here?' Vera was easing herself back into her chair.

'Well, she doesn't actually know she wants to work here. Not yet anyway. It's a long story, but to be blunt she's a soft touch and she's not been recouping what she's owed. Sounds like she's digging a bit of a pit for herself.'

Vera nodded. 'And what's this Rina to you two?' She looked at Rosie and then at Gloria.

'Her niece Hannah works at the yard,' Gloria explained.

'This Hannah,' Vera asked, 'was she one of the refugee children that came across a few years back?'

Gloria nodded. 'She must have only been about sixteen when her parents sent her over here to live with her aunty.'

'Just in time,' Rosie added, 'before Hitler decided that he wanted Czechoslovakia for himself.'

'And her parents?' Vera asked.

'Last Hannah heard they were in some kind of ghetto,' Gloria said.

Vera tutted.

'And you say her aunty can bake?'

Rosie and Gloria both nodded energetically.

Vera pushed out her chair and stood up for the second time. She looked over to see four of her customers were heading out the door, tired of waiting to be served.

'I'll bring a box over for the cake,' she said to Gloria and shuffled back to the counter.

After serving the customers who'd had the patience to wait, Vera headed back, box in hand.

'Let's give it a try then,' she said, packaging up the cake and handing it to Gloria.

'There's only one other problem,' Gloria said, smiling her thanks as she took the cake. 'We don't want Hannah or Rina to know we're behind this. They don't know we know—'

'About their money troubles?' Vera said.

Rosie and Gloria nodded.

'What part of Villette Road is she on?' Vera asked.

Her question was met by two smiling faces.

'Well, I'll be coming to Vera's with you every Wednesday just to see how this unlikely coupling manages to rub along. I just can't see it myself, but fingers crossed, eh?'

'I'll pop in next Wednesday,' Rosie said as they made their way back up High Street East, 'and if Rina's there, and it looks like it could work out, I'm gonna have a word with Basil and see if he can reduce the overtime Hannah's doing. Martha was telling me she's working herself to the bone.'

'I know, she never looks the picture of health at the best of times. I'm glad she's got that Olly though. He seems a nice lad.'

'I agree. She always seems happy when she's with him ... God knows, the poor girl could do with a bit of lightness in her life. She's certainly got enough worries on her plate, what with her aunty Rina, and from what Polly was telling me the other day about these so-called "labour camps", it's not good news.'

As they turned left down Norfolk Street, Gloria looked at her friend. 'How are you feeling? About Peter? It must be hard, not knowing how he is? Or where he is?'

Rosie sighed. 'I'm coping ... Well, at the moment, anyway. Peter didn't think he'd be going overseas for a while, but we're not far off March now so I don't think that'll be the case for much longer. It makes me realise how strong Polly's been this past year,' Rosie mused. 'It's a true saying, "You don't know what someone's going through until you've been there yourself."'

'I know.' Gloria was quiet for a moment. 'I didn't like the sound of his last letter either ... and she's not heard from him since.'

'What was it about the letter that was odd?'

'It might just be me looking too deeply into things, but Polly was over the moon because Tommy had told her how proud he was of her working at Thompson's. It just seemed to be a bit of a turnaround from his usual lament that she should work somewhere that was safer.'

'You don't think it was just a genuine change of heart?'

'It could be ... I dunno. I just had the feeling that there was something more going on.' Gloria waved her hand.

'Oh, ignore me, I'm turning into a right old worrier. It's probably me just being daft. Thinking the worst.'

Neither women said anything and although Rosie didn't think her friend was either 'daft' or a 'worrier', she sincerely hoped that in this instance she was both. For Polly's sake.

'Pol, come and share this cake with me.' Bel caught her sister-in-law coming through the scullery and into the kitchen.

'Oh, only if I must!' Polly said, deadpan. She had her thick dressing gown on and her hair tied up in a bun on top of her head.

Bel poured out two cups of tea and cut the slice of cake that Gloria had brought to her earlier on, pushing one half onto a small plate and handing it to her sister-in-law.

'I tried to do the right thing,' she said, 'and offered it round, but no one was having any of it. Agnes refused point-blank and said it was wrong to give a present to someone else and that Gloria would be offended were she to find out. Arthur agreed with her. Joe just laughed, told me he was sweet enough, gave me a kiss and went out to do his night shift. And Lucille has been playing up today so there was no way she was getting a reward for bad behaviour.'

Polly laughed as she sat down. Lucille was definitely becoming a handful of late. But she seemed so happy it was hard to be strict with her.

'I'm guessing you didn't offer the cake to your ma, then?' Polly teased, knowing that it wasn't only Lucille who was in Bel's bad books.

'You're joking, aren't you? Even if I wanted to, which I don't, she's never here.'

All of a sudden, they could hear Arthur's loud snoring start up. Bel chuckled as Polly leant over to the kitchen door, which led out onto the hallway, and pushed it shut.

Polly looked at Bel. 'Not that I'd ever be the one to stick up for your ma, but she does seem to be putting the hours in at the pub. And from what you've told me she's been pretty good about taking Lucille out whenever she's got a free moment.' Polly paused. 'And to be honest, I haven't seen her that out of it for a while. Tipsy perhaps, but not bladdered like she used to get.'

'You're right,' Bel backed down. 'She's not been that bad lately. I think I'm just feeling really resentful towards her at the moment.'

'Tell me more.' Polly leant back and could feel the tiredness starting to filter through her body. It had been a long day.

'Well, I know I sound like a broken record, but I just can't understand why Ma's so open with Maisie but so bloomin' evasive about who my father is – or was. She promised we'd have a chat about him, but that's never happened. She's never here. I've never known her to be so busy all the time.'

'Are you absolutely sure he didn't die when you were a baby, like Pearl's always said?' Polly asked, shovelling a piece of cake into her mouth and savouring it.

Bel moved her chair around a little so that she was facing the crackling fire that was now on the wane.

'Oh, yes,' Bel said with great certainty. 'I knew it anyway, but she finally admitted it a while back. Having said that, he might well be dead now, who knows?' She let out a quiet sigh. 'But, even if he *is* dead, I'd still like to know a little more about him. Golden-girl Maisie's been told all about her dad—'

'A sailor boy from the West Indies,' Polly interrupted, 'is not exactly a huge amount of information.'

'But it's more than I've ever been told,' Bel retorted.

Polly looked at Bel. 'Perhaps,' she hesitated, 'this isn't going to sound very nice, but have you thought that Pearl may not actually *know* who your da is?'

Bel looked at Polly but her face didn't show any anger at what her sister-in-law was suggesting.

'I have,' Bel mused, 'but I just don't think that's the reason she's been so cagey. I know she's not been exactly lily-white, but she was only sixteen when she had me. No, there's some other reason she's being so evasive about it all, but whatever her reasons, it's only fair that she tells me. And that this time she tells me the truth. If not, I'm just going to have to find out for myself.'

Bel got up and poked the fire so that it gave off a little crackle and a slightly tired burst of flames, while Polly went to wash up their plates.

Neither of them heard Pearl quietly tiptoe upstairs.

Nor had they any idea she had come in from her shift at the pub a little earlier than normal and had been standing quiet as a mouse in the hallway, listening in to the tail end of their conversation.

Chapter Twenty-Four

Glen Path, Sunderland

1913

The night Pearl was taken in and given the live-in job as a scullery maid, she had, not surprisingly, fallen into an exhausted sleep. When she woke the next day, though, there was a part of her that wished she had ended up in the park and, like the little match girl, seen wonderful visions and been taken to heaven by some kindly old grandmother.

Waking in her small box room in the servants' quarters, Pearl knew she should feel grateful she had found such a good job – one that would put money in her pocket every week, give her a roof over her head and leftovers from the kitchen. But as much as she tried to convince herself that she had fallen on her feet, the feeling of comfort she should have had was simply not there.

As the weeks passed, Pearl's body gradually returned to normal. The bleeding she'd had after giving birth ebbed away quite quickly, and her breasts stopped leaking and feeling sore. Her mind was not so quick to recover, though, and Pearl found herself unable to shake off the heavy cloak of depression that had wrapped itself around her.

Of course, she made sure no one was privy to her grief or the constant ache in her heart. She kept her head down, worked hard and watched her P's and Q's. She tried to scratch out the six months she had spent at Ivy House, where the kindness of the nurses had penetrated her hard outer shell, and the love for the unborn baby growing in her belly had slowly eased its way into her heart.

Most nights Pearl lay awake and quietly cried herself to sleep, reliving the moment she had given birth and the overwhelming love that had swamped her when she had held her newborn baby in her arms. She would imagine that she had her baby girl cuddled up against her chest, and when sleep finally came those fantasies would become dreams. Lovely dreams that brought Pearl such joy, but just like Cinderella, who was plunged back into her life of rags at the chimes of midnight, so Pearl was thrown back into the real world when she woke.

Unlike Cinderella, though, there was no prince waiting in the wings, ready to come and save her. There was to be no knight in shining armour for Pearl.

Far, far from it.

Chapter Twenty-Five

Park Avenue, Roker, Sunderland

Saturday 28 February

'Helen, darling, can you come and join us in the dining room, please?' Miriam shouted up to the top floor as she stood with both hands on the acorn-shaped newel cap that heralded the start of the ornate oak staircase.

Walking back into the dining room, she sat down at the table, which was littered with files and ledgers. Her father was sitting at the top end, right hand resting around a tumbler of single malt, a cigar smouldering in the crystal ashtray. In front of him was a thick parchment entitled 'The Last Will and Testament'.

Neither father nor daughter spoke while they awaited Helen's arrival.

'Grandfather!' Helen bustled into the room. She was dressed in a stunning deep green velvet dress that had been tailored to fit her figure perfectly. Mr Havelock pushed himself out of the high-backed dining-room chair.

'Ah, my favourite granddaughter!' He kissed Helen on the forehead.

Helen laughed. 'Your *only* granddaughter!' She paused. 'Actually, your *only grandchild*!' As soon as the words were out of her mouth, Helen was hit by an unwelcome vision of her baby sister. For the briefest of seconds whether Hope would be classed as a grandchild flitted across her mind, before she dismissed the idea.

'You may well be my only grandchild,' Mr Havelock took his cigar from the ashtray and puffed on it, causing swirls of smoke to fill the room, 'but even if I had an army of grandchildren, you, my dear, would always be my favourite.'

Helen brushed away her grandfather's comments with a self-deprecating wave of her hand and went to sit down.

'Helen, be a dear, won't you,' Miriam asked, 'and shut the door. We don't want anyone overhearing our private business.'

Helen got back up and walked over to the heavy dining-room door and shut it, even though she did not think it necessary. There was only Mrs Westley left in the house and she was in the kitchen, no doubt listening to the wireless, probably chuckling along to one of the comedy shows the BBC seemed so keen on airing, or that new music programme she'd been telling Helen about called *Desert Island Discs*.

'This all looks very serious,' Helen said, her eyes trained on the piles of documents strewn across the table.

'I'm afraid it *is* rather serious, my dear!' Mr Havelock took a small sip of his whisky. 'But it is all for your benefit in the long run. Much as I hate to even think about my own mortality ...' her grandfather's chuckle was followed by a dry cough ' ... it has to be done.' He looked at Helen. 'And recent events have propelled me into action.'

'Well, that surprises me, Grandfather,' Helen said, getting up and going over to the sideboard where she kept a packet of Pall Malls and a lighter. She picked up both and came back to the table. 'I thought you had all your affairs well in order?' Helen pulled out a cigarette and lit it.

'I did, my dear, but as I said, *recent events* have meant I have had to do a little reshuffling and make a few amendments to my affairs.'

Helen blew out a billow of smoke. '"Recent events" being?'

'Oh for goodness' sake, isn't it obvious, Helen?' Miriam's patience was now at an end, having endured an hour of boring legal talk with her father and the family solicitor, who had thankfully now gone.

'"Recent events",' she snapped, 'being *your father*.'

Helen looked at her grandfather. She saw the old man most weeks but not once had he mentioned her dad.

'Because of your father's recent infidelities,' he said, keeping his eyes firmly on his granddaughter. 'And because it would appear he has spawned an illegitimate child I've had to make sure the family money and your inheritance are safeguarded. And that has meant I have had another will drafted that makes it quite clear that your father is not to inherit a penny from the Havelock estate. I have also had to stipulate that although the bastard he has sired would not legally have any kind of rights to anything pertaining to the family, this is reflected in the will and would stand up in a court of law should any claim be made at any time in the future.'

Helen was staring at her grandfather, not sure what to say.

'In other words,' Miriam added impatiently, 'your father is being cut out of the will and anything else he may benefit from financially through his marriage to me. From now on he gets his wage and that's it. And to be honest, he's lucky to still be getting that.'

'Remember, Miriam,' Mr Havelock spoke to his daughter as though she were a petulant, spoilt child, 'this works out well all round. The family still retains its good name, and you and my granddaughter are able to keep face and still walk around town with your heads held high. The Havelock name will not be tarnished because of your poor choice in husbands.'

This was the first time Helen had heard her grandfather speak badly about his son-in-law. She had always thought, despite her grandfather's innate snobbery, that he had liked her father.

'I had thought ...' Mr Havelock took a puff on his cigar and looked at Miriam ' ... that as my own wife – God rest her soul – could not give me a male heir, one of my offspring might have given me a grandson.'

Helen looked at her mother, who was giving her father an unshielded look of pure animosity.

'And,' he continued, 'as your sister hasn't even been able to give me any grandchildren whatsoever, I'm now in a position where I am counting my lucky stars that I have at least the *one* grandchild.' He looked at Helen and smiled. 'And one who is working in a man's world.' He raised his voice as though rejoicing. 'One who is working in one of the most revered shipyards in the country ... One who is climbing the managerial ladder, and who, I know, will one day be running Thompson's. You, my granddaughter, may not have the Havelock name, but you have the Havelock blood coursing through your veins and that will have to suffice for this old man.'

Miriam watched as he took a final swig from his whisky glass and secretly wished he would choke on it there and then.

'Well, at least I've done something right.' She forced a smile. 'My dear mama and I have both failed to give you your male heir, but I've clearly come up trumps with the granddaughter I produced.'

Helen looked at her mother and then at her grandfather. You could have cut the atmosphere with a knife.

Mr Havelock crushed his cigar into the ashtray and picked up his will, folded it over the once and then pushed it into the inside pocket of his Savile Row jacket. He stood up, a little unsteadily, and gestured to the mess of papers and files on the table.

'If it's not too much bother for you, Daughter dearest, would you be so kind as to put all of this into some semblance of order and arrange for it to be sent back to the house.' Mr Havelock picked up his walking stick and leant on it heavily as he made his way slowly over to the closed dining-room door. Miriam hurried over to open it for him. She didn't want this meeting to end on a sour note. The last thing she wanted was for him to cut her out of the will as well. The old man's adoration of his granddaughter could well sway him into leaving the whole lot to Helen.

'Well,' Miriam said, guiding her father out into the hallway and then hurrying in front of him to open the main front door, 'you may get your male heir yet. Your darling granddaughter here is stepping out with a young doctor – a surgeon no less – who is up at the Ryhope, saving the lives and limbs of our brave soldiers.'

'Really?' Mr Havelock looked back at Helen, who had followed her grandfather as he made his exit. 'What's the chap's name?'

'Oh, you won't know him. He's not from here.' Helen knew her grandfather liked to be introduced to all the top doctors at the hospitals he donated money to, and he had given an awful lot to the Ryhope when it was being built last year.

'Well, where's he from? What's the young man's name?' Helen felt herself flush.

'He's from Oxford and his name's Theodore.'

'Theodore!' He laughed and coughed at the same time. 'Of course, where else would a Theodore hail from!'

And with that he stepped outside, still laughing at his own joke whilst focusing his concentration on negotiating the stone steps that led down to the little pathway.

When he reached the wrought-iron gate, he turned around.

'Bring young Theodore from Oxford round to meet me,' he commanded.

'And soon!'

Miriam waved as the car drove off, forcing a smile on her face even though she was pretty certain her father would not give either of them a backward glance. The chauffeur-driven car drove down Side Cliff Road, which led to the coastal road. It would have been quicker to turn immediately right along Roker Park Road, but Miriam knew her father always preferred the scenic route, even though it was pitch-black and the long stretches of sandy beaches were now cordoned off by ugly rolls of barbed wire. Hardly picturesque, but still, her father was a creature of habit.

'God! I need a drink!' she exclaimed aloud.

'Honestly, Mum, I don't know why you're so disagreeable to Grandfather.' Helen walked back into the dining room and lit herself another cigarette as her mother stomped over to the drinks cabinet and poured herself a large gin and added a small splash of tonic. Miriam looked at her daughter and her face softened into a pleading smile.

'You don't mind sorting out all this paperwork, do you?'

Helen tapped the end of her cigarette into the ashtray and started stacking the papers into a pile.

'Do you know *why* Aunty Margaret and Uncle Angus didn't have children?' Helen asked.

Miriam sat down in the chair her father had been occupying.

'My sister didn't have any problems getting pregnant. She just couldn't carry them. I lost count of how many miscarriages she had.'

Helen thought of her aunt and uncle and how kind they had always been to her, particularly during her last visit when she had gone to stay at their home in the Highlands.

'So, when am I going to meet this Theodore?' Miriam asked. 'His intentions must be serious – you've been seeing him long enough. How long's it been now, almost two months?'

Helen didn't say anything. Theodore had made it clear he wanted to meet her father as well, and the way he had said it implied that there were other reasons – like asking for her hand in marriage.

'Well, perhaps you will need to stay at home one evening, Mother, in order to meet him.' Helen grabbed a rubber band and snapped it around the pile of papers she had shuffled into order.

'Honestly, darling, you make me sound like some gadabout.' Miriam took a sip of her drink and seemed to be relaxing now that her father had gone. She would never allow herself to drink in front of him. It was acceptable for her father to have a Scotch at any time of the day or night, but not his grown-up daughter. She had learnt a long time ago that when it came to her dear papa, it was one rule for him and another for everyone else.

'Well, I want to meet him before your grandfather, who now clearly sees you as some kind of replacement male heir.' She glared at Helen. 'But I'm still your mother, so, if this Theodore does want to pledge his troth to you, then I want to meet him, and if *I* think he *is* suitable husband material, *then* we can make some excuse about your father and send him over to see your grandfather instead.

If you're going to be the old man's son by proxy, then he can be your stand-in father.'

And with that Miriam walked out of the dining room.

Helen heard her shouting for Mrs Westley, saying she wanted to discuss ideas for a dinner party. The time had clearly come to bring Theodore into the fold.

Chapter Twenty-Six

Ryhope Village, Sunderland

One week later

Saturday 7 March

'No, Theodore ...' Helen pulled away and sat up straight on the little sofa that was just yards away from the blazing gas fire. 'I think we should wait.' Her face felt flushed and she felt too hot. She also had that familiar feeling of tightness around her chest. Normally she would have felt the need to unzip the top of her outfit, but her dress was already undone.

Theodore's face was also flushed but his was due to a heady mixture of unrequited passion, frustration and anger. Helen was proving a harder nut to crack than he had at first anticipated. Although, in a strange way, this had fired him on. The chase had been longer and harder than he had predicted. Time, however, was running out. This evening when they had been chatting over a drink, before he had cajoled her to come back to his flat, Helen had mentioned meeting her family. He'd thought he had more time on his hands as it didn't appear as though her father was due back home any time soon, but now, from what Helen was saying, her grandfather had stuck his nose in.

'Helen,' Theodore traced her exposed back with his smooth, slender fingers, 'I think you and I are more than ready … We've been seeing each other for a long time now.' He turned her gently towards him so that he was looking into her deep green eyes. 'I *know* your body … Not just how beautiful it is – ' he traced the outline of her face so gently it sent a shiver down her ' – but how this is the perfect time.' Theodore kissed Helen and felt her respond. 'We're made for each other. Mind … and body.'

Tonight he was going to take his well-earned prize. It had been a long time coming, but as his hands felt her soft, ivory skin and he touched her in a way he had learnt she liked to be touched, he knew that it was going to have been worth the wait.

When Helen snuck home later on that night, she was as quiet as a mouse. There was no way she wanted to see her mother. She felt as though the events of the evening were plastered across her face.

As she hurried up the carpeted stairs, being particularly careful not to cause even a floorboard to creak when she passed her mother's bedroom, Helen felt a sudden urge to cry. She swallowed hard and tiptoed up the next flight of stairs to her own room. When she closed the door carefully behind her she exhaled. Her heart was thumping in her chest and she felt a little dizzy. She made it to the stool in front of her dressing table and sat down.

When she looked into the mirror she saw that all her make-up had come off and there were mascara smudges around her eyes. Her cheeks looked red and she realised Theodore's stubble had made its mark. As she continued to look at her reflection she saw tears pool in her eyes and then large blobs drop down onto the glass tabletop. She watched more tears roll down her face and did nothing to stop them.

Why did she feel so ghastly? Why did she have that horrible dark feeling inside her? She had thought making love with Theodore would fill her with love and happiness. She hadn't known what to expect but had thought it might be more pleasurable. She had enjoyed the times they had been intimate with each other; the act of making love, though, had not really felt like *making love*. But as Theodore had told her afterwards, these things took time to master – a comment that made her realise that Theodore had had other women before. And quite a few, by the way he was talking.

Why did that make her feel cheap?

She so *wanted* to feel special. To feel loved and cherished. Even more so as it was now more than evident that her father was totally lost to her. He had clearly either forgotten her or hated her for turning against him.

Her mother also appeared to have reverted back to her old self these past few weeks. All she seemed bothered about was going to the Grand with her friend Amelia, drinking gin and flirting with the naval officers there. She was outwardly a respectable, happily married woman whose husband had nearly lost his life trying to help his country win the war, but behind the scenes she was whooping it up and living the life of a single woman.

For Helen, her grandfather's visit last week had drawn a very definite line through her father's connection to the family. Once old Mr Havelock had gone, she'd had time to go over what had just taken place. Neither her grandfather nor her mother had shown any kind of consideration that the man they were cutting out of their lives was still her father. She did, after all, have Crawford blood running through her body as well.

As did Hope.

At the thought of her sister, a new batch of tears trickled down her face. Her eyes were now panda-like with the residue of watery mascara. Helen pulled out a handkerchief.

This should be a happy time! she chastised herself.

You are a woman. You have made love! It would only be a matter of time before Theodore proposed. He had intimated more than once that he would, and then she could run away from all this and start her own family. Away from here. Away from the constant memories of her father. Away from Gloria and Hope.

As Helen pulled off her dress, put on her nightie and climbed into bed, she forced herself to look at her future. At her escape.

She *would* be happy.

Her new life was just around the corner.

Chapter Twenty-Seven

South Docks, Sunderland

Three weeks later

Saturday 28 March

'Sorry ... Excuse me ...' Joe gently led the way through the crowds that had gathered on the south dock to see the latest launch from Thompson's.

'Daddy, Daddy!' Lucille was on Joe's shoulders and pointing over the growing crowd of spectators that had gathered just up from the ferry landing.

'Aye, there she is.' Joe cocked his head to look up at Lucille, who was staring in awe at the huge frigate that was sitting in the dock ready for her baptism.

'Mammy, Mammy!' Lucille shouted out behind her. Joe could feel her twist her body round as she looked for her ma. Her little arm was flailing, pointing ahead at the huge metal beast waiting to take her maiden voyage. Bel returned her daughter's look of excitement, at the same time hitching Hope up on her hip. Gloria's baby girl was now seven months old and seemed to be growing by the day. She was certainly more than aware of what was happening around her and had developed a love of crawling around at great speed. Bel and Agnes had to watch her every move. Even Tramp and Pup were giving her grasping hands a wide berth these days.

'Just say when you want me to take her.' Agnes had her arm interlinked with Beryl's. Her friend had only recently started to leave the house after the doctor had told her she had some kind of phobia and must try and go out at least once a day.

'I'm fine for the moment,' Bel said as Joe and Lucille made it to the iron railings of the quayside. Bel managed to squeeze up next to him and Agnes and Beryl gently edged their way through a group of elderly men to join their little party.

'Made it!' Beryl sounded relieved as they found a place overlooking an expanse of relatively calm water in front of them; the sunlight shining down as though a spotlight had been turned on for the midday matinee about to take place on the Wear.

'Iris and Audrey working today?' Bel asked Beryl, whose eyes were closed as she held her face up to the sun.

'Yes, they're working all hours.' Beryl turned her face away from nature's warm caresses and focused her attention on Bel.

'But they're enjoying it?' Bel asked. She knew Beryl's two girls had been taken on by the GPO just before Christmas. They had been put in the sorting office because they had only just turned fourteen and fifteen respectively, but they had both voiced their determination to become 'proper posties'.

'They're loving it,' Beryl said, 'but there's no end to the work. Constantly short of staff. Especially now they've pushed up the age of conscription to fifty-one.'

Bel looked across to see if she could spot Polly, Gloria or any of the other women welders on the other side of the Wear. Polly had said this morning, before she and Gloria had left for work, that they would try and stand somewhere prominent so they could wave to each other.

'Talking of the post, I'm guessing Pol didn't get anything this morning?' Beryl asked.

Bel shook her head. It had been months since Polly had heard from Tommy, and it wasn't just Polly who was becoming increasingly anxious about his well-being – they all were, though none more so than Arthur. The whole of the Elliot household was silently praying that the postwoman brought a letter – and soon.

'There they are!' Joe suddenly shouted, pointing across the river and waving his hand. His actions were mimicked by Lucille, who had become distracted by the large barrage balloon over the Wearmouth Bridge. Bel, Beryl and Agnes squinted against the sun's rays, their eyes searching the hordes of grey suits, denim overalls and, of course, flat caps.

'There they are!' Beryl shouted, spotting Polly waving her red scarf in the air as though baiting a bull. Next to her she could see four other headscarves of varying colours, which she guessed belonged to the other women welders.

Bel turned her attention to Hope and pointed across the water. 'There's your mammy!' Hope gurgled and stuck her hand into her mouth, feeling the build-up of excitement around her.

Bel looked at Joe and saw a sadness in his eyes. She nudged him gently.

'You all right?' Bel knew Joe desperately missed working in the shipyards. He would have given anything to be working again with his old squad of riveters. It had been his life. He and Teddy had spent their boyhoods down by the docks, trying to wheedle their way into the shipyards. The pride they had felt at being part of the town's revered shipbuilding industry had never diminished but had grown stronger as they had become men.

'Aye, I'm all right,' Joe said, moving his walking stick over to his left hand so he could take hold of Bel's. His gammy leg would never allow him to do what he loved. He just counted his blessings that he was here now, that his work with the Auxiliary Unit of the Home Guard gave him purpose, and that Bel loved him and had been able to allow herself to return the love that he had secretly felt for her his entire life.

'Are *you* feeling all right?' Joe asked. 'You look a little pale?'

It was coming up to five months since they had got married and Joe knew Bel thought she should have fallen pregnant. Perhaps a little naïvely, they both thought they would be giving Lucille a little brother or sister by the end of the year. Joe had seen the look on Bel's face this morning after she had come in from the washhouse and knew that her hopes had been dashed yet again.

Bel smiled and leant up to kiss Joe on the cheek.

'I can't keep anything from you, can I?' She looked up at Lucille, who still seemed entranced by the barrage balloon. 'I'm all right. Just a little disappointed.'

Joe squeezed her hand. 'It won't be long, I'm sure of it.' In reality, he wasn't at all sure. The war had taught him that nothing in life was certain.

'Yer ma working at the pub this afternoon?' Beryl asked as she continued to wave over to the women welders.

'Yes.' Bel looked at Beryl. 'I think my ma should just get herself a camp bed and stay there – she's rarely home these days. I've hardly seen her, only really hear her trying to be quiet when she gets in after last orders.'

Beryl laughed. She knew Pearl well and knew that although she might be working all hours, she'd also be enjoying the perks of her labour.

'You knew Ma when she was younger, didn't you?' Bel asked. Her question came out of the blue and both Beryl and Agnes looked at her.

'Aye, I did, pet,' Beryl said. 'When she moved round the corner to us when you were just a little bairn.'

'I don't suppose you knew anything about her before then?'

'No, not really.' Beryl wasn't entirely sure what to say. Pearl's reputation had certainly preceded her move to Back Tatham Street. Everyone knew she was a 'right one', always drinking, causing a nuisance, gadding about with some ne'er-do-well. Neglecting her only daughter. God knows what would have happened to Bel had Agnes not taken her in.

'What kind of thing do you want to know?' Beryl asked. She sensed Agnes shift about uncomfortably next to her.

'Well, Maisie was telling me that when Ma came back from London – you know, after she'd had Maisie and had to give her up?'

Beryl nodded.

'Well, Ma told Maisie that she got work as some kind of maid, and I was wondering if you knew where that was ...?'

'Actually,' Beryl said, her face suddenly lighting up, 'I do remember. Pearl's mate Sandra – I don't know if you know her?' Bel shook her head. The name rang a bell but that was all. 'Well, I remember Sandra telling me ages ago that Pearl had once worked in one of the big houses that overlook Backhouse Park.'

The words were just out of Beryl's mouth when there was an almighty cheer, followed by shouts of 'There she goes!' and 'God bless all who sail in her!'

'Yeah!' Lucille's jubilant cry sounded out alongside the clamour of voices and the sporadic blasts of the shipyard

223

horns. Men, women and children all celebrating the birth of a new ship. All captivated as it careered down the slipway and sliced into the placid waters of the Wear, in doing so creating two huge waves that rocked all the other vessels bobbing on the river's surface.

Bel looked up at Joe's face – a big smile showing his delight at the launch. No hint of sadness now, just pure pride at what his home town had produced. Bel stroked Hope's face and pointed out the small tugboats that were guiding the 440-foot-long vessel out of the river and into the North Sea. The little girl's face, which had crumpled at the sudden explosion of cheering voices, was now relaxed and smiling, soothed by Bel's gentle chatter and calming words.

As Bel looked back out at the flurry of life and activity on the river, it wasn't the launch that had her attention, but the short chat she'd just had with Beryl. And as she was gently jostled by the jubilant crowd around her, there was just one thought swimming about in her head.

Backhouse Park.

Chapter Twenty-Eight

Glen Path, Sunderland

1913

From the off, Pearl had realised that the mistress of the house was not in her right mind. It didn't take Pearl long to learn, due to the rest of the staff's relentless gossiping, that everyone else also thought that Mistress Henrietta was, in the words of Velma the cook, 'short of a few slices'. The mistress was, without doubt, one of a kind. Heathcliff, who was really called Eddy, said she was a 'different breed', whereas Agatha, the housekeeper, was less subtle and simply said, 'The woman's as mad as a March hare.' But Pearl also knew that Henrietta was not a bad person, and so she continued to keep her head down, smile when she needed to and simply exist.

Most of the time Henrietta either had her nose in a book and was not to be disturbed, or else would be flying around the house, full of endless energy and ideas. She went on huge spending sprees in town with delivery after delivery arriving at the house not long after she returned. These bouts of frenetic activity were usually followed by days of solitude. It didn't take Pearl long to see the pattern and predict the swing of her employer's moods.

Pearl also learnt that the master of the house worked away most of the time. (It was whispered that he did so out of choice rather than necessity.) And the couple only had two children, two girls, who were both away at something called a 'finishing school'. Pearl had no idea what this was until Eddy told her it was where they taught you how to be a lady.

The few times she had been upstairs, usually when one of the maids was off colour and needed a hand with the cleaning, Pearl had seen photographs of the daughters, who seemed to be around the same age as her. They were both blonde and pretty, with a look of refinement about them. Catching a glimpse of herself as she was dusting the large gilt-framed mirror, Pearl thought they did not look unlike herself. Perhaps this was why Henrietta had taken pity on her that day.

During those first few months, however, Pearl heard very little about the master of the house. It appeared that the rest of the servants were not keen to talk about him, and when they did, there was never any joy in their voices.

News filtered downstairs at the start of December that the master was definitely coming home for Christmas. As a result, over the ensuing weeks Mistress Henrietta seemed to be in a constant tailwind, swishing around the house in her colourful silk creations. She drove the cook mad by changing her mind every few days, and followed the maids around, getting them to check and recheck for dust, ripping off bed sheets and demanding they be laundered again. On the day the master stepped over the threshold, the house was in perfect order.

The atmosphere, however, when the news filtered downstairs that the master had arrived, was not, as Pearl would have expected, one of relief, but instead an uncannily tense one.

'And here, *Charlie darling*, we have our very own household cavalry.' Henrietta chuckled at her own joke and waved her hand from left to right across the half-dozen employees who were standing in a line in the large reception room at the back of the huge, twelve-bedroomed mansion.

'Charlie darling' was still in his jodhpurs and knee-high leather riding boots, having just returned from giving one of their fillies a good thrashing around Backhouse Park. Pearl had been told it was always the first thing he did on returning home after a spell away.

Pearl was surprised he was so old. He must have been easily fifty, much older than Henrietta, who she guessed was in her late thirties. For some reason Pearl had imagined him to be plump, probably because most rich men she'd seen were shaped like a barrel, but Charles was lean and wiry, and unlike many his age he still had hair – a covering of thin blond strands that were swept away from his narrow face.

'This is Heathcliff.' Henrietta giggled as she placed a hand out to show her husband who she was talking about. 'Of course, Heathcliff has not always been called *Heathcliff*, but we've grown quite fond of the name, haven't we, Heathcliff?'

Heathcliff gave a convincing smile and, as always, Pearl marvelled at the man's restraint. Henrietta treated him like he was her pet poodle. Pearl had asked him once how he managed to put up with it, especially as he had to spend so much of his day in her company, but Eddy said it didn't bother him. 'She means no harm,' he'd told Pearl. 'There's worse.'

'And this is Marian,' Henrietta said, her arm again reaching out as if to display her finest china. She looked at Charles and put a finger to her mouth like a little girl. 'Again I've been rather naughty and Marian isn't really called Marian, but, well, she is now – she's my Maid Marian!'

More giggles.

Everyone stood ramrod straight as Henrietta continued to introduce the staff to her husband. It was a ritual Charles had been forced to endure from early on in their marriage every time he returned from a prolonged period away, usually from some far-flung country where he'd been sent in his capacity as chief negotiator for one of the big shipping companies.

Henrietta's employees had changed over the years, although there were some stalwarts like Heathcliff and Marian, otherwise known as Agatha, who had been there for as long as Charles could recall. The names, however, were always based on some fictional character from one of the many novels his wife spent most of her day lost in.

Finally, Henrietta came to Pearl.

'And this is Pearl. She's our scullery maid!'

Charles had been inspecting each person as though they were livestock at a cattle market, and he looked particularly interested when his wife came to introduce the last of her employees.

'And do enlighten us, Henrietta ...' This was the first time the master of the house had spoken and six pairs of eyes stared at him in surprise. 'What is Pearl's *real* name?' His voice was deep and serious and had an almost imperceptible touch of menace to it.

'Ah,' Henrietta said, as if she was about to reveal an extremely closely kept secret. 'Pearl is *Pearl*.'

She looked wide-eyed and expectantly at her husband, waiting for the penny to drop.

'From *The Scarlet Letter*, of course!' Henrietta reprimanded him as if he had committed some terrible faux pas. 'By Nathaniel Hawthorne!'

Seeing the continued blank look on Charles's face, Henrietta tutted.

'In the book Pearl is symbolic of the act of love and passion and, of course, of adultery ... She is a beauty, not unlike our Pearl here, only dark-haired ...' Henrietta's mind seemed to wander for a moment before she snapped back to reality.

'Isn't she a real little gem?' She touched Pearl's cheek. 'Quite delectable.'

Pearl tried to emulate Heathcliff's convincing false smile, but felt it probably looked more akin to a grimace, not that Henrietta would have noticed as she was now rustling her way over to the drinks cabinet.

'She certainly is,' Charles agreed, copying his wife's action and tracing a line down Pearl's cheek with his finger.

Pearl's impulse was to swipe the master's hand off her face, but luckily she managed to stop herself. She wanted to keep this job, and although she still felt pretty much indifferent to life in general, she no longer wanted to bed down in the park and suffer the same fate as the little match girl.

'Oh my goodness me! Is that the time already?' Henrietta exclaimed. There was no clock in the room or watch on her wrist, but they all knew this meant it was time for the mistress to indulge in what she called her little midday 'pick-me-up'.

Pearl had learnt fairly early on while helping the cook that Henrietta survived on steak and caviar and a drip feed of various pills and potions taken at regular intervals throughout the day – all washed down with what she called her 'special Russian water', which was, in fact, vodka she ordered in from the town's top wine and spirit merchants, J.W. Cameron & Co.

'Shoo, shoo!' Henrietta flicked her hands into the air to show that her staff were being dismissed. 'My darling husband and I have *so* much to catch up on.'

She then turned around and scuttled towards the red-lacquered Chinese cabinet she'd had imported, which was where she kept her supply of 'Russian water' and a good stock of what she liked to call her 'essential remedies'.

Velma had told Pearl to 'keep clear of the master', but when Pearl had asked why, the cook had said he could get 'a bit nasty' when he'd had a few. Pearl had taken this to mean he had a temper on him, which hadn't perturbed her too much. Her own da had been free with the use of his hands and she knew how to get out of the way and avoid a good hiding. Besides, 'keeping clear of the master' would be easy. Her work as a scullery maid kept her pretty much entrenched in the kitchen, clearing up after the cook, scrubbing pots and pans, and running out to the vegetable plot, something she was particularly fond of doing as she had started to learn the names of all the herbs and vegetables that were grown out the back.

Christmas and New Year passed in a haze of sheer hard work as Charles and Henrietta threw back-to-back parties. 'The girls', as they were referred to, came back for the Christmas holidays from their finishing school in Switzerland. Pearl glimpsed them both a few times during their stay, but the two sisters never acknowledged the servants unless they needed something. Watching them come back from a horse ride with their father one day, Pearl was again struck by how much she looked like them, especially the younger girl. It was a similarity Agatha had commented upon.

Velma seemed to be in a bad mood the whole of the Christmas and New Year holidays and only cheered up once Charles had gone off to some country she'd never heard of and the girls went back to their school.

Chapter Twenty-Nine

Tuesday 7 April

'So, how was Charlotte?'

Rosie forced herself back into the here and now, her mind having slipped off on a rare daytime reverie about Peter. Taking a sip of tea and looking at her squad all sitting around the table, it took Rosie a moment to reply.

'That's a hard one to answer, Martha ... If I'm honest, I really don't know.' A frown creased Rosie's forehead as she spoke.

'But you've just spent the last three days with her?' Angie asked, confused.

Rosie laughed a little sadly. 'I know, Angie. You would have thought I'd have some idea how my own sister was after spending the entire weekend with her. If you'd asked me the same question a year ago – even just six months ago – I could have answered it without hesitation. But Charlotte's getting to that age, I am learning very quickly, which can be rather tricky.'

Gloria, Polly, Dorothy, Angie and Martha all looked at Rosie but were not able to offer her any kind of insight. They had all been fourteen-year-old girls once, but none of them could recall it being a particularly troublesome time. But then again none of them had lost both their parents on the same day when they were just eight years old, and none of them had spent the intervening six years residing permanently within the walls of a very posh, but very isolated all-girls boarding school. They had lived all their lives at home and by the time they were fourteen, they had left school and started work.

'What do you think is the problem?' Again the question was from Martha.

'That's what I'm struggling with.' Rosie looked at Martha. 'I just don't know. I'm not sure there is a problem, but she just seems to have changed.'

'In what way?' Dorothy asked, taking a sip of her tea.

'I guess she just doesn't seem as carefree or happy as she usually is. I've asked her if anything is wrong but she just keeps saying she's fine. But she says it in such a way as if she's anything but. I had a quiet word with her form teacher when I went to pick her up, but he said Charlotte was getting on well, her work was still of a high standard and she wasn't getting into any trouble ...' Rosie's voice trailed off.

'What did she say when yer told her you'd got hitched?' Angie asked.

Rosie didn't say anything.

They all looked at her.

'You didn't tell her, did you?' Polly guessed.

The women looked at their workmate and then back at their boss.

Rosie sighed. 'I know I should have. There just didn't seem to be the right moment.'

Looking up to the corrugated ceiling of the yard's cafeteria, Rosie sighed again. 'And then when there was a right moment, I suddenly got worried she might think that my marriage to Peter would somehow mean I didn't love her, that I might not bother with her so much—'

'Like Peter might be more important to you than she is?' Polly suggested.

'Yes,' Rosie said. 'That's it in a nutshell. And because she's been acting so strangely lately I just didn't want to do anything that might add fuel to the fire. Honestly, it's times like this I really wish our dad was still about. He'd talk some sense into her. He was always so good with her when she was small.'

'It seems to be a week for dads,' Polly said. 'Or rather the lack of them.'

Dorothy looked at Polly. 'What do you mean?'

'Oh, I shouldn't really say anything ...'

'Go on,' Rosie urged, glad to swing the attention away from herself.

'It's Bel,' Polly said. 'She's becoming totally obsessed with finding out who her real da is. She was telling me last night that she's sick of her ma not telling her anything and she's going to find him for herself.'

The women all looked at Polly, questions on their dirt-smeared faces.

'She reckons he's someone Pearl courted when she was in service,' Polly explained. All the women knew Pearl, or at least knew of her, and thought that Polly was probably being kind by using the word 'courted'.

'She's even talking about going knocking on the doors of houses where she thinks her ma might have worked. I tried to be as unenthusiastic about the whole idea as I could, but it didn't seem to deter her.'

Dorothy was just about to ask a question when Hannah came over and sat down with a heavy sigh. She appeared to be in an unusually unsettled mood.

'Blimey, who's got your goat today?' Angie said.

'Oh, it's nothing.' Hannah opened up her satchel and got out her sandwiches.

'It's clearly not "nothing", Hannah, so spit it out!' Dorothy commanded.

Hannah had her sandwich in her hands but didn't take a bite.

'It's Mr B. He says there's no more overtime.'

They all looked at each other. No one noticed Rosie and Gloria exchange loaded looks and shift about uneasily in their seats.

'Well, if there's no overtime, there's no overtime,' Martha said.

'There's always overtime,' Hannah said.

'Maybe there's always overtime when you ask Mr B, but there isn't really any overtime,' Martha persevered.

Now everyone was looking at Martha.

'Talk about speaking in riddles!' Angie gaped at Martha.

'Look, Hannah,' Rosie decided to interject. 'Perhaps it's worked out for the best. I'm sure there will be overtime in the future. Especially the way things are going. But perhaps this might be a good time for you to have a little rest. You've been working away like a little beaver for ages now. I think everyone would agree with me that you need to slow down a bit.'

There was a general nodding of heads as well as mumbled agreements.

'You could go out with young Olly,' Polly suggested. 'You like each other – why don't you spend some time with him, doing something nice? You could get him to treat you to tea at the Bungalow Café? It's really cosy in there. Then you can have a walk along the promenade ... Look out to sea.'

No one said anything, but they all knew that this was where Tommy and Polly had gone on their first date together. He had taken her on the back of his motorbike and they had stopped there for a pot of tea and a shared slice of cake. Everyone was quiet for a moment.

'Actually,' Hannah suddenly perked up, sitting up straight, 'I do also have some good news ... My aunty Rina's got a new job!'

'Really?' Rosie's voice was high and a little over the top, causing everyone to look at her.

'That's interesting!' Gloria jumped in. 'What's she doing?'

'Well,' Hannah said, looking to Rosie and then at Gloria, 'the strangest thing happened. My aunty Rina was shopping along the Villette Road one afternoon and this old woman comes up and starts talking to her.' Everyone was now listening intently. 'She said something like, "I hear yer know how ta bake?"' Everyone immediately burst out laughing at Hannah's attempt at speaking in the local dialect.

'So, what did yer aunty say?' Angie was sitting forward, hanging on to Hannah's every word.

'Knowing my aunty, she probably denied it and said she was no better than anyone else. But whatever my aunty said, this old woman wasn't having any of it, and she said that my aunty Rina sounded like she "dinnit like to blow her own trumpet".'

'She didn't want to boast that she was really good?' Angie translated.

'Yes, that's basically it.' Hannah smiled across at Angie. She had never actually worked with Angie – she had left for the drawing office before Angie had swapped the controls of a crane for a welding rod – but Hannah felt as though she had got to know her over this past year.

'So, why did the auld woman say that ta yer aunty?' Angie continued.

'Because,' Hannah again looked at Rosie and Gloria, 'she wanted her to work in her cafeteria making cakes and pastries.'

'Cor! That's good, isn't it?' Angie exclaimed.

'It is really good.' Hannah looked at all the women. 'Especially as, if I'm to be totally honest, my aunty wasn't doing very well as a credit draper.'

'So, where's this auld woman's café?' Angie asked, needing to hear the end of the story.

'Well, that's where there is a twist in the tale,' Hannah said, this time glancing across to just Rosie. 'The old woman's name was Vera and she runs the café on High Street East, just up from the south dock.'

'What? Not the one miss and her fella used to go to?' Again it was Angie filling in the blanks.

'And where Jack and Arthur used to go for their bacon butties?' Dorothy looked at Gloria.

'Yes, Vera's!' Hannah exclaimed. 'So, we're all going to go there and eat whatever my aunty Rina or the old woman has baked that day and drink tea.'

'That's great news,' Rosie said. 'I'm surprised Vera didn't say she was taking on someone new. When did your aunty start working? Can't have been long ago because I was in there the other week.'

'She's just started so I thought we'd let her settle in before we all go there "en masse", as it were.' Hannah chuckled at the thought of them taking over the place. 'But she seems to love it. The old woman sounds like a bit of a character, but my aunty comes back happy every day, so that can only be a good thing, don't you think?'

Hannah threw another curious look over at Gloria and Rosie as everyone smiled and concurred that it was, indeed, a very good thing.

'When did you go and see Basil then?' Gloria asked Rosie as they walked back to their work area ahead of the rest of the squad.

'Yesterday,' Rosie said quietly. 'He actually seemed relieved. He knew why Hannah needed the overtime. I didn't realise he lives at the bottom end of Villette Road and his neighbour is one of Rina's customers who seems to think buying stuff on tick means you never have to actually pay up. He said everyone round his way knew that Rina was a bit of an easy touch and there were more than a few taking advantage of her kind nature.'

Gloria tutted.

'Anyway,' Rosie continued, 'Basil was more than happy to tell Hannah there was no overtime, which there isn't. The poor bloke's been coming in early and making out there's work to do when there isn't. He's managed to get the extra hours past the paymaster's eagle eye, but I'd bet my weekly wage that he's not been claiming for the overtime he's been doing.'

'Looks like Rina isn't the only soft touch then,' Gloria chipped in.

'Mm, and I don't think we've managed to pull the wool over Hannah's eyes either.'

'I think you might be right there,' Gloria said. 'Well, as Angie would say, "All's well that ends well."'

'True,' Rosie said, 'but that still leaves us with finding solutions for Martha's, Dorothy's and Angie's problems.'

Gloria glanced at her friend. Hannah wasn't the only one looking tired. Only, unlike Hannah, Rosie's need to work flat out was not about keeping the debtors at bay, but her heartache.

'I don't want to sound like a defeatist,' Gloria said. 'But I don't think there is a solution to any of their secrets. We can't stop Angie's mum having it off with some bloke. And we can't undo the fact that Dorothy's mam's a bigamist. And we certainly can't change who Martha's real mother was.'

'That's one way of looking at it,' Rosie said a little cryptically.

Gloria laughed. 'What's going on in that complex head of yours?'

Rosie felt a sudden stab in her chest. Peter had often used the same words when he wanted to know what she was thinking.

'The way I look at it,' Rosie said, pushing back thoughts of Peter, 'Angie's mam and Dorothy's have both made their beds, but that doesn't mean others have to lie on that bed with them. The problems they have are their own problems – not their daughters'. If their misdemeanours are exposed, which they might well be regardless of Miriam, then *they* are going to have to be the ones to deal with the backlash. Not Angie or Dorothy.'

'But,' Gloria interjected, 'that's just the point – they're both going to get caught in the cross hairs if they're living under the same roof.'

'Exactly!' Rosie said. 'Angie and Dorothy will get dragged into the whole mess. And in Angie's case that could actually be quite dangerous.'

Gloria nodded grimly.

'So, the most obvious solution is ...'

Gloria's face lit up.

'Get them both out o' the road?'

'Exactly,' Rosie said.

'Perhaps we should put it in both of their heads that you and I needn't be the only ones to be moving house. Perhaps it's time for them two to get themselves a nice little flat or bedsit? They could afford it on both their wages and all the overtime they've been doing.'

Gloria suddenly hooted with laughter as she imagined the squad's 'terrible two' living together. 'I'm not sure whether that's a brilliant idea or a dreadful one.'

Rosie chuckled.

'The lesser of two evils, I think.'

'What are you both laughing about?' Dorothy demanded as she nudged herself between her two workmates.

'Eee, nosy parker!' Gloria elbowed Dorothy playfully, hoping she hadn't caught the tail end of their conversation.

'So, Glor,' Dorothy's voice had become serious, 'how much longer is Jack gonna have to stay up in Scotland? He's been gone an age.'

'He's hoping to get back soon.' Gloria tried to sound upbeat.

'That's what you said last time and the time before that. Don't they even give him the odd weekend off?' Dorothy dropped her voice. 'I thought you were going to tell Miriam? Especially now you're rid of Vinnie.'

'It's difficult. He's having to work every waking hour at the moment. We're trying to work something out.' Gloria hated lying. More than anything, though, she didn't know how much longer she could keep up the pretence that Jack was coming back.

'Come on, you two.' Rosie had been walking along quietly next to them both. 'Enough gassing. I need you two up on the main deck.'

'Talk about slave driver,' Dorothy huffed. 'The hooter's not even sounded out.'

As if by command the klaxon then bellowed out the end of the lunch break.

As the noise of the yard started up again, preventing any more chatter, Dorothy and Gloria headed towards the metal gangway and onto the injured cargo vessel they had been working on solidly since it had been dragged into the dry dock a few weeks ago. As Rosie watched them walk away, Gloria looked behind her and mouthed, 'Thank you.'

Rosie had heard the women talking occasionally about Jack and the length of time he had been gone; Polly had even mentioned Bel was getting concerned that Hope wouldn't recognise her father if she didn't see him soon.

Rosie knew that Gloria was going to have to make up a convincing lie – and sooner rather than later.

'I don't know what I'm going to do about Jack,' Gloria said as she bustled about the kitchen, making a cup of tea. Rosie was sitting in the lounge-cum-dining room, bopping Hope about on her lap.

'I know,' Rosie shouted through. 'I heard Dorothy quizzing you.'

Gloria came back in with two cups of tea and put them both down on the coffee table. 'Dorothy means well,' she said, taking Hope off Rosie. 'She's such a romantic. She's desperate to have me and Jack and her gorgeous goddaughter here. Together. One big happy family.' Gloria gave Hope a kiss on the cheek.

'I know she means well,' Rosie said. 'But knowing Dorothy, she'll keep on asking.'

'I'm going to have to think of something.' Gloria went back into the kitchen with Hope and got her bottle.

'What does Jack say?' Rosie asked.

'He's being remarkably positive.' Gloria sat down with Hope, the little girl now clinging to the bottle and gulping down her milk. 'He says that at least he's building ships and doing his bit, and that we'll find a way to be together, it's just going to take time. He keeps telling me that we are actually incredibly lucky to have found each other after all these years, and how terrible it would have been if that had never happened.' Gloria carefully reached over so as not to squash Hope and took a big slurp of tea.

'What *is* troubling him, though, is Helen.'

'In what way?' Rosie asked, looking at Hope, who was still sucking on her bottle but now with less fervour.

'He's been writing to her once – sometimes twice – a week. Whenever he writes a letter to me, he writes one to Helen, but she's not sent him back even one reply. *Not one.* He doesn't say as much but I can tell it's breaking his heart ... I know no one at work likes Helen, and to be honest there was a time when I couldn't abide the woman myself, but she really does – or rather *did* – adore Jack. I used to think Jack didn't really know what his daughter was like – that, like most parents, his child could do no wrong, that he was blind to the fact she was actually quite a horrible person, but now I know more, I really do think it's all a bit of an act.'

'Don't forget she's got her mother in her,' Rosie chipped in.

'I know ...' Gloria followed Rosie's gaze and looked down at her daughter, who was now simply lying with the teat of the bottle in her mouth, her eyes fluttering shut. 'There's no getting away from the fact that Helen has learnt a lot from her mother, but I honestly feel deep down she's not the hardened cow everyone thinks she is. None of you saw her that day she saved me from Vinnie. It took a brave woman to do what she did. Smacking Vinnie over the head with a shovel. Not knowing if he would turn on her. She saw someone in need and didn't think twice about helping them – or about the danger to herself. She's not so unlike the rest of us.'

'Mm,' Rosie said, with a lack of conviction.

Gloria stood up and carried Hope into the nursery, where she carefully laid her in the cot.

'Regardless,' she said as she came back into the room, 'Jack's worried about her. He might be thanking his lucky stars that we found each other again, and that we've got Hope, but I know he's distraught that it could be at the cost of losing Helen. I wish she would just send him a letter. It's been months now and not a word.'

'Which just proves my point,' Rosie said, standing up and picking up her gas mask and haversack, 'that Helen must be a hard and cold person to get all those letters from her dad and not reply. Not even once. I know you appreciate what she did for you, Gloria, but I still think the woman's got more of Miriam in her than she has her dad.'

Gloria hurried back into the kitchen and returned with a small brown envelope.

'Your rent, Mrs Miller.' She forced the money into Rosie's hand.

'Eee, honestly,' Gloria laughed, seeing the look of mortification on Rosie's face that she was taking money from her friend. 'You're going to have to harden up if you want to make it as a successful landlady.'

'I just hate taking money off you,' Rosie said.

Gloria gave her a cheeky smile as she opened the front door. 'Well, you'll just have to take a leaf out of Helen's book, otherwise you'll end up like Hannah's aunty Rina!'

Rosie put the envelope into the top pocket of her overalls and started walking up the steps.

'And,' Gloria continued her comparison, 'Vera won't take you on because you can't cook for toffee – never mind bake cakes!'

Rosie laughed as she reached the top step and turned around. 'You want to be careful, I might buy another flat from Mr Brown and rent it out to Dorothy and Angie! Fancy having them as your neighbours?'

Rosie was still chuckling to herself at the thought as she crossed the street and started walking up Toward Road.

After Rosie left, Gloria made herself a sandwich and switched on the wireless. She tried to concentrate on a news report from the well-known war correspondent Richard Dimbleby, followed by a discussion about the war in the Pacific, but it just made her worry all the more about her two boys.

When she tried to think about something other than U-boats torpedoing British ships, her mind immediately swung back to Jack and Helen.

Yesterday, before picking up Hope from Bel, she had nipped down Norfolk Street and into the GPO, where she had made a telephone call to Jack. It was only the second time they had been able to actually speak to each other since he had left at the start of the year. They'd tried phoning each other on other occasions, but it'd had to be organised with military precision. If one of them was just a few minutes early or late, they would miss the opportunity. Gloria had to call from a public phone while Jack had to wait by the one at work. It was wonderful hearing each other's voices, but saying goodbye was so incredibly hard.

If Miriam had hoped she might succeed in breaking up their relationship when she'd sent Jack away, she had thought wrong. If anything, they had grown closer, despite the distance between them. Their yearning for each other had only intensified, not diminished, and because they had to communicate more or less solely by letter, they had ended up telling each other their deepest thoughts and feelings. All of which could be read over and over again. Jack's words proved his love for Gloria was as strong as ever – perhaps even stronger. His determination that Miriam would not win came across loud and clear.

What had also been clear, though, were his worries about Helen. Yesterday when they had spoken, he had asked a lot about her. *Had Gloria seen her? What did she look like? Was she still looking thin? Was she still smoking lots? How was she getting on at work?* Gloria had been caught a little off guard, having become used to thinking about her replies. It was the one luxury writing gave you, thinking carefully before committing pen to paper. She hadn't known what to say. She couldn't tell the truth, that was for sure. She couldn't tell him that Helen was actually starting to look a bit gaunt. Of course, she was still stunning, nothing would ever take that away, but she *was* looking thin. And as for her smoking, well, she couldn't exactly tell Jack that she rarely saw her without a cigarette between her fingers, or surrounded by a halo of smoke. And Gloria knew she couldn't say anything about the arrogant young man she had met that night outside of the flat, or how Helen had been spotted coming out of some working man's pub half-cut. What would have been the point? She wouldn't be able to tell Jack the name of his daughter's new beau, or anything else about him. It would only worry Jack even more. If only Helen would write him a letter, it would put his mind at rest.

Thinking about Helen, and about Jack, Gloria then started to worry about Hope, who seemed to be mirroring her own restlessness and kept waking up demanding attention. The poor little mite had probably forgotten she even had a da. As Gloria picked Hope up out of her cot and started to slowly sway her in her arms, lulling her back to sleep, Gloria came to a decision. She might not be able to do anything about getting Jack back here, but she could at least try to get it across to Helen that just because her mam and dad were no longer together, that did not, in any way, mean that she and Jack had to be estranged.

By the time she had settled Hope back into her cot, Gloria was resolute. She was going to have a word with Helen and make her see sense. Make her realise that her father loved her dearly, that he thought the world of her, was incredibly proud of her, and it was breaking his heart that she was refusing to have any contact with him. She didn't quite know how she was going to get Helen on her own, or how she was going to broach the subject of her father's infidelity, but she knew she had to – somehow.

Chapter Thirty

One week later

Tuesday 14 April

'Mother, what are you doing here?'

'Can't I visit my daughter at her place of work?' Miriam looked around and ran her finger along the top of a tall metal cabinet. Her face crinkled as she looked at the dirt and dust that had been transferred to her fingertip. Helen caught her look.

'This is a shipyard, you know, Mother? Which means it can get dirty. Building ships does not take place in a sterile environment.'

Miriam rolled her eyes as though she were an obstinate child.

'What can I do for you?' Helen asked. Her patience was waning today.

'I thought you might like to come to the Grand with me for a little light lunch?'

Helen looked at her mother and realised she had no idea what she did day in, day out. Nor did she want to know.

'Mother, I have barely a minute to turn around at the moment, never mind go to the Grand and sit around eyeing up the latest Admiralty that has just shored up in town.'

Miriam jerked her head as though she had been slapped around the face. 'Now listen here, madam, I will not be talked to in such a manner!'

Just then Marie-Anne knocked on the office door and Helen waved her in. Knowing what she wanted, she took the order forms from her secretary's outstretched hand and signed them before handing them back. Sensing the tense atmosphere, Marie-Anne hurried back out and shut the door quietly behind her.

'Sorry, Mother,' Helen apologised, knowing she had overstepped the mark, something she was doing an awful lot of lately. 'It just seems to be one problem after another at the moment ... Just before you tipped up, Harold came to tell me there's another frigate due in that needs patching up, and speed, as always, is of the essence – which wouldn't be such a problem if the workforce wasn't so depleted.'

Helen stopped speaking, remembering that she had been looking for a list of the new batch of workers due to start next week. The news that they were getting more workers was a relief, although half were women and the rest men who should really be retired. When Harold had been in to tell her the news she couldn't stop herself snapping: 'Well, I guess beggars can't be choosers!' She had seen the look on Harold's face and immediately wished she had kept her thoughts to herself.

Having located the list, Helen focused her attention back on her mother, but seeing the blank expression on her face, knew she hadn't listened to a word she had just said.

'Mum, would you like a cup of tea?' Helen took a deep breath. She knew that her mother only wanted to take her out when she needed something. 'Have a seat. Tell me why you wanted me to go to the Grand?'

Miriam looked at the seat in front of Helen's desk with a stack of files on it and remained standing.

'I'll pass on the offer of tea, thank you. I just wanted to have a chat to you about your grandfather. You're obviously flavour of the month at the moment and he rang me yester-day asking to speak to you. Of course, you weren't in, as seems to be the case these days. I told him that you were more than likely out with Theodore and could I pass on a message.'

'So, what was the message?' Helen could feel her irritation growing again.

'He wants you to go round and see him when you have a moment.'

'What? That was it? Is it important? Can't he just ring me at work?'

'I did suggest that,' Miriam said a little defensively, 'but he said he needed to talk to you face to face. He's never been one to speak on the telephone at the best of times. And now I think he's getting paranoid in his old age and he keeps saying anyone can listen in to your private conversations.'

'Fine.' Helen sighed. 'When I have a spare minute I'll go round and see him.'

She looked at Miriam.

'Sorry, Mum, but is that all? I've really got to get on.'

Miriam straightened her back.

'Yes, I'm going! I know when I'm not wanted!'

And with that she turned, opened the office door and finally left Helen in peace.

As soon as her mother had left, Helen lit up a cigarette and walked over to the window. She blew out smoke and looked down at the yard.

Since her father had been exiled to the Clyde, her grandfather had started to involve her much more in the family business. Or rather the family finances. Her grandfather had sold or offloaded a good percentage of his business interests over the past few years. He'd had the sense to realise he was too old to keep up with the modern world, but he had been astute enough to safeguard his money. Helen also realised that her grandfather had relied heavily on her father, and that now he had been cut out of all of their lives, it had fallen on Helen to take over the reins. She wasn't stupid, though, and knew the only reason for that was because there wasn't anyone else to do it. Like she'd said to Harold – beggars can't be choosers.

As Helen stared out the window, she saw her mother hurrying past a squad of platers, their eyes to the sky, watching the huge arm of a crane slowly lowering a consignment of sheet metal to its designated area. Helen thought that her mother's need to get away from the dirt and grime of the yard might just surpass her eagerness to get to the Grand. After her father's infidelity had come to light, Helen had initially thought her mother would feel hurt. Rejected. But as time had gone on she'd realised her mother didn't seem to have been particularly affected by her husband's betrayal. If anything she seemed happier. She certainly seemed to be enjoying life.

Helen envied her mother. These past few months her own feelings of guilt had been in constant battle with her anger and resentment. In the end, though, it seemed that her guilt had finally been dissolved by the vitriol of her growing hatred. She had never believed she could ever hate her father, but she did now.

She was no longer the innocent young daughter who had sat by his bedside and willed him to get better. The one who had rejoiced when he had woken from his coma and had done what she could to drag his memory back from the depths of the North Atlantic. She was no longer that young girl. She had changed.

And, more than anything, she was determined her life would change. It wouldn't be long before she was engaged and then married, living nearly three hundred miles away in a city that could not be more dissimilar to this town.

As Helen tossed her cigarette end out of the window, she knew that leaving this place would be her only regret. This shipyard in 'The Biggest Shipbuilding Town in the World'. This chaotic mess of metal, this concrete expanse filled with hundreds of men – and women – all working together to build and repair these mammoth metal monsters that rode the waves. It made her heart lurch. For there would be no shipyards in her new life. No more deafening sounds of clashing machinery, no ear-splitting bursts of the riveter's gun, no shouting or bellows of laughter or banter, no ceremonies to mark the laying of keels or the launching of ships. She knew all about Oxford's architecture, its history, its treasure trove of culture, but it didn't have the untamed beauty of the North Sea, nor did it have a twisting and turning River Wear that ran like an artery through the town, bringing life to everything it touched.

Helen turned her back on the yard and walked into her office.

This place, this love of hers for it, she knew, was the one sacrifice she had to make for her new love – for her new life.

Chapter Thirty-One

The Cedars, Sunderland

'No, not today, thank you!' The housekeeper was just about
to close the heavy oak front door.

'I'm not after selling you anything,' Bel quickly said, putting on her best voice. She surprised even herself by how
posh she sounded. It obviously did the trick, as the elderly
housekeeper stopped the door from closing in Bel's face.

'Well, what do you want?' the old woman demanded,
folding her arms across her ample bosom, her eyes straying behind the young blonde on her doorstep to a battered-
looking Silver Cross pram and a little girl standing next to
it with a frown on her face.

'I'm trying to locate a long-lost relative.' Bel spoke
quickly so as to keep the woman's attention and to prove
to her that she meant no harm. 'And I believe she worked
in one of these houses.' Bel stretched her arm out and
pointed to her right, to the long line of mansions along the
road known as The Cedars.

'It was a while ago – about twenty-eight years, to be
exact.' Bel forced a smile on her face.

'Name?' the housekeeper asked sharply.

'Pearl Hardwick. She would have only been about fifteen at the time.' Bel again took care to pronounce her
words in her best King's English.

The old woman stood for a moment, thinking, before
slowly shaking her head from left to right.

'No. I've been here for well over thirty years and I can't recall anyone with that name working here.'

'Are you sure?' Bel couldn't stop the words slipping out. 'Sorry, I don't mean to be rude, it's just a long time ago.'

'I might be knocking on, pet, but there's nowt wrong with my memory and I can tell you for certain I'd remember if I'd had a young girl called Pearl in my charge.'

The old woman started to close the door.

'Of course, so sorry to bother you. Thank you for your time,' Bel said politely as the door shut and she heard the bolt being slid across the other side. She turned back to Hope, sound asleep in the pram, and Lucille, who was still wearing a frown.

'I want to go to park!' she declared.

Bel released the brake from the back wheel of the pram with her foot and started pushing the Silver Cross down the cobbled driveway.

'I *want* doesn't *get*, Lucille. You should know that by now.' But as she spoke Bel felt a twinge of guilt that she had dragged her daughter all the way from Tatham Street under the guise of going to the park as it was such a nice day, but so far they had spent the past half-hour knocking on doors.

When they reached the end of the driveway, Bel steered the pram left onto the wide pavement and started walking to the neighbouring house.

'We'll do two more houses, and then we'll go to the park,' Bel relented. She looked down at her daughter, who was holding on to the side of the pram as they walked. The frown was replaced by a big smile. Seeing the closed wooden gate of the next house, Lucille ran ahead to open it, now clearly in a hurry to get the next two houses done and dusted.

Bel was also glad they were almost done. This had turned out to be a completely demoralising task. It had seemed like a good idea at the time. When Beryl had told her at the launch that her ma had worked in one of the big houses up by Backhouse Park, Bel had actually felt quite excited about the idea of turning super sleuth and going in search of her father. She had told Polly, full of bravado: 'If my ma won't tell me, then I'm jolly well going to find out myself!' Polly hadn't said much, which Bel knew meant her sister-in-law wasn't in full support of her proposed actions. But Bel didn't care. Polly knew who *her* da was. Bel didn't. And she was determined that wouldn't be the case for long. She had made up her mind. Nothing was going to change it. She was going to find out who her father was, by hook or by crook.

'Sorry to bother you,' Bel began her now well-rehearsed speech. 'But I'm trying to find a long-lost relative.'

The dark-haired woman standing in the doorway looked harried. This house wasn't as big or as grand as some of the houses Bel had knocked on so far, but it was still impressive.

'Yes?' asked the woman, dressed in a neat, navy blue pleated skirt and matching cashmere cardigan, as she turned her head, distracted by the screams and shouts of what sounded like a classroom full of children. It turned out to be just three young girls, who had clearly decided to run riot while their mother's attention was elsewhere.

'Behave! The lot of you!' Her reprimand was followed by silence, before three pretty little faces appeared from behind their mother.

'Sorry, my dear, you were saying?' the woman asked Bel, pushing a strand of hair back behind her ear.

'I wondered if you knew of a young girl that may have worked here over twenty years ago. Probably as a maid.'

As Bel spoke the words she knew this was a no-go and was proven right fairly quickly.

'Oh, gosh, no, sorry, my dear. We've only been here ...' She paused a moment to think. 'Well, it can't have been much more than ten years.' Looking at Lucille, who was staring at her three daughters, she was unaware that they were all sticking out their tongues and pulling faces at the little blonde girl standing obediently next to the pram.

'And you can't remember anything of the previous owners?' Bel asked, without much hope.

'Oh, yes, I remember the couple who lived here before us, but they were old and they only had a housekeeper and a cleaner. I think they'd been here donkey's years, but from what I gathered it had never been a big household.'

'Oh, never mind.' Bel tried to sound chirpy. 'Thank you anyway.' She looked at the three faces still gurning at Lucille. 'Sorry to bother you.' As she turned to walk back down the steps she caught a glimpse of Lucille's scrunched-up face with her tongue sticking out, before it returned to an expression of angelic innocence.

'I'm going to pretend I didn't see that!' Bel whispered as she turned the pram around and pushed it back out onto the street.

As they started walking to the next house, they heard a familiar voice behind them.

'Bel! LuLu!'

They turned round to see Maisie, hurrying towards them. She was wearing a fawn-coloured suit dress and no overcoat, a sure sign that spring was here. Lucille ran to her aunty and flung herself at her.

''Aisiee!'

Maisie grabbed her under the arms and lifted her up, spun her around and then plopped her back down on the pavement.

'Well, this is a surprise. Don't often see you up this way?' She stepped towards Bel and gave her a hug, followed by a kiss on both cheeks. It was a habit she had acquired since starting work at Lily's.

'I know,' Bel said, feeling a little awkward. Maisie had become a regular visitor to Tatham Street and was actually getting to know the neighbours, as well as most of the locals in the pub, but she had never invited Bel to Lily's, which was, for all intents and purposes, her permanent home now.

'Aunty 'Aisiee come to park!' Lucille demanded.

'Ah, sweetie, I can't come today.' Maisie bent down to talk to her niece. 'I've got an appointment to keep.'

Bel raised an eyebrow.

'No, honestly,' Maisie said, standing up to talk to Bel. 'I would if I could. I really like the park. Never had one on my doorstep before. London may have many things, but it is lacking somewhat in greenery. And the parks they have are always so crowded.' They both looked across to the expanse of Backhouse Park, which consisted of two and a half acres of natural woodland and had been gifted to the town by a well-known Quaker banker who had lived in a huge mansion on the Ryhope Road that was now an art college.

'So, what's the appointment?' Bel asked, wanting to keep the conversation away from why she was schlepping from door to door along The Cedars with her daughter and Gloria's baby.

'Ah, well.' Maisie looked uneasy. 'It's not an appointment as such. Just going to visit an acquaintance.'

Bel looked at Maisie and felt herself blush, although why she should be the one blushing she had no idea. She had never talked to her sister about her employment at Lily's, and was happy to believe that Maisie's work was solely to do with the Gentlemen's Club.

'Oh, you got far to go?' Bel asked, more for something to say than for any other reason.

'Just round the corner to Glen Path.' Maisie looked down at Lucille, who was staring up at them both, taking in every word passing between her aunty and her mammy.

'Anyway, you didn't answer my question,' Maisie said, looking back at Bel. 'What are you three doing in this neck of the woods? Something tells me you're on some kind of mission? Especially as you all look like you're on your way to church, not just on a sojourn to the park.'

Bel looked down at her best coat, which she had pressed before leaving the house, and her black leather shoes that she had polished to a shine. She had also woven Lucille's blonde hair into two straight, tight plaits. Bel let out a sigh. There was no reason to lie to Maisie. Besides, she was the only one who really understood her need to find her father.

'Actually,' Bel lowered her voice, 'you're not far wrong.' She looked at Lucille, who had now got bored with the adult chatter and was on her tiptoes trying to look in the pram to see if Hope was awake, her intentions clear. If she wasn't, she soon would be.

'Beryl mentioned that Ma had worked around here, in one of the big houses, as some kind of maid,' Bel explained.

'What? So you thought you'd go all Miss Marple? Find the house and then what?' Maisie was intrigued.

'I dunno.' Bel now sounded deflated. 'To be honest, it's been a complete washout. I've felt like some kind of beggar with my two street urchins next to me knocking on all these doors.' Bel looked behind her at the half-dozen houses she had already called at.

'Honestly, I've felt about this small.' She put her thumb and forefinger an inch apart.

Maisie laughed. 'Yes, they can be a bit stuck-up along here. Lots of "old money", which generally means old people stuck in old ways. No time for working-class folk.'

'A woman just took one look at me and slammed the door in my face. God, I was so angry I had to stop myself banging on the door again and giving her a piece of my mind.'

Maisie chuckled again. She knew the only reason Bel probably hadn't was Lucille and Hope.

'So, Beryl reckons Ma worked in one of the houses along here?'

'I think her exact words were, "one of the big houses that overlook Backhouse Park".' Bel looked at Lucille, who was now pulling Hope's blanket down so she could get hold of her little hand.

Just then Bel was struck by an idea. 'You could ask your "acquaintance". See if he remembers a young girl called Pearl who used to work around here as a maid?'

Maisie stared at Bel for a moment as if a thought – and not a particularly pleasant one – had just occurred to her.

'Personally, I think you're looking for a needle in a haystack.'

As she spoke, Bel's face dropped.

'I know. It's crazy. Seemed like such a good idea when I was sat at home chatting to Polly.'

'I tell you what,' Maisie quickly looked at her watch, 'I've got to go now, but why don't me and you go out one day and knock on doors. Leave the "bairns" at home?'

'Ah, that would be really nice. Thanks, Maisie.' All of a sudden Bel didn't feel so hopeless. For the first time she felt as if she and Maisie were proper sisters. United.

'Mammy! Park. *Pleeease*.' Lucille's tone of voice had changed from demanding to outright begging.

'How can you refuse?' Maisie laughed.

'All right, LuLu, you win. The park it is!' Bel told her daughter, who removed her hands from inside the pram, although Bel feared it was too late as Hope was starting to stir.

'I'll pop by over the weekend and we'll make a plan,' Maisie promised, giving Lucille a hug and a kiss.

As Maisie hurried off down the wide, tree-lined pathway, Bel shouted out, 'Thanks, Maisie!'

Maisie turned around and blew them all a kiss before crossing the road and turning right into Glen Path.

As Bel started pushing the pram back down the street towards the park's main entrance, she took hold of Lucille's hand. The little girl was pulling her mammy forward with all her might.

Was it possible that her father was still here? Still alive? Still working in one of the big houses? If he was around her ma's age, perhaps a little older, he would be in his mid to late forties.

Suddenly Bel panicked.

The age of conscription had just been raised to fifty-one. There was a good chance her da would be called up – *might have already been called up!*

Her time might be running out.

Chapter Thirty-Two

As soon as Maisie had finished her 'appointment', she turned right out of the main gates instead of left, which she would have normally done had she been headed back to Lily's. This evening she was going to take a rather long detour home – via the Tatham. It was a relatively warm evening, and Maisie felt like clearing her head, so even though she knew it would be a good half-hour walk, she didn't mind.

She had asked her client, as she had been getting ready to leave, if he knew of a young maid called Pearl who had worked for a while in one of the houses overlooking the park. On hearing how long ago it was, though, he'd let out a snort of laughter, saying that at his age he was lucky to remember what he'd had for breakfast. When Maisie told him it was important and he had seen the look of earnestness on her face, he had sat back in his chair, filled his pipe and thought for a little while before declaring that, as far as he could recall, he had not employed any such maid. Maisie wasn't sure if he was telling the truth, or if it really was too long ago for him to remember. When she had continued to pursue the subject and asked if any of his neighbours had employed a skinny young blonde girl, he said, 'Even if I did have the mind of a younger man, it's highly unlikely, my dear, that I would see, never mind *know*, any of my neighbours' servants. We all tend to keep to ourselves around these parts.' Her client's use of the word 'servant' had made Maisie recoil, and she'd counted her money and left, forcing a smile on her face.

The walk along Glen Path and then The Cedars always seemed to be quiet, which Maisie found a little disconcerting. Being brought up in London and living there most of her life, it was rare to see an empty street without at least half a dozen cars or buses on it. Her spirits lifted when she reached Ryhope Road and crossed over to Villette Road, where she was hit by the buzz of life – a group of chattering Jews making their way to the synagogue, the usual shouts and screams of the local children running in and out of the Barley Mow Park, housewives carrying half-full bags of shopping, and the first trickle of workers heading home for their tea.

As Maisie cut through some of the side streets before coming out onto Tatham Street, she popped into the tobacconist and bought Pearl her packet of Winstons. By the time she reached the pub, it was just starting to get dark. Walking into the main bar, Maisie smiled and said her hellos to some of the regulars.

'Ah, Maisie!' Pearl's face lit up as it always did when she saw her daughter.

'Bill,' Maisie looked over at the landlord standing next to Pearl behind the bar, 'can I borrow your chief barmaid for five minutes, please?'

'Eee, yer dinnit need to ask his permission. I'm my own woman. I'll have myself a break if I need one!' Pearl said in outrage.

Bill raised his eyes to the heavens and Maisie shook her head in sympathy. 'That may well be, Ma, but Bill is still your boss.'

'Go and sit down and I'll bring your drinks over,' Bill said, as Pearl lifted up the counter and came round the other side of the bar.

'Ah, thanks, Bill. My mother doesn't know how lucky she is to have you as her employer.'

'Phut!' Pearl said, her eyes lighting up as Maisie handed her the packet of cigarettes. 'More like he doesn't know how lucky *he* is to have me here, working for peanuts, every hour God sends.' She then opened the packet, pulled out two cigarettes and handed one to Maisie with the words, 'Ta, pet!', sparking up her daughter's cigarette and then her own with the Ronson lighter Maisie had bought her in London. She exhaled smoke and spoke at the same time. 'So, then, to what do I owe this honour?'

Maisie turned around as she saw Bill coming over with their drinks. 'I don't think you'll be calling it an "honour" or be quite so chirpy when I tell you, Ma.'

'Here you go, ladies.' Bill handed Maisie a good measure of Rémy Martin from one of the bottles she had given him the other week. One was a gift, the other to be put behind the bar for her visits. Maisie had decided if the Tatham was to become her regular drinking hole, then she needed to be able to enjoy a decent drink.

'Eee, "ladies" is it now?' Pearl blew smoke up to the ceiling.

'Well, I could think of worse names to be called, Ma!' Maisie turned to Bill. 'Honestly, I don't know what's got into this mother of mine. I feel for you, Bill. Talk about a constant barrage of abuse.' Maisie turned her attention back to Pearl. 'Can't you say a civil word to the man?'

'Ah, he loves it!' Pearl chuckled, giving Bill a wink as he walked off smiling and shaking his head. 'Can't take ourselves too serious, can we?'

Maisie looked at her mother and took a deep breath.

'Well, I don't know if you'll be saying that when I tell you what I've got to tell you.' Maisie looked at the bulbous glass and took a sip of her drink. She wondered if Bill would be offended if she brought in her own glass too.

'What have yer gorra tell me, then, that's so serious?' Pearl took a long drag on her cigarette.

'It's Bel,' Maisie said. 'You wouldn't guess where I saw her this afternoon?'

Pearl's eyes were now focused solely on Maisie.

'Where?' she demanded.

'The Cedars,' Maisie said simply.

'The Cedars?' Pearl repeated. 'What was she doing up that way?'

Maisie took a deep breath. 'She was looking for her "da". Or at least trying to find where you worked after you came back from London. She heard from Beryl that you used to work in one of the big houses that overlook the park when you came back after having me.'

'And?' Pearl said. Her cigarette had burnt down to the butt and she tossed it in the ashtray.

'And,' Maisie said, 'she's done her maths and worked out that you must have fallen pregnant within a year of returning home. Which, in turn, probably means her father is someone you worked with ... Or ...' she blew out smoke ' ... someone you worked *for*.'

Pearl looked at Maisie and lit another cigarette. Her eldest daughter wasn't stupid, that was for sure. But more worryingly, neither was her youngest. It wouldn't take Isabelle long to come to the same conclusion.

'How many doors did she knock on? What did she find out?' Pearl was now perched forward on her stool, staring at Maisie, hoping upon hope that Isabelle's snoop along The Cedars had been fruitless.

'About half a dozen or so, but don't worry, she didn't find anything out. She seemed pretty down in the mouth, to be honest.'

Pearl wanted to say that she would be more than down in the mouth if she found out the truth, but she didn't. Instead she took a large swig of her whisky.

'She said someone even shut the door in her face. It didn't seem like anyone had been particularly nice to her. Or helpful,' continued Maisie.

For a moment Pearl was transported back to the day she too had trooped from house to house along The Cedars and then Glen Path. When she, too, had suffered the affront of having doors slammed in her face and being talked down to as though she was dirt. It hadn't bothered Pearl. She had been beyond caring. But it bothered her now, bothered her that people were being like that to her Isabelle. She was so kind, so pretty, and she had such manners. More than a lot of posh folk she'd come across. Her Isabelle shouldn't be knocking on doors, begging for information, like she herself had begged for a job and a roof over her head.

'Do yer think that's it, then?' Pearl asked. 'Do yer think she'll leave it at that?' But even as she spoke her words Pearl knew the answer.

'You're not going to get off the hook that easily, Ma. I'm afraid Bel's determined to knock on every door of every house that overlooks that park until she gets an answer. One way or the other.'

'Why doesn't that surprise me.' Pearl blew out another thick cloud of grey smoke.

'But,' Maisie sat back and smiled, 'this is when I deserve a big pat on the back.'

'Go on,' Pearl said, pulling another cigarette out of the packet and lighting it off the one she was just about to put out.

'I said I would go with her next time she decided to go door-knocking.'

Pearl's mind was working nineteen to the dozen. 'So you can tell me if she finds anything out?'

'Exactly!'

There was a moment's pause.

'That would take a load off yer auld ma's shoulders,' Pearl said, leaning across the table conspiratorially, 'even more so if you could keep her away from Glen Path.' She thought she saw a flicker of concern skit across her daughter's very beautiful freckled face. 'Is that gonna be a problem?'

Maisie shook her head. 'Any house in particular?'

'Nah,' Pearl said, as a large group of overall-clad workers she knew worked at Bartram's shipyard walked into the bar. 'Just keep her away from there. Just say you've already spoken to the people along that particular street. Make something up. Just don't let her go anywhere near those soddin' houses.'

Maisie watched her ma as she downed her drink and hurried back to the bar to help Bill out with the new influx of customers. As the pub continued to fill up, Maisie didn't make any attempt to move, but stayed there for a good ten minutes, drinking her brandy and smoking, deep in thought.

'She's like a dog with a bloody bone,' Pearl said. 'Just won't let it go.'

Bill nodded. They were both sat on stools by the bar, which was now empty. Customers had been chucked out half an hour ago and beer trays emptied.

'Maisie coming back has really upset the apple cart,' he mused.

Pearl's head snapped round. She hated to hear even the slightest hint of criticism or negativity about her daughter. 'Maybes, but I think this whole "da" malarkey would have happened regardless. If not now, then sometime in the future. Isabelle's always wanted to know who her father was. Always. Always mithering on as a child. She only gave up when she got in with Agnes and her clan. And now it's reared its ugly head again ... I just wish she'd get herself in the family way – might take her mind off all this. She should have fallen now, anyways.' Pearl did a quick calculation in her head. 'Married in November ... It's now April ... That's a good five months. More than enough time.'

Bill looked at Pearl as she lit up another cigarette and he could see she was anxious, something Pearl wasn't prone to. He also thought her use of the words 'reared its ugly head' had spoken volumes. There was something not nice, something *ugly*, about Bel's da. Disclosing who he was did not seem like an option for Pearl, but if Bel persisted, Pearl might not have any choice.

Bill took a swig of his beer and looked at Pearl's free hand resting on top of the bar. He was just about to put his own hand on hers, tell her that she was not alone and he was here for her. That he cared for her, had fallen for her; would go as far as to say that he loved her – all of her – regardless of her many failings and the life she had led. But as he moved his hand to show Pearl that what he felt for her was more than mere friendship, there was a bang on the door.

Bill stood up. 'We're closed!'

'It's only me – Ronald! Come to take that barmaid of yours off your hands. We need her to make up a game of poker.'

Bloody Ronald! Bill cursed under his breath as he went to let him in. *Him and his bloody card games and black-market whisky.*

As Pearl drained her drink and stood up to leave, she realised she wasn't going to be able to fob her daughter off any more. If Isabelle was a child playing a game of Hot or Cold, she would now be burning up. Pearl might have given herself a stay of execution by getting Maisie to throw her off the scent, but Pearl knew it was just temporary. She knew Isabelle, and when she didn't get her answers, she would go back and knock on all those doors again – including the ones along Glen Path.

It would just take one knock on one particular door and she would know. She would bet her bottom dollar that Agatha and Eddy still worked there, and if Bel met the master of the house, then one look at his face and she would see a reflection of her own.

Eventually Isabelle was going to find out the truth.

Pearl's hand was being forced.

Pearl lost every single game of poker. All she could think about was what to do next. Should she tell Isabelle a lie, only a more convincing one than she had told her when she was a child? This was not a game of poker, though. The stakes were so much higher. Besides, if it was a game of bluff, Pearl would probably still lose as Isabelle knew her too well.

No, Pearl had to face facts. There was nothing she could do with the dud hand she was now holding other than to chuck it in and admit defeat. She was going to have to tell her the truth.

Pearl sipped on her whisky. The sound of the card players' chit-chat filled the cramped front room, but Pearl wasn't listening. Her mind, as Ronald had already pointed out more than once this evening, was somewhere else.

Chapter Thirty-Three

Glen Path, Sunderland

1914

A week before the Easter holidays Henrietta announced to Maid Marian that Charles would be 'gracing us all with his presence', but that 'the girls' had sent a letter saying they had been invited to stay at a chateau in the South of France with the family of a friend of theirs. Agatha had smiled politely, but when she had repeated the news to the rest of the 'household cavalry', there had been a low rumbling of dissent.

'Flamin' Nora, we've only just recovered from His Majesty's last visit,' one of the stable lads said.

'You wanna be thankful yer dinnit work indoors.' Annie, one of the chambermaids, mumbled the words quietly under her breath.

'Well,' Agatha told them all, 'we've only got a week to prepare this time, so it's going to be a case of all hands on deck!'

A couple of days later Pearl was helping the cook pluck a goose when Agatha came into the kitchen all of a flurry.

'Bleedin' typical!' she said, looking about the kitchen and finding only Velma, Pearl and Eddy, who had managed to get an hour off as Henrietta was having one of her afternoon naps.

'Who's got your knickers in a knot?' Velma asked, giving Pearl a wink and a sly smile. Agatha was about as far removed from Robin Hood's love interest as one could get, and could be a bit of a tyrant as she ruled the roost both up- and downstairs. It wasn't often they saw her with her feathers ruffled.

'Little Annie has just been to see me with some cock and bull story about some old dying relative she's got to go and see. I told her I've never heard her talk about this ageing aunty before but she was quite adamant – as is her mam by all accounts – that she go and say her goodbyes.' Annie had earned the prefix 'little' because she was actually very small and skinny – skinnier than Pearl even – and looked much younger than seventeen.

Velma stopped plucking and went to wash her hands in the large white porcelain sink. Pearl thought she had gone rather serious all of a sudden.

'Oh aye.'

Velma always tried to speak properly so Pearl was surprised to hear the cook talking like she'd just stepped out of the east end.

'She's not got herself into trouble, like the last one? Has she?' Velma's tone was accusatory and Pearl noticed that Eddy had got up and sidled towards the back door.

'Course not!' Agatha glared daggers.

'Just off to have a quick word—' Eddy had disappeared out the back by the time his words were out. Both women ignored Eddy's hasty departure.

'Well,' Velma said, 'if little Annie needs time off for a bereavement, the lass needs it. Even if it is inconvenient that her auld aunty's decided to die at the same time as his lordship is due back.'

Agatha scowled at Velma.

'I've told Annie – and I've told her to tell that pig-headed mam of hers – that if the mistress of the house decides that she doesn't want to employ such unreliable staff then that's her prerogative.'

'Hah,' Velma let out a coarse bark of laughter, 'like Henrietta has ever given anyone the boot! If you sack that little lass—'

'Yes?' Agatha asked. 'And pray, Velma, what is going to happen to me?'

Velma huffed, knowing that at the end of the day she was just the cook and held no power over Agatha.

'Actually, I'm not going to give little Annie "the boot", as you put it. But take heed, her card is marked.' She walked over to the kitchen table and poured herself a cup of tea. She held the china cup up to her mouth and was about to take a sip when she stopped.

'Annie's position needs to be filled. Temporary though that may be.'

'Good!' Velma sat back down at the table and poured herself a mug of tea.

'So,' Agatha looked at Pearl, who was still silently pulling feathers and keeping her head down, 'I'm going to get young Pearl here to take Annie's place while she's gone.'

Pearl looked up, surprised to hear her name spoken.

'You'll do no such thing.' Velma was down her throat in an instant. 'I need her here with me. There's too much to do on my own.' She banged her mug down. 'No, Agatha, sorry, but you can't have her. She's mine!'

'It's already been arranged, Velma. You're just going to have to manage on your own.'

Pearl looked at the cook. She had never seen her so flushed and angry. Velma stood up and put her hands on her ample waist. She looked as though she was going to let loose, but she didn't. Instead she pursed her lips, turned on her heel, grabbed her smokes and went out the back.

She never allowed anyone to smoke in 'her' kitchen when there was food about. Not even herself.

'Annie leaves on Wednesday. The day before the master is due back,' Agatha said to Pearl. Her voice was calm and she was back in control of herself.

'Yes, miss,' Pearl said, not sure if this was a good thing or a bad thing. Not that it made any odds. If she wanted to keep working at the house, she had to do what she was told.

Chapter Thirty-Four

It had been two weeks since Gloria had made her resolution to speak to Helen about her father, and every lunchtime she had kept an eagle eye on the admin offices in case Helen left the building for her break. She never did, or at least Gloria had never seen her leave.

Gloria wasn't exactly sure what she was going to do if she did in fact see Helen; she just had a vague plan of catching up with her and asking if she could have a quiet word. It wasn't the most practicable scenario, especially as she would be taking the chance that they might be overheard, but what else could she do? She had hung back at the end of shift a few times, hoping she might catch her leaving, but it looked like Helen worked late most nights, and Gloria couldn't hang around as that definitely would look odd, and besides, she had Hope to pick up. She didn't want Bel to feel she was taking a lend of her.

Apart from catching her at work, Gloria didn't see any other scenario where she would be able to grab a few minutes with Helen to plead Jack's case. It wasn't as though Gloria could go and pay her a visit at home and ask to come in to have a cuppa and a natter.

'Yer in need of a bit supper there, hinny? I've gorra a load of crabs here and a few fillets of fresh fish gannin' spare?'

Gloria stopped the pram and had a look in Meg Shipley's huge wicker basket. The woman was a permanent fixture in the town and there were few who didn't know her. If she wasn't street hawking, she'd be down Corporation Quay waiting on the fishing boats. Gloria bought a piece of fish fillet and the two women went their separate ways – Maggie with her basket balanced on her head, Gloria pushing Hope in the Silver Cross.

Gloria had stayed for a little while at the Elliots' and enjoyed a chat with Agnes. It had been just the two of them as Bel had gone in search of washing powder, which Agnes said had become as precious to them – and as rare – as gold dust since it had been added to the ever-growing list of rationed goods back in February. Gloria had made a mental note to get them some, knowing how much they needed it to keep on taking in washing. It mightn't earn them a great amount, but with just Polly's wage and what Joe got paid for his Home Guard duties, every penny counted.

Once Gloria had turned left onto Borough Road, it was just minutes before she was back at the flat. She was looking forward to getting Hope bathed and settled, and then frying up the piece of fish she'd just bought, but as soon as she went to lift Hope out of the pram, her little girl suddenly started crying. She had gone from drowsy to making enough noise to wake the dead in a matter of seconds.

Gloria tried to soothe her daughter by gently stroking her two little rosy cheeks with the back of her hand, but it was pointless. Hope had been like this the past week and Gloria had tried everything to calm her down – cuddling her, feeding her, trying to distract her with one of the many toys that had once belonged to Lucille – but nothing had worked. It had only been by chance last night that Gloria had found the solution to her daughter's nightly tantrums. She had taken her for a walk round the block to give Mr Brown and the other tenants a respite from Hope's unrelenting vocals and within minutes she had stopped screeching. When Gloria had looked down at her daughter she had seen a very red, smiley face staring up at her. So, Gloria had kept walking and Hope had kept smiling and gurgling.

Tonight, rather than go through the usual litany of cuddles and cajoling, Gloria decided to simply head back out, even though it was the last thing she felt like doing. As soon as Hope was back in her pram being pushed along Borough Road, her screams subsided. As they passed the museum on their left and the bomb site that had once been the town's most exclusive department store, Hope was dribbling and giggling to her heart's content.

'You little terror, you're gonna take after yer godmother. I can just see it. Wanting to be up all night, gadding around town.'

Gloria decided to walk up Holmeside and past the Maison Nouvelle, not that she would be able to stop and see if Kate was still there, but she could at least look in all the shop windows and do a lap of the town centre. By the time she'd done that she was fairly sure her daughter would have finally dropped off to sleep.

At least, Gloria mused as she walked over the road by the south entrance to the railway station, it was now spring. The nights were light, the weather warmer, and there were plenty of people about.

'I'm so sorry,' Theodore took hold of Helen's hand and looked at her with puppy-dog eyes, 'but David – the doctor I was telling you about – well, his sweetheart is leaving tomorrow for her Wren training and this is the last night they'll be able to spend together for months. I know I'm a complete sucker, but I said I'd cover for him.'

Helen looked at the man she had given her heart, soul and, more importantly, her body to and forced a smile.

'Of course you must cover for David and his Wren. That's what I love about you so much. You put everyone else before yourself.'

Helen reached up and kissed him gently on the lips. They were standing on Crowtree Road outside the King's Theatre, which was showing *49th Parallel*, starring Laurence Olivier.

'I'm sure neither of us could enjoy the film knowing that we were doing so at the expense of their last evening together. We can go and see the film another night, can't we?'

'You are a doll, as the Yanks would say.' Theo's relief was audible. He had thought he might well have to argue his case as this was the first time they had gone to the cinema together. A date he had only agreed to as Helen had started to grouse about the fact they never did anything special. Her lament had not surprised him – far from it. Most women he knew would have been complaining fairly soon after they'd started courting that they never went anywhere appropriate for a couple of their class. One of the advantages of Helen being inexperienced was that she was easily steered and believed whatever he told her.

Theo knew he'd had a good run of it with Helen, just as he knew her demands to do what other proper couples did meant that time was now running out. He might be able to risk taking her to the cinema once, but he couldn't take the chance of taking her out to any of the town's more salubrious bars and restaurants. Places he might well meet people he, or Helen, knew.

'But that doesn't mean you're off the hook.' Helen forced her voice to sound light-hearted. Her mother had taught her never to appear even remotely clingy with a man as it was a sure way to lose him. She moved to the side to let a couple go pass, chatting away, oblivious to anyone else.

As she watched them hurry into the foyer, she felt an instant stab of envy, which perturbed her. *Why should she feel jealous when she had Theo? When her new life was just waiting for her around the corner – or rather, down in Oxford?*

'Come here.' Theo pulled Helen close and kissed her. As their bodies pressed together, he felt the instant pull of attraction. Helen might not be the most worldly-wise of women he had been with, but she had a natural sex appeal. He was going to miss her body, the way she excited him without really being aware of it. But it was time. This evening was the beginning of the end. And now he had started the ball rolling, he needed to make it as quick and as painless as possible.

'I won't be able to see you until next week,' Theo said when Helen pulled away. He could see by the look on her face that she was disappointed but was trying not to show it.

'I'll make it up to you, I promise.' Theo was now stepping backwards, making his escape. 'I'll ring you from the hospital next week. We'll do something nice.' Again, another empty promise.

'Don't forget the dinner party Mother's organising in your honour. She wants to set a date – and she won't give up until she's got one!' Helen shouted after Theo, who waved and smiled, but didn't say anything.

Helen watched her lover as he turned his back on her and walked away.

As Theodore hurried to the bus depot at Park Lane, he looked around and checked that no one he knew was about. It was unlikely, but all the same, he needed to make sure. The few people he did know up here were based at the hospital, but they were all well aware he was married. It just needed one person to see him, and then that one person to tell another, and then the Chinese whispers would be finding their way all the way back down south to Franny. *And there was no way she could ever find out. Certainly not in her present condition.*

As he jumped on a bus that had its engine running, ready to leave for a round trip to Ryhope, he had to admit that he had let this particular dalliance go on for much longer than normal, and if he wasn't careful he was going to get himself into trouble. When he had seen Dr Parker the other day he had told Theo all about the Havelocks – about Mr Havelock and his daughter, Miriam. How she had once been a great beauty and caused a bit of a stir by marrying below her station. Her husband was now a local hero, though, having nearly drowned at sea after being part of some maritime mission to America that had been organised by Churchill himself. For the first time, Theodore had felt a little worried. He might well have bitten off more than he could chew. Going to some dinner party that had been specifically organised in his honour was a definite no-no. He had to somehow cut Helen loose, and quickly.

Theodore checked his watch and saw he was only going to be a few minutes late to meet up with his new squeeze, Marion. Determined not to make the same mistake twice, this time he had found himself a woman who was not only far from innocent, but married too. It made life so much easier as she was equally keen that no one see her out with someone else, and therefore had no desire to be wined and dined, meet the parents or be taken to the blasted cinema.

Stop it! Stop it! Helen reprimanded herself. *You're behaving like a child.* She carefully wiped away a stray tear that had managed to escape and was now running down her cheek. *For God's sake, this is just one night.* It wouldn't be long before they were together all the time. In some lovely Georgian townhouse in Oxford. She had heard that the city was a bomb-free zone as rumour had it that Hitler had earmarked it for his new headquarters. She could escape everything. Her life and this bloody awful war.

But there was this niggle in the back of her mind. *Had Theo been telling the truth?* She'd heard him mention David before, but not his girlfriend. As soon as the thought came to her, she dismissed it. How could she possibly think something so awful? Honestly, she was getting paranoid. She should be pleased that the man she was going to marry had such a lovely nature as to sacrifice a night out for the sake of his friend's happiness.

As Helen walked back along Crowtree Road, she started thinking about her father. Just because he had rejected her didn't mean that every man would ultimately toss her aside. But as she walked she could feel the anger and hurt rise again. She stopped herself thinking about her dad, something she was becoming quite proficient at. She had even distanced herself from Rosie and the women welders. If she had next to nothing to do with them, it would also be easier not to think about Gloria – and Hope.

Halfway down the road she heard the braying of horses. The heavy sound of their hooves on the cobbles told her they were the Vaux horses, pulling the brewer's drays to deliver beer to the local public houses. As they trotted by she stood still and admired them. They never failed to take her breath away.

As Helen followed their journey down the main stretch of road, she saw others, like herself, staring at the two greys. There was one woman in particular with her baby on her hip, both watching the live early-evening street performance. The baby had a dark mop of hair and was waving a tubby little arm at the horse and squealing with excitement. When the woman's head turned she instantly recognised the child's mother.

Gloria!

Helen panicked. She should have turned then and there and carried on walking – away from the last two people on earth she wanted to see. But it was too late, Gloria had spotted her.

'Helen! Helen!' Gloria was shouting so loudly other pedestrians turned to look.

There was no escape.

After calling out Helen's name, Gloria stuck her hand in the air and waved frantically, wanting to keep her attention, to show her that she wanted – needed – to talk to her.

'Say goodbye to the horses!' Gloria kept her voice light and cajoling as she put Hope back into the pram, crossing her fingers that her daughter would not object and start screaming the street down. She let out a sigh of relief as she started pushing the Silver Cross up the street and Hope nestled back down. A picture of contentedness.

'Hi!' Gloria was out of puff by the time she reached Helen, who had not moved an inch since hearing her name shouted out.

'I'm so glad I've bumped into you.' Gloria looked at Helen's face and thought she looked sad. Her mascara also looked smudged. Had she been crying?

'Are you all right?' The words were out before she had time to stop them.

'Yes, yes, I'm fine,' Helen said, staring at Gloria and then down at the pram. The hood was up so that Hope was obscured from view.

'It's only that you look a bit upset?' Gloria's voice was soft and sincere. She hadn't seen Helen up close for a long time. She was done up to the nines, but still looked drawn and rather jaded. She had to stop herself reaching out and giving her a cuddle.

Helen opened her mouth and for a split-second Gloria thought that she was going to talk to her. *Really* talk to her. That her guard was down and the true Helen was going to show herself. But then she saw the change, which was dramatic yet fleeting. Helen's expression morphed as though another being had just stepped into her skin. Her back straightened, her eyes glowered with anger and her mouth went taut.

'I'm fine, Gloria!' The words were clipped and hard. If the real Helen had been about to come out, she had been knocked back and the door slammed shut.

Still, Gloria persevered.

'I wanted to chat to you, Helen.' Gloria took a deep breath. 'About Jack. About yer dad.' She tried to keep her voice kind. Unthreatening.

Helen glared at Gloria.

'What? Do you want to plead his case to overturn his excommunication?' Gloria had no idea what 'excommunication' meant, and did not have time to ask before Helen continued. 'Did you want to beg that he be allowed to come back?' Helen stopped for a moment as a young couple, both in army uniforms, hurried past. She cast them a quick look and felt yet more envy.

'Do you want him to be allowed to come back to you – to the child you have had?' As she spoke her eyes fell on the Silver Cross.

'Helen—' Gloria tried to speak, desperate to tell her that this was not why she had stopped her. This was not why she wanted to talk to her. This was *not* about her wanting Jack back home, but about *her – Helen and her dad*. She wanted to ask her why she was ignoring his letters. *Tell her how much her father loved her and would always love her.*

'Well, let me tell you this, Gloria.' Helen took a deep breath. Her voice was starting to tremble. 'I don't ever want to hear my father's name ever again.' Another scoop of air. 'He is *dead* to me. Do you hear me? *Dead!* I no longer have a father. He can be sent to Outer Mongolia for all I care – as long as I never have to set eyes on him again. I only wish Mother had got shot of you two as well!' She glared down at the pram.

'So,' Helen manoeuvred her way past Gloria and the Silver Cross, 'if you can do me the courtesy ...' Gloria saw Helen looking into the pram as she spoke ' ... of just walking past me if we ever bump into each other again. I really don't think we have anything more to say to each other. Ever.'

And with that Helen turned her back on Gloria and her baby sister, now happily snuggled up in the comfort of her pram.

Gloria watched as Helen marched down the road as fast as her high heels would allow her, before turning right into High Street West and out of sight.

Once Helen had made it around the corner she suddenly felt dizzy. Her vision was obscured by the sudden appearance of tiny glinting pieces of shiny metal. She felt the pavement shift under her and she staggered into the entrance of J.G. Scott's on the corner of West Street. Putting her hand on the taped glass window of the popular milliners, Helen managed to steady herself. She felt her body trembling. The familiar tightness was once again squeezing her chest. She stood for a minute until the dancing stars had disappeared. She opened her handbag, pulling out her lighter and packet of cigarettes. A wave of nausea came over her, but thankfully she didn't throw up. That would be her ultimate humiliation of the evening.

Helen stood and smoked her cigarette, looking out at the world from the confines of the shop porchway. Even though they were in the middle of a war, and one that they looked unlikely to win at this moment in time, people still had smiles on their faces and a spring in their step. She wished she was one of those people, instead of someone who simply wanted to go home, go to bed and forget everything and everyone.

Helen tossed the half-smoked cigarette to the ground and started walking, keeping her eye out for a bus that was headed over to the other side of the river. She'd only gone a hundred yards when she saw a green single-decker with SEABURN on the front. Putting her hand out, she was relieved to see the bus slowing down for her, even though she was nowhere near a bus stop. Public transport was still a novelty for her, but since there had been a ban on fuel for private cars she had been forced to use the Corporation's trams and buses. She still hadn't got used to waiting at a bus stop, but so far had found that if she smiled sweetly and waved a gloved hand out as though she were hailing a taxi, the driver would generally stop and let her on.

After she sat on the first spare seat she saw and paid her fare to the young clippie, Helen looked out the window as they chugged across the Wearmouth Bridge. She could see Thompson's in all its grandeur on the riverside, and as always when she saw her place of work, she felt a swell of pride. The lift in her mood that seeing the shipyard gifted her soon dropped, though, when thoughts of Thompson's led to thoughts of her father, which led back to her seeing Gloria.

She had told Gloria straight, hadn't she? She should feel good about her little speech and how Gloria had simply stood there and taken it all, but she didn't. She couldn't pretend it had made her feel even a little good. Far from it.

As she contemplated the whole sorry scene, she felt pretty wretched. There might have been a time when Helen would have revelled in putting Gloria down and giving her a good tongue-lashing, but all that had changed when she had seen Gloria being beaten. Now, every time she looked at her, she saw her bloodied face and felt sorry for her. Even seeing her kissing her father had not erased the memory of that afternoon and Gloria's heartfelt gratitude. Something had happened that day between them and Helen could not shake it.

'Side Cliff Road!' The driver's voice broke through her thoughts and Helen jumped off and walked the short stretch back home. She rang the bell, hoping that her mother would be at home to answer the door, usher her into the living room and ask what she had been up to. Helen waited, looking down at the little postbox that looked as though it had been there for ever now that the rosemary bush at the bottom of the stone steps had blossomed around it. After a short while, Helen gave up, got her key out and let herself into the main porch. She kicked off her heels, dumped her gas mask and handbag onto the tallboy and opened the inner door that led into the hallway.

'I'm home!' Helen's voice echoed around the house. She called out again but it was now obvious that no one was home. More than likely her mother was out with her friend Amelia, probably at the Grand, and as it was past eight Mrs Westley would have been long gone, especially as there was rarely anyone at home to cook for these days and her stews and shepherd's pies were no longer wanted.

And there it was again. Her father. There was no escaping him.

Helen walked into the lounge and over to the drinks cabinet. She knew she should probably have something to eat, a sandwich at least, but she just wasn't hungry. Not after this evening's fiasco. She'd have a gin and tonic and take it upstairs to her room. After she'd poured the tonic into the glass, she went over to the sideboard to retrieve the spare packet of Pall Malls she kept there. As she picked up a box of matches from the hearth, she saw that there were still a few embers glowing in the grate and what looked like the remnants of a couple of sheets of charred paper.

Her mother had obviously been having one of her clear-outs.

As Helen slowly made her way up the carpeted stairs to the sanctuary of her bedroom, she tried to cheer herself up with thoughts of Theodore and Oxford. Her heart lifted for a moment at the prospect of her new life, but by the time she reached the second floor and opened the door to her room, the little burst of joyful expectation had fizzled out.

Helen put her drink on her dressing table, unzipped her dress and sat down in front of the mirror to take off her make-up. She had been so pleased that he was finally taking her out on a proper date, just like other courting couples. It had become a bit of a bugbear of hers that they didn't go anywhere even remotely nice. Going to a variety of tawdry drinking dens in town had been a bit of a lark at first; it had felt like a game and she had been fascinated to see how the other half lived, but after a while the novelty had worn off and Helen had hankered after going somewhere more acceptable for people like themselves. Theodore had seemed keen but was yet to wine and dine her at the Grand, Palatine or Empress. He had invariably cried off going anywhere special, saying he was exhausted after a twelve-hour shift, and he had always managed to persuade Helen to simply spend the evening at his flat. At first this had been exciting and the few times she had allowed him to make love to her had been nice, although, in all honesty, it had not matched up to her expectations.

At least they had been careful, though, and Theo had reassured her that the 'natural family-planning method' they were following was 'a hundred per cent foolproof.'

Helen stood up and took off her dress and looked at her reflection in the mirror. Her body seemed to have changed since she had lost her innocence. She had become a woman in the truest sense of the word and she felt her body now reflected that. Pulling on her nightdress and climbing into bed, Helen tried to lose herself in a book, but her mind was too active. She gave up reading, switched off her light and lay surrounded by a swirl of gin-laced thoughts.

It wasn't Theodore, however, or even her father and Gloria, that she fell asleep thinking about – but the happy little face she had glimpsed staring up from the folds of her crocheted blanket, smiling at her.

Her sister, Hope.

Chapter Thirty-Five

'She just went off on one, saying that she never wants to see or hear anything about her dad ever again.' Gloria kept her voice low as she never liked to risk anyone hearing her talk about Helen or Jack.

'She spelled it out in no uncertain terms that I am not even to speak to her if I ever bump into her again, so there's not a lot more I can do.' Gloria sounded defeated. 'That girl's troubled, though. I just know it.'

'Oh dear.' Rosie didn't know what else to say. She hadn't been surprised by what Gloria had told her. She still sided with the other women in their belief that Helen followed in her mother's footsteps and could be incredibly hard, vindictive and totally self-centred.

'She said he was "dead" to her!' Gloria was still shocked by Helen's declaration, especially as Jack *had* nearly died.

Rosie looked across at Gloria as they walked over to the ladders that led onto the upper deck. They had been down to the lower deck to have a chat with the platers' foreman to see where he needed them next.

'Well, you've done all that you can possibly do.' Rosie let Gloria go up first. 'Now it's time to just concentrate on yourself,' Rosie grabbed the sides of the wooden steps and climbed up to the top, 'and Hope, of course.'

Gloria gave Rosie a hand as she reached the top step. They both stood for a moment, their hands shielding their eyes from the sun, admiring the bird's-eye view of the town, before walking over to the very tip of the bow where her squad had decided to eat their lunch. Dorothy was regaling the women with her and Angie's shenanigans from the previous night. Gloria and Rosie walked around a huge stack of metal piping and arrived at the women's makeshift picnic, by which time Angie had taken centre stage and was reading from a recent edition of *Woman* magazine.

'"I am serving in the Forces 'n find I'm going to have a baby."' Angie stopped and looked round at Dorothy, Polly and Martha, all sitting listening attentively, taking the occasional drink from their tin teacups. She smiled when she saw Rosie and Gloria approaching.

'And listen to this!' she said, her eyes wide. '"*Two men could be responsible!*"'

Her words were met with a loud tut from Martha.

'"*But I don't know which!*"' Angie looked up again to see Rosie and Gloria pull up two wooden crates as pews.

'Now, this is the part I can't believe. "*Both have offered to marry me, but I can't decide which!*"'

Dorothy let out a loud laugh. 'Go and tell them what she says at the end!'

'"*Would it be better to throw them both over and make a fresh start?*"'

Now they were all hooting with laughter.

'I don't believe that's a real letter,' Polly said, looking around at the women's faces.

'Nah, it's a proper letter.' Angie turned the magazine round to show them all, as if showing them the printed word was proof of its authenticity.

'I think they make it all up,' Polly said, refusing to believe a woman, and one serving her country at that, could be so wanton and have such loose morals.

'What does the agony aunt tell her to do?' Martha asked before taking a big bite of her doorstep spam sandwiches.

'Here, give it here!' Dorothy stood up and Angie relinquished the magazine. Dorothy pointed to the front of the magazine to show her audience the illustration of an attractive blonde woman in a brown ATS uniform, who was raising a perfectly arched eyebrow at a handsome soldier with a chiselled face and a mop of brown hair cut into a short back and sides.

'"You don't love either of them."' Dorothy had one hand holding the dog-eared magazine, the other raised in the air as though she were giving a sermon. '"Whoever marries you will never feel sure of you."'

She raised her voice dramatically.

'"Get over this trouble ... make up your mind to be morally stronger in the future!"' She suppressed a laugh. '"And marry when you find a man you can really love. Moreover, a man who will respect you before marriage."'

'Well, if that's meant to be real, I'll eat my hat!' Polly declared.

'Well, safe to say,' Dorothy said with a droll expression on her face, 'if women are having that much fun in the armed forces, I think Angie and I might well be downing our welding rods and signing up – pronto!'

'Don't you dare!' Rosie piped up. 'You're both needed here.'

'Yeah, speak for yourself, Dor, I'm gannin' nowhere. I'm quite happy here, thank yer very much.'

'Well, if the letter is true, I think it's shameful behaviour.' Polly was still shocked that women could behave in such a way.

'More like *stupid* behaviour!' Angie said through a mouthful of cold corned beef and potato pie.

Gloria looked at Dorothy and Angie and was glad to hear that both seemed to have their heads screwed on properly. She would hate to see them getting themselves into trouble.

'God, I hope they don't have women like her over in Gibraltar,' Polly said suddenly. She had never thought that Tommy might have met someone else.

'Don't be daft!' Gloria said. 'That lad's only got eyes for you. You've no worries about that.'

There was a general murmur of agreement.

'Still no letter?' Martha just came straight out and said what they'd all wanted to ask.

Polly shook her head.

'I just keep telling myself *no news is good news*.'

'I know I'm repeating myself,' Gloria said, 'but there's loads of reasons you've not had a letter. Last year I didn't hear from my boys for months – they'd sent me a letter but it's never arrived to this day.'

'Yes,' Rosie chipped in, 'and you don't know if he's been sent somewhere and he can't write to you. A bit like Peter.'

'Mrs Crawley, the woman who lives next door to Clements the photographers on our street,' Polly said, her voice despondent, 'she got a telegram the other day saying her Anthony had been declared "missing in action".'

'That doesn't mean he's dead,' Martha said sternly.

'Aye, the auld woman down our street, yer know the one who's got the fruit and veg stall in Jacky Whites Market?' Angie said.

They all nodded.

'Well, she got a telegram a few weeks back saying her Harry her youngest's a POW.'

Dorothy glared at Angie.

'I think what Angie is trying to say, in a roundabout way, is that if Tommy's a POW he won't be able to write, but if that is the case, which I'm sure it isn't, well, at least he's still alive.'

The women fell silent as they realised their words of reassurance were becoming anything but. They all knew the war was not going well, that every day in the newspaper there were more names of those killed in action, and there was not one of them that didn't know at least one person who had lost a loved one.

'Have you heard or read anything of what's happening over there?' Rosie perked up. They were more than aware that Polly's obsession with world maps, and just about everything to do with the war, was her way of coping with Tommy being away and doing such a dangerous job. Looking at Polly now, Rosie wondered which the greater torment was. Waiting for a letter, or knowing you weren't going to get one?

'I've not heard anything about Gibraltar,' Polly said. 'Everything I read seems to be about the war in the Pacific, about the Japanese taking over everywhere – the Philippines, Singapore ... The Germans taking Malta and North Africa. None of it looks good. And that's just what they're telling us.'

Feeling an even heavier mood descend on her squad – and herself – Rosie stood up and brushed off the crumbs from her overalls.

'Right, we've got twenty minutes left before we're back at it, so I reckon we nip down and see Hannah.'

They all followed orders, screwed their cups back onto their flasks, stood up, and swung their bags and gas masks round their shoulders.

'How's Arthur managing? I've not seen a lot of him when I've been round yours lately,' Gloria asked Polly as they made their way down the ladder one by one, their hobnailed boots clomping onto the steel decking as they jumped the last few rungs.

'Worried sick,' Polly said, tying up her long brown hair into her turban. 'Not that he'd ever admit it. He's been busy at the allotment with Albert. The pair of them are not just "Digging for Victory" for all they're worth, but I think they're also trying to produce enough fruit and veg to feed the five thousand.'

The women, who were all listening in to the conversation, chuckled.

'And what about Bel?' Martha's voice was low and her tone tentative.

Polly let out a heavy sigh.

'Oh, worse than ever. She's not going to rest until she finds her da, that's for sure. She's actually been knocking on doors up near Backhouse Park – she's convinced he was in service with her ma in one of the big houses there. She's even roped Maisie into looking for him.'

'I don't understand why she needs to know?' Martha said, puzzled.

'Me neither, Martha,' Polly said as they all trooped along the metal gangplank that led down to the main yard.

'I don't know who my real dad – or my real mam – is, but I've never wanted to find out who they are.' As Martha spoke she was unaware of the slightly alarmed look Gloria gave Rosie.

'So you *are* adopted?!' Angie couldn't contain herself. 'Eee, me and Dor always wondered, didn't we?' She looked at Dorothy, who was looking unusually mortified.

Martha let out a loud guffaw.

'Of course, I'm adopted, yer daftie! I would have thought it was really obvious?'

Angie didn't know what to say so looked at Dorothy.

'Well, you know, we didn't like to ask you, Martha. These things are personal, aren't they?' She looked around at Polly, Rosie and Gloria for moral support. For once she got it as they all nodded back, agreeing that this was, indeed, a subject that many would probably not want to discuss. Especially walking across the middle of a shipyard.

'So, you don't know anything about your real parents?' Dorothy asked, encouraged by Martha's openness.

'I call them my *biological parents*,' Martha corrected. 'But no, I don't know anything about them. Nothing.' This time Martha *did* catch the loaded look Rosie gave Gloria, and demanded: 'Why the funny look?'

'Oh, Rosie and I were just talking the other day about something similar, weren't we, Rosie?' Gloria looked at Rosie, who nodded back. 'And we are of the opinion that some stones are best left unturned.'

'Eee!' Polly chirped up as they arrived at the drawing office. 'My ma said exactly the same thing when Bel was going on about finding her da. She said, "Bel, you get to my age and learn that sometimes some things are best left well alone."'

Chapter Thirty-Six

Glen Path, Sunderland

1914

As expected, Charles returned to the house the day before Good Friday. This time, though, there was less pomp and circumstance. The staff were all the same and still had the same pseudonyms that Henrietta had chosen for them before his last visit, so there was no need to go through the whole rigmarole again.

Velma had told Pearl at least half a dozen times that if she wasn't needed upstairs, she was to come straight back down to the kitchen to help out. She had even told Pearl that if she managed to do so, she would make sure she kept some choice leftovers aside for her.

Pearl was chuffed. Since she had started work here she had tried all sorts of delicious foods, some of which she had never even heard of before. Velma had told her that she had hollow bones as it didn't matter how much Pearl ate, she was still 'as skinny as a rake'.

Each day Pearl would steadily work her way through the long list of tasks that had to be performed in her new, albeit temporary, job as chambermaid, starting with sweeping the halls at six thirty, then drawing baths, opening shutters, and airing beds after breakfast. Henrietta had her own maid, which meant Pearl really only had the master's bedroom to tend to and the guest rooms on the odd nights they had people stay over.

Agatha had told Eddy, who had then told the rest of the staff, that Charles's refusal to employ a valet was a sore point between the master and mistress and that they'd had an almighty argument about it on the first day of Charles's return.

Pearl liked the fact she had been given a new maid's outfit that consisted of a smart navy blue dress with white collar and cuffs, along with a starched white apron and cap. Henrietta had made a great show of giving it to her, telling her that it was her 'afternoon livery', but she could wear it all day, and she could keep it after she had finished her short stint as a chambermaid as she might well be required to do more work upstairs in the future, since 'maids these days seem to be fly-by-nights' and it would be good to have a stand-in.

Pearl knew most girls would have loved to have been promoted to a position upstairs, even if it was just on an ad hoc basis, but she didn't enjoy it anywhere near as much as downstairs with the cook, where the atmosphere was warm and there always seemed to be chatter and laughter, which had the bonus of stopping her from thinking too much about Maisie. Her baby girl still paid her frequent visits in her dreams at night, but it was now almost nine months since she had given birth and although she still carried the pain and heartache with her, she had started to accept that she really had not had a choice in giving up her daughter. She would never have been able to afford to feed her, never mind keep a roof over her head. And whenever she started thinking *But what if ...?*, she forced herself to remember Evelina's words: the couple would bring Maisie up properly, they were wealthy and respectable – working here and seeing how the other half lived had certainly made Pearl think about all the luxuries her daughter would have in life – and, most of all, they were coloured, which meant that Maisie would be accepted.

Generally, Pearl worked alone when she was upstairs. She made sure she did what she had to do well, but also as quickly as possible, adhering to Velma's instructions to come back downstairs as soon as she was finished with her chores so that she could help in the kitchen. And, as promised, Velma always put some little treat aside for her.

During the first week of the Easter break, Pearl would occasionally bump into the master of the house while she was hurrying along the corridor or coming out of one of the bedrooms. He would never speak to her, or even acknowledge her, but Pearl could feel his eyes on her until she had disappeared from view. Once he came into his bedroom after returning early from a ride and found Pearl turning down the counterpane. She apologised and made to leave the room, but he'd told her to 'Finish what you're doing!' His voice was deep and cold and Pearl had quickly fluffed up the pillows, closed the shutters, and made to leave. Again his eyes had followed her and he'd made no effort to move out of the doorway, forcing Pearl to squeeze past him. As she'd done so, she'd caught the sweet aroma of his aftershave, mixed with the distinctive smell of the stables. Coming out of the room, she'd been accosted by Agatha, who was hurrying along the corridor with a worried look on her face.

'There you are!' She seemed angry and Pearl wondered what she had done. 'Get your skates on! There's work to be done! Get downstairs and give the cook a hand. She's run ragged down there!' But when she arrived in the kitchen, having rushed down two flights of stairs, she'd found Velma humming away to herself, nonchalantly stirring a variety of pots she had on the hob of the Aga, looking as far from run ragged as could be.

During the second week the house seemed to be constantly busy with visitors, mainly sombre men dressed in smart, expensive suits who spent hours in Charles's office, talking business and foreign affairs. Most evenings were taken up with dinner parties or having friends or work acquaintances around for drinks.

As the second week came to an end, Henrietta informed Agatha that Charles was due to leave on the Tuesday and she wanted to throw a farewell party for him on Monday. An air of relief seemed to emanate from the staff; a sense that the finishing post was in sight and they couldn't wait to get there. Pearl was also glad her time as a chambermaid was nearing an end. She would never say so, but she found the work boring, and had also started to feel a little uncomfortable around the master. He would often appear unexpectedly, and had taken to returning from his rides or trips into town just in time to catch Pearl as she was carrying out her late-afternoon chores.

'Just one last push!' Agatha told them on Monday morning. 'Mistress Henrietta has told me she wants to make the party this evening the best yet, so we've got our work cut out!'

All day the house was abuzz with people coming and going; crates of wine, port and Henrietta's best 'Russian water' were brought in through the tradesmen's entrance at the side of the house. The butcher boy arrived early, barely able to ride his bike it was so heavily laden with just about every type of meat imaginable. This was not to be a sit-down meal, but rather a constant drip feed of what Pearl had heard were called 'canapés' or 'hors d'oeuvres'.

After doing her regular chores in the morning, Pearl was then tasked with cleaning and preparing the reception room where the party was to be held. Everyone was working themselves to the bone to make the evening as extravagant and as lavish as Henrietta's tastes dictated.

When the first guests started to arrive, Pearl was given a quick brush-down and a new apron to cover her navy dress. For the next few hours Velma slaved over vol-au-vents stuffed with salmon, and what looked like miniature Scotch pancakes laden with duck pâté or dollops of cream cheese with carefully crafted strips of ham.

It was Pearl's job to carry all these wonderful concoctions up to the party on a large silver tray. It didn't take long before the tray was empty and she was returning to the kitchen, swapping it for another. Pearl was surprised to see the master of the house so jovial and animated. He was like a different person when he was in company and she wondered if perhaps they had all got him wrong and that he was just quiet when he was on his own.

By nine o'clock the party was in full swing. All the food had been consumed and Henrietta told Agatha that they would manage just fine for the rest of the evening.

Everyone made a beeline for the kitchen, where they slumped around the table, exhausted, but also content now their work was done; both the master and the mistress seemed happy with the fruits of their labour, and, moreover, Velma had kept aside enough leftovers to go around. There was also a bottle of brandy that hadn't made it upstairs, as well as a big pot of tea in the middle of the table.

'Well, pet,' Velma said to Pearl, 'it'll be good to have you back where you belong – down here!' She let out a hoot of laughter, suggesting she had been at the brandy already.

Pearl was glad too. As glad as she was tired. So tired, that after eating her fill of leftovers, and slurping down a cup of sugary tea, she slipped off to bed – the first to leave the merry little party in the kitchen.

Pearl practically crawled into her bed and immediately fell into a deep sleep. Images of her beautiful, dark-skinned baby seeped through from her subconscious and she saw Maisie crawling towards her, smiling and gurgling – her distinctive mop of curly brown hair dishevelled, as though she had just woken. She was reaching out with her two pudgy arms, her little hands clenching and unclenching as she tried to grasp her ma.

Pearl tried to reach out and pick her up, but for some reason she couldn't, something was stopping her. Panicking she felt her arms being pulled backwards. With all her might she tried to free them. Pearl cried out, but no sound could be heard. Her neck was hurting. There was something around her neck, stopping her from moving, from shouting out, from breathing! Her panic intensified as she furiously gulped for air.

The vision of Maisie's face desperately trying to get to her started receding into the darkness. Pearl caught one last look at Maisie's confused little face as her light hazel eyes frantically searched for her.

Only then did Pearl wake up, expecting to be free from what had fast been turning into a nightmare.

Only then did she realise that the night terror she was experiencing was real.

There was no Maisie, but she *was* suffocating. And her hands *were* behind her back – held there by someone who was gripping both of her wrists so tightly she thought her bones would break. A hand was around her neck and was squeezing it with increasing pressure.

Her face was being squashed into the pillow. She was choking. Pearl managed to lift her head a fraction and gasp for air, her eyes straining to see who was behind her. And that was when she caught sight of a strand of blond hair – and then the flash of a man's profile.

It was the master.

He was pressing his whole weight on top of her. He was stronger, much stronger than she would have imagined a man of his stature could be. He was strangling her and then releasing his grip, allowing her a few precious seconds to suck in air.

And then she felt an awful pain – the searing violation of her person.

She screamed but her desperate pleas for help were silenced as he pushed her head down into the pillow to muffle her cries.

Pearl was trying desperately to thrash her body around with every ounce of energy she had. Her arms flailed as she tried to grab and scratch. Anything to get free.

She knew it was hopeless, but she kept on and on, until the hand around her neck squeezed her more tightly. Until her vision clouded over and darkness prevailed.

Only then did the pain stop.

When Pearl woke she had no idea what time it was, only that it was still dark outside. Her mouth was so dry she could hardly swallow and every part of her body felt sore and bruised. She slowly rolled herself on to her back. She was still wearing her cream cotton nightie, and her bedclothes looked ruffled, but no more than normal.

For a second Pearl thought that she had simply woken from some horrendous nightmare, and that was all it was. Her little bedroom looked the same as it always did. Her nightie was covering her modesty. Her bedclothes were even pulled right up to her shoulders.

So why did her body feel like it had been pummelled, pushed and pulled out of shape?

Pearl sat up, but as soon as she moved, her head started to bang as though an invisible fist was punching it over and over again. She reached for the glass of water she always kept on the bedside table. It was still there. She picked it up and took a large glug. It relieved the dryness but it still hurt when she swallowed.

Grappling around for the matches, she found them on the floor by the side of the bed. She reached down and picked them up. For some obscure reason, Henrietta's voice calling her 'the little match girl' came into her head. It seemed to take all of her energy to simply strike the match and light the candle.

Again, Pearl looked around her and everything appeared just as she had left it before she had fallen into bed that night.

But still she knew everything was not as it had been when she went to bed.

She stood up and had to sit back down for a moment.

Again, she attempted to stand up. This time she succeeded and managed to take two steps to the dressing table, where she picked up her small hand mirror.

She looked at her reflection.

Her neck was bright red and starting to bruise. She put the mirror to her back and saw more patches of purpling skin.

She put the mirror down, and cautiously pulled up her nightie. In the flickering candlelight Pearl stared down at the bloodied and bruised markings. She stood in the semi-darkness, statuesque, clutching her nightie, looking at her body, or rather *a* body – one that no longer felt like her own.

She stayed like that for what felt like a long time. Her mind whirring, her eyes darting about her as if to check that he was not still in the room. Stupid, she knew, as there was barely enough room to swing a cat, never mind hide, yet still the fear gained momentum. She dropped down on all fours and looked under the bed. Nothing. She pushed herself back up onto her haunches and stayed crouched down on the floor, listening, terrified that he might return.

The house was quiet. When she had fallen asleep last night it had been full of life and laughter. She'd heard the music and had thought it sounded nice. Now the quietness felt deathly; even the old copper pipes weren't making their usual lament.

It took Pearl ten minutes to clean herself up, put on her clothes, and stuff what few belongings she had into her big cloth bag. She left the maid's outfit that Henrietta had made such a show of giving her. She did not want to take anything from this place.

Not one single reminder.

And then she left.

As Pearl stole out the tradesmen's entrance, quietly tiptoeing down the gravel path by the side of the house, her heart in her mouth, her head thumping, petrified that the master would come and drag her back in, she was not to know that she had, in fact, left with something from that godforsaken house – and that 'something' would be a constant reminder of the horror, the violence and the injustice of what had happened to her that night.

Chapter Thirty-Seven

Thursday 30 April

Since he had seen Helen last – or rather since he had cancelled his date with her over a week ago – Theo had thought very carefully about what he knew he had to do and where would be best to do it. He had shied away from asking Helen to come to his flat for two reasons. First and foremost, he was worried she might cause a scene and alert the neighbours, who might even come knocking.

The second reason was that his resolve, and moreover his willpower, might fail him, so that on seeing her he might well end up trying to take her to bed one last time. And if he did that, he really would be skating on thin ice. He had bumped into Dr Parker the other day in the staff-room at the hospital, now a regular occurrence since he had requested a permanent transfer from the Royal to the Ryhope, and 'young John', as everyone seemed to call him, had started chatting about Helen. It could have been a case of paranoia, but there was something in his tone that suggested he knew more than he was letting on. Either way it had panicked Theo a little and strengthened his resolve to end his fling with Helen once and for all.

When he had rung Helen at work, he had made out he was taking her to watch the film they were meant to see on their last aborted date. In reality, when they met up he was going to suggest they go for a walk instead, and then he'd tell her. He wasn't looking forward to the inevitable flak he'd get afterwards, though. He knew he had slipped up with Helen. He should have simply stuck with the married Marions of this world; he'd known from the off that Helen was high-risk. He had seen it the first night he'd set eyes on her, the way she had clearly had the goo-goo eyes for Matthew, and then later on that evening when he had found her outside that grotty pub down from the museum, dithering whether or not to go in. She was not your average young woman. But perhaps that had also been the draw – it had been risky and therefore more exciting.

Helen had been too much of a temptation. She had got his race pulsing. His need for a new high had won over the possible pitfalls, and he had revelled in the adrenaline buzz of seducing and then bedding this beautiful, intelligent and very sexy woman. A woman whom most men would give anything just to date, never mind sleep with. He had initially told himself to walk away when he realised that Helen was still a virgin – he had been surprised to find that behind that magnificent bosom, swaying hips and veneer of confidence, there was, in fact, a naïve young girl.

When she had come back to his flat for the first time and he'd realised she had barely even been kissed before, he knew the sensible option would be to end it there and then. But he hadn't. The temptation had been too great. He had wanted and desired Helen. And he'd had her.

He loved his wife and he enjoyed making love to her, but it was not the same as the passion he felt when he slept with other women, and certainly nowhere near the heights of passion he'd experienced with Helen. But now his hourglass was just about empty; his time with Helen had come to an end.

However, this was not going to be easy, and he had not reckoned on her having such a powerful and influential family. Nor had he banked on her determination to live a picture-perfect married life in Oxford.

As he splashed his face with cold water and put a comb through his hair, he looked at his reflection in the mirror and saw a worried man looking back at him.

It was time to pay the piper.

Helen put on a thick layer of red lipstick, and then looked at herself in her full-length mirror. Pleased with her reflection, she made her way down the stairs and out of the house, which was, as usual, deathly quiet.

As she stepped out into the fresh air she felt the evening sun on her face and felt happy. Or at least happier than she had been this past week while she had waited for Theo's phone call. This had been the longest she had gone without meeting up with Theo. Perhaps it was because of this that doubts had started to creep into her head. Worries that he might be losing interest in her. She'd had to stop herself from picking up the phone at work, dialling the number for the Ryhope and asking for a message to be relayed to him. That would have smacked of desperation.

Her mother had told her that she was arranging a dinner party in Theo's honour next week and that this time there were to be no excuses. There had been two occasions lately when it had been arranged for Helen and Theo to go to the Grand and have a drink with Miriam, who was still insisting on meeting Theo before her grandfather. 'I am your mother!' she had declared. 'Your grandfather will just have to wait his turn.' But both times Theo had apologised profusely when he had met Helen, telling her about the terrible traumas he had witnessed that day in theatre and how he was in no fit state to make polite small talk. Helen had gone on to the Grand alone to tell her mother, who had not been at all impressed.

The dinner party was going to be Theo's introduction to the family. It might even precipitate a proposal from Theo. These days, dating for nearly four months was a long courtship and weddings were often taking place within just weeks of a couple going on their first date.

Getting on the tram that ran the stretch of the coastal road as far as Seaburn, Helen paid her fare and climbed the iron spiral stairs to the top deck. She had developed a love of riding on the trams since being forced to travel with the hoi polloi, especially now they were heading towards summer and the chewing winds from the North Sea, although still pretty constant, were not as bitingly cold.

As the tram trundled down Dame Dorothy Street, Helen looked across at Thompson's. She had almost burst with pride today at work when Harold had come to see her to tell her that they were officially the second-busiest yard, behind Doxford's, and that if they kept going the way they were they'd be looking at breaking a thirty-six-year-old production record. At least, Helen thought, I will leave the yard on a high when the time comes to move to Oxford. After Theo's proposal, her next aim was to get him to apply for a transfer back down south. She was sure they were just as much in need of surgeons in Oxford as they were up here. And if he couldn't make it happen, she was sure her grandfather would be able to pull a few strings.

Stepping off the tram in Fawcett Street, Helen cut through the town centre. She felt a little nervous that she might bump into Gloria and Hope again, but reckoned that if she did, Gloria had got the message and would simply pretend she had not seen her. Still, it would be better not to see her and Hope, full stop. It would only dampen her mood and she wanted tonight to go smoothly, especially as she had to break it to Theo that the dinner-party date had been set and he *had* to be there, come hell or high water.

Hurrying up Blandford Street, she admired her reflection in the shop windows before turning right onto Crowtree Road. As she did so, she spotted Theo almost immediately, pacing up and down in front of the main foyer.

'Hello, gorgeous.' Theo walked towards Helen, taking her arm and directing her away from the theatre.

'Darling,' Helen said, looking back over her shoulder at the entrance, now partially hidden by the congregation of cinema-goers. 'It's lovely to see you, but I thought we were going to the flicks?' She stared at Theo's face and saw that it looked unusually serious. 'Dear me! Why the stony face?' She let out a tinkle of laughter.

'Where are you taking me, Theo?' As she spoke, Helen found herself being practically marched back down Blandford Street. 'I can only go so fast in these heels!' she tried to joke.

As they turned right down Waterloo Place and then left into Holmeside, Helen saw the museum and then the penny dropped. *Theo was taking her back to the place he had first set eyes on her.* The evening, he had told her, that he had fallen for her 'hook, line and sinker'. She was so silly! The reason for the sombre look was actually that he was nervous. He was going to get down on bended knee and propose to her. Obviously he couldn't do it in the back row of the theatre – which meant he must be taking her somewhere special.

'Let me guess,' Helen purred. 'You're taking me to the museum?'

Theo looked at Helen as though he had no idea what she was talking about.

'I'm guessing it's open late tonight. Some exhibition on?' Helen let Theo take the lead as they crossed over the road.

Theo finally spoke. 'Actually, we're going for a walk in the park.'

Helen couldn't help but feel a little disappointed. She had loved the Winter Gardens and Mowbray Park as a child, but they were looking a bit sorry for themselves as of late, their mix of landscaped and natural beauty pockmarked by a recent smattering of incendiary devices.

Crossing over the busy Burdon Road, Theo took Helen's arm and guided her through the side entrance.

'Helen, I need to say something to you,' Theo said, finally stopping as they reached the edge of the large man-made lake. It passed through Helen's mind that there could have been more romantic spots for a proposal, but that didn't matter. Theo was finally going to ask for her hand in marriage.

'Yes, Theo?' Helen asked, coyly. 'What did you want to say?'

'It's rather difficult,' he said, taking hold of Helen's hand and then dropping it.

Helen took hold of his hand. He obviously needed a little help.

'I'm so sorry, Helen.' Theo looked at Helen through the same puppy-dog eyes he usually tried to seduce her with, but this time he was hoping they would bring him clemency.

Now it was Helen's turn to look serious.

Proposals did not start with an apology.

'Sorry?' Helen's voice was as sober as her look.

'Yes, I am sorry, truly sorry.' Theo paused. He had been practising this speech for the past hour and knew it was important to give Helen a chance to absorb what he was telling her.

'I'm afraid I have misled you rather terribly ... I have been what they call in the films a "cad" ... A number-one, prize cad, in fact ... But it was not through any kind of maliciousness that I have found myself acting in such a way, but because I did fall for you – like I have told you before, I fell for you truly, madly and deeply.'

Helen was now staring at Theo, failing to take in what he was saying.

'But I'm afraid I can't be with you. Not now. Not ever.' Another pause. Helen looked stunned. Speechless.

'You see, when I left Oxford last year, I also left behind a sweetheart. Someone I've known most of my life, and who I have been with since we were little more than youngsters.'

'Sorry?' Helen couldn't quite believe what she was hearing. 'You've what? You've got someone else?' Helen's face had flushed red. Her chest was also falling and rising and she could feel herself starting to hyperventilate.

'I'm so, *so* sorry, Helen, I know I should have told you from the off ... What I have done is inexcusable ...' Theo felt her let go of his hand. He looked around and saw a bench nearby. 'Helen, sit down, please?'

In a daze, Helen turned and walked over to the park bench and sat down. Theo perched on the edge, his hands clasped in front of him – inwardly praying this was not the calm before the storm. He had seen it before – shock followed by a huge eruption of fireworks. And unlike normal fireworks, these were not a pretty sight.

'I must stress that this was in no way intentional,' Theodore continued. 'I have never been unfaithful before. *Never.* But then I saw you, and you took my breath away ... And it all seemed so unreal ... Being here. So far away from home ... doing the job I do ... all those poor souls whose bodies and limbs have been scarred, mutilated, irreparably damaged.'

Theo stopped speaking. This was the part of his speech he wanted Helen to really listen to. So that she would see him as a worn-out, psychologically marred surgeon who was only here to save lives and had strayed from the path of good just this once. So that the life-saving work he did would go some way to helping her to forgive him this indiscretion.

'These are such strange times.' Theo took Helen's hand, but she instantly pulled it away. This was not a good sign. Theo braced himself for a potential explosion.

'I got lost,' he continued, hoping he might still be able to forestall the detonation. 'I got lost in *you*. You are the most amazing, beautiful, intelligent woman I have ever met.'

Helen's mind was working at a rapid rate, trying to adjust to the gargantuan reversal in which the complete opposite of what she had thought was taking place was actually happening. Her world had just been turned upside down. *He was breaking up with her!*

And not only was he dumping her – *he had another love!*

His words churned around in her head.

She had been deceived.

Lied to.

Cheated on.

As Helen sat there, an icy calm seemed to wash over her. A strange kind of disjointed reality that made her feel as though she was watching herself sitting on the bench, looking at Theo clenching and unclenching his hands, his face pleading and doleful. Helen's head shifted ever so slightly, her glistening emerald eyes bore into his and she heard herself speak – her voice low and calm, and a little unnerving.

'If that's the case, Theo, if you "got lost" in me, if you fell "truly, madly and deeply" in love with me, then why aren't you having this conversation with your Oxford sweetheart? Telling her that you no longer want *her*, but *me*?' Helen raised her eyebrows questioningly before continuing in the same cool and composed manner.

'If you are offered a choice of caviar or cod's roe, you don't opt for the roe, do you? Or do you, Theo?' Helen cocked her head to the side, demanding an answer.

'If I am more "amazing", more "beautiful" and more "intelligent", then why are we sat here now, having this tête-à-tête?' As Helen spoke she could feel the anger simmering under the surface.

How dare he do this? How dare he lie to her?

All this time he had *another lover*!

Worst of all, he was choosing the other lover over her!

When he still didn't speak, Helen continued. 'If you *really* meant what you said, and you *really* did have all these wonderful feelings for me, then why don't you tell your Oxford sweetheart that you've met someone you love more?'

Theo again tried to hold Helen's hand, and again failed to do so, before finally he spoke.

'Because, Helen, my darling, I know I would never be enough for you ... You might think I am now, but I know you would soon get bored ... Someone better than me would come along and then you would be stuck in a loveless marriage, resenting me and wishing you had played the field more. Found someone more your equal.'

This was the second stage of Theo's planned speech. The part where he convinced Helen that he was actually doing her a favour by ending their courtship.

'You're wrong.'

Helen's voice had softened and Theo sensed a minor triumph. He might stop the detonation yet.

'I think we could be perfect together.' All of a sudden Helen saw the images she had played over in her head again and again every night to help her sleep. 'We could have a lovely marriage, a wonderful house, a family, in Oxford—'

'But that's just the point,' Theo interrupted, 'you might like it down in Oxford at first, but you would miss your home town, I know you would. You might think you'd like it amongst the "dreaming spires" you keep describing, but it's different down south, the *people* are different. You'd grow to hate it.' Theo took a deep breath.

'But most of all, you love it here. That's as plain as day. You love your shipyards. You'd be lost without them.' These were the only true words Theo had spoken in all the time he had been with Helen. They also heralded the moment when he unwittingly pulled the pin out of the grenade he was holding.

'How dare you tell me what I would and would not feel!' Helen stood up so that she was glaring down at him.

'You have no idea! No idea what I want or don't want! It has obviously escaped your notice, even though I would have thought it was as clear as day, that I *can't wait* to get shot of this place!' She flung an arm around her as if to demonstrate her point more succinctly. '*Can't wait* to leave here. To start a new life somewhere different!' Helen's words were spoken with such passion that spittle came out of her mouth.

Theo stared at this woman and realised that he really didn't know her at all. He'd known she was determined to move to Oxford – but not how *desperate* she was to do so.

'I'm sorry.' Theo stood up so that they were at eye level. 'I'm so sorry. I just don't know what else to say—'

They looked at each other for a moment. Theo knew he had done the hard part. There was no going back now, and they both knew it. Helen knew it was finished. And he knew it had never really begun.

Theo watched as Helen turned on her heel and walked like a model on the catwalk down the shale pathway and back out of the park, taking what little dignity she had left with her.

Theodore waited a few minutes before he left the park himself. All in all, he mused, it hadn't gone at all badly. There had been no real hysterics, no awful shouting and screaming, no causing a scene in public that he'd had to smooth over. He'd actually come out of it all relatively unscathed.

As he walked to catch his bus back to Ryhope, he checked his watch. He was easily going to make it back to the flat in time for Marion's visit.

Stepping out of the park, Helen felt her body slump. Her legs felt like jelly and she had to stop for a moment and steady herself by the small wall that ran around the park's perimeter.

'Are you all right, miss?' An elderly gentleman touched her gently on the shoulder. Helen felt like collapsing into the old man's arms and sobbing her heart out, but, of course, she didn't.

'Yes, yes, thank you,' Helen said, forcing her mouth into a semblance of a smile. 'I'm fine. Just came over a little dizzy, that's all.'

The grey-haired man, who was dressed in a slightly shabby-looking three-piece suit and sported a lopsided dicky bow, was looking with concern at Helen over the top of his gold-rimmed spectacles.

'Come for a sit-down and a cup of sugary tea. I'm just meeting my daughter Georgina in the café up Holmeside.'

'That's such a kind offer,' Helen said. 'But I think I'm best getting myself straight home.'

The old man tipped his hat and crossed over Burdon Road, while Helen walked straight ahead and waited until it was safe to cross the wide expanse of Borough Road. As she waited for two trams to pass by, she wished, more than anything, that it was winter and there was a blackout so that no one could see her; she could simply fade into the darkness. But it was a lovely spring evening, just gone half seven, and the town was still enjoying daylight.

The road now clear, Helen hurried across to the other side, looking right as she did so, her eyes seeking out the entrance of the public house where she had first met Theo. She couldn't stop her eyes shifting left to the large Victorian house where Gloria lived in her little basement flat. She thought about the day she had bumped into her there, and then again the other week when she had seen her in town, and for a ludicrous moment she had an urge to veer off to go and see her.

What is wrong with you! Helen immediately scolded herself. She really was losing it if she was thinking about going to see Gloria, of all people.

God, was she becoming some kind of masochist?

Helen forced herself to walk up Fawcett Street, past the town hall, where a bus and tram were unloading a few dozen passengers all done up for a night out on the tiles. Not wanting to get on any kind of public transport for fear of having to talk to anyone, Helen kept on walking. She felt as though she was wearing her heart on her sleeve, and that anyone who so much as cast a glance in her direction would see her bare-faced distress.

By the time she reached Bridge Street, she seemed to be surrounded by couples, many of them in some kind of military uniform, hurrying past her arm in arm, laughing and chatting. When she saw even more happy faces waiting expectantly at Mackie's Corner under the big clock, Helen decided she could stand it no more and hopped on a tram. It was only half full as most people were going into town at this time, not heading home like she was. To a home, Helen thought, depressed, that seemed so cold and empty these days now her father had gone.

Still, tonight it was probably a blessing. She couldn't face telling her mother that the dinner party was off, and that Theo had not only just dumped her, but had also been two-timing her.

Tears started to build. In the space of an hour all her hopes and dreams had been obliterated. Marrying Theo and setting up home in Oxford had been her salvation and now it was clear that dream had been a fantasy.

Passing the harbour, Helen had a brief thought of walking along the north pier until she reached the lighthouse, where she would throw herself into the slapping, frothing folds of the North Sea and simply be no more. But she knew she couldn't do that, not because both north and south piers had been cordoned off since the start of the war, but because she knew she didn't have it in her to take her own life. Like this old metal workhorse of a tram, she knew she would just have to keep trudging on.

Helen forced herself to get up out of her seat and make her way down the spiral staircase. When the tram stopped on the corner of Side Cliff Road, she got off. She knew what she would do when she got inside, knowing that the place would be empty. She would pour herself a large gin and tonic, take it upstairs and finally simply cry her heart out without having to worry about anyone hearing her.

As she opened the front gate, she looked at her mother's postbox. She saw a white envelope sticking out of the opening and went to pull it out, but it had been pushed too far in to retrieve without tearing it, so she left it there.

As she put her key in the front door, Helen hated to admit to herself, but it was at times like this that she really missed her dad.

Chapter Thirty-Eight

'You here for an interview?' Alfie leant out of the window of the timekeeper's cabin so as to be heard above the noise of the shipyard. The pretty blonde woman standing at the gate looked puzzled.

'You here for a job?' Alfie shouted out, pointing up to the admin building, the top of which was just visible.

'No, no,' Bel said, raising her sister-in-law's lunch box in the air by way of explanation. 'Polly Elliot – one of the women welders – forgot her lunch.' Bel kept her explanation short as it was nigh on impossible for her to hear her own voice, never mind for anyone else.

'Who?' Alfie shouted back, his hand to his ear.

'Polly,' Bel yelled. 'Elliot.'

The expression on Alfie face's changed, showing he had heard. He waved Bel through the main gate with a smile.

As soon as Bel entered the yard she stopped in her tracks. The sight that greeted her took her aback. She had been brought up within walking distance of most of the town's main shipyards, had seen them from a slightly elevated perspective whenever she'd crossed the River Wear, but she had never actually been *in* a shipyard.

For a few seconds she simply stood and stared. The hit on her senses had the effect of taking her breath away momentarily. The sight of so many flat-capped workers – hundreds – working mostly in groups, a smattering on their own, others standing communicating with their hands – the sign language of the shipyard. The sound of the machinery, clanking and hissing, banging and clashing, was overwhelming, but strangely enough it was also oddly musical – disjointed and chaotic, but occasionally rhythmic. And then there was the smell, a familiar one she had come to recognise as the smell of the shipyards from all the times she had washed Teddy's overalls and, more recently, Polly's.

As Bel started walking, looking about her, trying to find Polly and the women welders, the loud, deep blare of the klaxon sounded out the start of the lunch break. The whole yard changed in an instant. It was as though someone had waved a magic wand – the noise stopped, and a calm descended.

'Who yer looking fer, pet?' an old man, rolling himself a cigarette as he stood at the foot of a massive crane, called out.

'Rosie's squad …' Bel started towards the man. 'The women welders.'

The man pointed over to the quayside, the half-made cigarette scissored by his blackened fingers. Bel glimpsed the top of a bright orange turban. 'Thank you!' She smiled at the man and walked the hundred yards over to the women. As she neared the quayside she saw Martha sitting on a large wrought-iron cleat, sandwiches in her lap, chatting to Dorothy and Angie, who had commandeered the top of a wooden workbench, legs dangling, their hobnailed boots not quite touching the ground.

'Bel!'

Bel turned her head slightly to see Polly walking towards her.

'You're a star!' Polly was looking at the lunch box her sister-in-law was holding. 'But you shouldn't have. I could have just grabbed something from the canteen.'

'Not without this.' Bel pulled Polly's little cloth purse out of her coat pocket.

'Eee.' Polly shook her head. 'I think I'm going doolally.'

Bel laughed. 'You've always been doolally, Pol. Nothing new there.'

'Bel!' Rosie had just come back from chatting to the plater's foreman. 'What brings you here?'

'I forgot my bait – as well as my purse,' Polly said, sitting down on the stack of pallets and patting a space for Bel to join her.

Bel shook her head. 'I'm not staying long.'

'Bel!' Dorothy and Angie shouted out in unison and she looked up to see the pair jumping off the bench to come and see her, followed by Martha.

'Everything all right, Bel?' Gloria was walking towards her, having just returned from the women's washroom.

'Yes, Hope's fine,' Bel was quick to reassure her. 'Agnes is looking after her today. I'm just dropping off Polly's lunch and then I'm off to meet Maisie.'

'Ah, she said she was going out with you this afternoon,' Rosie said. 'You two off anywhere nice?' Maisie was now well and truly part of the furniture at Lily's, but she still kept her cards close to her chest, never giving too much away about her personal life.

Bel looked at the women.

'Well ...' she hesitated. 'Actually, we're on a bit of a mission.'

'Ohh, sounds interesting!' Dorothy said as she and Angie sat down next to Polly, who was making a start on her sandwiches.

Bel felt herself blush. 'It sounds silly saying it out loud ...' She looked at Polly.

'They're gonna try and find her da,' Polly said through a mouthful of ham and pease pudding.

Bel looked at the women, whose eyes had all widened in surprise.

'Well, good luck!' Martha said.

'Thanks, Martha.' Bel looked around her self-consciously. 'I know it's a long shot ...' Her voice trailed off.

'Well, I think it's nice that Maisie's helping you,' Gloria chirped up. 'It's what sisters are for.'

Everyone nodded their agreement, although Rosie thought it was rather odd for Maisie to do something when there wasn't anything in it for her.

'Eee, well, it's great to see you all!' Bel said, looking around at their surroundings. 'And to see you all at work as well!'

'Come on,' Polly said, putting her sandwiches to the side. 'I'll walk you out.'

'See yer later on.' Gloria went to sit where Polly had been.

'Yeh, 'n good luck on yer mission!' Angie shouted out.

'Bye, Bel!' Dor and Martha added their farewells as Polly and Bel turned and made their way back across the yard to the main entrance.

'That's the platers' shed,' Polly pointed out as they walked along the length of what Bel thought looked like a huge metal cathedral. 'That's where the platers' squad and the frame-benders shape the template designs for the ship's hull.' Bel caught a glimpse of thick sheets of steel and rows and rows of metal chains and hooks hanging from the high ceiling.

'And over there,' Polly redirected Bel's attention as they neared the entrance, 'is where Hannah and Olly work in the drawing office. And there,' Polly lowered her voice in a mock-conspiratorial manner, 'is the admin building where *you know who* works.'

They both looked up.

Polly took a sharp intake of breath. 'Talk of the devil. There she is now.'

'Where?' Bel asked, intrigued. Even though she had never seen Helen before, she felt as though she knew her.

'There, on the top floor, by the window. Smoking,' Polly said, trying not to look in case Helen spotted them both gawping at her.

Bel glanced up to see Helen, her shoulder-length black hair loose in gentle curls, looking stunning in a cherry red dress pulled in at the waist by a thin white belt that perfectly complemented her curves. She was taking a drag on her cigarette and blowing it out of the half-opened window. She seemed miles away.

'Golly me,' Bel said as she pulled her gaze back to Polly. 'She looks exactly like I thought she would!'

'I know, pretty stunning, eh?' Polly said as she tugged Bel's arm and guided her around a heap of scrap metal. 'Heavens knows why Tommy chose me!'

Bel threw Polly a look of reprimand. 'She's not a patch on you!'

'Ah, Bel,' Polly chuckled, 'you're nothing if not loyal.'

Bel turned and gave Polly a big hug.

'I'll see you later.'

And with that Bel left the world of the shipyard and re-entered the one where she hoped she would find what she was looking for – the man she had wanted to meet all of her life.

Her da.

Chapter Thirty-Nine

Zone Occupée, France

'*Billet, s'il vous plaît.*' The ticket collector waited for Peter to hand over his train ticket before quickly clipping it.

'*Merci.*' Peter took back his ticket and put it in his leather wallet along with his false French identity card and passport, glancing up to see the inspector move on to the next passenger.

As the train cut through the flat, lush green countryside of the Loire region, Peter eased back into his seat and looked out of the window. Seeing an elderly couple tending the front garden of their modest chalet, Peter felt thankful that he had been able to make Rosie his wife and hold her in his arms one last time. It had now been fifteen weeks since he had said his final goodbyes to Rosie; sometimes it felt like just the other day, other times as if it had happened in another life.

It had hurt to have to tell her that there would be no contact, but now he was glad of it, for even if he had been able to chat to her openly, he wouldn't have wanted to. He certainly wouldn't have wanted to tell her about what he had been taught at Wanborough Manor, that he now knew how to use a variety of weapons and explosives, as well as how to silently kill a person.

He also wouldn't want her to know that a number of agents had already been caught, and either tortured or killed.

He had never agreed with the theory that ignorance is bliss – until now.

The three weeks he had spent at Wanborough had been intense. Then Peter and all but two of the original recruits had been sent up to the north-west of Scotland for commando training. After that it had been down to Ringway in Cheshire for basic parachute training, and then on to Beaulieu, another stately home, on Lord Montagu's estate in the New Forest in Hampshire. There Peter had learnt all about personal security, communication in the field and how to maintain a cover story and act under police surveillance.

Two days ago, Peter had been put up in a hotel where he had spent his last night on British soil before being ferried to RAF Tempsford in Bedfordshire, a secret airbase that had been designed to look like an ordinary working farm. The SOE was using the cottage opposite as its base and it was there that Peter had received his final briefings and checks before being taken to a barn on the airfield's perimeter and issued with his firearms.

Peter's objective was clear – once he was over enemy lines in occupied France, his task would be to head up what was called a 'circuit' in Paris – a small group of men, and sometimes women, who would develop a resistance force in the heart of the city. There was already a network of these circuits, or *'réseaux'*, and each one was made up of a leader, a wireless radio operator, and a courier to carry and gather information. His particular circuit had been given the name 'White Light'.

Last night Peter had been flown across the Channel in a Whitley bomber by two pilots from 161 Squadron, hurling himself out in the dead of night and landing, as planned, in a field near the town of Mer, roughly 100 kilometres from Paris. The resistance fighters who had picked him up had thick accents, but having been forced to speak more French than English these past few months, Peter had no problems communicating.

After being taken to a safe house, then a railway station early this morning, Peter had boarded the eight o'clock train to Paris.

It was now nearly eleven o'clock and the scenic views from his carriage had been replaced by pictures of city life. As the train slowly pulled into the Gare du Nord, Peter stood up and made his unsteady way to the end of the carriage, where there were already half a dozen travellers, along with two German soldiers, waiting to disembark. Peter had seen a number of Wehrmacht uniforms, and even more swastikas, and had envisioned what the future might hold for England. It was an image that both repulsed and bolstered him. If ever there was a time to put one's life on the line, it was now.

As Peter stepped onto the platform he was pushed along by the swarm of passengers eager to be on their way. As he looked over their heads, he saw a man dressed in a rather shabby pair of trousers and a worn waistcoat, the traditional navy blue beret on his head. He caught sight of Peter and waved at him as though he were an old friend. As Peter neared him, he threw his arms out in an embrace.

'Bonjour, Pierre,' the Frenchman said.

'Bonjour, ça va?' Peter asked as the two men gave each other cursory kisses on both cheeks before walking back down the platform and out of the station, as though they had been friends all their lives and didn't have a care in the world.

Chapter Forty

Lily's, West Lawn, Ashbrooke, Sunderland

2.35 a.m., Friday 1 May

Rosie was woken with a start by the sound of sirens. She lifted her head from her desktop and the pillow of her folded arms. This wasn't the first time she had fallen asleep whilst poring over the bordello's ledgers, but it was the first time in a while since she had been woken in the dead of night by the mournful wailing of the air raid warning. Over this last week the Luftwaffe had started another blitzkrieg in retaliation for the British bombing of Lübeck. Exeter had been its first target, followed by a three-day onslaught on Bath, which had resulted in more than four hundred people being killed. It was inevitable that Sunderland would also come under attack. It was just a matter of when.

'Rosie?' The heavy oak door opened a fraction and Kate's head peeked round. 'You coming?' Her voice was tired but her large, doe-like eyes looked wide awake, despite the dark circles that seemed to have settled there of late. Rosie wondered whether her friend had been working late, or was just unable to sleep.

Rosie stood up and looked about the room, a little disorientated. What she would have given to simply stay there and sleep. She felt exhausted. But exhaustion was her sole aim at the moment, and that meant working flat out for as long as she could, so that when it came time to go to bed there was no argument – her body's need for sleep would easily overcome the galloping of her mind and its compulsion to keep churning over the same litany of worries.

Where was he now?

Was he all right?

Was he alive?

She knew Peter would have completed his training by now. He had told her that not everyone 'cut the mustard', but there had been no doubt whatsoever in her mind that he would be more than up to scratch.

Walking over to the door, Rosie smiled at Kate and followed her down into the cellar. The mood was subdued, which wasn't surprising as everyone had just been shaken from their slumber and parted from the warmth of their beds. Everyone had on thick dressing gowns and either woollen socks or slippers. Vivian and Maisie had also each brought a pillow with them and were nestling down on two narrow wooden beds that had been brought down after the last air raid, when it had finally been agreed that the war did not look likely to end any time soon. Lily had said they looked unsightly and took up too much room. She had finally got the cellar looking cosy and stylish, with its chaise longue, wind-up gramophone and drinks cabinet, but as George had pointed out, this was an air raid shelter, not an extra room for Lily to indulge her passion for interior design.

'You, *ma chérie*, should really be at home in your own bed, or rather your own cellar,' Lily chided Rosie on seeing that she had been right in getting Kate to see if Rosie was still in her office. 'You are working too much. You're going to wear yourself out and then you'll be no good to anyone.'

Rosie had heard Lily's lament numerous times these past few months, and she let it float over her head.

322

'Anyone for a snifter?' George asked, going over to the drinks cabinet while Lily sat down at the little fold-up wooden table and started shuffling a pack of cards.

Lily signalled that she just wanted a small one, and everyone else muttered a tired 'No, thanks.'

As George splashed Glenfiddich into two tumblers, Rosie sidled up to him. 'You heard anything?' She didn't have to say more.

'All quiet on the Western Front,' George said quietly. He had decided that should he hear any bad news about anything that might be happening in France, he would not tell her. Instead he would tell her only good news. Some might see this as dishonest, but he didn't care. He saw it as his responsibility to keep Rosie buoyant while Peter was 'doing his bit', and a bloody brave bit at that. If something happened to Peter, Rosie would be informed soon enough.

Trusting what George had told her, Rosie felt a little relieved and went to sit down on a threadbare but comfy settee that had a little side table at each end with gas lamps that were throwing out a good light. Rosie picked up a book she had purposely left there. It was a 'how to' book on all things business and finance. George had given it to her shortly after she'd got back from Guildford, knowing that Rosie's way of coping was to keep herself busy.

Rosie looked at Kate, who was curled up like a cat at the other end of the sofa. In her hands, as usual, were a needle and thread and a piece of fabric. Kate's hands always fascinated Rosie. Thanks in part to Lily, Kate had metamorphosed into a chic young woman who looked more French than English, with her short dark hair and simple black dress. It was her hands, though, that gave away her former life – gnarled and calloused, the nails bitten down to the quick.

'Any more news about Charlotte?' George asked as he sat down opposite Lily and waited for her to deal the cards.

'I got a letter the other day.' Rosie looked up from her book; she was reading but not really taking in the words. 'It was basically a few sentences on school and what she'd been up to, followed by a page and a half of reasons why it would be "best all round" if she were to come back here and live.'

'Oh, for Gawd's sake, Rosie,' Lily slammed her cards down on to the table, 'let the poor girl come home!'

George let out a nervous cough. 'Now, now, ladies, no arguments tonight!'

Discussions about Charlotte's return had caused Lily and Rosie to exchange more than a few harsh words, but although it had hurt Lily to hear that Rosie was a little ashamed and afraid of introducing her sister to Lily and the bordello as a whole, it had also cleared the air.

'Rosie and I have spirited discussions, George, *not arguments!*' Lily corrected.

George raised his eyebrows and took a drink of his whisky.

Seeing that Maisie and Vivian were wide awake and listening with interest to the conversation, Lily shot daggers at them. 'I thought you two were getting your beauty sleep over there. I need you in tip-top shape tomorrow. We've got that council bloke round about the Gentlemen's Club. It's going to be a busy day – bombs or no bombs.'

As if on cue they all heard a very distant, muffled explosion. The cellar fell quiet.

'Bloody Jerry!' George couldn't contain his anger.

They all looked up at the ceiling as if it would help them to find out where the bombs had just landed.

'I think I'll have that snifter now, George,' Maisie said, getting up but keeping her blanket wrapped around her. Her thoughts were with her ma, her sister and her little niece. She didn't mind admitting it now, but she would be devastated should anything happen to them. Maisie took her drink off George and sat back down on her temporary bed, telling herself that Joe would have made sure they all got to an air raid shelter in time. They would have had to have been quick, though. There had only been about twenty minutes – at the most – between the sirens going off and the series of blasts they'd just heard.

'Well, my advice to Rosie,' Maisie said, forcing her own and everyone else's thoughts away from what might, or might not, have just happened, 'would be to bring Charlotte back home, enrol her in that all-girls school up the road, and just bide your time ... Introduce her to us lot when it feels right.'

Rosie looked at Maisie, Vivian, Lily, George and Kate, who were all staring at her. She knew they were dying to meet Charlotte, as they had heard so much about her, and she felt terribly guilty that they knew about her reticence over bringing Charlotte to meet them all.

'I know you think I'm ashamed of this place, but I'm not,' Rosie told them. 'Not now ... I might have been a little before, when Lily and I had our "cross words", but things change.' A pause. '*I've* changed.'

Everyone was listening intently as it wasn't often Rosie opened up and spoke so frankly – especially about personal matters. 'I'm just not sure what the best thing to do with Charlotte is at the moment. Not sure what it is that's making her want to come back here.'

'Maybe she just wants to be with her big sister,' Vivian said. Tonight there was not a hint of Mae West about her, she was just a girl from the Wirral. 'Yer the only family she's got. She must feel like a missing part amongst all those little princesses with their mummies and daddies and more money than sense.'

'I wouldn't have put it quite like that,' George spoke up, 'but I think there might well be an element of truth in what Vivian says. She's at the age when she's got her own mind, her own thoughts, and perhaps, like Vivian's just said, she doesn't feel like she belongs and has decided that she wants to come home.'

Lily was sitting up straight, her pink floral dressing gown pulled tight around her and her black sleeping mask on her forehead. She didn't say anything, but didn't need to, the look of self-satisfaction that she had been right all along was clearly plastered across her face, along with smears of the white cream that had been applied before she'd gone to bed, but not rubbed in properly.

It wasn't too often that Rosie paid much heed to what came out of Vivian's mouth, but what she'd just said had struck a chord. Sometimes you needed to hear something without the sugar coating. 'Well, I think I'm going to have to do something, as this is not just going to go away like I'd hoped,' she acquiesced.

Knowing that there wasn't anything more to add to the discussion, Lily and George picked up their cards and continued their game of rummy. Vivian and Maisie were half chatting, half snoozing, and Rosie had her nose back in her book. Only Kate seemed unsettled. She sewed a few stitches and then stopped, before doing another few stitches and stopping again. After about ten minutes of the stop-and-start stitching, she gently pulled on Rosie's sleeve. When Rosie looked up, Kate could see that she had been dropping off to sleep whilst still holding her book.

'Sorry, Rosie, I thought you were reading,' she apologised.

'Don't worry,' Rosie said, seeing the look of concern through the flickering of the gas lamp. 'Are you all right?' She kept her voice low, sensing that Kate wanted this conversation to be just between the two of them.

'No, not really,' Kate admitted.

Rosie felt herself become more alert. Kate never admitted to feeling anything but fine and dandy. Rosie looked at Kate's pale, anxious face.

'What's up?' Rosie asked, her voice soft and cajoling. She shuffled a little nearer to Kate and tried to take her hand, but Kate pulled away.

'You won't want to be nice to me when I tell you what I've got to tell you,' she said. Her voice was now a whisper and croaky, as though she was on the verge of tears.

'I'm so sorry, Rosie ...' Kate's words were followed by an intake of breath as she tried to hold back her tears. 'I feel *so* terrible. *So guilty.*' Pools of tears were now starting to brim over and run down her pale face.

Rosie shuffled nearer, put her arm around her friend and pulled her close. It felt as though she was cuddling a child. Kate had always been waif-like; it was something she hadn't outgrown.

Another torrent of tears was precipitated by Rosie's show of love.

'And you won't be wanting to give me a cuddle when I tell you what I've got to tell you,' Kate said through her tears. Lily and George had heard and seen Kate's upset, but didn't let it show and instead carried on with their card game.

'I'm sure nothing can be that bad,' Rosie tried to reassure her friend, although she knew it must have been something serious.

Kate took a deep, slightly juddering breath, and pulled herself into a cross-legged position. Rosie gave her the space she needed and put her hands in her lap.

'Just before Peter came to see me, to give me your letter,' Kate began, 'I had someone come into the shop that I hadn't seen in a long while.'

Rosie was watching her friend's face and could see how hard this was for her. 'Who was the visitor?'

Kate looked at Rosie with sad, slightly frightened eyes. 'Sister Bernadette. One of the nuns from Nazareth House.'

Rosie tried to keep the shock from showing on her face. Kate had not had any dealings with the nuns since she had left their so-called 'care' and gone to live on the streets.

'That must have been a bolt out of the blue?' she said.

Kate nodded, her eyes now trained on Rosie's.

Lily and George were still holding their cards, but were no longer keeping up the pretence of playing and were quietly listening.

'Yes, it was … To be honest, it really knocked me for six. It was the first time I've seen any of the Poor Sisters of Nazareth since I left the home. I might well have seen some of them when I was on the street, but if I have, I can't remember … I didn't know what to say or do. I just stood there like a right lemon.' Kate's north-east dialect was now surfacing.

'She actually said to me, "Cat got your tongue, Kate!", but even then I still couldn't say anything, not that I think she would have been interested in anything I had to say.'

Rosie could feel her blood starting to boil. Kate had never talked about her time at the children's home, but Rosie had seen her as a child with bruises and welts on her skinny legs and over the years she had heard about some of the cruel and sadistic punishments the nuns had meted out to the girls and boys who lived under their roof.

'So,' Rosie asked quietly, 'what did this Sister Bernadette do?'

'Oh, she didn't do anything,' Kate said. 'I don't think she'd have dared. Not with me being grown-up 'n all. She just let loose a load of nasty words, yer know, the usual...'

Rosie didn't know and shook her head.

'Oh, it was always the same with Sister Bernadette: "You're the devil's child, Kate, spawned by Jezebel" ... What did she say? That was it ... I'm "doing Satan's work by dressing women like whores". All of that kind of thing.' Kate paused. 'Honestly, when I think about it now, it's almost laughable.'

Rosie didn't think it at all laughable.

Neither did Lily, from the look on her face.

'The thing is,' Kate said, her face clouding over, 'I felt like I was a child again. I hate to admit it but I was terrified.' Tears of frustration and shame appeared in Kate's eyes as she thought about how she had been so petrified she had wet herself while Sister Bernadette had beaten her down with words.

'I just stood there the whole time and didn't do or say anything.' She took a deep breath. 'And then, literally seconds after she slammed the door and left, Peter came in – with your letter. I can't remember a word he said, just him giving me your letter and asking me to pass it on to you.' Kate's face now showed pure guilt. 'But I didn't, did I? I shoved it in my pocket and I completely forgot. I shut up shop and came straight back here ...' She hesitated, knowing she had to tell Rosie everything, but knowing the shame it would cause her to do so.

'And I went straight into the kitchen, got the bottle of cooking brandy and took it up to my room and drank until I passed out.' Silent tears were now falling down Kate's cheeks as well as Rosie's.

'Oh, come here.' Rosie put her arms back around Kate and pulled her close. She cast a quick glance across at

Lily and could see that although her eyes had not filled with tears, they shone with pure anger. George was holding Lily's clenched fist in his own hand to try and subdue her. Lily had made Kate vow never to touch another drop again after she had helped her get through the awful withdrawal she had suffered coming off the drink.

'When I woke up and saw the letter, still stuffed in the pocket of my skirt, I was mortified.' Kate didn't say she had been sick in her sleep, nor that she had dry retched as she had panicked and pulled on clean clothes and then, despite a thudding head and waves of nausea, practically run all the way to Thompson's.

'I was so ashamed of what I'd done.' Kate became aware that Lily and George were also listening and she looked guiltily at Lily, who tried to put a look of reassurance on her face. It was hard, though, as all she wanted to do was get out of the damned cellar, march across town and give Sister Bernadette what for – and all the other nuns while she was at it.

'I felt so angry with myself,' Kate said, looking up at Rosie, 'so angry for being so scared and pathetic. So ashamed that I'd gone back to the drink and forgotten all about Peter's letter.' Another batch of tears came tumbling out. 'And when you went running off to catch Peter leaving on his train and you missed it, and it was all because of me, I just wanted to die. I felt so guilty.'

Kate looked across at Lily; it was clearly not just Rosie she felt as though she had let down.

'I didn't know what to say. I'd ruined everything and there was no making it better. I was trying to pluck up the courage to tell you – and Lily.' Another shame-faced look. 'And then you came bustling into the shop, telling me Peter had sent you a telegram and you were leaving for Guildford that afternoon. I was so happy for you, and so relieved that I hadn't totally ruined everything.'

'Oh, Kate, you didn't ruin anything at all!' Rosie reassured her. 'If anything you actually helped matters.'

Kate raised her head up to Rosie questioningly. Her tears had started to dry up and her body had stopped juddering.

'Well,' Rosie explained, 'it was only because I didn't get the letter, and didn't get to the station in time, that Peter sent me that telegram. And if I hadn't gone to Guildford I would never have had such a wonderful few days with Peter ... and he would never have proposed to me and we would never have got married.' Rosie looked down at Kate, who was listening intently.

'So, really, I should be thanking you for forgetting to give me the letter!'

Kate let out a choked laugh that was followed by a deluge of tears. Tears of relief that she had finally made her confession and been unreservedly forgiven.

She sat up and wiped her eyes with the back of her sleeve. 'I've wanted to tell you for so long now. There just hasn't been the right time. And you've been so busy with the bookkeeping and everything that I haven't wanted to disturb you.'

Kate's words unwittingly struck a chord of guilt in Rosie as it suddenly occurred to her that her need to run away from her problems had actually also caused her to alienate those closest to her.

'Well, don't ever worry about "disturbing" me, as you put it. There's more important things to life than ledgers and work.'

They both laughed at the irony, for it was their work that kept them both going.

It was their raison d'être.

*

Two hours later when the all-clear siren sounded out, everyone in the cellar woke with a start, gathered up their belongings and made their way single file up the stone steps and back into the hallway, from where they all trooped into the kitchen and plonked themselves around the table.

George went to use the house telephone, which was on the desk in Rosie's office. It was only ever used in an emergency, or on occasions like this. The switchboard operator put him through to the person he had asked for and they spoke for a very short while before George hung up.

Walking into the kitchen, he was met by five anxious faces.

'Four bombs. One landed in Mayswood Road, Fulwell. One on Fulwell fire station. One on the Fulwell Club and Institute. One on Ferry's dairy farm. Two dead.' George knew that none of the women round the table had friends or relatives in any of these places and he could see the looks of relief on their faces. He didn't tell them that it was a married couple who had been killed in a home-made shelter, nor that their son, who had delayed going to the shelter, had been saved.

'Right, I'm going to try and get a few hours' kip,' Maisie said, standing up now that she knew the east end had escaped intact.

'Me too.' Vivian followed suit.

Kate turned to Rosie and gave her a hug. 'Thanks,' she whispered in her friend's ear. 'Thanks so much for everything.'

Rosie gave Kate a hug back. 'You've nothing to thank me for.'

Watching Kate hurry back upstairs to her room, Rosie looked at Lily. 'I'll be getting off then.'

'I'll see you out.' Lily bustled out of the kitchen and down the hallway. She put her hand on the latch but didn't open the door. 'Those bleedin' nuns, they make my blood boil. As if there isn't enough evil in the world without them trailing around in their bleeding black habits pretending to be holier than thou. It's them that's doing "Satan's work"! I could throttle them with my own bare hands, I could.'

'Well, don't,' Rosie said. She wouldn't put it past Lily. 'It would only make Kate feel even worse than she already does, especially if they got the boys in blue on you.'

'You sound just like George!' Lily's mouth tightened and she finally opened the door to let Rosie go.

'At least now I know why she's been so jumpy every time someone enters the shop,' Rosie said.

'And has those bags under her eyes,' Lily added.

'I think we need to keep an eye on her, though,' Rosie said quietly as she left the house. 'And make sure she doesn't go back on the drink.'

Lily nodded.

As Rosie made her way down the steps, Lily called out: 'And you take care of yourself in that shipyard. Accidents happen when you're tired!'

'Yes, *Mother*!' Rosie shouted back over her shoulder, as she reached the front gate.

She didn't see the smile that appeared on Lily's face as she watched her go on her way.

As Rosie walked home it was starting to get light. Despite the lack of sleep, she felt awake and her mind was turning over what Kate had told her. *Wait till I tell Peter.* As soon as the thought passed through her head, reality slapped her across the face. Perhaps she was more tired than she thought.

333

As she sauntered down Tunstall Vale, she could hear the birds' early-morning songs and she wondered what Peter was doing at this precise moment. She knew France was an hour ahead of England, which could mean he might be getting up now and having breakfast. Reaching the little gate that heralded the start of Brookside Gardens, Rosie thought about the evening that Kate had drunk herself into oblivion and forgotten to give her Peter's letter. Despite not getting his letter that night, something had still compelled her to go and see him, and she had walked to this very spot and argued with herself whether or not to knock on his door. It was only her hard-headedness that had stopped her.

Closing the gate quietly behind her and walking quickly to her front door in case Mrs Jenkins was still up, Rosie's mind wandered to her last few days with Peter. She thought about their wedding day and the young couple who had been married after them, and the look of delight on the bride's face when she'd given her the bouquet of pansies.

Rosie wondered what had happened to them both. Had they managed to have time together before they were parted? Were they both still alive and well? Or had the ATS bride joined the country's growing list of young widows?

Was Rosie destined to join the swelling ranks of war widows?

Shutting the door behind her, Rosie pushed away a feeling that kept on coming back to her, no matter how many times she tried to bat it away.

A feeling that Peter did not expect to see her again.

Chapter Forty-One

General Post Office (GPO), Norfolk Street, Sunderland

One week later

Thursday 7 May

'It's been five months now – almost to the day!'

Gloria had the telephone receiver jammed against her ear, needing to feel as close as possible to the man who was both her lover and her friend. She didn't need to strain, though, to hear the total frustration and utter exasperation in Jack's voice.

'Five bloody months 'n I've not set eyes on you, or Hope, or Helen. The three most important people in my life! And one of those most important people won't even write to me, never mind talk to me!'

Gloria knew that the hurt cut deep with Helen. Very deep.

'The girl's not even met her little sister! Never held her. Never even said a bleedin' hello to the little mite!'

Gloria heard Jack sigh heavily. 'I know, Jack. I know.' There wasn't anything else she could say. Their situation felt hopeless.

'I'm of a mind to just jump on a train 'n come 'n see the three o' you. Sod the consequences!'

Gloria felt a shot of panic. This was not just about them. The lives and wellbeing of her friends – and their families – were at risk.

'Jack, you can't!' Gloria's voice was louder than she'd anticipated. She looked at the person in the next booth, fearful that she might have overheard. As far as they knew Miriam had no idea they spoke to each other on the phone, and she wanted to keep it that way.

'It doesn't matter how careful you are, someone would be bound to see you. To recognise you.' Gloria dropped her voice. 'We're even taking a risk chatting over the phone. She'd go mad if she found out.'

'There must be a way round this,' Jack argued the case. 'From what you've said, Hannah's future is more stable now that her aunty's got a new job … and if Dorothy and Angie get their own place, they'd be out of the firing line … And she can't exactly shame Rosie for courting an older man when she's married the bloke!'

'But that still leaves Martha,' Gloria said. 'God forbid the truth about her mam comes out. And it wouldn't just be Martha that suffered, but her poor parents.' Gloria took a deep breath. 'And God forbid Tommy thinks Polly's dilly-dallying off with some other bloke …'

'She's still not heard anything from the lad?' Jack asked.

'No, nothing,' Gloria said simply.

'Bet you Arthur's worried sick.' It was a statement rather than a question.

'Polly says he doesn't show it, but that's Arthur—'

'—tough as an old boot,' Jack finished off. 'Hard on the outside, but soft as clarts on the inside. Bet ya the old man's in bits.'

There was silence down the phone, but Gloria could sense Jack's disquiet.

'I hate to be defeatist,' Gloria said, 'but there is no way round this. Even if we somehow overcame the Martha problem and could put a stop to Miriam making up lies about Tommy, Hannah would still be devastated if she was forced out of her job in the drawing office. And there would still be Dorothy's mam – and her little 'uns – to think about. Can you imagine what would happen if she got found out? And Angie's mam. What would happen to her if her husband found out she's been having it away behind his back?' Gloria bristled as she thought of the violence she had been subjected to in her own married life. 'We couldn't have that on our conscience.'

'God!' Jack erupted. 'I could murder Miriam! As if we've not got enough to worry about with this goddamn war, without that bloody woman making life harder still!'

'I know, I know,' Gloria agreed, resignedly. 'It's madness. The whole world is in turmoil and all she can think about is herself.'

'And then there's Helen. I've no idea what's happening in her life. I've lost count of the number of letters I've written to her, but nothing! Not even one reply – not even a letter telling me to go to hell 'n stop bothering her!'

Gloria didn't say anything. Didn't know what to say. He would hate to see the person Helen was becoming in his absence. She certainly couldn't tell him the truth that Helen seemed to be turning into a replica of her mam, that she had been a nightmare at work – especially this past week or so, snapping at anyone and everyone. God forbid one of her staff make even the smallest of mistakes as they'd instantly find themselves on the harsh end of her tongue. Even her secretary, Marie-Anne, had started seeking refuge in the canteen at lunchtime, forcing herself to overcome her shyness just to get away from her sniping, bad-tempered boss.

'You not seen or heard anything from her, then?' Jack asked. The despondency he felt was clear.

'No, nothing,' Gloria lied. She still felt guilty, had done ever since she had seen Helen that evening in town. But what else could she do? She couldn't exactly tell him that she'd seen Helen and that his daughter had told Gloria she wished he was dead. That really would break Jack's heart. Well and truly. Sometimes it was kinder to lie. Gloria sighed to herself. She seemed destined in this life to be the keeper of secrets.

'You heard anything from yer boys?' Jack asked. His tone had softened. He knew how much Gloria worried about Bobby and Gordon, and how she kept those worries to herself.

'No, but I'm not expecting to. I've only just replied to their last letter.' Gloria heard voices in the background.

'Aye, all right!' Jack shouted back and Gloria knew their time was up. Jack always spoke to Gloria from the phone at the yard because that was where he now spent every waking moment.

'Sorry, Glor. I'm gonna have to go. Sounds like there's a problem. Give Hope a cuddle from me.'

'I will,' Gloria said.

'And, Glor.' Jack paused. 'I love you. Don't know what I'd do without you.'

After Gloria hung up and made her way to Tatham Street to pick up Hope, she couldn't help but think that Jack might be a lot better off without her. If she hadn't come back into his life he would still be here, working at Thompson's, and Helen would still love him and not want him dead – and the secrets of her friends would all be safe.

When she reached 34 Tatham Street, the door to the Elliot household was open.

'Only me!' Gloria called out. As she walked down the hallway, Bel appeared with Hope in her arms.

'Look who it is!' Bel was looking at Hope and waving at Gloria at the same time.

Seeing her daughter's happy, innocent face, as she leant towards her, arms outstretched, Gloria knew that she had been wrong. If she had not come back into Jack's life, then she would never have had Hope.

This little girl – their daughter – put everything into perspective, made everything worthwhile, worth enduring, and worth fighting for.

Chapter Forty-Two

One month later

Monday 8 June

Stepping through the front door and into the wide, terracotta-tiled hallway, Helen dumped her gas mask and handbag down on the mahogany console. As she did so she caught her reflection in the overhanging mirror. She looked awful. Her hair was a mess and seemed to have a will of its own these days. Her victory rolls had been well and truly defeated by the unrelenting winds that never seemed to give up, no matter what the season. And she had dark bags under her eyes, brought on, no doubt, by her inability to get a good night's sleep. She seemed to spend the whole night tossing and turning, and then when she did fall asleep, she'd have terrible nightmares and wake up covered in sweat.

'Anyone home?' Helen called out.

Expecting the usual silence, she was surprised to see Mrs Westley bustling out of the breakfast room.

'Ah, petal! Perfectly timed!' Mrs Westley turned, beckoning with her hand for Helen to follow her back through to the kitchen. 'I've just made yer favourite! Come on, or it'll get cold, flower!' Mrs Westley's voice cajoled. She had purposely stayed late. She hadn't seen much of Helen lately, but the past few times she'd not looked particularly well, and she certainly didn't seem at all happy.

Turning away from the mirror, Helen walked through the breakfast room and into the kitchen, where she was immediately immersed in the smell of Mrs Westley's home cooking and the gentle warmth of the Aga.

'Come and sit down, hinny,' Mrs Westley told her, putting a plate of steaming shepherd's pie down on the kitchen table. Helen did as she was told and when she started eating, realised just how hungry she was.

'You keeping safe at work?' Mrs Westley was of the mind that women shouldn't work in a shipyard, even if it was in an office.

Helen nodded whilst blowing on a forkful of hot mince and mashed potato.

'Well, don't you be overdoing it now. You're looking a bit peaky, if you don't mind me saying, pet.' Mrs Westley had known Helen since she was a baby and couldn't help but cluck over her like a mother hen, just as she did with her own children, even though they too were all grown up.

'I've been listening to the Radio Doctor every morning on the wireless,' Mrs Westley shuffled into the breakfast room to set the table for the morning, 'and he's all for looking after yourself.'

Helen had heard the cook mention the new programme, which was part of the Ministry of Food's popular *Kitchen Front* show, but so far she had only really heard Mrs Westley talk about the doctor's 'lovely, soft voice', rather than any of the pearls of wisdom he had thus far bestowed upon his audience.

'Mm,' Helen muttered through another mouthful of pie.

There was a comfortable silence between the two as the cook continued to put away pots and pans and wipe down surfaces, and Helen continued to enjoy her supper.

Their amicable quietness, however, was broken by the unexpected arrival of Miriam.

'Cooeee!' Her shrill voice sounded through the house, followed by the clip-clop of her heels stomping their way down the hallway, becoming more subdued as they hit the Windsor rug that covered the wooden floor in the breakfast room.

'Ah, Mrs Crawford!' Mrs Westley wiped her hands on her pinny when Miriam appeared at the doorway. 'I wasn't expecting you. Would you like a bit of supper?'

Miriam shook her head vehemently, her eyes glued to Helen and the shepherd's pie she was eating.

'Honestly, Helen! You're just like your father! That was always his favourite.' Miriam swung her attention back to the cook, throwing her a look of pure admonishment. She didn't need to say what she was thinking.

'Well,' Mrs Westley said, reading her employer's thoughts, 'like I was just telling Miss Crawford here, we've got to keep our strength up.'

Miriam glowered at her daughter, who was putting another forkful of food into her mouth.

'Don't stop on my account, Helen. God, you'll be the size of a bus if Mrs Westley has her way.'

Helen stopped eating and put down her knife and fork.

'Well, Mother, to what do we owe this pleasure? I thought you'd be at the Grand?' She got up and scraped the rest of the shepherd's pie into the bin, adding, 'I don't know why you don't just move in there.'

'I'll be getting myself off, then, if I'm not needed?' Mrs Westley had already removed her apron and was putting on her coat.

'Yes, yes,' Miriam said, waving her hand at the cook as though shooing her away. 'And don't forget. From now on, no more pies of any description – or stews.' She crinkled her nose. 'They really do stink the place out. I thought I was walking into some working man's canteen just now.'

Picking up her handbag and gas mask and hurrying out the back door, Mrs Westley made a silent wish for the immediate return of Mr Crawford.

Something told her, however, that her wish was not going to be granted any time soon.

'Come and join me in the front room for a quick G and T before I have to dash back out. I only popped back to check up on you as I've not seen you for so long. Passing ships in the night, we are!' This was, of course, an outright lie. The sole reason for Miriam coming back home was to see if there was any post. The last few letters from Jack had been stuffed half in, half out of the little postbox, and could have easily been pulled out by Helen. And that was the last thing she needed. Then the cat would be well and truly out of the bag.

'Well, you needn't have bothered, Mother, I'm absolutely fine.' Helen followed Miriam through to the living room.

'Well ...' Miriam had reached the drinks cabinet ' ... if you don't mind me saying, darling, you certainly don't look "fine".' She poured out two large gin and tonics and handed one to Helen.

'You look the epitome of "all work and no play".' She screwed her eyes up as she scrutinised her daughter further. 'And what's going on with your hair? I think it's time for a trip to the hairdressers, don't you?'

Helen sighed and put her drink down on the coffee table.

'If you've just come back to pull me to pieces, Mother, then you might as well get yourself back to the Grand, because to be honest, I can't be bothered to stand here and be picked to shreds. I'd rather get myself upstairs and put my head down and get some rest.'

'Well, you could certainly do with some beauty sleep, that's for sure!' Miriam knew she had hit below the belt and immediately apologised.

'Sorry, darling!' She walked over to where Helen was standing by the fireplace. The cast-iron grate had been stacked up with kindling and coal but had not been lit.

'I'm just a little concerned about you, that's all.' She put a manicured hand gently on Helen's shoulder. 'You've just not been yourself since you ended things with that two-timing toerag.'

'*He* ended things, Mother. Not *me*.' Helen bent down to take a sip of her gin, but it tasted strange so she put it down again. 'I might have felt a little better had *I* been the one to call it a day, but I wasn't even given that minor victory.'

'Darling, you have to kiss a lot of frogs before you get your prince.' Miriam tried to sound empathetic.

Helen looked at her mother. A part of her wanted to tell her that she had actually done a lot more than kiss this particular two-faced, two-timing frog, but she didn't.

'Oh, darling, I do feel for you.' Miriam forced the words out, trying to sound sincere when really she just wanted to get back to Amelia, who was waiting for her at the Grand, and enjoy another evening of being fawned over and flirted with. 'You know, I do *know* what it feels like.'

She paused and lowered her voice even though there was not a soul who could possibly hear her.

'What your father did to me broke my heart.' Miriam tried to make her eyes water but failed. She squeezed Helen's shoulder before going back to retrieve her drink. 'But, darling, you just have to put on a brave face, dust yourself down and carry on.' Miriam took a big swig from her crystal tumbler.

'And it's not as if you promised yourself to him in any way, is it?' The question was rhetorical, but if Miriam had

344

been more concerned about her daughter than herself, she would have seen Helen tense.

'Women of your standing,' continued Miriam, 'have to keep their standards. It's fine to flirt. An unmarried woman is like a perfectly wrapped parcel. You can undo the bow, even take a little peek, but that is it. The present is not revealed until there is a thick twenty-four-carat gold band on your wedding-ring finger.'

Helen would have liked to have pointed out that this appeared to be another case of her mother's 'do as I say and not as I do' advice as she had clearly let her father unwrap the parcel well before walking down the aisle. However, all Helen could wonder was why had her mother not chatted to her about these things before now?

A part of her wanted to confide in her mother, tell her that Theodore had unwrapped his parcel on more than a few occasions. To explain that was why she was so hurt. So down. She had given herself to a man she had thought was going to marry her and take her off to another part of the country, to another life.

She wanted to ask for a hug, for some comfort, for her mum to stop her from feeling as though she were falling from a great height, like in the dreams she was having. To cushion her when she did hit rock bottom.

Helen looked at her mother, but the words got stuck. She was so confused. One minute she believed one hundred per cent that Theodore had quite simply been a total 'cad', as he'd put it, using her while his sweetheart was down in Oxford. Other times, she replayed his words and believed what he'd said, that he thought Helen would tire of him and life down south. A few times she'd had to stop herself from running to the hospital to tell him that he was wrong – that she would love him for ever. *That he was the one for her.*

'Right, darling, I better get myself off. Amelia will think I've deserted her. And besides,' Miriam touched her daughter's face tenderly, 'I think you do need to have a good night's rest.' As Miriam finished off her drink, she headed towards the door and picked up from the console the handbag in which she had another letter to Helen from Jack.

'Oh, I forgot to remind you,' she said, poking her head back into the living room. 'It's your grandfather's birthday tomorrow. He's going to be seventy-eight and he wants us to go out with him for dinner to celebrate. He wants to go out early, like these old people always do, so I've arranged for his car to pick you up from work at five.'

'But I don't finish until half past,' Helen objected.

'Really, Helen!' Miriam now had her coat on, her gas mask and handbag were over her shoulder and she was edging towards the front door. 'I think when you tell Harold the reason for your early finish he will be more than accommodating. Your grandfather still does carry a lot of weight in this town, you know – even if he is well and truly over the hill.'

Helen watched her mother leave and it occurred to her that Miriam always had to make at least one barbed comment about her own father whenever he was the topic of conversation. Walking over to the sideboard and pulling out a Pall Mall from the packet she kept there, she thought of how much she loved, or rather *had* loved, her own father, and wondered why her mother had never seemed to care too much for hers.

Chapter Forty-Three

The following day

Tuesday 9 June

'I've *really* had enough, Dor.' Angie sounded totally disheartened and dejected as she and her best mate were pushed along in the early-morning drove of workers. They were becoming more squashed the nearer they got to the bottleneck that always formed at the timekeeper's cabin.

'Has your dad been kicking off again?' Dorothy asked, automatically inspecting her friend's face for any signs of a backhander.

'It's not just him—' Angie's sentence was cut short as she was pushed from behind, causing her to stumble forwards. Her head snapped round at the perpetrator.

'Watch it, yer greet big clumsy clot!' Her voice was loud and angry.

'Ah, keep yer knickers on, pet,' the man jeered from behind.

Dorothy saw Angie's hand ball into a fist and thought for a moment she was going to lamp the poor bloke.

'Come on,' Dorothy tugged her friend's arm, 'it was an accident.'

After they spotted Alfie at the hatch and were given their time boards and released into the yard, Dorothy linked arms with her friend.

'So, come on, who's ruffled your feathers this morning? You're not normally so ratty.'

'I dunno, Dor. I just feel fed up. Fed up and knackered. Mam's never about, so me and Liz are getting lumbered with the kids and are having to do all the cooking, cleaning and washing. It's not fair. And now Liz is talking about packing in her job at the munitions factory and joining the bleedin' lumberjacks – jills … whatever they're called – and I'm sure it's 'cos she'll have to move out and go and live in the country … get shot of us lot.'

'Where's your mam, then?' Dorothy dropped her voice. 'Or shouldn't I ask?'

Angie looked across at her friend. They had never really talked about Angie's mam, although they had both spotted her one afternoon disappearing off with some bloke down one of the back lanes when she was meant to be at work.

'She's making out she's working all hours at the ropery, but I dinnit believe her.'

'And your dad, do you think he believes her?'

'Clueless,' Angie said simply

'Well, let's hope he stays that way. I wouldn't want to see him if he ever found out.'

'He'd go ape.' Angie shivered even though it was a warm summer's morning.

'*Dorothy! Angie!*'

They both looked back to see Hannah and Martha hurrying to catch them up.

'You two all right?' Martha asked, although she was looking at Angie.

'We saw a little – oh, what did you call it, Martha?' Hannah asked.

'A kerfuffle.'

'Yes, that's it. Great word. *Kerfuffle*. We saw there was a bit of a kerfuffle in the queue back there?'

For once Dorothy didn't answer for her friend.

'Ah, just some clumsy git nearly tripping us up with his greet big plates of meat,' Angie explained.

'Ah.' Hannah nodded as though it made sense, even though she hadn't understood a word of what Angie had just said.

'Oooh!' It was Gloria, who had just appeared from behind with Polly by her side. 'Are they what I think they are?' She was looking down at two square cardboard boxes, tied with some string, that were dangling from Hannah's hands.

'Cakes and pastries!' Hannah chirped up. 'A present from Aunty Rina and Vera.'

'Ah, that's really kind of them,' Polly said.

'So,' Hannah stopped walking as they had now reached the entrance to the drawing office, 'I'll bring them round at lunchtime.'

'Don't be late!' Martha joked as they left their little bird and made their way over to their own workstation.

'Morning all!' It was Rosie, standing by the hut they had commandeered just down from the platers' shed, within a stone's throw of the quayside. The hut was small but big enough to keep their coats, bags and some surplus welding equipment in it.

'Hannah's bringing cakes over at lunchtime, courtesy of her aunty Rina and Vera,' Dorothy informed Rosie.

'Lovely,' Rosie said, casting her eyes across her squad. 'That gives us something to aim for.'

'And something to cheer us up,' Dorothy said, making eyes at Angie, who was angrily rummaging around in the shed for some spare welding rods.

By the time the klaxon sounded they were all dripping with sweat due to the overhead welds they had all been doing,

349

which after four and a half hours left even the strongest of men in need of a rest.

'Eee, I'm knackered!' Angie declared as they all switched off their machines and dumped their welding masks on the ground.

'Here they come!' Martha declared, looking across the yard as Hannah and Olly dodged the usual obstacles to get to them. The women were working on the lower hull of a ship that had what resembled a huge bullet hole through its mammoth metal flank. Rosie, Gloria and Martha pulled up a few wooden crates for them to sit on, while Polly waved over to the little tea boy. Dorothy and Angie dragged a workbench across in place of a table. Dorothy took the two boxes off Hannah and Olly and proceeded to open them, tearing up the boxes to make paper plates.

'Cor, these look gorgeous!' Angie said.

'Glad to see something's put a smile on your face!' Dorothy nudged Angie as she took the first bite of her cake, smearing some of the icing on her face. Everyone chuckled.

'So, come on then, Angie,' Rosie said, taking a slice of Victoria sponge. 'Why the gloomy face today? It's not like you to be down in the dumps?'

There was a murmur of agreement.

'Ah, it's nowt, miss,' Angie said. Everyone looked at Dorothy for an explanation.

'Ange's just fed up at home.' Dorothy looked at her mate. 'She's being put on all the time by her mam, who's never there, and her and Liz are having to do their own jobs as well as play nursemaid to the kids and do all the housework as well. I think she's just sick and tired of it all. Aren't you, Ange?'

'And yer dad can be a bit handy as well, can't he?' Gloria added, breaking off a piece of her oatmeal pastry and popping it into her mouth.

Angie looked at Gloria and knew she understood. She nodded but didn't say anything.

'Thanks, Mikey,' Polly said as the tea boy arrived, carefully balancing his seesawing pole of metal cans across his narrow shoulders. Rosie pressed some coins into the little lad's dirty hand as he was leaving.

Rosie took a sip of her tea and looked at Dorothy and Angie. 'Have you two thought about the possibility of getting your own place?'

'Wot? Just me 'n 'er?' Angie said.

'What just the two of us?' Dorothy echoed.

'Sounds like a good idea to me,' Gloria chipped in. 'It's not as if yer bairns any more. How old are yer both now? Twenty? Twenty-one?'

'Twenty,' they said in unison.

'Nearly twenty-one,' Dorothy added.

All the women, and Olly, who was listening attentively, were looking at Dorothy and Angie and then back at Rosie and Gloria.

'How would they find somewhere?' Polly asked, genuinely curious.

'The local paper?' Olly suggested.

'I could ask the rabbi if he knows of anywhere round our way,' Hannah added.

'I could ask George as well,' Rosie volunteered. 'He keeps going on about never being at his flat in town because he's always with Lily and that he should rent it out.'

Dorothy clapped her hands in excitement, and Angie smiled for the first time all day.

'Eee, you and me, living together! Having our own pad! Sounds like a brilliant idea, doesn't it, Ange?' Dorothy raised her eyebrows at her friend.

'And I'll bet you George's place is dead swanky?' Dorothy was now looking at Rosie.

'Not too posh, though!' Angie butted in, sounding a little panicked. 'We don't want to be somewhere that's too la-di-da.'

Dorothy rolled her eyes. 'The grander the better, that's what I say. If we can afford it, who gives a toss!'

'Did you see Helen leaving *early* today?' Polly said to Rosie and Gloria as they headed down the embankment towards the ferry landing.

'Harold told me it was because it's Mr Havelock's birthday. Some kind of family celebration,' Rosie said.

'Is it just me, or does Helen seem to be avoiding us all lately?' Polly asked.

Gloria cast Rosie a quick glance.

'She used to be on our backs all the time,' Polly said, thinking back to when Helen had tried to split up the squad after unsuccessfully trying to break up Polly's relationship with Tommy.

'If she's got a bloke, which Dor and Angie seem to think she has, that might be taking her mind off giving us hassle,' Rosie said as she looked up at the seagulls, who seemed particularly verbose that day.

The three women were momentarily separated during the usual skirmish to get to the bobbing paddle steamer. Once they had reached the ferry landing, Gloria made a point of changing the subject.

'Do you reckon George'll rent our terrible two his flat?' she asked.

'Well, I don't see why not. He's met them both a few times now – he says he thinks they're a "hoot".'

'I don't think I know of anyone our age who's got their own place,' Polly said. 'I think someone Bel used to work with on the buses rented a room, but that was with a landlady living there.'

'It's not exactly the norm,' Rosie said, 'but—'

'—these aren't normal times.' Polly finished the sentence for her. Her voice sounded sad. She couldn't help but think that if these *had* been normal times, she would probably be looking for a home to move into with Tommy. 'Well, I think it's a great idea,' she perked up, trying to shake herself out of a maudlin mood. 'Neither Dor nor Angie are happy at home. Dorothy was saying the other day that she hadn't even seen her ma for nearly a week – even though they live under the same roof!'

'And it would be good to get Angie out of harm's way,' Gloria added as they stepped onto the ferry and gave Stan their fare. The old man smiled at Polly but didn't ask her about Tommy, something he had stopped doing a while ago. He knew Polly would tell him when she did hear something. Good or bad.

The three women looked out at the glistening waters of the Wear and at the ship they had been working on that day, as well as all the other vessels lining the riverbanks, waiting to be either fixed or built, or to have their bellies filled with coal and other cargo.

'It's nice to see Hannah so happy,' Polly mused as she watched one of the fishing trawlers offloading its catch by the quayside. 'That was a piece of luck her aunty getting a job in that café you and Peter used to go to.'

Rosie felt her heart quicken at the mention of her lover's name, but tried not to let it show.

'I'd heard through Beryl,' Polly continued, 'that Hannah's aunty Rina wasn't doing at all well as a credit draper.' Polly looked at Gloria and Rosie, who feigned surprise. 'Quite the reverse in fact ... So the job came just in the nick of time.'

'And Martha was telling me today,' Gloria added, 'that Hannah's aunty has heard from their rabbi that her mam

353

and dad are still in that ghetto she told us about – the one none of us can pronounce. By the sounds of it, it's an awful place to be, but it's better they're there than being shipped off to one of the labour camps, by all accounts.'

'Poor Hannah,' Polly said. 'What a worry.'

As the three of them continued looking out at the river, their thoughts naturally drifted to the people they loved and about whom they, too, were worried sick. Gloria's two boys were always at the forefront of her mind, and every night she asked a God she didn't believe in to keep them safe. Tommy was constantly on Polly's mind, day in, day out, although strangely enough she didn't dream of him at night. For Rosie the opposite was the case: she somehow just about managed to keep her thoughts of Peter at bay during the day, but at night her dreams of him were constant and not always a comfort.

Chapter Forty-Four

Wanborough Manor, near Guildford, Surrey

'Come in!' Major Roger de Wesselow bellowed at the closed door of his office, which was jam-packed with overflowing boxes and stacks of books, maps and files.

When Conducting Officer Sergeant Searle entered the room, there was a blast of noise and activity as the F Section of the SOE had just taken on another half a dozen recruits. They had arrived much later than anticipated. It had now gone five thirty and everyone was piling into the old library, where their introductory talk was just about to take place.

Shutting the door behind him, Sergeant Searle walked over to the Major, saluted and held out an envelope to his superior officer.

'Update, Commander, on Circuit White Light.'

Major de Wesselow tensed. Taking the proffered message, he put on his spectacles and sat down.

His face remained expressionless as he read:

Circuit White Light. Disbanded due to enemy infiltration.
Five members captured. Whereabouts as yet unknown.
 One killed. As yet identity unknown.
 Two escapees. Believed to have made it to the unoccupied zone. Again, no information available regarding identities.

The Major looked up at Sergeant Searle, his arms straight by his sides, at attention, awaiting his orders.

'As soon as we have names, I want to be informed. Night or day. Then you can inform next of kin.'

'Yes, sir!' Sergeant Searle saluted, then turned and left the room.

Neither man needed to say more. Both hearts were heavy. And seemed to be getting heavier with each passing week.

Chapter Forty-Five

The front door slammed shut.

'Isabelle!'

Bel stopped what she was doing, surprised to hear that her ma was back home so early. She normally kept out of the way between her afternoon and evening shifts at the pub.

'I'm in the scullery, Ma!' she shouted back.

Bel could hear her mother's footsteps down the hallway and then saw her appear at the doorway to the kitchen. Tramp and Pup went to greet her, but she ignored them as they sniffed around her feet and wagged their tails in expectation of either food or love.

Bel took her hands out of the sink where she was peeling potatoes for the hotpot Agnes was going to make when she got back from Beryl's. Aggie's nursery had more or less moved permanently next door. Beryl had said it made sense as Iris and Audrey were now working full time, which meant the house was empty during the day – whereas there were people coming and going all the time at Agnes's, and they had been taking in so much washing of late that everywhere you moved there were piles of laundry.

'You're back early?' Bel dried her hands and walked into the kitchen, causing Tramp and Pup to try their chances with her.

'Aye, I am.' Pearl did not move from the doorway.

Bel stared at her ma, who, she thought, seemed uncannily subdued.

357

'You all right there, Ma? Did you want something?' Bel reckoned she was on the beg as normally she would have simply snuck off to her room, changed quickly and gone back out without anyone being any the wiser. Bel went to check on Hope, who was starting to get restless in her cot. When she looked back, she caught her ma looking at her watch.

'You waiting for someone?'

Pearl ignored the question, and instead told her daughter, 'Me and you's going for a walk.'

Bel was in the middle of picking up Hope; she stopped dead and stared at her mother, a puzzled expression on her face.

'Are we now?' Bel laughed a little incredulously. '"Me and you" going for a walk?'

'Aye. And no bairns.' Pearl looked at Hope and then out the kitchen window at Lucille, who was playing hopscotch in the backyard.

As if sensing she was being watched, Lucille looked up from the number ten square she had just hopped onto and saw her nana through the window. She immediately abandoned her game, and seconds later was bustling through the back door.

'Nana!' she shouted. 'Hopscotch!'

Pearl laughed, which, in turn, started off her smoker's cough. 'I'm too auld for all that kind of malarkey, pet. Anyways,' she told her granddaughter, 'me and yer mam's gannin' out fer a walk.'

'Me come too!' Lucille demanded.

'Sorry, pet, not today. Another time. Yer nana needs to have a good chatter to yer mammy.'

Bel looked at her ma and that was when the penny dropped. And as it did so, butterflies started fluttering around in her stomach. She took Hope into the scullery and started to fill her bottle. The house felt quiet; the air tense and full of expectation.

The stillness was broken by the sound of the front door clashing open.

'About bloody time as well!' Pearl exclaimed as soon as Polly and Gloria appeared. They both stood and gawped at an unusually serious-looking Pearl. Polly could feel her hackles rise – an effect Pearl regularly had on her.

'I didn't know we were expected back for anything?' Polly said as she and Gloria walked down the hallway, edging round the Silver Cross and then past Pearl, who had moved out of the doorway to let them through to the kitchen. Just then Bel came out of the scullery with Hope in her arms.

'There we go,' she said, waving a freshly made-up bottle of milk at Gloria. 'One bottle and one happy little baby girl. In fact,' she said as she handed Hope over, 'she was just telling me how much she was dying to see her mammy.' Hope gurgled as if agreeing with Bel.

'Ah, thanks, Bel. Have I told you you're a real star?' Gloria said, looking down at Hope all wrapped up and ready for the journey back home.

Bel smiled. 'Just a few dozen times.'

'So, Pearl,' Polly had her hands on her hips, 'what's all this it's "about bloody time"?'

Pearl bobbed down to fetch her handbag from under the kitchen table, ignoring Polly's question.

'Ma wants me and her to go on a little walk,' Bel answered instead, her eyebrows arching and her big blue eyes widening as she looked from Polly to Gloria. They both returned similarly perplexed looks.

'I can see yer all *making faces*,' Pearl said, her head swinging back up, her hand clasped around her handbag. 'I've told yer before – eyes in the back o' ma head.'

359

'Well, I'd better get myself off,' Gloria said, aware of the strained atmosphere.

'Let me see you out,' Bel said, as she slipped through to the hallway and opened the front door while Gloria got Hope settled in her pram.

'Thanks again, Bel,' Gloria said as she bumped the Silver Cross down the front step. 'See ya tomorrow.'

'See you tomorrow,' Bel said, but just as she was about to shut the door, she spotted Maisie hurrying down the street.

'Maisie!' Bel said, surprised. 'Everything all right?'

Maisie gave her a light kiss on both cheeks. 'Can I not come and see my gorgeous little niece when I fancy?' As if on cue, Lucille, who had heard her aunty's distinctively genteel-sounding voice from the kitchen, came running down the hallway.

''Aisiee!' she cried out excitedly as Maisie bent down and hauled her up into the air. 'Gosh, this little girl seems to be getting bigger by the day!' she exclaimed, giving Lucille a tickle and making her squeal even louder.

Bel watched as Maisie walked down the hallway and into the kitchen with Lucille on her hip, chatting away to her little niece. Following her, Bel felt a sudden nervousness. She was pretty sure why her ma wanted to go out – and it looked like a degree of forethought had gone into it, since Maisie had clearly been asked to act as babysitter.

Five minutes later, Maisie had got Lucille ready and the pair headed off up to the town. Bel shouted to Maisie not to spoil Lucille, but her sister and her daughter pretended not to hear.

Bel grabbed her gas mask as well as Pearl's, since her mother was doing her usual last-minute search for fags. After going upstairs to her room she found a spare packet

360

she had stashed away, and finally they both left for their 'walk'.

Polly stood on the front doorstep and waved them both off. She had a good idea what was going on, and just hoped, for her sister-in-law's sake, it all went well.

Chapter Forty-Six

Pearl hadn't realised she was with child until she was well into her pregnancy. She bled lightly on and off for months after the rape and had actually felt relieved, believing that she was having her monthlies. It wasn't until she went to see the old woman, thinking she had something bad growing inside her belly, that she was told she was with child. She would never forget her disbelief – had actually refused to believe it for a while afterwards. Until, that was, she felt the baby move. Only then did she finally accept that she was in the family way.

Over the next few months she worked like a Trojan, doing any kind of labouring work she could find, keeping her bump well concealed, which hadn't been too hard as she was not particularly big. Not like when she had blossomed with baby Maisie and the girls at the maternity home had joked she was as wide as she was tall and that if they pushed her over she'd just roll away.

Everything about this pregnancy was different. Even her boobs didn't get particularly big. A part of Pearl felt, or perhaps it was more a question of *hoped*, that this baby wouldn't go full term – that all the pushing and pulling she did during her stints at the ropery or the glass factory would somehow prove too much for the little mite inside of her. But it wasn't, and her baby was born just as it had been conceived – in the direst of circumstances. Pearl knew she had nearly died – was amazed she hadn't when she saw the amount of blood she had lost. But somehow, regrettably, she did not.

It took her weeks to name her second child – unlike with Maisie, whose name she had decided upon weeks, if not months, before her birth, knowing instinctively she was going to have a girl. This time she only did so when she went to register the birth, and only chose Isabelle when it was suggested to her by the clerk, who had become impatient at Pearl's indecision.

Pearl had considered having Isabelle adopted out, but after what she had gone through with Maisie she knew she couldn't. The old fishwife who had sewn her up after Isabelle's birth had told her she wouldn't be having any more children. Perhaps that went some way towards her decision to keep her baby, she wasn't quite sure.

And so, aged just sixteen, Pearl became a single parent to an illegitimate baby girl. She never experienced the joy of motherhood, that feeling of falling in love she'd had after giving birth to Maisie, but worse still, in place of what should have been maternal happiness, was anger.

Anger that a man had forced himself on her, and that she had now been forced to have his child.

Anger that she had lost all control over her body, and also her life.

Anger and hatred became her constant companions.

Hatred for Charles. A monster who had taken what he wanted.

And anger towards herself for being so bloody blind. For being oblivious to what had really been going on in that house in Glen Path. She had been so wrapped up in her grief over Maisie that she had not seen what was happening in front of her very eyes. She should have read the warning signs. The change in atmosphere whenever it was announced that the master was coming back home;

Velma's initial warnings to 'keep out of the master's way', and her attempts during Charles's visit at Easter to keep her downstairs.

Of course, Pearl now realised bitterly, there was no dying aunt to whom little Annie had had to go and pay her last respects. Annie had obviously found herself prey to Charles's perverted sexual needs when he had visited the previous Christmas. *Had Pearl been the only person in the house not to realise that?*

The more Pearl kept replaying her time under Henrietta's employ, the more her anger spread to the rest of the mistress's 'cavalry'. *Why had no one warned her?* And then, of course, there was the question of Henrietta's culpability. *Did she know what her husband was doing?* She wondered if Henrietta had purposely chosen her because she knew of her husband's predilection for young – very young – blonde girls. Or whether she was so off her rocker that she didn't have any idea about what was happening under her own roof. Pearl recalled the mention of a previous maid who had got herself in the family way. Was that baby also Charles's? Which begged the question, how many other bastards had he sired in the town during his lifetime? For Pearl was fairly sure she was not the first, and nor would she be the last, to be left with a permanent reminder of the violence that man enjoyed inflicting.

Pearl would never know. What she did know, though, was that any chance she might have had for a normal life had now been destroyed. Who would want her with the encumbrance of a bastard child? Pearl might be a looker, but she was no catch.

The ultimate nail in the coffin was the fact that even if she did manage to find a fella to love her and marry her, she would not then be able to give that man his own family.

And as much as Pearl could be a pretty tough nut when necessary, she knew she could never be so cold and calculating as to lie and pretend that she could bear any future suitor a son or daughter.

As Isabelle grew older, the more she looked like Charles. She had the same nose, the same pale skin, slim build and blonde, slightly curly hair. It was a constant reminder of that harrowing night. And to make matters worse, her daughter seemed to be different to the other youngsters around the doors. She was never quite sure whether Isabelle tried to speak better than her friends, or whether it just came naturally to her. Regardless, she never developed the strong local accent of their neighbours in the east end, nor did she really behave like them either. She was always a little distant, as if she didn't belong, and the other children seemed to sense it too.

She tried to love her daughter, tried to be like other mothers, but it was no good. No matter how hard she tried, she simply couldn't do it. And the more she tried, and the more she failed, the more of an outsider she felt. After a while, *feeling* like an outsider led to her *being* an outsider. Drink and men became her escape, and that escape became her life.

For the first five years of Isabelle's life, Pearl found it hard to settle, and so she dragged her daughter around with her, never staying in the same bedsit or tenement for long. When problems came, she ran – just like she had that fateful night. It was only when she moved to a room in Back Tatham Street – and Agnes ended up taking Bel under her wing – that Pearl decided to stay put.

Bel had often questioned Pearl about her father, but had eventually stopped. Perhaps she just got tired of hearing the same answer. The same lie. Perhaps it was no longer important once she had found a new, better family in the Elliots. Who knew? All Pearl was aware of was that it was a relief. Finally, she could leave the past dead and buried.

Until now.

Now, the past was nipping at her heels, and she had no other option but to turn around and face it.

Chapter Forty-Seven

'So, Ma, are you going to tell me where we're going? Or is it a mystery?' Bel tried to inject some humour into her voice as they turned right down Tatham Street. Pearl huffed by way of reply. They had left at what was probably the busiest time of the day, when the shipyards had just sounded out the end of the day's shift and hundreds of workers were hurrying either straight home or to their local for a quick pint before their tea. As they battled against the tide of those going into town, or were pushed forward by the current of those heading towards Hendon, Pearl was glad of the crush of people for it meant there was no opportunity to talk. That would come later.

As they started down Suffolk Street, Pearl glanced across at her daughter. She had not had the easiest of lives, but she had managed to remain relatively unscarred by the hardships she'd had to endure.

It angered Pearl that she herself was now going to be the one to inflict a wound on her daughter that she knew would mark her for ever.

'Villette Road!' Pearl shouted across to Bel, who had become separated from her in the mob of workers. Bel nodded across to her ma as she stepped onto the road to let an old woman pass, her shoulders stooped with the weight of two bags of groceries. Once they were halfway up the street, the crowds started to disperse and a relative quietness descended. All the shops along both sides of the street had shut up for the day, and as it was now teatime, there were no children about.

'Hold yer horses a moment,' Pearl said, as she stepped to the side of the pavement to light a cigarette.

'I hate coming out at this time,' Bel said, taking a big breath and forcing herself to relax.

Pearl puffed on her cigarette to get it going and looked at her daughter through a fog of smoke. Isabelle's attention, she noticed, had been drawn to a heavily pregnant woman pushing a pram down the other side of the street.

'You've not managed to fall yet then?' Pearl said. Following Isabelle's wedding to Joe they had all assumed it wouldn't be long before the happy couple were announcing that she was expecting. But looking at Isabelle now, still slim as a pin, this was clearly not the case.

Bel glanced across at her mother.

'No,' she said simply.

Neither woman spoke. Instead, mother and daughter walked in silence, past the Barley Mow Park and then across the wide breadth of the Ryhope Road. As they reached the first mansion in the long row of huge detached homes that made up The Cedars, Bel felt a nervous excitement.

So, she had been right after all! It was as she had thought. The answer to the puzzle of her paternity was right here, in one of these houses overlooking Backhouse Park. It had been here all along, her whole life, right on her doorstep. Bel kept up with her mother as they walked shoulder to shoulder at a steady pace along the wide pathway.

Sneaking a look at her ma, Bel saw that her face had gone deathly serious.

As they passed house after house Bel thought about the lifetime of wondering and wanting to know the truth about her father. These past few months it had become nothing short of an obsession. And now, finally, she was going to find out the truth.

As they passed the house where the harried mother and her three daughters lived, Bel stared. She had been shocked when Polly had told her this was Dorothy's home, that the dark-haired woman who had answered the door and the three energetic girls who had joined her were, in fact, Dorothy's mother and sisters.

After about another hundred yards Pearl slowed her pace, checked that there was no traffic and hurried across the road.

She had been trying to avoid this moment for months now. But Isabelle was always strong-willed, as a child and as an adult. If she'd been honest with herself, Pearl had known she was on borrowed time from the moment Isabelle had mentioned her da not long after Maisie had come careering into their lives. Now, finally, the time had come.

She couldn't stall any longer. It was time to tell her daughter the truth.

The only dilemma in her mind was whether or not she should tell her the whole truth.

Bel followed her ma, but was surprised when she started walking down the long stretch of road called Glen Path. She hurried to catch up.

'Where're we going, Ma?' Bel felt a little perplexed. Maisie had told her that she had knocked on all the doors along this street and everyone had been definite that they had not ever employed a young girl called Pearl. Most of them, Maisie had told her, still had the same staff they'd taken on before the First War.

'I know,' Pearl said, 'you're thinking to yourself that Maisie knocked on all these doors and there was nothing doing.'

Bel looked at Pearl, who had stopped shortly after they had crossed over the road and started walking round the bend that stretched the quarter of a mile or so to the Queen Alexandra Road.

'Well, she lied,' Pearl said, scrabbling around in her handbag for her cigarettes and lighter. She looked at Bel and saw outrage and disappointment on her face.

'But dinnit be getting all irate now,' Pearl continued. 'I asked her to.'

Pearl took a cigarette out. She looked up and made eye contact with her daughter.

'*I* wanted to be the one to tell you. No one else,' she said.

Bel's mind was now all over the place. *So, Maisie had lied. Her sister had been in cahoots with her ma all along.*

As if reading her daughter's mind, Pearl told her: 'So, don't go sounding off at Maisie when you see her next! She was only doing what she thought best for you.' She lit her cigarette and blew out a thick stream of smoke.

Bel heard something different in her ma's voice, but she couldn't put her finger on it. She looked at her as Pearl snapped her handbag shut and flung it over her shoulder, causing it to bash against her gas mask. The fading light had given her an almost ghostly look, exacerbated by the cigarette smoke curling around her. She looked even more gaunt and worn than she did normally.

'Are you all right, Ma?' Bel asked.

Pearl ignored her daughter and they both walked another hundred yards in a taut silence.

When they were halfway along the road, Pearl's pace slowed. She took one last puff of her cigarette before tossing the butt to the ground.

Bel looked around her, taking in her surroundings. Lining the street on both sides were two parallel rows of trees, all standing straight and tall like sentinels awaiting the arrival of their king or queen. Behind them on one side, beyond the wall, there was a wealth of trees, all different types, shapes and sizes, standing still and quiet – the natural arboretum that made up Backhouse Park.

Even though the sun was only just starting to drop, it seemed as though Bel and her ma had become separated from the light, enclosed in the shadow of the centurion trees – and there was now a chill in the air. Any kind of expectant feelings, any butterflies that had been fluttering around in her stomach, had died. For the first time since she had started down this road in search of her da, Bel felt a little afraid of what she might find out. *Perhaps she shouldn't have harangued her ma so?*

'We don't have to do this, you know?' Bel's growing ambivalence was clear as day.

'Eee, Isabelle, yer a funny one,' Pearl said, but her tone lacked its usual bite. 'You've been mithering me no end about yer da,' she said, lighting up another cigarette. 'Well, for once in my life I'm going to do something you've asked me to do.' Again the tone was almost gentle, verging on self-recriminatory.

'Yer see this house here?' Pearl said, waving her cigarette at the house directly opposite them on the other side of the street. They both stared at the wide gravel driveway that led to the palatial Queen Anne-style red-brick house – its bright red front door bordered by two stone pillars. Pearl's heart was thumping. She had lain awake last night and gone over and over in her head the best way to tell Bel the truth, but there didn't seem to be any 'best way'. Before she had finally fallen into an exhausted slumber in the early hours, she had resolved to simply bring her daughter here – to this place she had not been to since that terrible night – hoping that once she was there she would find the right words.

Now that she *was* here, though, she doubted the wisdom of this plan.

'I came here when I got back from London, right after I'd had Maisie,' Pearl began. Her tone was faltering, unsure.

'I didn't want to go back and live with my ma and da, so I went looking for a live-in job, 'n I got one here.' Pearl tried to keep her voice light, but it was a struggle. She could feel the darkness of that time start to press down on her.

Bel looked at her ma and knew not to interrupt; that the time had come for her to find out who her father was.

'I think the mistress of the house was a bit touched in the head.' Pearl was suddenly hit by a vision of Henrietta all dolled up, dressed up in some outrageous outfit, flitting around the house as if she was onstage.

'She called me the "little match girl" when she first saw me. I didn't have any idea what she was talking about to be honest ... Course, I know now. I've even read the story to LuLu ...'

Bel looked at her ma, who now seemed a million miles away. She was looking straight ahead at the house.

'She meant no harm though.'

Pearl stopped speaking, as if unsure what to say next.

Bel noticed her ma was shaking.

'Do they still live there now?' Bel asked, looking at the house and thinking that it looked well-kempt, lived-in.

Pearl wrapped her flimsy summer coat around her skinny frame. For a second she considered lying and telling Isabelle, *No, they moved out years ago.* She could even embellish the truth and tell her that the master of the house had some top-notch job overseas, and that the family had moved to go and join him in some far-flung country. But Pearl knew Isabelle would see through her deceit.

'I believe the master of the house still lives there ... I'm not sure what happened to Henrietta ...' Pearl's mind was starting to wander again. She had never heard anything about her dying, but then again that wasn't so unusual. She had lived a good part of her life down south. Her old mate Sandra was about the only person she had kept in touch with and she wouldn't have thought to have told her if she had. Why would she? No one knew of her connection to the family.

'So, there was the master and the mad wife – I'm guessing they had children?' Bel prodded.

Pearl looked at her daughter – her delicate features, her pretty face and pale skin – and saw Charles's face. Bringing Isabelle up would have been so much easier if she hadn't looked quite so much like him.

'Aye, they did,' Pearl said. She could feel her mouth going dry. 'Two girls. But they didn't really live there. They were at some posh school abroad. They only came back home every now and again.'

'So, Ma,' Bel asked, nudging her mother in the direction she needed to go, 'were you courting anyone while you worked there?'

Pearl looked at her daughter and realised that she had no idea what her mother was going to tell her. She wasn't as streetwise as Maisie.

'Nah, Isabelle,' Pearl said, taking a step backwards so that her back was touching the uneven brick wall. 'I wasn't with anyone at that time.'

Bel was looking at her ma, her mind spinning with questions.

'So, what was the name of the master of the house, Ma?' Bel kept her voice soft.

Pearl hesitated. She had never said his name aloud after that night. Ever. After a silence that felt like an age, Pearl gave her daughter the answer to her question.

'Charles.'

She said the name, but as she did so she felt her throat close up. Even now she could still feel the squeeze of his hands around her neck.

Bel was looking intently at her mother as she spoke and thought she caught her flinch. She stepped forward and gently touched her mother's arm.

'Ma, is Charles my father? Is that what you're trying to tell me?'

'Aye,' Pearl said. She looked down at the cigarette that was smouldering between her fingers and then back up at her daughter.

'Aye,' she repeated. 'It was Charles.'

There was a moment's silence.

Bel stood still, taking in her mother's confession.

A few moments passed.

'So, what happened, Ma?' Bel wanted to know everything. 'He must have been quite old if he had two girls away at school. And you were still very young – you must have only been about fifteen?'

'Aye. Fifteen.' Pearl's shoulders had started to stoop as if the weight of remembrance was getting heavier by the second.

Bel struggled to put the pieces together. She desperately wanted this to be some kind of tragic love story whereby the master of the house, in a loveless marriage with a woman who was a bit touched, falls for the pretty but poor scullery maid.

'Were you both in love?' Bel asked.

Pearl's body stiffened.

Bel scrutinised her mother's face.

There was something there, but she couldn't read it.

Pearl looked at her daughter. Should she tell Isabelle the horrible, vile truth of her conception? How she had been created during a moment of violence. How she had come into being because a man who had been old enough to be her father had violated her in the worst way possible.

Had nearly strangled the life out of her while creating life inside of her?

Pearl looked at her daughter. Her beautiful, genteel daughter. And it came to her. She knew what she had to do. *She* had lived with this her whole life. *She* had suffered because of one man's perversions – but she was damned if she was going to let his poison spread to her daughter and infect her with his darkness.

'I was young, Isabelle. And dinnit forget,' Pearl started her untruth, 'those were different times.' The words came easier now she knew what she had to do, but still she was aware that what came out of her mouth next had to be convincing. Had to sound genuine. Truthful. Her daughter wasn't easily fooled.

'He was the master of the house. I was the young skivvy he took a liking to.' Pearl drew hard on her fag and forced the words out alongside a thick grey billow of smoke. *'And I took a liking to him.'* Pearl took one last drag of her cigarette as though wanting to scorch the words from her throat. 'I was young and stupid, without the brains I should have been born with. He was rich ... handsome.' Pearl tossed her fag butt to the ground and crushed it into the pavement.

'It was a very brief affair.' She had to push the words out. *How it hurt to say them.* But she knew the truth would damage her daughter so much more. 'Just the once.'

She looked at Bel and could see that she was taking in every word, and most of all, believing everything she was saying.

Listening to her ma's words, a strange relief had come over Bel. The feeling of fear and dread that had crept up on her earlier had now gone.

She had been the result of a love affair – a love affair of sorts –
although one that clearly had been doomed from the start.

'So, what happened?' Bel was now entranced. So much
so that she did not see a shiny black Jaguar turning into
Glen Path from the main road. Pearl, however, *had* spotted
the car and turned slightly so that if the passengers in the
car did spot them, all they could see would be the backs of
two women standing having a gossip.

'I felt so guilty.' Pearl looked her daughter straight in
the eye, wanting – needing – to keep her attention. 'He
was a married man, dinnit forget. And I had always liked
Henrietta, even if she was a few slices short.' Pearl was
now starting to speak faster as the car approached. 'So, I
just packed my bags and left one night and never went
back.' Panic was now coursing through Pearl's body and
she felt herself shake even more.

The car was slowing down!

'It wasn't until a good while later I realised I was pregnant with you,' she continued.

The car was now turning into the driveway, its wheels
crunching on the gravel.

Bel turned to see the flash of red brake lights as the car
slowly came to a halt outside the stone steps that led to the
front door.

Pearl desperately wanted another fag but didn't dare
move. The shaking was getting worse now. She hadn't
banked on this. *Why hadn't she thought this through more*
carefully? She had heard the old man hardly went out these
days. That he was always coming down with some ailment
or other that kept him housebound.

Don't be stupid, it's probably just visitors. She tried to calm
herself.

'Come on, Isabelle.' She took hold of her daughter's arm
and pulled her gently.

Bel's face swung round to look at her mother.

'Is this him? Is this Charles?' Her face was flushed with excitement. At last, she was going to see her father. She might even get to meet him.

'It's probably just house guests,' Pearl said. She tugged her daughter's arm again but she didn't move. Bel had no intention of going anywhere.

'I just want to see him,' Bel whispered, although she would have had to shout for the man getting out of the car to hear her.

Pearl closed her eyes for a moment, wanting all of this to disappear. When she opened them again, she saw a chauffeur helping Charles out of the car. It shocked her how old and frail he had become. His blond hair was now grey. He was still thin and wiry, but his posture was bent – no longer the straight-backed horse rider.

'Gosh, Ma, he looks so old.' Bel mirrored her mother's thoughts. Her face was no longer expectant, nor enthused with excitement.

As Charles put one hand on the top of the car to steady himself and watched the driver walk round to open the other passenger door, Bel caught his profile. It was still light, the sun only just going down, so she had a good view. Her eyes narrowed as she inspected his face.

'He looks familiar.' She turned her head slightly towards her ma, who was still gripping her arm, all the while keeping her eyes peeled on the man who she now knew was her da.

She knew this man. She was sure of it.

'Where do I know him from?' Bel turned, this time looking at her ma. She was shocked to see Pearl's face was drained of colour. She was as white as a ghost. Bel glanced down at her mother's hand, clamped on her daughter's arm. She could feel it trembling. This was so unlike her. Her ma was never afraid of anything.

When Bel looked back across the road she saw that there were, in fact, two other passengers getting out of the back of the Jaguar. Two women. One dark-haired, the other blonde. The older, fair-haired woman seemed to be a little unsteady on her feet, a little tipsy perhaps, and was checking her perfectly coiffured hair with a small compact, while the other, younger woman was rooting around for something in her handbag. A few seconds later she pulled out a cigarette and lit it.

Bel let out a gasp of disbelief.

The woman blowing out a plume of smoke into the early-evening air was none other than Helen.

And then the penny dropped.

Of course she knew his face! He had been photographed for the local newspaper enough. Always at some charity function or being pictured cutting a red ribbon, or receiving some award for his charitable work.

Charles – the man who was her father – *was Mr Charles Havelock.*

Bel stood there, stunned. Not quite knowing what to think.

Her ma and Mr Havelock? A love affair?

Bel's mind was whirring

Something didn't feel right now she had seen him with her own eyes. He must be well into his seventies ... her ma was just in her early forties ... that made a thirty-five year age gap between the two, at the very least.

They could easily have been father and daughter.

If her ma was just fifteen when she'd had her affair, that would have made him in his early fifties.

A fifteen-year-old girl and fifty-year-old man?

Had it really been a love affair?

Bel felt a shiver go down her spine.

She looked at her ma, who seemed to have dropped into some kind of a trance as she watched Mr Havelock, his daughter Miriam and granddaughter Helen make their way into the house. Miriam's shrill, arrogant voice shouted more orders to an elderly butler who had opened the front door and helped unburden the chauffeur of presents.

Bel and Pearl stood and watched, statue-still, as everyone piled into the house and the bright red front door clashed shut.

There was a few seconds' silence before Bel spoke.

'I don't know what to say, Ma.'

The feeling of unease and dread Bel had felt earlier had now returned in full. She watched as her mother turned to look at her and, realising she was still holding on to Bel's arm, released her grip.

She didn't say anything. Instead she fished out her last fag.

As Bel looked at her mother hunching over to light her cigarette, everything fell into place.

A rush of nausea hit her as it dawned on her what had really happened between her ma and Charles.

There had been no love affair.

She knew fear in a person when she saw it and she had seen it in her mother as soon as her ma had set eyes on Mr Havelock. She had felt the tremors of terror in her ma's body as she'd clung to her arm.

Her ma had been raped.

And she, Bel, was the product of that rape.

That was why her ma had lied to her all these years.

Her ma had been trying to protect her.

As the pieces of the jigsaw fell into place, Bel understood why her ma had found it so hard to love her, yet so easy to love Maisie.

For her firstborn had been created by love – whereas her second had been spawned through violence and hate.

Bel felt tears prick her eyes.

Tears for herself, but also tears for her ma.

She felt nauseous at the thought; at the realisation. She wished more than anything that she could take that knowledge back. But it was too late. There was no going back. She had pushed and pushed, forced her ma's hand, and finally got what she wanted.

Now she wished, more than anything in the world, that she had simply left well enough alone. Done as Agnes had said – *let sleeping dogs lie.*

Bel turned to look at her ma. Her eyes were dry, but they looked bloodshot, and they showed a deep sadness it hurt Bel to see.

'Come on, Ma,' Bel said. 'Let's go home, eh?'

'Aye, let's go home, Isabelle,' Pearl agreed. A sense of relief washed through her body, followed by an incredible tiredness. She had been running away from the memory of Charles and what he had done to her for so long now. Seeing him today, in the flesh, had brought her to a sudden standstill. And now all she wanted to do was rest.

As they both trudged away from the Havelock mansion, Bel's mind was spilling over with a cascade of questions she wanted to ask her ma, but she knew this wasn't the time.

As they turned into The Cedars, the early-evening sun started to shine through the avenue of trees, guiding their way back home, causing Bel's eyes to water more than they were already.

What she had just learnt had struck at the very core of her being, and she knew the shock waves of that revelation would continue to reverberate for a long time yet – perhaps for ever.

There was, however, one comfort that she would take out of all this darkness – and that was the knowledge that her ma *did* love her.

Perhaps not like other mothers loved their daughters – but her ma had loved her in her own way. She had loved her enough to keep her when she was a baby; she had not given her up and had her adopted out or left her on the steps of the local orphanage like many women would have done.

Her ma had brought her up as well as she could, but most of all she had tried her hardest to protect her from the truth.

And in keeping that truth from her – a terrible truth she was still trying to keep from her even now – her ma had given her something that she had always yearned for, always wanted – *craved* – but never felt she had ever had. Until now.

A mother's love.

Chapter Forty-Eight

As Polly sat down at the kitchen table she poured herself a cup of tea. The house was quiet. Even Tramp and Pup were gently snoring in their basket by the range. Apart from Joe, who was out on some kind of all-night exercise with the Home Guard, and Pearl, of course, who wouldn't be back until after last orders, everyone else was in bed.

Normally, this would be the time that she and Bel would have a natter and a catch-up, but this evening when Bel had come back from her walk with her ma she had said she was really tired, and that it had been 'one of those days' and she just wanted to get Lucille ready for bed and hit the sack herself.

Tired out from her trip into town with her aunty Maisie, and happy with the doll she had been treated to from Saxons, Lucille had offered up no resistance when Bel had told her it was time for bed and that tonight she was going to be allowed to sleep in her 'mammy and daddy's bed'.

It struck Polly that this was the first time that Bel had referred to Joe as 'daddy'. She wondered if her acquiescence was due to tiredness – she certainly looked shattered – or if something had occurred on her walk that had led to her change of heart. Whatever the reason, Polly was glad Bel had given Joe his much-deserved title of Lucille's 'daddy'. Joe might not be the little girl's biological father, but he was her da in all the ways that mattered. Polly might be biased, but she thought Joe was the best daddy any child could ask for. *Had something happened this evening that had made Bel realise this too?*

As Polly took a sip of her tea, she reached into the pocket of her dressing gown and pulled out Tommy's letter – the last letter he had written to her and one she had reread too many times. The rustling of the paper caused Tramp to open one eye to see where the noise was coming from.

Polly straightened the paper out on the top of the table, which was covered with an old oilcloth. As she read the words that she now knew off by heart, she gave free rein to her tears, knowing she wouldn't be disturbed.

I just want you to know how proud I am of you.

A big salty teardrop suddenly landed on the letter and punctuated the end of the sentence. Polly panicked in case Tommy's words to her would be erased. She scrabbled around in her other pocket for a hankie. Finding one, she carefully blotted the letter and then dabbed her eyes, but she couldn't stop the tears.

She imagined Tommy writing these very words, telling her how he was always boasting to his mates that his fiancée was *building ships that are saving our backsides* and how they would, in turn, poke fun at him, saying that he was *telling porkies* and that *my Polly* was just *a figment of my imagination*. She still felt a pull when she read his words: *. . . it doesn't matter to me whether they believe me or not. I know you are real. And I know you are mine!*

Polly thought of the afternoon when they had all been chatting at work and she had thought for the briefest of moments that perhaps the reason she hadn't received a letter from Tommy for such a long time was because he had fallen in love with another woman. How could she even have considered such a thing? She felt as though she had betrayed him just by thinking about it. But it was now over five months since his last letter and her hope was fading fast. So much so that a part of her would actually be willing to make the trade. For him to have found another sweetheart rather than be 'killed in action'.

Polly felt Tramp push against her bare leg and she automatically put her hand down to stroke her head. She looked down to see the dog's eyes staring up at her, demanding that her owner offer up reassurance that she was all right.

Looking back at the creased letter, now watermarked but still legible, Polly continued to stroke Tramp while her free hand traced Tommy's words:

> ... I just need you to look after yourself and make sure you get to the nearest air raid shelter as soon as the sirens start up.
>
> It's good to hear that Arthur's doing well and keeping Agnes well stocked up on fruit and veg – and fish, of course! I know I've said this a few times before but I am so eternally grateful to your mam for taking Arthur under her roof. She really is the best. Tell her I'm missing her gorgeous stews and dumplings!

There was just something about the words ... Was he making sure her ma knew how much he appreciated all she had done for his granddad in case he never got to tell her himself?

> Talking of your ma, I know she will hate me for writing this and a part of me thinks I should tell you to do the complete opposite – but keep building them ships! And keep sending them out into that great North Sea.
>
> I am so very proud of you and you must keep doing what you have always wanted to do (even before this war).

You are a shipbuilder! Just like your brothers, and your dad, and his dad before him.

I can't stress just how very proud I am of you.

When Polly had first read Tommy's letter she had been so chuffed. His words confirmed that she really was a part of the war effort, that she really was making a difference. Even if she was just a very small cog in a very big wheel, she was a cog all the same. Lately, though, when she reread the letter, she had done so through different eyes. Of course, she still saw the love there, and the fact that he was genuinely proud of the work she was doing, but she now read something else – it was as though he *needed* to say this to her ... As though he was worried that this might be his last letter.

'*Stop it!*' Polly told herself. 'Stop this now!' Her words woke up Pup, who pulled himself out of his basket, padded over to the table and pushed himself between Tramp and Polly's leg.

There had to be a reason for her not getting Tommy's letters. There just had to be! They mightn't be able to get post out of Gibraltar, or the ship or aeroplane in which his letter was being transported had, God forbid, not made it back to British shores. She repeated the mantra: *No news is good news.*

Polly sat for a few moments before taking a deep breath.

Just because his letters weren't finding their way to her, that didn't mean her words of love weren't going to find him.

Polly pushed herself out of her chair. Walking over to the dresser and pulling out the top drawer, she got a sheet of airmail paper and a pen. She then went and sat back down at the table, folded up Tommy's letter, and shoved it back into her pocket.

As was her way before she put pen to paper and wrote to her fiancé, Polly closed her eyes and imagined that the man she loved was sitting right next to her, smiling and listening to her as she wrote and told him all her news.

As Tramp and Pup curled up at her feet under the table, Polly opened her eyes and said out loud:

'Time for me and you, Tommy.'

Chapter Forty-Nine

'Was Bel all right after her "walk" yesterday?' Gloria asked as they hurried down to the ferry along with the early-morning mass of workers. Gloria had guessed the reason for the mother-and-daughter outing, knowing that Bel had been on at Pearl to come clean about who her father was for some time now. But seeing Bel this morning after dropping off Hope, she wondered if perhaps Bel might now be wishing she had left this particular stone unturned.

'Do you think Pearl told her who her dad is – or was?' Gloria raised her voice slightly to be heard above the squawks of the seagulls excited by a couple of trawlers arriving at the fish quay.

They both nudged their way on to the waiting ferry.

'I think so,' Polly said, handing over her penny fare to Stan, 'but to be honest, I'm not quite sure.' She followed Gloria as she pushed her way through a gaggle of men so that they could reach the railings on the side of the boat. It was Gloria and Polly's favourite spot as they liked to stand and look out at the river.

'It was hard to tell when they both came back,' Polly mused. 'They seemed all right. They weren't sniping at each other like they normally do, which was *highly* unusual considering they'd been in each other's company for at least an hour or so. Probably a record for them two.' Polly looked at Gloria, who was listening but looking across the river. 'But I could tell Bel didn't want to talk about it, so I didn't push it.'

Gloria turned to look at Polly, a question on her furrowed brow.

'She's like that sometimes,' Polly explained. 'Always been like that – even when we were little. If Bel's got something on her mind, she tends to stew on it for a while.'

Gloria listened. She knew Bel had depths that she liked to keep covered up.

'She'll chat about it,' Polly added, 'when she's had time to work things out in her head.'

Chapter Fifty

Two weeks later

Monday 22 June

Helen shut the door to the doctor's consultation room quietly behind her. As she had already paid her five shillings beforehand, she made her way straight to the front door. She guessed she must have been the last appointment of the day as the little waiting room was empty and the secretary already had her coat on and was standing in front of the mirror, adjusting her headscarf.

As Helen closed the heavy oak door behind her, she again did so carefully, making sure it didn't slam. She felt a need to keep all noise to a minimum as the rushing sound in her head was so loud and overwhelming.

Walking past St Thomas's Church and turning left onto Fawcett Street, Helen saw the number 12 bus waiting, its engine running. It was jam-packed with shoppers and workers all heading home for their tea. As soon as Helen stepped on board, it pulled away. Paying her fare, and then squeezing herself into the only spare seat she could find, Helen stared out of the window, not wanting to catch anyone's eye. She had no desire to draw attention to herself. If she could have one wish at this moment it would be to be invisible, or, better still, to simply disappear off the face of the earth. It would be a solution to all her problems. This, she thought to herself, as the bus trundled up Toward

Road, must be what it feels like to be in purgatory. Living in your own personal hell, without the relief of death anywhere on the horizon.

Twenty minutes later the bus drew to a stop on the Stockton Road, within a stone's throw of the Ryhope Hospital. Waiting until the rest of the passengers had disembarked, Helen shuffled out of her seat, quickly walked down the aisle and got off. Pulling out her cigarettes and lighting one, she watched as those she had been travelling with hurried off in various directions. Behind her the bus pulled away, leaving the air thick with exhaust fumes. Walking over to a bench on the periphery of the hospital grounds, Helen sat down and smoked her cigarette. Then she smoked another.

Knowing what she had to do, she took a deep breath, got up and walked up the slightly winding pathway to the main entrance of the hospital and let the revolving door deposit her into the large foyer.

Having never been in this hospital before, Helen felt disorientated and looked around before setting her sights on the small reception area.

'Good afternoon,' Helen greeted the woman positioned behind the counter. 'I'm here to see Mr Theodore Harvey-Smith.'

The receptionist, a well-made-up woman who looked to be in her mid-fifties, gave Helen a look like the summons, before demanding, 'Have you an appointment with Mr Harvey-Smith?'

Normally Helen would have enjoyed pulling this mutton-dressed-as-lamb receptionist down a peg or two, but today she simply ignored the question and told her straight: 'Tell him Miss Helen Crawford is here to see him. Mr Havelock's granddaughter.' Helen watched as the receptionist's mouth tightened and she picked up the receiver of the black Bakelite phone. She was not able to hear what was being said as the woman was speaking quickly and quietly, but when she finished talking she put the phone down and turned to Helen. 'Mr Harvey-Smith cannot be located at this moment. Perhaps you'd like to take a seat and wait until we can find out where he is?'

Helen glared at the receptionist. Not deigning to give her an answer, she turned on her heels and walked over to the large wooden board where all the names of the different departments and wards had been written. Finding 'Surgery' and an arrow pointing to the left, Helen hitched her handbag and boxed gas mask onto her shoulder and started down the long, white corridor. It had no windows and was infused with the distinctive smell of disinfectant, a smell that never failed to remind Helen of her father and the many weeks he had been in the Royal. And, just like the Royal, the place was teeming with people – doctors in white coats, stethoscopes hanging around their necks, nurses in blue uniforms walking faster than most people could jog, visitors looking confused and scared, and the odd patient either hobbling on crutches or being pushed in a wheelchair. The only difference was that in this hospital all the patients were young, they were all male, and they were all soldiers.

After a hundred yards or so, Helen came to more signs, with more headings – and more arrows. When she came to yet another set of signs she began to feel as though she was in some kind of oversized rabbit warren, and with no windows showing the outside world, she was hit by an increasing sense of being hemmed in. Trapped. She looked around, hoping to see someone she could ask, but everyone seemed to be walking so quickly. Busy, too busy to stop and give her directions. She looked down the list of departments and wards, but the words all seemed to merge into one. She stared down the corridor that branched off to her left and then down the corridor that led to her right. She had no idea which one to go down. Her breathing grew laboured again and she began to feel the familiar tightness in her chest. A few seconds later the panic set in, bringing with it tears of helplessness.

'Helen?' The voice seemed to come out of nowhere.

'Helen? Are you all right?'

It took her a moment to focus on the face in front of her. The young, slightly pale face was not handsome, or ugly, and was framed by a thatch of straw-blond hair.

'Helen, it's me, Dr Parker. Are you all right? Do you want me to find you a seat?'

Unable to speak, Helen stared at the young doctor.

'Here, come and sit down for a moment.'

Helen found herself being ushered into a room that was small and had a desk and two chairs – but most importantly there was a window. Seeing daylight and a glimpse of the hospital grounds helped bring Helen back to reality. She looked up at Dr Parker, who was half perched on the front of the desk, a concerned look on his face.

'Gosh, I don't know what came over me then.' Her voice sounded raspy and not like her own.

'Have you come to visit someone?' Dr Parker asked.

'No, no ... I mean, yes.' Helen paused. 'I've come to see Theo ... Theodore Harvey-Smith.'

Dr Parker looked at Helen. He had seen various sides to Mr Crawford's daughter. He had seen her tired, weary, worried and upset. He had seen her happy, relieved, thankful, and later on, when Mr Crawford had been discharged and he had bumped into Helen at various charity dos, he had seen the confident, Hollywood-starlet Helen – with the attitude to match.

He had never, however, seen her like this. And he would wager he knew exactly who was responsible for putting her in such a state.

'Theodore?'

Helen nodded, took out her cigarettes and lit one.

Dr Parker handed her an ashtray.

'Theodore's gone, Helen. He's been sent back down south. I believe they were in dire need of surgeons at the Radcliffe Infirmary in Oxford. And as that is his home town, where he belongs, and of course where his family is, he was a prime candidate. Besides, I don't think he ever saw being here as long-term.'

Helen felt bewildered. She had not thought for even one moment that he wouldn't be there.

'Oh, that's strange. I thought he said he was due to stay for at least another year?'

Dr Parker shifted a little uncomfortably.

'Well, I think that was the plan, but I believe it was a combination of factors, not just the fact this position came up.'

'Such as?' Helen asked. There was something in Dr Parker's tone, as if he was purposely holding back information.

'Well, I think his wife needed him back home.' He paused. 'Having said that, to be honest with you, we were all a little surprised he has been allowed to go back as this hospital is still pretty short of surgeons.'

Helen felt as though she had just been punched in the gut.

'I'm sorry, what did you say?' Her voice was breathy.

'We were all surprised,' Dr Parker repeated, 'as this hospital's short of decent surgeons. Actually, surgeons full stop – decent or otherwise.'

'No,' Helen's voice had fallen to a whisper, 'I meant about his wife? He has a wife, does he? Theo's married?' Helen had gone as white as a sheet.

'Yes.' Dr Parker looked at Helen and knew his suspicions were right. Helen had been Theo's latest squeeze.

'Yes, he has a wife. A wife *and* two young children.'

'He's got two children?' Helen could not hide her disbelief.

'Yes, a boy and a girl. Stanley and Tamara.'

Helen looked down at the ashtray in her lap and the cigarette that had burnt down to the stub.

They were the names of his brother and sister. The ones he lived with at home with his mother and father.

'Tamara and Stanley,' Helen repeated the names.

Dr Parker looked at Helen. It was the first time he had ever felt sorry for her.

'And, you say, his wife needs him in Oxford?' Helen's mind was struggling to comprehend everything she was being told.

'Yes,' Dr Parker felt a reticence about telling her everything, but knew she needed to hear this.

'It would appear his wife is expecting again. Their third. That's why she wants him back down there, and it was one of the reasons, I believe, that he was put ahead of a long line of other candidates. Oxford, as you can imagine, is quite a sought-after place to work.'

'Theo's wife is expecting?' Helen repeated the words more to herself than for any kind of affirmation. 'Their third?'

Dr Parker nodded. 'It sounds like she might be near her due date.'

All of a sudden the door swung open.

'Bloody hell! Parker! There you are! You're needed in trauma. Emergency.'

Dr Parker stood up and looked at Helen.

'I'm so sorry, Helen, I'm going to have to dash. Are you all right?' He could see that she wasn't. He quickly took the ashtray off her lap and took hold of both of her hands and held them tight.

'If you need me for anything,' his voice was serious, 'just phone, or come to the hospital, there's not many hours in the day when I'm not here.' He tried to force her eyes to focus on him. He didn't like the slightly vacant look she had.

'Even if it's just for a chat. I'm here. All right? Do you understand?'

Staring up at him, Helen nodded before Dr Parker rushed off and she was left alone in the small room, with its small window, in a state of complete and utter shock.

The second shock she'd had within as many hours.

Chapter Fifty-One

Helen somehow managed to retrace her steps through the maze of windowless corridors and found herself stepping out of the hospital's main entrance and into what was a rather perfect midsummer's evening.

In a daze she walked down the long path, through the hospital grounds and out onto the main road, where she spotted a single-decker bus, its engine idling. Stepping on board, she paid her fare and took a seat. Gazing out the window as though in some kind of hypnotic state, she felt the bus jerk into first gear, and then second and third, and she watched the changing scenery as she and a bus half-full of passengers were transported from the village of Ryhope back to the centre of town.

Getting off the bus and walking up Fawcett Street, she stopped for a moment and looked up at the Italian Renaissance clock tower that made up part of the town hall. Standing stock-still, her neck craning, it took a few moments for her mind to register the time – it was just a few minutes before seven o'clock. Only when a group of chattering merchant navy sailors accidentally knocked into her were her eyes forced away from it.

'Sorry, darlin'.' The sailor's cockney voice was genuinely apologetic.

Helen watched as the group of petty officers carried on their way.

Two highly explosive bombs had just gone off in her life – one straight after the other. She felt as though she were wandering around in the debris with no idea what she should do, or where she should go next.

She looked around her as if she might find her answer on these streets, but all she could see were women like herself, young and dressed up, and men, either in uniform or smart suits, heading off for a night on the town. In all her life, she had never felt so completely alone, so desperate, so confused – so burdened. But most of all, in so much dread of what life now held for her.

For an instant she considered going to work, until she remembered the town-hall clock. It was late. Too late to go to work.

Home. Just go home! a voice in her head commanded, but every part of her being rebelled. The prospect of going to an empty house with just her thoughts for company filled her with dread.

Walking past Meng's French restaurant, which was considered the finest place to eat in town, Helen recalled how she had suggested to Theo that they go there. She had even dropped hints that it was known as the best wedding venue a girl could want. But, of course, they had never set foot inside the place. Just like they had not set foot anywhere that was even half decent.

Finally, Helen allowed her anger to break through and surge forward.

God, how Theo had taken her for a ride! Helen felt like screaming the words aloud as she forced herself to walk past the huge glass windows with their tiers of cakes and confections on display.

But then hot on the heels of her anger came a plethora of self-recriminations.

What a fool you've been!

You stupid girl!

Of course, Theo didn't want to go anywhere like this!

397

Of course, he had laughed his way out of it, joshing her along, telling her that they were young and should experience life – a different side of life.

Of course, he had only wanted to take her to working-class pubs, like the Burton and the Wheatsheaf, because they were places he would not be recognised. Places he would not risk bumping into someone who knew him. Someone who would expose him as being *a married man.*

With two children.

And another on the way.

How stupid she was to have been so easily coerced into *letting her hair down,* into seeing *how the other half lived* – into believing it was all just *a bit of a lark.* Like an idiot, she had gone along with it.

And, by God, it all had just been a game to him.

The going out.

The staying in.

The lovemaking.

He had used her. No. Worse still. He had *conned her.*

Conned her into going out with him.

Conned her into thinking he would marry her.

Conned her into bed.

Conned her into believing there was another life awaiting her.

Well, there was no arguing the toss now – there certainly was *another life* awaiting her. That much was for sure. But it was certainly not the *other life* she had so desperately craved.

As Helen continued walking up Fawcett Street, she felt the outrage and the fury gather momentum inside her. Stepping onto the cobbled main road that led to Bridge Street, Helen was immediately deafened by the sound of a blaring horn and the screech of brakes. She jumped out of her skin.

'Open your eyes, yer stupid mare!' the driver's enraged voice shouted at her.

Helen hurried over to the other side, this time checking to her left and her right for any other oncoming vehicles.

Stupid! Yes, she was. The most stupid woman on the whole of this planet. Stupid. Stupid. Stupid.

Just before she reached the pavement she went over on her heel. The pain was excruciating but she managed to stay upright and not go sprawling on all fours. She hobbled to the shop doorway on Mackie's Corner and grimaced with pain, waiting for it to subside. She looked ahead of her: St Mary's Church was on the left, and there, on the right, where a shiny black Rolls-Royce was pulling up, was the Grand Hotel.

Of course – why didn't she think of that before? *Her mother.* She would go and see her mum. She was bound to be at the Grand now. She would go and see her. Tell her everything. Tell her about Theodore. How he had used her, lied to her, conned her and then cast her aside like a piece of rubbish. *Her mum would help her!* She would know what to do. Her mum was strong. Stoic. Look how she had dealt with her father's betrayal! But most of all, she was her mother, wasn't she? And if ever there was a time she needed her mum, it was now.

Despite the pain in her ankle, Helen practically ran the remaining hundred yards to the entrance of the hotel. She hurried up the front steps and pulled open the heavy glass front door before the doorman had a chance to do it for her. Hobbling into the main foyer, she looked around her at the reception area and lounge bar, which was filled with oversize potted plants and plush hide-covered furniture, the hotel's famous stained-glass windows framed by swish velvet curtains.

Panic shot through her.

Her mother wasn't here.

But she was always here! Wasn't she? Seeing the front desk, Helen staggered a little towards it.

'Is Mrs Crawford here?' she asked, not even attempting to keep the desperation out of her voice.

The young woman sitting behind the wide leather-topped desk looked at Helen warily.

'Yes, she is, who should I say is here to see her?'

'I'm her daughter!' Helen snapped. 'Where is she?'

The receptionist faltered for a moment.

'She's with the Commander on the first floor.'

Helen limped towards the wide sweeping staircase. Grabbing the thick wooden handrail, Helen made her way up the carpeted steps. She could hear the receptionist's voice calling after her, somewhat belatedly, telling her she should wait for Mrs Crawford in the downstairs bar.

Reaching the top of the stairs, Helen looked about her. There was another bar and a buffet, which, judging by the number of men in uniform, was solely for the use of the Royal Navy.

All of a sudden Helen heard a burst of laughter from behind a large blue door. The slightly guttural laughter she knew to be her mother's after she'd had a few. Helen's ankle was now throbbing but her need to get to her mother and offload all her troubles was now all-consuming. Helen didn't think she had ever needed her mum so much in all her life.

Without knocking, Helen swung the door open. As soon as she spotted her mother, standing in the middle of the room with a drink in her hand, Helen rushed towards her.

'Oh, Mum. Thank goodness you're here!'

Miriam stared at Helen in disbelief. Her mouth had dropped open. How had her daughter known to come here? To the Commander's room? *That bloody dim-witted girl on reception!*

'Helen, darling?' Miriam forced herself to give her daughter the clearly required hug and gentle tap on the back.

'My goodness, what's happened? You look in a state!' she added, conscious of the interested looks coming from the Commander, with whom she had been enjoying a rather flirtatious relationship for a while now. His second in command was cosied up on the chesterfield with Amelia.

Helen suddenly became aware that they were all staring at her.

'Oh, gosh, I'm so sorry for just turning up like this.' Helen looked imploringly at her mother. The atmosphere in the room had gone from light and frivolous to a stunned, slightly embarrassed silence.

'Don't you worry about that, my dear.' The Commander, who had been by the drinks cabinet, put down his glass and walked over to Helen, who was now standing by her mother's side. He took her hand and patted it.

'Looks to me as though you need to have a private moment with your dear mother here.' He smiled at both mother and daughter.

'Yes, yes,' Amelia agreed as she was helped up from the sofa by her lieutenant, 'you two just take your time.' Helen noticed her mother's friend was flushed. 'We'll leave you to it.'

Helen watched as the three of them walked out of the room and quietly shut the door behind them.

As soon as the coast was clear, Miriam rounded on her daughter.

'What the hell's got into you, coming in here? Just barging in like that. God, what a total embarrassment!' She strode over to the cherrywood drinks cabinet and poured herself another gin, only looking up to shoot daggers at her daughter. She made no attempt to offer Helen a drink.

'I didn't know where else to go,' Helen started to defend herself as she watched her mother slosh a good measure into her glass.

'What about *home*!' Miriam snapped. 'You could have gone *home*, like any other normal person would have done.'

'But I didn't want to go home.' Helen heard her voice become child-like. 'I needed to see you ... Wanted to see you ... To talk to you.'

Miriam finished mixing her drink, turned round and scrutinised Helen.

'Look at the state of you! God knows what people are going to think of you, coming here looking like this.' She took a large gulp. 'Have you seen the state of you?'

Helen caught her reflection in the art deco mirror that was taking up a good part of the wall opposite. The vision shocked her. She looked like she had been dragged through a hedge backwards, and her make-up had either worn off or was smudged.

'Oh, Mum.' Helen felt tears start to well up in her eyes. 'I've got myself into the most awful mess.'

'Well, I can see that!' Miriam said, walking over to the chesterfield and perching herself on its wide arm. 'And I can guess exactly what it's about. Or rather, *who* it's about.'

Helen looked at her mother, stunned.

'You know?'

Miriam's eyes went to the ceiling. 'Of course *I know*, Helen!'

'What? About Theo?' Helen asked. She was still standing on the same spot in the middle of the room.

'Yes, "about Theo",' Miriam repeated.

'You know?' Helen started. 'You know—'

'Of course I know!' Miriam hissed. She wanted to shout at her daughter, but didn't want anyone to hear.

'I know that your *darling* Theodore from Oxford – the one I went to an awful lot of trouble to organise a dinner party for in the expectation that I might finally get you married off – *is actually already married!*' Miriam almost spat out the words in disgust. 'Honestly, Helen, how on earth you didn't realise is beyond me!'

'You knew he was married?' Helen's voice was quiet. Saying the words made them all the more real.

'But I don't understand. How did you know?' Feeling her legs starting to shake and the ankle throb even more than it was already, Helen staggered a little to the armchair adjacent to the chesterfield and sat down. She dumped her handbag and gas mask on the patterned oriental rug that was as big as it was beautiful. She started scrambling around for her cigarettes. Finding them, she pulled one out and lit it.

'To be honest, I'm surprised I didn't find out sooner than I did!' Miriam leant forward, her legs crossed, both hands nursing the thick glass tumbler.

'How? How did you know? When did you know?' Helen implored.

'Your grandfather. He wanted to tell you before. I actually came to Thompson's to tell you that he wanted to see you *face-to-face* because he didn't trust telephones, but you never went, did you? Too busy *working.*' Miriam said the word as though it was something to be ashamed of.

'By the time you did see him, you and "married Theodore from Oxford" had already broken up, so your grandfather, thoughtful soul that he is, didn't see the need to make the whole debacle even more painful for his darling granddaughter.'

'How did Grandfather know?' Helen was becoming confused. Theo's marital status had come like a bolt out of the blue to her just over an hour or so ago, and now it would seem that every man and his dog knew. Even those who had never met him before!

'You know your grandfather.' Miriam rolled her eyes to the ceiling. 'He might look decrepit, but the old man's still as sharp as a pin. And he still wants to feel like he's in charge. When we told him that you were stepping out with one of the doctors at the Ryhope and that he was called Theo and he was from Oxford, he took it upon himself to find out just about everything there was to know about the man.' Miriam paused to take a drink.

'The sad thing is, from what I can gather, your grandfather was quite excited about the prospect of you finding a suitable husband, especially one that was a surgeon, from good stock – *and hailed from Oxford*. To all intents and purposes, Theodore Harvey-Smith, which I gather is his full name, was an exceedingly good match – or might well have been, *had he not already been married!*'

Miriam took another drink to calm her nerves.

'Thankfully your grandfather managed to get shot of him before he could cause any embarrassment to the family. Sent him packing, back to Oxford, back to his wife and his two – soon to be *three* – children.'

Helen suddenly thought of what Dr Parker had told her. That a position had come up at the Radcliffe Infirmary and Theo had been lucky to get the position. Clearly, neither luck nor his wife's impending labour had had anything to do with it.

'Let's just be thankful for small mercies,' Miriam continued, 'that no one else knew about the whole charade. God, I can just see the gossips now, loving the fact that my daughter was naïve and idiotic enough to be taken in by a married man.'

Helen stared at her mother, struggling to take on board the vile words falling out of her mouth. But worse still was the realisation that all her mother was really bothered about – all she had ever been bothered about – was her reputation. It was always her, her, her. And always would be.

Well, she was in for one hell of a shock.

Her mother might have successfully managed to brush the scandal of her husband's infidelity, his mistress and their baby under the carpet, but my goodness, she was going to find it nigh on impossible to keep this latest diabolical turn of events under wraps.

'Mother.' Helen stood up and put her cigarette out in the ashtray in the middle of the glass coffee table. 'There's something else … Something I don't believe you know about. Something no one else knows as I only just got to know myself this afternoon.'

Miriam, who had stood up at the same time as her daughter, had wandered over to the mirror and was checking her make-up, forcing a few stray hairs back into place.

On hearing what her daughter said next, Miriam swung round.

Her face contorted into disbelief.

Her hands automatically going to her mouth to stop herself from screaming the place down.

'I'm pregnant mother!'

'You're what!' Miriam whispered, dropping her hands to her side, her eyes glued to her daughter. A part of her was desperately holding on to the hope that this was some kind of cruel, sick joke. There was a moment's silence when, as if perfectly timed, the gramophone that had been playing quietly in the background suddenly stopped; the clunk of the arm could be heard returning to its resting place.

'I'm pregnant, Mother,' Helen repeated. There was no emotion in her voice. This was the second unpalatable truth that Helen had been forced to verbalise in the past ten minutes.

'You stupid, stupid girl!' Miriam stormed over to her daughter and slapped her hard across the face.

Helen's hand automatically went to her stinging cheek. She could feel it burning red, but the rest of her body felt oddly cold. She should have known that this would be her mother's reaction. If she had thought about it before rushing in here, jumping in with both feet forward, she could have saved herself the hurt and humiliation that were already weighing her down.

Who was she kidding, coming here, thinking that her mother would help her? Would shoulder her burden? Would tell her everything was going to be all right?

Of course, she was idiotic. Idiotic to expect anything different from her mother.

'My God! The shame of it!' Miriam was now stomping across the room. She turned and stomped back again. She glared at her daughter.

'You're going to ruin my life!' She spat the words out. 'Just as I had finally got my life back! Finally got everything sorted! God, the trouble I went to in order to clear up the mess created by your bloody father and his tart! And now you!' Miriam suddenly let out an evil laugh that was untouched by any kind of mirth.

'Ha! You two. What do they say? Like mother, like daughter? *I don't think so.* More like, like father, like daughter! He's had a *bastard* with a married *woman*, and now you're about to have a *bastard* with a married *man*! A married man that doesn't even want you!' Another slightly hysterical laugh.

'Well, you couldn't have made it up, could you? Mm?' Miriam took a dramatic swig of her drink, before slamming it down on the table.

'Two bastards! That's all I need! Two bloody *bastards* in the one family!'

The fourth mention of the word 'bastard' was too much for Helen.

This time it was her turn to swing her arm back and give her mother a hard, stinging slap across her face.

It stopped the vitriol dripping out of her mother's mouth long enough for Helen to pick up her handbag and gas mask, turn on her heels and walk out of the room.

Feeling a strange kind of calm come over her, head held high, Helen made her way through the open lounge bar, down the two flights of stairs, and across the main foyer.

This time, though, she waited until the porter reached the heavy glass-panelled front door first and opened it for her.

As Helen stepped out of the Grand and looked up to the aqua blue skies above, she let go of the desperate need that had driven her here. The need for support, the need to be cared for – the need of a mother's unconditional love. If there had ever been a time when she'd needed this, it was now. But it hadn't been there, and it never would be. Accepting this harsh, hurtful truth, though, brought with it a peculiar feeling of liberation. And with that liberation came a sense of strength. The strength to look reality in the eye and not shy away.

Standing there on the pavement outside the Grand, Helen felt lighter, free of the constraints she had felt she had been wearing these past few months.

As Helen turned and looked down the long stretch of road that led back to the town centre, she knew the time had also come for her to face up to something else, or rather, to *someone else*.

Someone she had been running away from for a while now.

The time had come for her to accept her life – a life that she might well feel she'd had foisted upon her, but it was a life she could no longer ignore.

Still hobbling a little due to her injured ankle, Helen started walking towards the town centre. As she cut through West Wear Street and then Bedford Street, crossing over High Street West – this time making sure she looked before crossing – it was as though she was seeing her surroundings for the first time – the trees, the public houses, the little boutiques, the cobbled streets – and at that moment she felt as though she was viewing the world around her with great clarity.

She was finally giving in to the yearning she had been feeling these past six months. She had tried to outrun it, but now realised she had been wrong to do so. What she should have done from the start was to turn around and embrace it.

Walking down Frederick Street and turning left onto Borough Road, Helen finally reached her destination. Carefully making her way down the small flight of stone steps to the basement apartment, she heard the faint sound of the wireless and the comforting smell of home cooking.

Taking a deep breath, Helen raised her hand and knocked on the door.

Chapter Fifty-Two

Having got Hope down for the night, Gloria was just putting a bowl of stew that Agnes had kindly given her into the oven to warm up, when she heard a knock on the door. At this time the only person she could guess it might be was her neighbour, old Mr Brown, so when Gloria went to open the door and found Helen standing there, you could have knocked her over with a feather.

'Helen!' She took a step back, not quite believing her eyes.

'Hello, Gloria.' Helen's voice was a little frosty, but not antagonistic. 'Can I come in?'

Gloria immediately stepped back and opened the door wide, showing Helen that she was welcome. 'Of course, come in!' She watched in slight disbelief as Helen walked over the threshold and into her home.

Shutting the door behind her unexpected guest, Gloria suddenly felt at a loss for words. She looked at Helen – her lover's daughter, the woman who had saved her from being beaten to a pulp, the woman who had told her that she should not even acknowledge her should she see her on the street – and she had no idea why she was here.

There was, however, something different about Helen. Something about her had changed, but she couldn't put her finger on it.

'I've come to see my sister.' Helen just came straight out and said it.

Gloria didn't think it was possible to be even more shocked than she already was. She was speechless, and instead simply nodded and went to get Hope from the back bedroom.

Returning a few moments later, carrying her daughter, who was clutching a pastel pink crocheted blanket, Gloria smiled.

'Hope, say hello to your big sister.'

As she spoke, Gloria handed over her daughter.

Helen reached out and took Hope, holding her for a moment, before slowly walking over to the sofa and carefully sitting down. Not for one moment did she take her eyes off her little sister.

As Gloria stood quietly and took in the sight of Helen and Hope together on the sofa in the front room of her modest little home, she thought how well Helen looked, much better than she had for a long time now. Her complexion looked rosy, and she had her curves back, as well as her bosom.

And that's when she realised what was different.

'How far along are you?' she asked gently.

Helen immediately looked up; tears had filled her startling emerald-green eyes and were threatening to spill over.

'How did you know?'

Gloria smiled, but didn't say anything.

'The doctor reckons only a couple of months,' Helen said, looking up at Gloria for just a brief moment before her eyes were drawn back down to Hope, who was grasping at her sister's thick raven hair, demanding attention.

There was another brief quietness between the two women. Gloria hesitated before she spoke again, knowing that the words that came out of her mouth next were important.

'Everything'll be all right, you know. You'll manage,' she told Helen, trying to sound as reassuring as possible, whilst all the time trying to hide her shock.

'Your dad loves you, you know. He'll be there for you ... And I will be too ... If that's what you want.' There was so much Gloria wanted to say to this troubled young girl, but instead she said, simply:

'Sometimes life takes an unexpected turn, but you'll deal with it. You're strong. And you're brave. Very brave.'

Helen's head was bowed and Gloria could see that her body had started to judder slightly. Gloria walked over to the settee and sat down next to her.

She looked at her baby girl's little face, full of glee and laughter as Helen's tears splodged onto her, which in turn caused Helen's muffled sobs to turn into a half-laugh, half-cry.

'I think she likes you,' Gloria said, trying her hardest to keep the tears from her own eyes.

'I think I like her too,' Helen said, her tears now falling freely down her face, causing Hope to giggle even more.

And the two women and the baby all cried and laughed and cried some more.

Epilogue

On the last day of the month of June 1942, two women in Sunderland stepped out of their front doors on their way to work at one of the town's biggest shipyards – J.L. Thompson & Sons. It was just a quarter to seven in the morning, but the sun was already up and proving that this day, like the one before, was going to be hot and sweaty.

Both women were just in time to catch their respective postwomen making their early-morning deliveries.

The older of the two postwomen, who had been working for the GPO for some time, was turning into number 34 Tatham Street when she bumped into a young woman hurrying out the front door. The pretty girl was wearing a colourful headscarf and denim overalls, and had a boxed gas mask slung over her shoulder along with a haversack.

If an outsider was watching the women, they would rightly presume they knew each other by the ease of their greeting. The younger woman was about to go on her way when the postwoman stopped her and handed her an envelope, on which the young woman's name and the address were typed.

The postwoman lingered for a short moment, which was unusual for her as she was not one to idle. She touched the young girl's arm gently before going on her way.

The young woman tore open the envelope and stood, stock-still, as she read the few paragraphs that had been typed onto the single sheet of paper.

If anyone had been watching they would have observed that she stood and read it for longer than was needed.

For a moment it looked as though the young woman was going to turn and go back into the house from which she had just come, but she didn't.

Instead she reached into the top pocket of her overalls and pulled out what appeared to be a ring and put it on her left hand. As she did so, the small sheet of paper she had just received in the post floated freely to the ground, and a short blast of air swept it under an oncoming tram.

The young woman didn't make any attempt to chase after the piece of paper that had escaped her grasp, but instead stepped onto the pavement and joined the throng of workers who were all heading towards the shipyards that lined the banks of the Wear.

If anyone had looked at the face of the woman with the ruby engagement ring on her finger, they would have seen tears rolling down her cheeks unchecked.

But nobody noticed, so nobody asked if she was all right, and she walked in her hobnailed boots to the ferry that would take her to her place of work.

A place of work where people *would* notice that she had been crying, and would ask her why, and who would comfort her – just as the young man who had given her the ruby engagement ring knew they would.

The other postwoman, who was delivering in an area of town officially classed as Ashbrooke, was dithering a little as she had never been down the little stretch of houses known as Brookside Gardens.

The postwoman held in her grasp a letter for number 4 and as luck would have it, the person living in that house was just coming out of her front door.

413

The postwoman thought the blonde, overall-clad woman who was now striding down the wide, gravelled pathway looked very determined.

The woman worker slowed down at the sight of the postwoman, who was waving the letter in the air as though it was a flag. She stopped, smiled politely and took the envelope before thanking her and going on her way, walking on until she reached the little gate. It was only then that she stopped in order to open the small white envelope.

She stood and stared at the envelope as though it were a gift from the gods above, and, with hands that had started to shake, she slowly and carefully prised it open.

For a moment it looked as though there was nothing inside.

But then the woman turned her hand so that her palm was facing the blue skies above and she shook out the fragile contents.

From afar it would have looked as though butterflies were escaping from the restrictive confines of the thick white envelope, but anyone standing nearby would have seen that what had fluttered so gently into the woman's upturned hand were actually petals – very dry and fragile petals, but petals all the same.

And those who knew their flora would have seen that these ivory-coloured petals were from a cluster of pansies.

And as the petals fell into the woman's hand she started to cry – only her tears were borne of true joy and happiness.

And as she cried unabashed tears of love, she raised her hands to the morning sun and blew the dried petals gently into the air, and whispered in the wind:

'I'm thinking of you, too, Peter.'

Dear Reader,

If you have been with the shipyard girls from the start of the series you will now have accompanied them over a two-year period from August 1940 to June 1942, and you will have been with them through all their various highs and lows.

I hope you will continue to join them as they battle on and help each other cope with everything life throws at them – both in their personal lives and because of the tumultuous times in which they live.

All of the books in the Shipyard Girls series focus on the women's ability to triumph over adversity. Sometimes that triumph is simply to keep going.

I hope if you are experiencing hardships, or any kind of tragedy, or you are just simply having a tough time at the moment, that you too can see there is light at the end of the tunnel, and that you are able to keep going until you reach the light.

Until next time.
With love,

Nancy x

History Notes

Out of the seven hundred women who worked in the Sunderland shipyards during WWII, a number of those – like Angie before she joined Rosie's squad of women welders – worked as crane drivers.

Here is one such woman – Miss Eileen Reay.

This photograph was used in one of the very few articles I have been able to find which tells us of the brave and inspirational women who worked in the country's shipyards during wartime. The article 'Women on the Wear' can be found on the BBC website and was written by contributor Angela Stevenson.

Acknowledgements

A special thanks to the Sunderland Antiquarian Society – in particular Linda King, Norm Kirtlan, and Philip Curtis – for providing the wonderful background image used on the cover of *Victory for the Shipyard Girls*.

Thank you also to all the lovely staff at Waterstones in Sunderland, researcher Meg Hartford, Jackie Caffrey, of Nostalgic Memories of Sunderland in Writing, Beverley Ann Hopper, of The Book Lovers, journalist Katy Wheeler at the *Sunderland Echo*, and Suzanne Brown and fellow members of the Sunderland Soroptimists. As well as 'Team Nancy' at Arrow, publishing director Emily Griffin, editor Cassandra Di Bello, my wonderful literary agent Diana Beaumont, and, of course, my parents, Audrey and Syd Walton, and husband, Paul.

Thank you.

Want to know what happens next?

Look out for the next book in the series…

Courage of the Shipyard Girls

Nancy Revell

21 March 2019

Order your copy now in paperback
or e-book today

Hear more from

Nancy Revell

SIGN UP TO OUR NEW SAGA NEWSLETTER

Penny Street

Stories You'll Love to Share

Penny Street is a newsletter bringing you the latest book deals, competitions and alerts of new saga series releases.

Read about the research behind your favourite books, try our monthly wordsearch and download your very own Penny Street reading map.

Join today by visiting
www.penguin.co.uk/pennystreet